A
Kind of
Vanishing

LESLEY THOMSON

D1381696

Myriad Editions

First published in 2007 by

Myriad Editions
59 Lansdowne Place
Brighton BN3 1FL

Reprinted 2011, 2014

www.myriadeditions.com

3 5 7 9 10 8 6 4

A CIP catalogue record for this book is available from the
British Library.

ISBN: 978-0-9565599-3-7

Printed on FSC-accredited paper by
CPI Group (UK) Ltd, Croydon, CR0 4YY

For my Mum and Dad – May and Bill –
special parents.

And for LMH for so very much.

Part One

June 1968

One

'One... two... three... four... five...'

L ater Eleanor would describe to the Scotland Yard detective how it had been her turn to hide and she hadn't had long. Now that the counting had stopped Alice would come at any moment.

She heard a crack, a twig or the sound of plastic breaking. Someone was there. She squeezed through a gap in the bushes and plunged recklessly into the tangled undergrowth, wincing as thorny tentacles scratched her skin. Finally she nestled into a space, concealed deep in the branches.

Eleanor was glad to have got away from Alice, even for a few minutes. She was not enjoying playing with her. Eleanor usually invited friends down from London where her family lived, but that Whitsun all possible candidates had been quick to say they were doing other things. She wouldn't have minded being on her own, but her parents were convinced that Eleanor, the youngest Ramsay and officially designated as a 'problem', would benefit from calm and mature companionship. The perfect solution had been Alice, the daughter of Steve Howland, the village of Charbury's new postman. Alice's family had just moved to Charbury from Newhaven, ten miles away, and she knew no one. She was understood to be sensible and well behaved, the kind of girl who would stop Eleanor being a nuisance or getting into scrapes. In the Ramsay family, Eleanor was the benchmark against which her brother and sister measured their behaviour and took their allotted roles. Gina was the eldest; at nearly thirteen already loftily occupying a different world to her siblings. Lucian was the only boy; he would be a doctor like his father, a self-imposed destiny, for his mother wanted him to be an artist. Then there was Eleanor, who talked too fast, got red and hot after playing, with a foghorn voice that heralded a slipstream of chaos wherever she went.

Eleanor Ramsay would be nine years old in 1968, although that day, Tuesday, the fourth of June, she was eight and counting the days – a vast twenty-four more – until her birthday. Her sister Gina had said Eleanor was too old for hide and seek, which ensured that Alice, who had been nine for three months and who always agreed with Gina, was a grudging, even obstructive participant.

Although Eleanor had hidden, she was upset at Alice's treachery in stopping counting. Balanced on her haunches, she fulminated at the injustice. Eleanor set huge store in playing fair. She was reluctant to admit something bad in someone else, so it was with dismay that she silently formed the words.

Alice had cheated.

With her chin resting on bony knees, Eleanor crouched low and waited.

Since they'd met, only four and a half days earlier, Alice had tried to keep things ordinary. Eleanor was speechless when Alice said there were no robbers or ghosts, no dragons or kings and insisted they play hopscotch. She watched, dumbfounded, as Alice marked out squares in coloured chalk on the concrete by the swings in completely straight lines. After Alice had won five times in a row, she had made Eleanor watch her skip a hundred skips non-stop. She had put out a hand like a policeman barring the way when Eleanor quickly whispered, for someone might come, about the dangerous mountain ranges waiting to be explored and the child-eating monsters they must fight and vanquish. Alice's voice came through her nose as she declared Eleanor's scary jungle was a dirty green sofa and that she had done a project on Sussex and there were no mountains. Eleanor gaped uncomprehending when Alice had screamed 'yuk!' at the cat hairs on the cushions and the crumbs underneath. She would only sit on the sofa after Gina had flounced in and flung herself into a corner hugging a cushion, scoffing at her younger sister. Later Alice said she hated dirt and mess, implying Eleanor was to blame. Now as Eleanor stared up through the roof of criss-cross branches, half closing her eyes so that the shapes of light became a fuzzy kaleidoscope, she decided Alice didn't know anything, whatever she said.

Eleanor had brought Alice to the Tide Mills village the day after they first met. Four and a half days was a lifetime to the nearly-nine-year-old, and now while she lay in wait for Alice to come looking, Eleanor could barely remember her life before she knew her. She pictured the many-levelled stretch of time, packed with evil witches, gnarled branches, and dark hiding places lurking with mythic murderers and strutting Sindy dolls with hairdos like Alice's mother, with growing despondency. It was only Tuesday; she had at least four more days of Alice before they went back to London. Eleanor didn't know how she would bear it. Her whole half term had been wasted. The Tide Mills village had been her last resort: a place where the ghosts of children now old and dead might lure Alice away from skipping and talking about dresses and dancing. It had been a big sacrifice for Eleanor to reveal her most secret place.

Eleanor would come to think of this decision as a mistake.

Every time Eleanor visited the deserted village, which was a quarter of a mile from the White House, she found something new: a 1936 sixpence, a perfume bottle, and one Christmas a great triumph, the discovery of the name 'Herbert' scratched into a wall in the communal wash and mangle house. The squat building had no roof, and rotting rafters let blocks of light slant across the walls, still lined with chipped and cracked white porcelain tiles. At the far end, in the shadow of a twisted pear tree – evidence of an orchard – were two bent and rusting mangles appearing to grow out of the chalk. Alice had hung back, arms folded, as Eleanor fervently related the tale of Prince Herbert's four straining stallions. The magnificent beasts were, she informed her hoarsely, even now tethered to a huge ring fixed to the granary wall, eager to canter to far off corners of his kingdom. Alice had retreated out into the sunshine with a shrug as Eleanor paced out the scene, talking rapidly and raising her voice as her audience drifted away. In the end she decided to skip the story and get straight to explaining the rules: each time a hiding place was discovered they lost a life. They each had three lives and after that they were truly dead. The first one to die must give up.

The one thing that Eleanor would never forget was that she had described these rules quite clearly to Alice. When they had first played hide and seek last Sunday afternoon, in the lane near her home, Alice had spied on her while she was still counting to see where Eleanor hid. This had made Eleanor very doubtful that Alice would play properly this time. But that last morning, as they did exploring and excavating, because Eleanor was practising to be an archaeologist, Alice had been quite obliging, at least for the first couple of hours.

Whenever Eleanor talked, Alice ogled the sky with saucer eyes, doing peculiar things with her mouth. After only two days, Eleanor had spotted that when this happened, Alice was being Gina, using the same voice her sister put on to talk to her horse, where words did a kind of swooping. This gave Eleanor an uncomfortable feeling. A phantom Gina was there too. Most people tried to be like Gina. A fact that absolutely baffled Eleanor, who found nothing in her older sister worth imitating.

There was no further sign of Alice coming to find her. Eleanor pushed and patted loose soil into a comfortable hillock, as she considered how there was no point to skipping. Alice would get ready for what was in effect a Skipping Show with the studied care of the famous: tossing her long hair back Gina-fashion and tugging at her skirt to keep her stupid frilly knickers hidden. Eleanor wondered why Alice breathed so noisily: taking huge breaths as if she was suffocating.

'*I like coffee, I like tea…*'

The matchstick legs in white socks had blurred, as the rope whirred round and round, slapping the ground. Alice never let Eleanor use her rope for anything except skipping, and certainly not for tying up bandits. It was new and clean and a present from her Dad. As she had dutifully watched Alice perform skipping feats in the village playground, Eleanor waited on the baking asphalt for a rescue party that never came.

Someone watching the two girls as once more they prepared to play hide and seek on that Tuesday might have guessed that apart from their age, they had little in common. One stood stiffly sentinel with reedy arms folded across her budding chest. Her pinafore dress was a primrose-yellow cotton column, while white socks with no wrinkles were strapped to the cut out figure by their paper folds. The other girl was recklessly boyish in a huge grass-stained shirt, with short sleeves that reached to her wrists. An observer might have frowned at the cropped haystack hair which stuck up at one side, imagining a mother's neglect. It would be hard to make sense of this child's erratic behaviour. She darted back and forth around the other girl, gesticulating urgently like a director allotting actors their strict space and choreography: leaping, jumping, pointing. An onlooker might have marvelled at the poise of the cleaner, party-dressed child, pale skin rendering her ghostly against the tumbledown buildings, as the goblin creature cavorted indefatigably. The pose of suffering tolerance endowed this child with calm maturity beyond her years.

Then the boy-girl belted away over the hill towards the sea leaving the Angelic One alone. Abruptly, she put hands to her face, an action that was heart rending until she began to count in a cooing voice with quavering tones that lacked conviction.

Eleanor could hear the echo of Alice's voice in her head, although it must be ages since Alice had stopped. There was still no sign of her. She had pronounced each number with the hesitant chant of an infant class still learning to count. Eleanor pictured Alice's words as jewels that – like Alice's three Sindy dolls – she kept stored in a cupboard for special occasions. Eleanor always knew what Alice was going to say because her sentences had belonged to other people first.

'*My favourite colour is pink, what's yours? My best dinner is roast pork. I hate girls who climb trees. When I grow up I want to be a nurse, who do you want to be?*'

Eleanor had not known who she would be. Alice had made it clear she didn't believe her by tutting and sighing. Eleanor was telling the truth, but to please her she finally lit upon Mickey Dolenz, which had disgusted Alice.

Eleanor never knew the right answers to Alice's questions. She pondered now, one foot wedged against a tussock. How could Alice hate girls who climbed trees when she didn't know all of them?

Eleanor stopped breathing and jerked her head up.

There was the unmistakable sound of someone walking on the path, treading quietly so as not to be heard. Eleanor shut her eyes to better hear the click of Alice's shiny shoes on the flints. She could have seen her if she had lifted the branches, but with her eyes shut, Eleanor was cloaked with invisibility. The footsteps crunched past and faded away.

One, two, one, two.

Eleanor's ears were pounding and to stop the sound she clapped her hands over them and pummelled away the memory. She slumped against a bush, relaxing into its armchair comfort, shifting until the springy branches stopped poking into her back.

She felt guilty for bringing Alice to the empty village again. They were playing illegally because their parents had forbidden them to go there. It was overgrown with tall weeds and overblown with untold dangers. Eleanor's father had said the ground was subsiding and that eventually the whole lot would fall into the sea. There were rumours in the village of an attack there after the war, a child's strangled body found at the bottom of the cliff and no one caught. Eleanor had taken all her friends there.

On the first day Alice's mother had told them to play nicely on the village green where there were swings, and a lumbering roundabout that was hard to push and hard to stop. Eleanor hated the square of tarmac surrounded by yellowed grass, with no hiding places, dotted with benches for dead people whose names Alice said she knew off by heart. Skipping and hopscotch were the only things to do there, since Alice didn't play football. Eleanor couldn't skip, her legs caught up in the snaking rope, but Alice's mother had said Alice must stay clean and tidy and not crumple her lovely new dress. This meant she refused to move around much. While her Mum was giving instructions, Alice had smoothed the cuffs and stroked her fancy dress with pointy pink fingers and, doing what Eleanor considered a stupid smile, had turned into the ancient Mrs Mahey warbling nursery rhymes with the infants in their school play.

'...*six, seven, eight, nine, ten, then I put it back again...*'

Eleanor heard her holiday clang shut.

When she was at home in London, Eleanor would make up stories of perfect afternoons at the White House. Everyone would sit together in the shade of great-uncle Jack's willow tree, planted after he was gassed in the trenches in the First World War. The sound of her father pouring tea, as she traced jigsaw patches of sunlight on the stained tablecloth – in her fantasies always piled with cakes – made her stomach buzz. Shutting her eyes and lifting her arm slowly, Eleanor could feel the weight of the jug of freezing lemonade, and the smooth curvy handle on her dead grandmother's bone china teapot that was more like a friendly person than crockery. She knew her Dad felt the same way about it, although he never said. Instead he would tell her Mum they shouldn't use it because one day they would break it. This would make her mother use the smile she could snap off suddenly like a trick.

'This is supposed to be a home not a museum stuffed full of your dead relatives.'

Mark Ramsay was right, for one day the teapot did get broken. By that time, a morning over thirty years later as the sun shone brightly on a new century, so much was different that while the Ramsays stared dumbstruck at the smashed china scattered across the kitchen tiles, they felt nothing at all.

As Eleanor lay in bed back home in Hammersmith she would wander around the White House's large garden, smelling the lawn just mowed by Leonard, the very old man who also did the grass in the churchyard where his wife had been 'sleeping by the west buttress for forty years'. Tripping between the long rectangular beds, past the caged sweet peas, the nets weighed down by fallen leaves from the oak tree above, she would bury her face in her pillow to muffle the silence from the floors below. She would think of the newly dug soil and the scent of roses that her mother loved and by concentrating, conjure up the clinking of cups with chipped lips and knives with blotches like snowflakes on the blades. The windows were always open wide, tattered curtains ballooning out in the breeze like sails. Her parents would be laughing, her sister snorting like a horse, and her brother sprawled back on his tilting chair in fits at Eleanor's jokes. By concentrating hard, Eleanor could give these vaporous figures substance.

The Tide Mills ruins belonged to Eleanor. She had never seen children from the village there and only once a grown-up. Last holidays she had come across an old tramp in a torn donkey jacket, with long grey hair combed over his head like Bobby Charlton, waiting by the disused level crossing for an approaching train. It was because of the tramp that her parents had absolutely forbidden her to play at the Mills.

Last year when they were in Sussex for the summer, Eleanor had rushed straight down there while everyone was unpacking and unaware that she had gone. She trotted round checking on the state of the buildings. Once a grand house with a porch and three storeys, only a section of the ground floor remained of the Mill Owner's home. There was one corner of the upper floor, as if someone had pared away the rest with a knife. A complete tiled fireplace was attached to the snatch of wall, the paper long gone, the dado had rotted to a stain.

Eleanor had traced the disgusting smell to a half eaten cat on the floor of what had been the kitchen. It nestled on terracotta tiles with coarse tufts of grass pushing between them. The lower half of the cat's furry face was missing. As Eleanor knelt down, its eye sockets blinked and she tumbled backwards as a cloud of blowflies rose up around her. The carcass buzzed like a gigantic bee. A doctor's daughter, she had meticulously examined the stiff matted body, poking into the dried fur with a stick, quite free of emotion. The floor was encrusted with oyster shells and tiny bones, coke tins, beer bottles, jagged bits of coloured plastic, cigarette ends and suspicious gobbets of tissue – several generations of rubbish that formed clues to lives long dead or now lived elsewhere.

Honeysuckle and goose grass grew up one wall forcing the remains of a window frame further from the brick. A low wall was all that was left of a row of workman's cottages opposite the mill. Eleanor had run along the top, leaping over gaps for windows and doors. The cottage furthest from the sea, in the shelter of the granary wall, had survived. It was a Hansel and Gretel house with its little windows and low doorway. Someone, perhaps Bobby Charlton, had been in the front room. There were squashed triangular milk cartons and leathery banana skins all over the floor. The staircase was missing, so there was no way up. She heard skittering and scurrying as she crept inside. The glass had long gone from the windows. She thought of the house as a skull, a vacant home gaping out at the countryside. During that summer Eleanor had begun weeding, pulling at the stalks that thrust through cracks in the sun-baked flagstones. Her efforts at restoration were slow and haphazard. One evening she had picked out the prettiest weeds. Mrs Jackson had said that nothing was a weed if you liked it. It all depended where it grew. As Eleanor hopped and jumped along irregular railway sleepers in the track that used to run up to the Seaford and London line, she had paused to add scabious and red clover to a sweaty bunch of nodding dandelions and daisies to present to her Mum.

She had planted seeds at the back of the Mill House in a bit of soil she had cleared, unaware that a hundred years earlier a portly widower had taken as much pride in dahlias growing in the same spot. The next time she visited the ruins, Eleanor hurried to see if the seeds had sprouted and was greeted by a tangle of red and orange nasturtiums. She had never grown anything before and was ecstatic, but she had to keep quiet about it because she wasn't meant to be there. Until Alice she had never shown anyone.

The tiny garden was her secret.

When Alice had seen the long thin mound with its straggling nasturtiums she had shuddered dramatically and pronounced it was like a grave. There was, she had crowed, absolutely no point in having flowers in the middle of rubbish. Also she had done nasturtiums at school. Whatever that meant.

Eleanor preferred the Tide Mills to anywhere because it was full of places to hide and make dens. She was never alone. As she sat on the worn front step of the cottage or trailed along the old railway line, she saw the shadows of what, until the extension of Newhaven harbour at the end of the nineteenth century, had been a thriving community of several hundred people.

Eleanor would hear the clanging bell warning of a train and then a fantastic silver locomotive would steam by, sneezing and puffing, with a handsome name like *Alexander the Great* or *The Flying Horseman*. There would be Summer Holiday trains, hammock racks bundled with suitcases and a rainbow jumble of beach things smelling of warm, soft plastic. The train would stop at the halt, with 'Bongville' painted in uneven sloping letters on a large concrete sign, breaking the country silence with a clattering of doors and bundling of cases, as the ticket barrier framed a parade of faces sporting a deathly London pallor.

Eleanor seldom reflected that she invented the most exciting bits of her life. The whimsical world in her head was real, the life she lived a dull perseverance in comparison. When Alice had insisted she was lying, Eleanor hadn't understood.

Eleanor had in fact rarely been on a train. In June 1968, Doctor Ramsay drove his family down to Sussex in his brand new racing green Rover, which Alice had said made her feel sick when he had brought them home from the swings the second time they played together.

Until that June, when everything changed, the Ramsays had spent every holiday at the White House, a three-storey detached house fronted by a sweeping circular drive that was reached by entering through two huge wrought iron gates. The house had been built by Eleanor's great-great-grandfather with money her mother said he got through slavery, just as Mark's father, Judge Henry Ramsay, whose scary portrait hung in the chilly dining room at the White House, had made his money through hanging people. That made her Dad go on about how James Ramsay was rich because of his share in the Tide Mills and investment in Newhaven harbour and that Henry (he always referred to his father by his first name) had wanted to create a better world through the rule of law. The children would sigh and exchange looks because the history lesson about James Ramsay and the stained-glass-lamb-window in the church was coming next. To make the story friendly, Doctor Ramsay's youngest daughter pictured James Ramsay as a white woolly lamb with her cat Crawford's fluffy front paws.

This year seagulls had splattered the outside walls of the only remaining cottage at the Tide Mills with gashes of berry-red and scattered fluffy feathers on the rubbled floor, which had also made Alice feel sick. Fat pigeons jostled and clattered in the larder of the cottage, their wistful voices amplified in the enclosed space. Gorse and blackberry bushes, nettles and dandelions made it hard to walk along the pathways between the buildings. Lichen and moss had moved like a tide over the worn stone, which peeped out like bone through tissue in places where the ground dipped away. Once, ferreting in the undergrowth, Eleanor had discovered an iron key as big as her hand and, easing and tugging at it with a patience no one knew she possessed, had got it out from between the stones without disturbing the tiled floor of the Mill Owner's hallway. It fitted the rusted lock of the outhouse door, but would not turn. She put it in her Box of Secrets.

The Box of Secrets came from South Africa, and was an unwanted present to her mother. The cedarwood was always warm and smelled of Saturday mornings perched on her Mum's bed listening to snippets from *Vogue* or *Nova* and examining pictures of beautiful women. This image greeted Eleanor as she slipped the gold catch and opened the lid, and cheered her whatever her mood.

The secrets included three train tickets found in the waste paper basket in her father's study, an ivory compact still with traces of rouge that had been given to her by an actress friend of her parents. A Victorian Bun penny, two farthings and the sixpence from the Tide Mills were wrapped in tissue paper and kept in a soft leather bag with a drawstring. Tucked in next to this was a silver case shaped like a plump cushion. It was lined with a nest of red velvet on which rested a tuft of grey fur from her rabbit, killed and mostly eaten up by a neighbour's cat when Eleanor was seven. She had snipped off the fur from the leftovers. After this Eleanor promised herself never to mind things again.

Eleanor acquired her most cherished treasure a few days before meeting Alice. The brand new penknife had a sharp blade, and a fan of gleaming tools. She had stolen it from the gun shop where they had gone to buy a new riding hat for Gina. Eleanor had not known she was going to take the knife. Her hand whipped out when the man went to get more hats from the stock room. Once she held it, cold and heavy, she could not put it back. No one was looking as she slipped it into her pocket. Eleanor believed that the knife made her capable of anything.

Later she told the police she had the penknife with her the last time they played hide and seek. She realised too late that she shouldn't have mentioned it because when they asked to see it, she couldn't find it.

Eleanor kept the Box of Secrets under a floorboard in her Sussex bedroom; and when she couldn't sleep in London would make a mental inventory of its contents. After the light was switched off, she waited for the hunched ghouls to become the chest of drawers, the toy cupboard and the wardrobe. Sometimes they never did. Then she composed a spell to lift her bed over London, and fly away across the Sussex Downs to Charbury where it was always summer. There she could lie and listen to the push and hush of the waves, tucked up safely. Eleanor never got back to London; she was already asleep as her bed landed by the sea.

That Tuesday Eleanor had said Alice could hide first. She had hidden ridiculously. As Eleanor reached 'ten' and started to search, she straight away spotted Alice peering round from behind the crumbling wall of the Mill House. Eleanor was relieved. She preferred hiding to seeking.

As warm breezes brushed the brambles of Eleanor's hiding place, they carried the scent of lavender, wild roses and blackberries and bluffed around her like her Mum's best hugs. She rubbed her nose to stop the tickle. She mustn't sneeze and give herself away. She didn't want Alice to find her.

Then after a few moments it dawned on Eleanor that there was no point in hiding. Alice wasn't looking for her any more. That much was clear. Eleanor pushed aside brambles, and slithered along the floor of the leafy tunnel on her stomach, moving further away from the path. Thorns tore at her skin; soon beads of blood dotted the scratches. Eleanor's mouth was dry. She was miles from civilisation. It could be days before she found drinking water. She had signed a pledge in blood. *My mother will die if I fail.* She had a new task and would return – like Odysseus (or was it Hercules?) – to the darkened room where Isabel Ramsay lay only when it was completed.

Isabel Ramsay was unaware of the swollen rivers crossed or mad monsters vanquished by her small daughter in her name. Eleanor would tiptoe into her bedroom against her Dad's instructions and kiss the creamy, scented cheek. In Eleanor's story Isabel was always glad to see her and leaping out of bed would tug back the curtains and gasp at the bright sun making elongated shadows across the lawn.

'*What is the time? It was morning when I went to sleep.*'

'*You have been asleep over a hundred years, under a wicked spell.*'

She would explain about spells.

'*After much trouble I have released you.*'

'*That long? It seems like a minute. Thank you, darling!*'

Then her mother would see the tea table with the white cloth under Uncle Jack's tree. Her handsome husband and two other children would wave all together in a row. Hearty family waves like rainbows; a collection of cheery hats and bright summer clothes. Eleanor would lead her Mum out into the sunny garden, doing the slow, traily walk practised in her bedroom. She would give her Darjeeling tea in her favourite cup with the wafer thin edge.

After a few minutes Eleanor crawled into blinding sunlight. She was only inches from a drop of six feet to the beach. With a moment's hesitation, she scootered around to face the other way and inched over the edge on her stomach, feet first, feeling for toeholds. She found one. As she trusted her weight to it and felt for the next one, it gave way in a spray of chalk and she shot down, and crash-landed on the shingle, bruising her knee and jarring her ankles. She heaved herself into a sitting position, relishing the pain as part of the massive task she had to fulfil. Her palms were stinging. But she was alive. She wiped her forehead with her handkerchief, dashing the cloth across her face, the way her Dad did.

The beach was enclosed by a chalky outcrop at one end, and a towering pile of rocks at the other that few people climbed. When the policeman asked her to recall details of that day, Eleanor said the beach was empty. A rusting boat, slouching dark and sulky against the sky, interrupted a stretch of pebbles that dropped in terraces to a finger of wet sand at the shoreline. She told him it was a cloudless day full of colours: yellow, blue and red.

Chief Inspector Hall did not appreciate these vivid observations; the little girl's stream of words made the stiff-suited man shuffle about uneasily on his chair. He thought that there was something strange about her and got stern when Eleanor told him she liked to paddle in the water, and wasn't frightened of the tide returning because she had a tide-table book. He didn't know any other little girls like her, and was especially irritated when she took this comment as a compliment.

Eleanor collapsed back on the stones, keeping her knees bent to avoid the scorching pebbles, with one hand flung over her heart, as the wound from the sword grew worse. She was badly hurt, but must keep going, she had a long journey ahead to find the Indian Amulet stolen from the King's crown. She must return with it or her mother would die of the curse.

This last bit was based on reality. The day before, Eleanor had searched her bedroom and the playroom for the amulet given to her by Mrs Jackson, who used to live next door in St Peter's Square. Without it Eleanor knew she too would be cursed. She had begun to suspect that Alice stole things. She had to find it. She had better find Alice first.

Eleanor particularly hated the way Alice said her name: in a sing-song voice not as a real name tripping off her tongue well worn and well loved, but like a thing held in delicate and disgusted fingers. Most people called her Elly; until Alice, no one had called her Eleanor unless they were cross, or a teacher.

The tide was coming in so she couldn't go on to the beach, instead, she tramped back up the cliff path. She would go home through the Tide Mills.

The distant hoot of a train on the London line sounded across the fields. Now there were no birds in the sky and nothing moved. The day they arrived, there had been swifts but Lucian said they had gone to Africa. Eleanor wished she could fly to Africa whenever she wanted. She aimed powerful, accurate kicks at stones as she dodged and skipped back up the track. She was Georgie Best as she scored the winning goal.

If Alice was hiding, Eleanor considered it was really unfair. It wasn't her turn. She chased up the six wooden steps to the short village street and began pacing from one end of the ruins to the other. She knew she was being watched, so she walked with her hands behind her back, like the Mill Owner checking the great wheels were turning in the deep pond under the arches of the bridge before going in for his tea in the big house behind the high wall.

She could forget about Alice and go on playing.

Eleanor tiptoed around the cottage and kicked open the back door. It swung inwards and crashed against the wall. Someone had oiled the hinges. A pigeon flapped down from a hole in the ceiling and flew past her, its wings breezing near her face. She kept perfectly still, listening to the silence. There was no sign of Alice.

She stepped back outside. Then she saw her. A figure was standing near the halt, half hidden behind the Bongville sign. Everything shimmered in the blistering heat so that at first the person and the tall thistles appeared to be doing a strange swaying dance. One minute they were all thistles, the next people. As she got nearer, Eleanor forgot that to be quite fair she should give Alice one more chance. She forgot that Alice had two more lives to go as she crept forward on grandmother's footsteps, clasping her penknife. All she could think of was the huge task she had to accomplish if she was to save her Mum and release everyone from the curse. She began to count, in a voice loud and low:

'Five... four... three... two... one... COMING!'

Two

Crawford disappeared at parties. As people came in through the front door he rushed out the back, leaping over the garden wall and out of sight. He never returned until it was over. Only Eleanor minded. She longed to show him off to the guests, more for the reflected glory she presumed being seen with him would lend to her, than for Crawford's personal attributes. Once she had tried to make him stay by enticing him with food, but when he heard the door knocker he tore out of her bedroom and she was caught chasing down the stairs after him, her footsteps thundering, her face too red. Her parents particularly hated it when their children went out of control. Looking back at her childhood, Eleanor later decided that as children they had been expected to play the same role for Mark and Isabel Ramsay at parties as Crawford had for herself. They must shed different and flattering lights on their parents, the younger ones decked in Kids in Gear corduroy, Gina in her first Biba dress. Isabel had declared one party utterly ruined when she was forced to send Eleanor to bed in front of the guests.

When Eleanor blocked the cat flap, Crawford wriggled out through the small window in the downstairs lavatory. As each strategy failed, Eleanor got less scrupulous about her methods of keeping him indoors. One evening she trapped him inside a washing basket in the utility room, but felt ashamed, so let him go. It was fortunate for Eleanor that her efforts were unsuccessful. The production of Crawford, with his tendency to bite, at one of Isabel's intricately orchestrated events was too terrible to contemplate. If she had not become so engrossed in the challenge of getting him there, Eleanor would have been the first to warn others off the idea. Few of the people invited to a Ramsay party would have enjoyed hearing the story of the shredded ear, or of the headless mice and dead birds regularly left beside the morning cornflakes on the kitchen table.

Crawford was a sturdy orange and white cat sporting a red leather collar and an attitude of outrage. The only person whose lap he would grace was Isabel Ramsay. The rest of the family had given up on him. Only Eleanor kept trying.

When Eleanor was seven, Mrs Jackson moved in next door to their house in St Peter's Square. She lived in the dark basement flat in the house of her son who, to Eleanor's indignation, had refused to let her bring her cat because his wife was allergic to it. So a few weeks after Mrs Jackson arrived, Eleanor, taking the advantage of surprise, had snatched up a preoccupied Crawford, and lugged him, paws spilling over her bare arms, to visit her. He had struggled, growled and spat as she hopped from one foot to the other, waiting for Mrs Jackson to open the door, and in another minute would struggle free. But once inside the flat he became a different cat. He shrank and felt softer, he stopped spitting and clung to Eleanor, even climbing with silent intent further up her shoulder. When she placed him on the rug in front of the gas fire, he leapt up onto her lap, purring noisily, then curled up close to her. She was enchanted. At Mrs Jackson's, Crawford was the cat Eleanor had dreamed of.

After this she always took Crawford when she went to see Mrs Jackson. Eleanor went more often. She looked forward to the warm weight of him as busy paws kneaded her jumper and a hot rough tongue licked her hands. In the green subterranean light of Mrs Jackson's living room, she gazed down at him over her glass of orange squash and worked her way through a plate of Jaffa cakes that did not have to be shared with anyone.

Eleanor found she could talk to Mrs Jackson about what was important and instead of being told not to be silly or having the way she pronounced things corrected, Mrs Jackson listened to her. She even laughed at her jokes. Eleanor promised

Mrs Jackson that she would take her to the Tide Mills and asked her advice about the secret flowerbed. She related the story about the wicked Mill Owner who locked little girls in the Granary, dressing them out in the finest ball gowns and making up their hair, so that they became a collection of secret princesses. Then one day he had fallen down dead on the train to Brighton, which meant his ghost could not rest but must keep haunting although never arriving and the girls were released and allowed to go free and live happily ever after. Mrs Jackson was genuinely concerned about ghosts and took the matter just as seriously as Eleanor who had seen him pacing the bridge over the millpond.

One day Mrs Jackson gave Eleanor a small cardboard box daintily wrapped in silver cigarette paper. She had placed it beside the biscuits on the spindly-legged table. A present! Eleanor was nervous and her hand trembled as she lifted the lid. She wanted to like it. She did not want to have to pretend to be pleased. She need not have worried, for lying on a wad of cotton wool was a round lump of green glass. She put out a finger and gently touched it. It was cool and smooth and shone like a jewel. Glancing at Mrs Jackson and receiving an encouraging nod, she took it out and cradled it in her palm. She looked up and was taken aback to see Mrs Jackson smiling like a young girl. Overwhelmed, Eleanor practically flew at Mrs Jackson and hugged her tightly, telling her truthfully it was the best present she had ever been given. No one had ever given her something so special. She called it an amulet and swore she would keep it always.

For a moment Eleanor divined that Mrs Jackson, as if by magic, knew just who she was. Then the moment was gone and the empty plate, the glass and the ransacked present box returned to normal. Only years later, staring out of a lace-curtained window, would Eleanor briefly allow herself to return to that afternoon, and see that Mrs Jackson had known her even better then she had known herself. By then it was too late.

But each time they got home, Crawford would be worse. When Eleanor scooped him up, he would fight more fiercely to escape. He was harder to catch because he bolted as soon as she approached. The guilt Eleanor would feel when she did finally recapture him was always obliterated by her blind indignation that Crawford had forgotten who she was. Once she had chased after him, grabbing him by the tail as he raced past, dragged him back and smothered him in a towel to stop him struggling. She noted clinically how his high-pitched cry of pain as her hand gripped his hind leg was like the sound of seagulls.

'What have I told you, Crawford?' The words fizzed through clenched teeth. 'Now you are making me very cross indeed. This is an incredible waste of my time. Your co-op-er-ation would be appreciated.' She shook the towelled bundle in time to her words and squeezed him, telling herself as well as Crawford how this treatment was for his own good. 'Behave!' she hissed at the whimpering inert lump.

Then one day as Eleanor reached up to ring Mrs Jackson's bell, Crawford freed a paw and lashed out, gouging her neck. She yelped and hurled him across the paving slabs. For a second a shapeless mass seemed to fly, four limbs and tail spreading like ragged wings, then he thumped heavily against the dustbins, knocking a lid to the ground with a terrible clang, and vanished over the wall. She stared after him dizzily as she nursed her wound. She was scared that the Jacksons had heard the noise and she wanted to run away too, but couldn't move. There were marks in the patches of moss on the flags. Eleanor traced one with the toe of her sandal – making a coded sign of contrition for anyone who could decipher it. After a while, when it was clear no one was coming, she was disappointed. She wanted Mrs Jackson to open the door and take her in, but with Crawford gone there was no point in pressing the bell. Mrs Jackson would ask where he was. She wouldn't like Eleanor if she found out what she had done. She would tell her never to come again. Behaving as if this scene had actually taken place, Eleanor staggered home with tears dribbling down her cheeks and blood from the cut on her neck staining her shirt. She reached her room without being seen and curled up on her side on her bed, her face to the wall. As she lay with lavatory paper clamped under her collar to stop the bleeding, visceral emotions set hard as lava. No one would be allowed to get close to her again.

Crawford was missing for three weeks. His absence threw the Ramsay family into frenzy, and a rare state of unity. Gina drew posters and stuck them to trees and in the windows of as many shops in King Street as would let her. Lucian was at boarding school, but used up his pocket money ringing every night to check on progress and give painstaking advice to whoever answered the phone. Mark Ramsay patrolled the square every night whistling and calling. Sometimes Isabel joined him. Only Eleanor appeared not to care. She slunk about the house, wearing a series of polo necks to hide the nasty scratch on her neck. She bore the less tangible secret of how evil she was like a rucksack of rocks. Inside her head, sentences of explanation, speeches of atonement, of love and confession evaporated before a judge as harsh as her grandfather had been. She was certain that despite being a cat and unable to talk, if he came home, Crawford would give her away.

Then one Saturday morning while they were all in the kitchen eating breakfast, Crawford tipped open the cat flap with his nose, waited briefly then eased himself in and things went back to normal. Except that Eleanor avoided him, even leaving a room if he padded in, and she never visited Mrs Jackson again.

Mrs Jackson eventually plucked up the courage to ask Isabel if she had offended Eleanor. Isabel, barely aware that Eleanor knew the old lady in the basement next door, dismissed the possibility with strident politeness. She reacted with such astonishment that an old woman, reputed to be going senile, could imagine she had any sort of relationship with a chaotic seven-year-old, that Mrs Jackson abandoned the idea of sending Eleanor a small note. A few weeks later Mrs Jackson accidentally left the gas on. It was a mistake anyone could have made, her mind was on other things, but her son decided she could no longer live on her own. For her own sake he put her in a residential home in Woking and let the flat to a young actress with a crush on Vanessa Redgrave and a small part in *The Newcomers*.

The Ramsays were celebrated as gifted hosts able to put guests at their ease. They lavished undivided attention which, though fleeting, still bathed the recipient in a rapturous glow of self worth for the duration of the evening. People drifted down the worn stone steps of the tall Georgian house convinced they had seen more of the Ramsays than they had and were more valued than they were.

The parties were noisy, crowded affairs packed with people from every sector of public life: top financiers and famous actors, prize-winning novelists and emerging landscape designers were mixed strategically with primary school teachers, nurses and riding instructors. No one was allowed to latch on to familiar groups, they were guided by gentle hands, beckoning looks, floated on wafts of Isabel's light perfume, or seduced by Doctor Ramsay's lilting brown voice into life-changing decisions – new lives. Isabel styled herself a thoroughly modern Ottoline Morrell, although she hoped she attracted greater respect from those she helped than her private role model. Business and romantic partnerships were forged against all odds, deals of international importance were struck, diffident geniuses unmasked, promotions enabled, while lucky breaks came to those who had given up or given in. Old friendships were rekindled from damp ashes of long held enmities and life long relationships were toasted to the clink of glasses of sparkling white wine from the ripest Italian summers. Decades later Ramsay parties would be remembered as interludes from life, or as rare glimpses of true life where conversation knew no limits and the dancing was wild and free. The walls in the St Peter's Square house were hung with the latest discoveries: a Hockney in the drawing room, a Jim Dine over the drawing room fireplace, and an early Warhol in the downstairs lavatory. As young men and women emerged into the sleeping square in the blue hours before dawn, they were baffled to find themselves on drab streets in a drizzling Hammersmith, looking in vain for taxis or a stray 27 bus in the chill morning air. Only those too ill to get out of bed, or too naïve to know what they were missing, refused an invitation to a party at 49 St Peter's Square.

Eleanor loved it when her parents gave a party. She knew nothing of the social and political machinations running like well oiled engines beneath the surface of the chatter and champagne, and believed parties were thrown for fun. She soon learnt the signs of one approaching. Her mother would get excited and talk very fast. She would insist she must see Clara, she had to catch up with Tarquin, oh! and of course, Charles, whose conversation she absolutely craved. She adored his latest book, so clever, so true! She must see them all. She ruffled and pulled at Eleanor's hair and caught her up into a rapid jig around the table. They must have a party.

When her mother was organising an event it seemed to Eleanor that Isabel Ramsay became a new person. She stayed out of bed all day, cuddled her children impulsively and even appreciated Eleanor's jokes. She ran up and down stairs, calling orders to Lizzie, their live-in help, all the while singing and doing different voices as she juggled with a variety of lists, pausing only to draw neat lines through completed tasks with a flourish. Revising and devising, with gimlet eyes and pen poised, she plotted the evening from start to finish. She did not stop talking: making and taking telephone calls from her bedroom in a low voice with the door shut, or chatting in a small girl's voice into the wall mounted telephone in the kitchen. Her voice rang out across the square as she called imperiously to deliverymen from the doorstep. She muttered to herself as she planned and barked orders to Mark, and yet again rewrote the guest list, impatient at his response, or concerned for his opinion. She scribbled the latest developments and tiniest reminders on a white plastic notice-board hanging by the fridge in bold black felt marker. The spikes and loops in the words reminded Eleanor of the purple graffiti daubed high up on the stage doors of the Commodore Bingo Hall on the corner of King

Street. She developed the hazy assumption that her mother was responsible for both. Isabel would absently stretch the telephone cord across her children's heads as she reached for her wine, or a mug of tepid coffee. She chain-smoked, pacing the kitchen, ripping open envelopes of acceptance, slamming drawers and rummaging in cupboards, in search of the one thing that would make the party perfect.

Gina was willing assistant, finding things that were lost, filing letters, appeasing shop owners, fending off phone calls from over-eager guests. Lucian was usually away at school. Eleanor tried to make the most of this time when her mother was out of bed, so friendly and nice. She was desperate that each party should be the best ever. This time the food would be truly scrumptious, her mother's favourites would come, with no one to bore her or get on her nerves and make her cross. Everyone would be happy. Afterwards, her mother would never be sad again. Eleanor imagined hearing the shouts of laughter as she lay in her bedroom, lulled to sleep by the dips and peaks of music and voices, waiting for her Mum to come and tuck her in and leave butterfly kisses on her forehead. On party nights Eleanor would not have to lie rigid to fool the monsters into thinking she was dead because her Mum would be there to keep them out.

After the party, Eleanor promised herself that everything would be better.

Mostly Eleanor didn't let herself think of afterwards.

She was allowed to help Isabel dress because just before the party Gina disappeared into her bedroom until she was called. Eleanor scoffed inwardly at her sister who would emerge, stuck up straight like a brush handle in a trance to hang limply on their Dad's arm. Or Gina would parade around holding a glass of watered down wine, peering at the pictures on the walls as if she hadn't seen them every day of her life already. Eleanor would stump after Gina – clop, clop, clop – up the stairs to be introduced to the early guests. She couldn't believe that Gina bothered to spend ages putting on stupid make-up so she could look like a lunatic.

With Gina out of the way, Eleanor could sprawl contentedly on her parents' bed, creeping amongst the squashy pillows, sniffing lungfuls of her mother's scent that mingled with the smell of cotton sheets, and watch her get ready.

Isabel sat on the edge of a low Victorian nursing chair to put on her stockings. She leaned back into the chair, raising one thin, shapely leg then the other as she unfurled each stocking along the length, pointing her toes upwards like the ballerina she should have been.

Eleanor stared at her mother's hands as her fingers tipped with pink nail varnish swept up with a swoosh along the calves and around the thighs, smoothing out the silky wrinkles. She held her breath for the snap of the suspenders, as her mother dipped down to clip her stockings into place.

Isabel moved with precision and elegance. A fleeting frown betrayed a woman rehearsed in every gesture and action, and conscious of everything she did. Isabel could not afford spontaneity. She might have been gratified, yet disbelieving, to know she had long succeeded in appearing the woman she wanted to be. Her bosoms (a word Eleanor could not say out loud) pushed up over the black lace bra. Eleanor knew the skin was soft and warm, and as she glanced furtively at the dark space inside the bra she would picture the battles she had fought, the creatures she had slain mercilessly to save her mother's life.

Eleanor would stroke her forehead and tell her everything was all right.

'*Soon your headache will go and you'll be happy.*'

Isabel turned this way and that as she tried on different outfits. She never planned her dress in advance. Even if asked, Eleanor dared not say she liked something. If her mother didn't feel right, she would be cross with Eleanor and might send her out of the room. She watched with trepidation as Isabel yanked clothes off their hangers, discarding rejects on the bed and shoving others along the rail to find what she wanted. Eleanor knew that all the days of preparation could fall to ruin if her mother wasn't wearing clothes that made her happy.

Finally Isabel was ready. She stood with one hand on her hip in front of the wardrobe doors and ran her hand over her stomach, stroking it downward, over and over, in the way that made Eleanor's father angry. Eleanor recoiled at the crushing sensation in her tummy at the sound of him shouting in the White House garden last summer. It was the first time her mother had been out of bed the whole holiday.

'*For pity's sake, Isabel, take your hand off your fucking stomach!*'

'*And where do you suggest I put it?*'

He had snatched at her wrist and held it, shaking it as if it didn't belong to her, staring wildly at the thin flapping thing. There were white marks on her mother's skin when he let go. The children had played statues until it was over. Isabel got up from the table as if nothing had happened, and Eleanor watched her go across the lawn in her short white dress and vanish into the house. Everyone chewed and swallowed in silence until it was all right to get down.

Isabel was unaware of her human shadow as she studied her reflection, making reparation for perceived flaws with restless hands. Eleanor traced her own hipbones through her pinafore dress with the flat of her palm. With a faraway look, Isabel put her hand to her nose and sniffed the tips of her fingers and thumb as if confirming her own existence. Eleanor sniffed her own fingers, the smell was comforting: a mixture of her guinea pig and the tuppenny lasting lolly she wasn't allowed because her Dad said it was pure sugar.

As she copied her mother, Eleanor learnt how easy it was to be someone else.

That night, for the party vaguely intended to celebrate the departure of the Ramsays to Sussex for Whitsun, Isabel had chosen a black shiny dress with no sleeves and a zip up the back. She let Eleanor do it up. As she balanced on the bed to reach, Eleanor dreaded her father coming in and taking over. She could hear him next door, striding about in the ironing room where he kept his clothes. She clutched her mother's bare shoulder to steady herself.

'Eleanor! Get off, you're cold!'

Eleanor briefly nursed her hand, blowing hard on it. The shape of Isabel's body appeared as the zip pulled the slippery fabric together and it tightened over her hips and waist, to reveal contours of muscle and bone. She lingered over the fastening of the hook and eye at the top.

Now the make-up.

Eleanor had prepared the dressing table while her mother was in the bath. She lined up what her mother called her 'condiments' including the tiny bottle of scent the children had bought for her birthday that was still full. An expert assistant, on these occasions Eleanor never got it wrong.

Her mother handled the brushes like an artist, shading in colour with deft flicks of soft sable. She pouted at the three-way mirror as with a magician's sleight of hand, she drew an accomplished bow with a lip pencil, and filled in fleshy lips with glossy lipstick. She took a tissue from her daughter without acknowledgement and stained the paper with a crimson kiss. Taking another bottle of perfume from her handbag, she squirted it behind her ears, on the inside of each wrist and between her breasts. She dropped the bottle back in her bag and snapped shut the clasp.

Isabel was ready to meet her guests.

Eleanor studied Isabel, anxious to miss nothing. It was one of the facts of life that her mother was clever, witty and beautiful. She had overheard a woman say Isabel Ramsay could turn men to stone. It was obvious to Eleanor that the tall woman adjusting her bra through the neck of her dress as she stepped into high heels was capable of everything. Her mother was a project Eleanor could have got top marks in. She knew her better than anyone. Better than Gina who went on the shopping trips, better than Lucian when her mother rubbed his back after cricket and told him he was her favourite man. As Eleanor followed her out of the bedroom, she swiftly pocketed the crumpled hanky. Later she hid it in her Box of Secrets with the others.

After Alice disappeared, Eleanor was not allowed to help her mother dress.

29

The doors dividing the drawing room in half were thrown open to make a space the length and breadth of the house. The furniture had been pushed back to the walls or removed. Her mother prowled the room, her stilettos clicking on the polished floorboards, rearranging chairs and repositioning ornaments. She touched surfaces and looked tetchy, but Eleanor knew Lizzie had done a good job.

Isabel was never happy.

Eleanor took up position by the French doors, and peered through a pane of warped Georgian glass. The road was fragmented by the swirly shaped gaps in the wrought iron balcony. She would spot the first cars. She loved the start of parties as the house filled up with excited, colourful people, their faces flickering in candlelight. Yet it was with mixed feelings that Eleanor anticipated the first knock at the door. It signalled her countdown to bedtime.

Suddenly her mother was upon her, stroking her hair, adjusting her dress and wrenching up the socks with the horrible flowers Eleanor had purposely rolled down. Clawing nails grazed her skin. Eleanor sniffed her mother's hair: apple blossom and warm spring although outside a cold, spotting rain marked the end of May. Her breath caught as Isabel squeezed her round the waist, bending so far over her that Eleanor could not see and her tummy hurt. She didn't want to cry out or it would end.

'You're my very own darling! My gorgeous, delicious little baby. You love me best, don't you? You love your Mummy… so, so…' Her voice grated in a half whisper. Eleanor was unable to respond.

Then it was over.

Her mother strode over to the coffee table and snatched up a cigarette from a silver box placed at an acute angle on the glass. Mark and Isabel's initials were engraved on the lid: a chunky 'I' and 'M' fitted around each other like building blocks, a shape so familiar to Eleanor that it had nothing to do with letters or with her parents. Isabel lit the cigarette before Eleanor could do it for her and stood with one hand on her hip as she sucked on the filter, tossing her head back to exhale smoke rings that broke into ribbons above them.

The banging shook the house. Isabel shuddered at the noise then snapped into action, stubbing out her cigarette in a huge speckled marble ashtray and checking her face in the mantelpiece mirror. She left the room, smoothing her stomach with fluttering hands. Eleanor chased after her, only remembering as she was about to take the stairs two at a time, to adopt her mother's languid indifference.

When Eleanor reached the hall Isabel was giving what her children privately called her 'too hot to touch' hugs to a woman with dark hair in a green mini dress, who had the skinniest legs Eleanor had ever seen. Her Dad wore the saggy tweed suit her mother hated because it made him look 'stodgy'. The suit meant he was in a bad mood and Eleanor felt helpless as she watched him shake hands with a man in a flowery shirt and tight yellow trousers who had a mass of long curly hair, making Eleanor think of an exotic bird. Her mother presented her face to the man to be kissed. They kissed on the lips and then Isabel briefly touched the man's cheek, as if correcting a mistake.

Eleanor stayed on the bottom stair, hanging from the newel post. The man obviously didn't know her mother hated to be kissed like that when she had her make-up on. She pulled a face and glancing at her Dad saw that he too had seen the other man's mistake.

Soon Gina would appear, tottering like a doll on stilts in her new pointy shoes and there was a danger they would send Eleanor to bed. She kept still and hoped no one would notice her. Then Isabel beckoned to her:

'Harry, you'll have to say hello to my youngest. This is me at seven. To a tee. I'll have to find a picture. Elly is the ghost of me as a girl, the others take after Mark.'

Years later, flicking through photographs, Eleanor would see quite plainly that she took after her father. The likeness was striking. Yet Isabel had always insisted that Gina had Mark's eyes and that Eleanor had hers. It made her suppose that Isabel had perhaps loved her after all. But by then too much had happened.

'I'm nine in thirty-one days.' The words were lost as her mother's voice soared, she was holding the man's hand which was all right for crossing a road, but looked stupid indoors. She signalled urgently to her:

'Darling, come here. Now! Come and meet the next poet laureate!'

Eleanor didn't want to go near the man who in any case was staring at her mother. Isabel pulled her forward with a jerk and held her by the shoulders.

'This is my last baby. She's growing up far too fast. Don't you hate the way they lose that puppy look? The best bit is over so soon.'

Eleanor tried to smile but his eyes were on Isabel so it didn't matter. She kept still, in case her mother let her go. The man remarked that she had grown. Eleanor was about to say he had grown too, she had planned this would be a good answer for a question she was sick of, but the man was speaking to her mother so clearly their chat was over.

Isabel led the way up the stairs. The yellow-plumed bird-poet followed. Her Dad gave a slight bow to let the stick-lady walk in front, then without looking told Eleanor to go to bed, reassuring her that he would tuck her in. Eleanor looked to see if her mother had heard; if she had, she might let her stay up longer. The banishment was too early tonight. She was not to be at the party at all. She got the sick feeling that came the day after parties, so couldn't answer when the lady commented how lucky she was to have such a kind daddy.

Eleanor loitered around on the landing outside the drawing room, hoping Isabel would appear and take her in. She could not know Eleanor had been told to go to bed. But the knocker banged again, so she gave up.

It was all over.

Tomorrow her mother would stay in bed refusing to be touched. Tomorrow things would go back to usual, except Isabel was crosser after parties.

Eleanor did not want tomorrow.

Things were different after the business with Alice. Eleanor's parents never allowed her downstairs when they gave a party. Nothing was actually said, certainly Alice was never given as the reason. Eleanor just knew she must keep to her bedroom. At first she would sit on the top stair listening to the muffled music and laughter. Through the landing window she would count the double-decker B.E.A buses going back and forth to London Airport on the Great West Road. The noise swelled each time the drawing room door opened and she hoped it was her Mum coming to fetch her. It never was. Instead she had to be ready to rush back to bed when Gina floated up the stairs, walking like Isabel.

After Alice vanished, Eleanor dreaded parties. She wished that, like Crawford, she could escape out the back door until everything was over.

Three

Alice was there. No matter what Eleanor did. Alice was there, smiling.

As soon as Eleanor clicked off the bedroom light Alice arrived and would not go. Eleanor tried everything to make her disappear. She jammed her knuckles into her eye sockets to shut out Alice's smile, but as her eyes began to ache and sting, Alice's disembodied head still hung in the spangled darkness like a Chinese lantern, her face swollen and peculiar. Now Alice had new powers. She made shadows glide around the room. Her skin was translucent white, the eyes a grey see-through jelly. The hair was solid like the bust of Beethoven on Lucian's piano. Eleanor tried opening her eyes and staring hard to make Alice vanish again. This almost succeeded, but then Alice returned bit by bit, in the carved pattern over the wardrobe mirror. First two eyes, then the nose and finally the curly bit in the corner became a ghastly grin. Other times Alice floated like an escaped balloon outside the window where the moon should have been. Her bloated, gloating face lit up the room with a bluish light like Mark Ramsay's surgery at the hospital where Eleanor believed she had once slept, although it may have been a dream.

Then things got worse. Alice came in the day too. She was there when Eleanor's father shut the curtains in the evening, hovering in the fabric. Earlier, Eleanor had found her lying under the sofa, her face cupped in chubby hands. She was using all Eleanor's secret places. Alice was spying without taking turns, which was not fair. She was hiding really well, for only Eleanor had found her.

After Alice didn't come back from hide and seek, Eleanor's parents kept the newspapers away from her. If Eleanor pattered into the sitting room when the news was on, they leapt up to switch off the television. Yet they didn't work as a team. They disagreed about what to shield Eleanor from. They wanted to see the news themselves, so were unreasonably infuriated with her for causing them to miss it. Finally Mark took to ordering Eleanor out of the room. In the midst of this, both Mark and Isabel underestimated the resourcefulness of their youngest child. Simply by remaining single minded and alert Eleanor learnt to pick an erratic course through the fog that descended on the Ramsays after Alice went, to find out what she needed.

Alice's disappearance forced the Ramsays to stay on in Sussex while the police interviewed Eleanor. The press got wind of this and so Isabel had barred her from going into Charbury and even from being at the front of the house where she could be seen from the window. She could go in the back garden because it was screened by a high wall, reinforced by holly bushes and trees planted by the Judge, a private man and, as the executions mounted, a paranoid one. Now his paranoia would have been justified, for journalists outnumbered inhabitants in the lane beyond his wall. Vans and cars were parked nose to tail along the verges leading from the station right to the church, ploughing up the village green.

Lean-eyed men lounged against the counter in the village stores and queued outside the telephone box beside the Ram Inn. They perched on the church wall to scribble frantically in notebooks, or prowled around the narrow streets, lifting dustbin lids, parting branches and peering through windows and questioning everyone like pretend police. From her lookout post high above them all, Eleanor, spying out of the playroom window with a notebook of her own, was rewarded by the sight of a line of constables in white shirtsleeves, poking long poles into hedges and ditches, the way her father checked the oil in his car.

With Alice gone, Eleanor had no one to play with and there was no more talk of suitable local children. Lucian and Gina could go out but must not speak to anyone, even people they knew, like Iris Carter, the new lady at the stores who looked like Lulu. This ban effectively stopped them buying sweets. Gina might go to the stables if accompanied by her father, which made her furious. Lucian went to the river, returning in the evenings smudgy and cross with no fish. The rules made no sense to Eleanor; she knew they would never find Alice by stopping her leaving the house. Yet she kept to the regime with a devotion that went unnoticed. Their self-imposed curfew put the Ramsays in a sour mood.

Isabel stopped having headaches and was possessed with the organisational energy associated with parties. She learnt the names of the police, fended off reporters, deciding who to give interviews to and how best to present her family, as she always had. Mark and Isabel's friends would have been astonished to hear that it was Mark who crumpled. Although he was of no interest to the police because he was a doctor, Mark was irritable, shouting at objects, and swearing when the telephone rang.

On the morning after Alice disappeared, Eleanor was making her way along the passage from her bedroom to the stairs, hoping to overhear something useful about Alice, when she came upon her Dad on the landing. He was staring at Crawford, who, unaware of his rapt audience, was very slowly crawling along the carpet, his nose up close to the skirting board, his tummy touching the floor. He began sniffing the wood, pausing now and then to give a scratch at it with his paw. He was following a mouse trail. Eleanor wished that Alice would return just to see this. Alice hated mice. Then Mark Ramsay, unaware that he in turn was being watched, gave Crawford a hefty push with his boot making the animal yelp and shrink back in a snarl of fur. At the same time Mark caught sight of his daughter at the corner of the passage.

'Scram!' He growled at Crawford who, pausing briefly to spit at him, lolloped awkwardly away down the stairs, obviously in pain. Eleanor was perplexed. How she had treated Crawford during the Mrs Jackson campaign was her terrible secret. Perhaps it had not been so bad. Yet if she had kicked Crawford with pointless cruelty just for being a cat, her Dad would have been livid. She didn't think it fair.

Mark and Eleanor eyed each other, as if a long held enmity was now being laid bare before Eleanor obediently trudged on up the stairs to the playroom.

In the days that followed Eleanor slunk about feeling like an unwanted guest, pausing outside rooms, loitering on the landings, always retreating to the playroom. At meals she chewed dainty mouthfuls ten times, persisting though no one praised her as they had Alice. The Alice-Head hovered, invisible to the others, demanding Eleanor saw through its eyes. Eleanor became ruthlessly tidy and forced to ignore fanciful possibilities, her life shrank to a tedium. Alice had made Eleanor a fugitive in her own home.

Later that Wednesday Eleanor had succeeded in sneaking into the sitting room, and was building a tower with playing cards in the corner while her parents fluttered restlessly about the room. Her mother held a book, but wasn't reading it, while Mark had given up on the newspaper, saying that since the Kennedy shooting it was full of old news, and was pacing back and forth in front of the fireplace. Eleanor, who had been keeping quiet in the hope they would fail to notice her, was startled into attention when he blurted out to Isabel how absurd it was that one child got so much attention when there had been an assassination attempt on a presidential candidate. Isabel said it was an awful thing to happen twice, and that if the Senator died there would be no hope for America. She mumbled something about Alice going missing being the last straw and looked so upset that Eleanor did not like to ask how the Senator could die twice. She reconsidered her hide and seek rule of having three lives. Maybe two would do.

'The world is falling apart and they are wasting their time on this.' Mark drew the curtain to cut out the view of the gates, where a straggle of journalists had been camped since the previous evening when news of Alice's disappearance became public.

'What's the matter, worried because Kennedy's your twin so you'll lose half your self? I thought you weren't superstitious.' Isabel sneered.

'Don't be ridiculous.'

Eleanor meant to keep quiet to avoid annoyance, but she couldn't resist speaking. Until now she had only known about her Dad's younger sister, she didn't know he had a twin brother, let alone one that had been shot. No wonder he was so cross.

'What twin? Is he your brother, this Senator?'

'Now look what you've done.' Mark rounded on his wife.

'She doesn't understand.' Isabel always took the time to explain things when it was to make a point to Mark and she turned to Eleanor now with exaggerated patience: 'Robert Kennedy, this man who has been shot, is exactly the same age as Mark. It's always given him a power complex. Except today it's given him a headache!' She laughed and rubbed her face. No one was meant to find anything funny since Alice had gone.

Eleanor was grateful for being noticed so she nodded sagely.

'It's a damned sight more important than a girl going AWOL.' Addressing the gap in the curtain, Mark added: 'She's missing. Until they find her, what more is there to say? I'm being practical. We hardly even knew her so why don't they leave us alone?'

'You know why.' To Eleanor's alarm, her Mum had started crying and she spluttered in horrible jerking sobs. 'What if one of your children disappeared off the face of the earth?' Isabel shifted around so she could see Mark, who was now standing behind her, and kicked over the Bagatelle board that Eleanor had left propped against the sofa. It fell with a crash spilling ball bearings all over the floorboards. Isabel carried on:

'Her parents don't have any other children. It's over for them if Alice isn't found. I feel for her poor mother.' She fished up her cardigan sleeve for a tissue and blew her nose loudly at Mark Ramsay's implacable back, the material tightening around his bottom as he shuffled change in his trouser pockets.

Eleanor was anxious to stop her mother crying – her Dad hated crying – so she asked why 'it was over for them'? He scowled at Eleanor as she scuttled around the room retrieving ball bearings.

'You are only a mother if you have a child.' Isabel massaged her tears into her face with a forefinger because, as she had once told Eleanor, tears were good for the complexion. 'If Mrs Howland hasn't got Alice, she has no one to mother. At her age it's probably too late.'

'Stop talking bilge!' Mark closed the curtains entirely. They were in the dark until he snapped on a light. 'She's only about thirty! She has at least five child-bearing years yet.'

Eleanor dropped a ball bearing. It hit the side of her tower of cards bringing the whole lot down. She hovered over the cards making comic gestures of powerlessness to mitigate the mess and disown the pettiness of her game. Mark Ramsay rounded on his wife:

'Whatever happens she's still a fucking mother!'

Alice had said swearing was rude. Her teacher had told her it was a lazy use of language.

'It's irrelevant whether your children are dead or alive! Since when did you care about Alice Bloody Howland? You hardly bother with our lot. It's me who ferries them about and is driven bonkers by the inane chatter of them and their friends!'

'Oh and a few car rides makes you the perfect father, does it? If you think she's dead, why did you insist last night she was probably just hiding or had wandered off? Make your mind up!' Isabel caught Eleanor gaping at her and slumped back in her chair, adding too wearily to convince, 'Daddy doesn't mean it', before subsiding into silence.

Eleanor spoke fast to ward off more tears:

'Is the man going to be okay?'

'What?' Mark Ramsay stared at his daughter.

'The Senator Man. Is he going to get better?'

'No.' Doctor Ramsay pronounced a death sentence. Eleanor shuffled the pack of cards. She had boundless confidence in her father's powers, medical or otherwise.

'You don't know that.' Isabel pulled a face at him. She assumed it must be bad for her children to hear unpleasant news even about people they had never heard of.

'I do.' Mark was firm.

'They said on the radio earlier that Senator Kennedy saved his son from drowning days before he was shot. He managed to grab him as he was being swept away and get him to shore. He was a good man.'

'What would you expect him to do, let him drown?' Mark was impatient.

Isabel pursed her lips and turned away from her husband.

'Does that mean if he dies then his son will die now too?' Eleanor couldn't conceive of the consequences of a person's actions remaining intact after they had died. If after saving him, his Dad died, wouldn't the son die too? Surely all trace of a dead person having lived vanished when they died.

Like footprints in the sand washed away by the tide.

Eleanor dared not admit, even to herself, that she wished very much that this was the case.

'Where do you get these ludicrous ideas, Eleanor?' Isabel glared at Mark.

'But what about all of his children?' Forgetting her resolution to be neither seen nor heard, and that she wasn't meant to have seen any news, Eleanor was overtaken by her fevered curiosity. Hiding behind the sofa when *The World At One* was on the radio, she had been particularly impressed by the information that the man who had been shot had ten children. 'If their Dad dies, does that mean they're not children any more?'

'That's not amusing, Eleanor.'

'I only meant is he going to get better?' Mark's small daughter countered lamely. This was the best question she could have asked a doctor.

'It's astonishing what punishment the human brain can take. Actually there are large tracts of the brain that can pretty much be dispensed with. But he's suffered damage to major blood vessels.' Mark Ramsay smiled pleasantly, an expression

Isabel knew he wore beside a sick bed. The look still made her want to have sex with him: 'From the bulletins we're hearing this afternoon, I'd say he'll be brain damaged if he does survive, the right cerebral hemisphere is destroyed. The likelihood of any kind of recovery is remote. If he lives he'll be a vegetable. But I doubt he'll make it.'

Eleanor was reminded of the moment on her eighth birthday last year, when the tin mould was removed and she had held her breath in case her mother's raspberry cat flopped into liquid as it usually did. It must set, or there would be no birthday. Eleanor had dug her fingernails into her palms willing it to work. With a brief wobble it had stayed upright. She had been so relieved, she had accidentally joined in singing 'Happy Birthday' and Gina had called her big-headed. She had the same dread of collapse now as her father warned:

'The next twenty-four hours are critical, the bullet was a massive shock to his brain.'

Twenty-four hours was a day. It was the same length of time that Alice had been hiding. Eleanor arranged the cards in suit order. It would look unfeeling to actually play anything with them. In another day, Robert Kennedy might get well and Alice might come back nicer.

She began to build another tower.

That evening Eleanor formed a plan. She banged her head with some force on the wall by her bed six times before going to sleep. The next morning, Thursday 6th June, she woke promptly at six, in time to catch the newspapers at a quarter past. Her Mum had reacted swiftly to the crisis and insisted they order *The Times* as well as the *Guardian* to get what she called 'a comprehensive picture' of how Alice's disappearance was being reported, so as to ensure things did not get out of control.

In the deathly quiet of the sleeping house, with only Crawford for company, Eleanor found Alice's fixed smile on the hall mat, folded inside *The Times*. The head was slightly tipped to the side like a good girl. There were two small photographs on the inside pages, the one of Alice and, to Eleanor's surprise, one of herself next to writing about the missing schoolgirl who had vanished leaving no trace. Eleanor was a confident reader and she scanned the text easily, pausing over 'excavation' and 'interfered with', which baffled her, but didn't stop her making sense of the story. She hadn't thought of Alice as a 'schoolgirl'. School didn't have much to do with Alice since they had met in the holidays and Alice behaved so old. Eleanor didn't think of herself as a schoolgirl. Alice had been different, perhaps being a schoolgirl had been the difference.

The writing said Alice was pretty and innocent. Eleanor couldn't see why she was innocent and wondered if it was to do with being good at ballet. Lizzie had said 'poor little mite she wouldn't hurt a fly'. Eleanor knew this wasn't true. As she knelt on the doormat, the stiff brush pile stinging her knees, Eleanor wondered if the story said she too was innocent. She scoured the inky words with a stubby finger, but found no mention of herself as an innocent schoolgirl. But then after the incident with Judge Ramsay and the bambi, Eleanor she knew she was not.

Isabel Ramsay was vague about checking whether her children had done their homework. She might forget entirely until a letter came from a teacher. Then she would lurk around them making the work last twice as long with relentless questions and corrections. Despite this they preferred their mother's scrutiny to their father's. Mark Ramsay was impatient and irritable, reducing them to blank and panicky beings, whereas Isabel's wafty presence did sometimes provide room to think and even learn. A hidden Ramsay fact was Isabel's acute grasp of maths and music theory. She could spot a mixolydian or locrian scale after a few notes and whip through a simultaneous equation, slashing out numbers with dazzling speed and accuracy, her calculations a mouse's tail down the page.

No one in the family could do needlework.

Last Christmas, six months before Eleanor would meet Alice, she had been sent home with the template for a brown

42

and beige felt bambi, to be completed in the holidays. Eleanor not only hated stitching, she despised the whole idea of sewing. She wanted to do woodwork, but girls were not allowed. While the boys made useful, interesting objects like chairs and boxes, the girls had a choice of gonks or bambis. Eleanor had sulkily agreed to the less silly of the two options, privately planning to do neither. But when at the end of the holidays, the folded pieces of felt were discovered still in their paper bag, Eleanor had been exiled to the austere dining room in the White House where she was given three hours to produce a fully fledged bambi. The Ramsays were going back to London that evening after the rush hour. In a burst of maternal authority, Isabel laid out cotton, thimble, scissors, buttons for eyes, and old stockings for stuffing. Eleanor had to cut out felt in the shape of the cardboard template, then sew up the two halves, leaving a hole to stuff the stockings through. She accidentally attached the back legs to each other with uncharacteristically neat blanket stitch and then, in a fury of unpicking, undid all she had achieved. Needlework was really stupid she growled, as at last she managed to guide the sodden end of cotton through a needle with the biggest eye her mother could find. Then she pricked her finger. She stifled a scream of rage. It was then Eleanor had realised she wasn't alone.

She was being watched. The oil portrait of Judge Henry Ramsay eyed her grimly, his judicial wig giving him the advantage. The gilt framed painting hung over the gigantic marble fireplace and at night was lit by a tarnished gold down-light. The Judge sat in a high backed chair, with his arms folded. He held a thick blue book, his bony hands obscuring the title. Mark Ramsay had told his children this was Aeschylus' *Oresteia*, his father's favourite, while Isabel said it was the telephone directory. On the first day when Eleanor had been made to give Alice a tour, she had taken the time to explain that the Judge's book was about justice and that the man who wrote it had changed drama by using the chorus in a different way, although in response to Alice's persistent questioning, Eleanor was hazy about the details and couldn't say how or why because it was Lucian who listed facts. Alice had come alive at the mention of a chorus and informed Eleanor that she had been placed at the front of the chorus for her school production of *Joseph and the Technicolor Dreamcoat* so she understood exactly how important one was. Eleanor had nothing to add to this, and had instead pointed out to Alice how the Judge's eyes swivelled so that wherever a person was in the room he was always staring right at them. To her satisfaction Alice had not liked this.

Judge Henry saw everything.

The Judge had watched her struggling with her embryonic bambi. She wanted him stopped.

Eleanor had climbed off her chair and lugged it over to the fireplace. She retrieved the bambi from the grate where it had landed, and mounted the chair, the needle in her left hand, the bambi dangling from the knotted thread. Standing on tiptoe, she could just reach the Judge's face. She pushed the needle firmly into one eyeball then the other. She eased it around to widen the holes. Then she abandoned method and began stabbing the pupils, piercing the canvas over and over.

He was still staring; now his eyes had a blank quality that was much worse. Perhaps the Judge was as mad as her Mum said. With wild criss-cross stitches, Eleanor had then hurriedly assembled the bambi, shoving in the silk stocking stuffing and scampering from the room.

The bambi and the Judge knew Eleanor was not an innocent schoolgirl.

Eleanor was briefly ashamed of the buzz of excitement she felt at seeing her own face in the newspaper. She had got this feeling when she was The Narrator for the Nativity play, aged only six and a half. She had been the youngest child to do narrating in the school's history so was made a fuss of. The headmistress told her father, who had arrived when it was all over, that Eleanor 'had embraced the responsibility with unbridled enthusiasm'. With her hand pressing on Eleanor's head, she had told Doctor Ramsay that Eleanor had vocalised with confidence and clarity.

'What a shame Mrs Ramsay couldn't get here either. Eleanor said that you were very busy, but she insisted to me that her Mummy was coming.'

'My wife gets headaches.'

'Oh, Doctor Ramsay!'

Eleanor had known, by the way her Dad fiddled with his watch, that he sniffed a criticism. Good doctors should be able to stop headaches. Her mother had been well enough to go out for a meal that night. As The Narrator, Eleanor sat next to her and was allowed to choose her own pudding.

In the photograph, Alice was in school uniform. Her hair was bunched in pigtails with bows neatly tied. The crisp newspaper without tears and creases made Eleanor forget that Alice couldn't have posed for her picture after going missing. Alice gave a big smile for the camera, showing off clean white teeth that Eleanor knew she brushed every morning and every night. *Up down, up down, not too hard so they are pearly white.* Her own face was above the words '*The tomboy who courted danger and excitement*'.

Alice had said Eleanor looked like a boy in the photo they had found in a packet at the back of a drawer in the games cupboard, and left out on the sideboard in the dining room. This was the clumsy snapshot that Mark Ramsay snatched up when the police asked for one of his daughter. Lucian had only taken it to finish the film. Few pictures of Eleanor were taken on purpose. She was a liability, likely to squirm and be smeared with dirt as well as pink and sweaty from getting over-excited. She had cut the crooked fringe herself with unwieldy kitchen scissors, and tufts peeped out of the sides of her beloved denim sailor cap, pushed jauntily back. People examining her over their breakfasts assumed the sun-dazzled scowl was evidence of ill temper and waywardness, and formed the toast-crunching opinion that she was not the kind of girl they would let loose on their own children.

Eleanor's boisterous presence was in stark opposition to Alice's angelic absence. Eleanor was placed in a different species category to Alice.

The previous night, after the police had been, Eleanor had overheard her mother telling her father off. Isabel Ramsay had an acute sensitivity to the importance of public perception. She was adept at constructing a potent and plausible story with little scenery and scant characterisation. As she berated her husband for his careless choice of picture, Isabel knew exactly the damage he had done to her family.

Alice had flipped through the photographs and made a gurgling sound at one of Gina leaning against a stable door with Prince, her horse. Eleanor clutched her stomach for the giggles they would share, for it appeared that Gina had a horse's head growing out of her neck. Instead, Alice had said Gina was beautiful in a strangled voice. When she saw the snap of Eleanor she had sniffled into church-steepled hands, saying her cap was too big and she looked like a boy.

So, Alice wasn't laughing now.

Eleanor remained on the chequered tiles in the hallway, hidden by the coat stand, her skin tinted red by the dawning sun coming through the stained glass fanlight. Blurred back to front sentences like a crudely coded message were imprinted on her bare arms from the newsprint where she had leaned on the paper, but she was too engrossed to notice. She turned back to the front page and read the thick black words about Senator Kennedy. '*Kennedy Clings To Life After Brain Operation.*' She didn't know what a Senator was, but now discovered that apart from having ten children he had another on the way.

He might die without ever seeing his baby.

She peered closely at the picture of the man lying on the floor with his hands resting on his chest. He looked asleep in the sun like her Dad except he had on a suit and tie and wore polished black shoes. His jacket was twisted and crumpled. His eyes were like the Judge's and stared at something frightening on the ceiling. Eleanor ran a finger along the words: '*They rested his head on a plastic boater hat, with a band that said: "Kennedy Will Win". The blood from his wound ran down over the hat, and mixed with the pool on the floor.*' He had been shot at twenty minutes past midnight, Los Angeles time.

She blinked and rubbed her nose with a grubby fist. There was another picture of Robert Kennedy making a speech minutes before he got shot. He looked happy with his wife Ethel beside him. Eleanor thought he must be a nice dad to have and wished she was one of ten children with one on the way instead of three with no one else expected. Then Eleanor knew with a certainty beyond her years and outside the bounds of rationality that if Robert Kennedy were to live it would be all right. Alice would come out of her hiding place, all of her not just her head and her hands and her smile, and this time they would play properly. They would even be friends.

It was just as she thought this and was turning the pages of the paper so as to leave it neatly that Eleanor saw the small headline. She froze.

'"*Alice*" *Grave To Remain. The grave of Mrs Alice Hargreaves who was the model for Lewis Carroll's* Alice in Wonderland *is safe.*' The story was about a council saying it would 'level all graves and remove headstones' to make space for more bodies. Eleanor wondered where it planned to find these bodies. People had complained and stopped them. It hadn't occurred to Eleanor that Alice had a grave. Up until now it had been a game that ended happily with Alice no longer here to bother her. Eleanor conflated the smiling face on page two with the item about the grave and went cold.

How could a grave ever be safe?

She heard a sound, a tiny creak from one of the many rooms above her head and hastily arranged the newspaper on the mat to look like it had fallen there. This minute action was the start of a policy of disguise and concealment that would seal fates and change lives. No one heard Eleanor scamper back to bed on small, soundless feet.

Eleanor lay facing the open window, gradually warmed up by the morning sun slanting on her pillow, and in a bid to banish thoughts, she whispered a story to herself about her real father, the handsome Senator with the crack in his chin. 'He was shot eight times at close range and lay injured by the freezers in the kitchen. He moved a little; once he licked his lips slowly,' she hissed hoarsely, demonstrating a photographic memory unrecognised by her teachers or family. 'The kitchen was *"boiling with people"* but *"Senator Kennedy and three other wounded lay terribly quiet in the midst of the uproar".*' She propped herself up on one elbow. 'They think he spoke, he asked everyone to move back to give him air!'

As Eleanor knelt beside him she stroked the Senator's hand, he smiled up at her and squeezing her fingers he muttered:

'*I'm so proud of you, Alice.*'

'It's Eleanor!'

After that Eleanor formed the routine of checking the newspapers each morning. Then every night after everyone was asleep and it had become too late to make anything better, she would tiptoe down to the kitchen, and as her eyes grew used to the dark, she would skitter across the stone flags, to pull the newspaper out from the pile under the sink and stuff it up her pyjama jacket. She was astute in her assumption that the rackety habits of the Ramsay household carried on despite everything. Used to her home as a harbinger of secrets, Eleanor had learnt to keep her own while negotiating the repercussions of others. Her pyjamas crackled as she marched stiffly up to the playroom at the top of the house. Scissor blades flashed in the shimmery light from a rubber waterproof torch balanced between the chimneys of the doll's house as she snip-snipped around the article, leaving neat windows in the paper.

She would lay her growing collection of images out in a row on the floorboards. Robert Kennedy sitting on a carpeted staircase in smart shoes that must squeak when he walked. He looked tired. Eleanor's favourite was a close-up of his face with the dent in his chin that she had invested with magical significance. Finally, smoothed flat, the three she had found of the Senator sprawled between freezer cabinets in the Los Angeles hotel kitchen, a still shape glimpsed between shoving bodies lit by a frenzy of flash bulbs. In the last, his shirt had been undone exposing a hairy chest. Her Dad's chest was hairless. As an afterthought, Eleanor had cut out the story about Alice with both their pictures in it. She had left the one about the grave.

After scrutinising her private gallery, she would slip everything into the space between the floor and the skirting board behind the doll's house. When they returned to London, Eleanor intended to take them all out and put them in her Box of Secrets. But when the time came she forgot and later, as often happened with her secrets, she forgot what they were or where they were hidden.

Four

Eleanor had been introduced to Alice one sunny Friday morning on the last day of May that year. The Ramsays had arrived from London late the night before intending to spend the first week of June at their house in Sussex. For all of them the day they got there was always the best, rich with hope and anticipation. The hope dissipated even as Lizzie opened all the doors and windows to chase out the damp. By the next morning everyone had gone their separate ways: Gina to the riding stables; Lucian to the river; Mark retreated to his study with the door locked and Isabel was planning the food with Lizzie in the kitchen. Eleanor had been called downstairs just as she started sorting out the doll's house. On the way down to Charbury, squeezed between her older brother and sister, she had planned to rearrange the furniture to give the inhabitants a new lease of life. She would draw new pictures for the rooms and paint the front door bright red. With this in mind, she had packed her box of enamel paints. The doll's house was a loyal friend awaiting her. She told herself she had no need of other friends ever again.

Eleanor's grandfather had made the doll's house, an obsessively faithful replica of the family mansion called the White House, over thirty years before for Mark Ramsay and his younger sister, Virginia. It was an uncharacteristic act of paternal attention from the adamantine high court Judge, who enthusiastically donned the black napkin until prevented by the demise of capital punishment itself. The loss of so final a tool of retribution had made Judge Henry permanently peevish. In

1957, the enactment of the Homicide Act effectively curtailed his power to propel a man or woman to meet their maker and drove him into brooding retirement. He clung to his memories and to the almost permanent seclusion of his workroom, a shed in the orchard, which like his study was acrid with the smoke of the 'Regency Segars' he received every month in a brown paper parcel from Fribourg and Treyer in the Haymarket.

When Judge Ramsay died on 13th July 1958, exactly three years after Ruth Ellis became the last woman to be hanged in Britain, a month before his seventieth birthday and too soon to know about the birth of Eleanor, no one had the courage to clear out his den. Isabel had turned up at the door of the shed, clanking with cleaning materials, intent on sweeping away the last vestiges of her hated father-in-law and transforming it into an artist's studio with which to tempt Lucian with its chalky light. She had quailed at the sight of the immaculately laid out bench, the labelled shelves stacked with tools, and books on architecture and model building. Towers of wooden cigar boxes were filled with tiny objects: drawing pins, nails, screws and pen nibs. Isabel's nerves were finally shattered as her cheek brushed against the Judge's black wool jacket hanging lifeless from the door, and as she jumped back the metal bucket clipped the doorjamb with a fearsome clatter. Defeated, she had abandoned the shed to become an inadvertent shrine. Over the years people claimed to have caught glimpses of the Judge through the grimy windows, a giant concentrating crow perched on his high stool, shrouded in his jacket.

Deep among the plum and apple trees where the Judge couldn't hear the incessant squall of children, and – before she died when her eldest child, Mark, was nine – the high pitched call of Rosamund his wife, he would work into the night. At last with reluctance, he had presented the doll's house to two catarrhly bemused children whom he had expected to be semaphorically appreciative of his gift. His son's reaction particularly enraged him. Mark walked around the butcher's block on which the house was placed, his hands behind his back, the nonchalant pose actually a desperate demonstration that he recognised its significance. At last Mark had gleefully pointed out the clue. There was always a clue. The Judge didn't approve of unfettered generosity so every present he gave them was a test. In each of the two playroom windows in the big house there were six bars giving the long wide room the oppressive air of a prison cell. But in the doll's house playroom windows there was none.

Mark Ramsay never forgot the look of contemplative fury his father gave him for revealing his mistake. The Judge had not imagined the playroom with bars on the windows because he had avoided the room once his parents had made the gardener install them, thus making them pointless for the rest of his childhood as he was the only surviving child. Now his own son had unmasked his father's apparent labour of love as a labour of atonement. Although only ten years old, Mark Ramsay knew utterly that an irrevocable severance had taken place. From that moment, until his own death, he was the Judge's greatest champion. His defence reached evangelical fervour in the face of Isabel's scorn.

Mark and Virginia could only play with the house under the Judge's supervision; they did so with the highly tuned attention of bomb disposal experts. Soon they dreaded the sight of it standing on its grisly plinth in the playroom like a body on a slab.

Judge Ramsay had constructed each storey separately to slot into the frame of the house like a shelf into a fridge. He spent days reproducing the fretted stonework that hung like a web between octagonal pillars to recreate the geometric shadow on the wall of the actual house. The Ionic pillars supporting the pediment of the front porch were particularly hard to get right, and took him months. The front and back were effectively large doors, and he saw that his first idea of using hardboard was impractical, for it would quickly deteriorate with constant opening. In the end he chose pine, with fascias of oak where dark paint wouldn't do. He became skilful on a lathe despite a discouraging start, which included severing an Ionic column in half along with the top of the middle finger of his left hand.

One obituary incorrectly attributed this injury to a letter bomb sent by a relative of a man who had been hanged. Thus did myth become truth.

The Judge was most proud of the priest hole that ran from the minute study on the second floor to emerge behind a wood panel on the landing. It was operated by pushing a knob in the centre of a Tudor rose to the right of the mantelpiece exactly like its real counterpart. It comprised a tiny chamber behind the study wall with a narrow airless passage leading away from the study along to the landing. It had been particularly complex to construct, but after several weeks the Judge had achieved it. He didn't tell Mark and Virginia. This well-kept secret was his big test. He hadn't known of the existence of the priest hole until finding the plans. He would reward whoever discovered his clue.

If one of them did, they never confessed.

Until his son exposed his error of the windows without bars, the Judge had considered the plasterwork his one failure. Time was lost as he wrestled with tiny renditions of the intricate mouldings for the ceilings on the ground floor. Eventually he relented and commissioned a craftsman. He told no one that the work was not his own, but was given away by an obsessive commitment to administrative order. He had filed the invoice and Eleanor found it after his death. This was proof to her that Henry Ramsay wasn't the great man Mark insisted he was. The Judge had lied. Isabel's dislike of the Judge dated from before she met him, in jealous response to Mark's uncritical devotion to 'Henry', which seemed far stronger than for herself. She rationalised her emotions into principle and on their visits to Charbury she would rashly engage the Judge in fierce arguments about capital punishment until Mark ushered her away. However, Mark assured Isabel she had misjudged the Judge. Mark explained to his family that the invoice had been the Judge's clue.

Judge Ramsay left the White House and its replica to his son on his death. The Judge had used the White House as a country retreat for weekends and holidays. It was after the sudden death of his wife that he began work on the doll's house. He told himself he was granting Rosamund her dying wish that he take good care of the children, but he knew he was building the house for his own reasons. Had she known of this promise, his daughter would not have considered it fulfilled.

Virginia Ramsay was astonished that her brother had forgotten the stolid meals round the dining table, the compulsory evening recitals of poems, the tiptoed silence that enabled the Judge to work in his study and his fury if one of them mentioned their dead mother. Once she was old enough to leave home, Virginia shunned all opportunities to return to the White House and only came back when she was old and could be sure that everything would be different.

Mark exorcised his father by whipping up a hectic family life involving dizzying sessions of charades, Scrabble, Monopoly, and Racing Demon, and long striding walks along the coast towards Brighton or up into the South Downs. He hated it when Isabel had a headache and the children had to be quiet, sneaking around like prisoners, careful not to slam doors, for then his childhood returned as if it had never gone away.

Mark Ramsay did not impose his father's numbing laws of 'playing with the house' on his own children. Perhaps he unconsciously hoped it would disintegrate through hours of hectic attention. It did not. The outside grew as weathered as the original, paint peeled and the plasterwork under the eaves chipped and powdered, as each child made it their own.

At first Eleanor could only touch the house under Gina's stern direction, occasionally being ordered to move a doll or a chair. She was never allowed to do any of the dolls' voices, because Gina said she got them wrong. Now Gina, like her Aunt Ginny before her, thought the doll's house stupid, and spent most of her time at the stables, or sticking horse posters up around her room and reading books in which horses featured heavily. Eleanor was frightened of horses, a secret only Gina knew, but had so far not made use of. So only a few months before meeting Alice, Eleanor became sole custodian of the doll's house. She had taken possession with a flourish, installing her Matchbox cars in the bedrooms and initially interring the dolls in a shoebox, although she did later exhume them and give them minor parts.

The furniture had been copied from furniture still in the big house. The long green velvet sofa and rickety rocking chair were identical to ones in the living room. Only the table and chairs in the kitchen were from a shop, the originals lost or broken, even the tiny plates and cups were exact versions of the crockery piled in teetering towers in the church-like wooden unit in the kitchen.

Out of her Box of Secrets came postage stamp pictures of Crawford and pencilled family faces split by joyful laughter. Singing and chatting to herself, Eleanor hung them from threads of cotton in all the rooms.

Minute bedspreads had been fashioned out of squares of material. Her Mum had stitched them one winter afternoon earlier that year. The house was freezing and they had huddled together in the kitchen, close to the Rayburn like conspirators. As a surprise, Isabel had embroidered Eleanor's initials in the middle of one square: 'E.I.R' – Eleanor Isabel Ramsay. Eleanor had laid it on the huge double bed in the main bedroom.

'One day you'll show this to your children and tell them their grandmother made it,' Isabel had pronounced briskly. 'They'll treasure it.' She was always mindful of leaving footprints for the future. Eleanor didn't choose that moment to tell Isabel she didn't want children.

Soon Eleanor's replica White House had been transformed into a cosy home welcoming in plenty of sunshine and quite safe from intruders. Her cars were content there.

That Friday morning, Eleanor had been eager to finish breakfast and embark on her proposed changes. She insinuated herself into the gap between the playroom wall and the house and inched the heavy structure across the painted floorboards until it was about four feet from the wall. A happy rush of anticipation galloped through her as she cleared out every room and gathered the contents in a heap on the rug by the fireplace. She would spend the afternoon painting new pictures for the walls; the main bedroom could also do with a chest of drawers. She knew how to make one out of matchboxes with paper studs for handles. Her Mum might help again.

Then Lizzie called out that she had a visitor, 'a surprise person', she would say no more. A selection of perfect people paraded through Eleanor's mind, starting with Aunt Ginny who only ever visited when they were in St Peter's Square because she hated the dead Judge and who always brought wild adventure, perhaps a ride in her Austin van with Aunt Ginny's friend Maggie, all of them singing songs by Cilla Black in shouty voices and swearing at other cars without being told off. After this the list tailed off for it couldn't be her best friend, Lucy. Perhaps it was the girl at the village shop yesterday afternoon, who had blown pink bubbles with her gum until one burst covering her face like a mask. She had left it there, plastered over her cheeks until her Mum noticed, just as Eleanor would have done.

But the surprise was none of these.

What Eleanor saw from the top of the stairs was a ghost with chalky-white skin in a yellow dress, fair hair fanning out over its shoulders so that Eleanor thought its head was a triangle. Then she saw it was a girl standing to attention in a patch of sunlight outside the porch, smiling with the tops of her cheeks. She had on what Eleanor soon discovered was her new favourite dress; the flimsy frilly frock adorned with lacy bits filled Eleanor with foreboding. The girl was entirely still, her bony knees close together, her feet in black patent leather pumps with no specks of dirt, proving she had flown to the White House without touching the ground.

Like her grandfather, Eleanor wasted no time drawing conclusions, and she instantly wished that she had hidden when Lizzie called. She slowed down for the last few stairs but had inevitably to reach the bottom one.

Mark Ramsay lounged in the porch rocking back and forth on his heels, hands in the pockets of his favourite country trousers. Eleanor was sure he was trying to keep a straight face as he listened to the girl's mother, who talked very fast then stopped with a hiccup to give way to bursts of cockerel laughter. His genial doctor's voice kept saying, 'I see' and 'Is that right?' Then she saw that he didn't laugh when the woman laughed which meant he wasn't listening. This was normal. Eleanor relaxed.

'Ah, Elly, there you are. What kept you?' He scrumpled up her hair, gently urging her forward out of the shadow of the porch towards the ghost girl. 'Well, now you can stop sulking around the place moaning. We've found Anna.'

'Alice actually. Nearly right!' Eleanor was impressed that the woman could move her neck like a pigeon. She splayed her hands in the direction of her daughter as if introducing a circus act.

'Like *Alice in Wonderland*! Your favourite book, isn't it, Alice!' She gave a squeal.

At this Alice moved her head, which startled Eleanor, as she had grown used to the idea that she wasn't real. She guessed, without forming the words, that her father made Alice's mother scared. A lot of people behaved strangely with him. The glistening lady with damp hands, who had tried to teach Gina the flute, got a blotchy neck after encountering him in the hall. Her mother had said it was because he was a doctor and they were idiotic enough to think he could see them without their clothes on.

Suddenly Eleanor remembered hearing about Alice. She was the girl who had moved into the cottage next to the village shop. Her Mum was receptionist at the local surgery, and her Dad was Charbury's new postman. The bubble gum girl had confided to Eleanor that there was an Alice who could stand on her head for over fifteen minutes. It must be this one. For a moment Eleanor's unalloyed admiration for this supposed feat overcame her objection to the proposed arrangement.

She was astonished to find her mother outside too. Isabel was walking up and down outside the dining room window, her arms folded tightly as if she was cold; her high heels crunched small holes in the gravel. She was dressed for going out in her turquoise trouser suit and full make-up. Eleanor had thought she was in bed and, although pleased she was up, she was disheartened that she would soon be gone.

Isabel's two eldest children were too grown up for the ruthless tactics they had adopted four years earlier when Lucian and Gina, aged six and eight with a tearful Eleanor in tow, had hidden their mother's jewels in seed trays stacked in the potting shed to stop her leaving. The plan had failed. The jewels were found and the gardener was dismissed on the basis that he had boasted to Lucian about stealing a car when he was a boy. The children said nothing, not even to each other and the secret grew like a deadly plant. Gradually they stopped playing together and only formed expedient, if uneasy alliances. These were fluid at first; any two of them might side against the third or close ranks against outsiders, but as they got older Gina and Lucian sealed an unspoken pact, freeing them of guilt and adroitly placing amorphous blame on their little sister. Isabel was smoking, eyes hidden behind sunglasses that reflected the group clustered around the porch. She addressed no one, her voice husky from smoke and hours of silent darkness:

'She'll stop my daughter getting into mischief. Gina's too old to play, although she'll keep an eye. I am sure Alice is a sensible girl.'

Eleanor's heart sank as her mother gave one of her very short smiles, which made the girl in the dress shimmer with lacy trembles. She glared at Gina, leaning triumphant against an Ionic column, acting too old to play. They avoided looking at each other in case it was all too clear what was really in their minds.

The four years between the sisters was beyond argument, but this chasm, usually represented by Gina's devotion to horses, had been widened recently by new differences in their experience. The past week had seen Gina clamped to a hot water bottle with period pains and the failure of a boyfriend (who her family said didn't exist) to appear at the Hammersmith Wimpy as arranged. Eleanor and her friends' only interest in boys was around how to win back Eleanor's champion marble from Chris Thornton who had unfairly refused to risk it in further games. The sisters had little to say to one another.

It was proposed that the friendship between Eleanor and Alice start immediately. Eleanor's mother had her 'out-of-bed' voice: higher than usual, with one 'darling' every minute, listing rules like other Mums. She made Eleanor promise not to do anything foolish and to make sure that every day they were back in time for tea.

Every day? Was Alice going to be there from now on? Eleanor's spirit was dampened. In resigned tones she enquired: 'What time is tea?'

'Four. Same as always, darling!'

Eleanor had flinched as hands tugged at her hair, straightened her collar and smacked invisible flies off her chest and arms. Looking up she could see herself reflected in her mother's sunglasses: a dark shape with no face. She mechanically took Alice's outstretched hand and glumly led her upstairs to where they were to play, properly like good girls, until Alice's mother, who was called Kathleen, came to collect her.

Alice and Eleanor were only months apart in age and with the odd logic that people apply to everyone but themselves, this broad commonality identified them as like-minded and inevitable soul mates. Alice quickly established she was born three months and three days before Eleanor and this fact became the basis of a discussion, in which they quizzed each other vigorously, gleefully unearthing differences with no inclination to find shared ground. Alice archly informed Eleanor that the age gap meant that she was already on solids by the time Eleanor was born. By the time Eleanor was walking, Alice was winning prizes for dancing.

The two girls hoisted markers that, besides their material worth, set important basic cornerstones. Both of them were seasoned experts at judging the social implications of owning three Sindy dolls with full wardrobe, versus a scratched pick-up truck complete with a winding handle and a dirty length of string which could lift cars right up into the air. Alice led the way on primary facts, rapping out questions and nodding with pursed lips at Eleanor's garbled answers, or providing the answers herself while Eleanor cast about for a hilarious response.

Alice had smaller feet than Eleanor, which she declared an advantage for ballet. She had just won a prize at school, presented only yesterday, for her dance to 'Up, Up and Away in my Beautiful Balloon'. Eleanor knew that things were beyond hope when Alice began swooping around the doll's house singing in a high-pitched reedy voice. She was especially unsettled, but dared not look away as Alice did a circle with her hands above her head for the balloon. There was more: last year Alice had received nine commendations for tidiness and clean hands. (Eleanor's school did not give commendations.) Alice had been presented with her Sindy dolls on her eighth birthday, three months and three days before Eleanor's birthday, which that year Isabel had forgotten. Eleanor announced that all dolls were sissy and that she preferred cars. She did not tell Alice that Gina had a Sindy doll with a cracked tummy from where Eleanor had bicycled over it by accident. Gina would be cross to be mentioned at all. All Eleanor's cars had names, and were boys or girls with ever-changing relationships. Alice laughed at the names. Eleanor was incredulous as Alice assumed a starey-eyed expression and covering her mouth, sniggered through her fingers. This stopped Eleanor from telling her about the Citroën called Sophia who was married to the flat bed lorry called Desi, after Lucille Ball's son, Desi Arnaz Junior. She had been bursting to tell Alice that Sophia's family cut her off without a penny because Desi was half Cuban. It was so thrilling but she was confounded when she realised that Alice wouldn't understand.

Eleanor knew the difference between each day because of their colour and feeling. Monday was thick and yellow like cheese, which she didn't like. Tuesday was orange with netball and piano lessons, which she sometimes enjoyed. Best of all was Friday: toffee flavoured and deep red with a story before home time. She would rest her head in her arms on the cool pencil-smelling desk, and listen to Miss Galliver. She wished Fridays would never end, and wondered what happened to Miss Galliver at the weekends. She didn't say any of this to Alice.

Alice liked yellow best except in sweets when she preferred strawberry. This was one thing they agreed on. Alice let

Eleanor have a red Opal Fruit from an unopened packet as soon as they were upstairs, which gave Eleanor a burst of hope. After that it was always lime or lemon at the top when Alice reluctantly waved the sweets at her. Eleanor hated these two flavours but said yes to be friendly. When she suspected Alice of rearranging the sweets, she got the pain in her ribs like when her mother didn't join them for supper.

Alice pulled a face when she saw the doll's house, insisting it was scruffy and dirty; but admitted she liked the green sofa. She wouldn't help put back the furniture because everything should be washed and cleaned, or they would just be rearranging the dirt. Like a surveyor, she pointed out scratches all over the front of the house, and showed with the bat of a hand how the top of the porch was splintered, the dining room windowsill was hanging off, and with the prod of another finger, drew attention to a crack in the staircase. When Alice rubbed a window ledge, and thrust her finger under Eleanor's nose, Eleanor nodded meekly at the grey fluff. She never thought about keeping things spotless. She got on with playing.

After that, Eleanor had to answer Alice's searching questions about Gina, whom Alice had seen at the stables. Alice said she wished Gina was her sister, and with a tired sigh, breathed that Gina was so-o-o very pretty. Eleanor decided that it was the way Alice popped a strawberry sweet in her mouth and screwed up the paper between fussy palms, that made everything she said true. She tried it after Alice had gone, exactly mimicking Alice putting a sweet between pouting lips, using a wrapper Alice had left in a neat ball on the window seat to round off the effect. Immediately Eleanor was Alice.

'She looks so different to you. I can't believe she's your sister. She's just like a princess. I heard one of the riding instructors say she will be a beautiful woman when she grows up.'

Eleanor shrugged. She was revolted at the idea of Gina being any kind of woman. She was especially irked to hear that Gina had astounding poise on a horse and would be a famous equestrian one day. Alice pronounced each bit of the word 'eck-wes-tree-an' so that it took ages and put Eleanor off asking what it meant.

Alice wouldn't play with the doll's house, nor would she touch the cars or be spies. There was no game that suited them both, so after a tour of the house they had ended up each end of the wide seat in one of the playroom windows, looking down on the garden through the metal bars. Eleanor leaned forward, drumming her heels against the seat. Alice sat up straight. They avoided looking at each other as they dissected the differing merits of their teachers, the children in their class, and compared school dinners and favourite pets. It was a lifetime later when Lizzie called out that Alice's mother had come to take her home.

Everyone said what a great success the visit had been, so Alice would just go home for lunch and come straight back afterwards. In fact it was decided that Eleanor would play with Alice every day. In those brief four and a half days Eleanor got to know every expression, every gesture: every little thing that made up Alice. Yet after Alice disappeared Eleanor didn't give the police any clue as to where she might be, or think of anyone she might have gone off with. Eventually, to please them Eleanor had decided to let the policemen see two of her dens, knowing Alice would not be there.

Eleanor didn't tell the policeman he was wrong when he said she must miss her friend. Nor did she confess that she was relieved she no longer had to play with Alice. But she wanted to get the answers right because then he gave her sweets. She wanted him to be kind because he had a crack in his chin like the Senator. She didn't admit that when she thought of Alice she got a pain in her ribs. Alice's words hurt like the chunks of flint hidden at the Tide Mills that were sharp enough to cut up Crawford's horsemeat:

'I know a secret about you.'

Alice had been sure she knew everything, but she was wrong about the secret.

It had rained on the Saturday afternoon so, after their illicit trip to the Tide Mills that morning, the girls had ended up in the dining room, at the long oval table, doing pictures with oil pastels and the pencils that Eleanor loved because they went like paint when the ends were wetted. The mess created by the boxes of crayons emptied on the green baize tablecloth, the crumpled sheets of discarded efforts strewn around the chair legs, was at odds with the chilly formality of the room. Over the years Isabel had redecorated most of the White House but Mark had not allowed her to touch this room, presided over by the thickly daubed oil portrait of Judge Henry Ramsay.

They had come close to their first argument during a debate about whether it was better to be deaf or blind, a subject brought up by Alice and on which she had, as usual, a firm opinion. Although later Eleanor couldn't think what Alice had replied. She did remember that Alice had refused to answer when Eleanor asked if it was better to be alive or dead. Just as Eleanor had wondered if they could get away with being silent until it was time for Alice to go, she had spoken so quietly that Eleanor nearly didn't hear:

'I know a secret about your family.'

'Secrets are stupid.' Eleanor leaned closer to her picture: the Tide Mills from a small plane. She was the pilot, in goggles and a leather helmet.

'I don't care if you do.' But she did care because she knew what the secret would be. It was what the secret always was and so really no secret at all. This time though, because she had been careful never to leave Alice on her own or with Gina, Eleanor had thought the secret was safe.

'Not all secrets are stupid. If this was my secret I would care.' Alice had on her teacher's voice: stern and disappointed. She pulled her bubble-gum pink cardigan tighter around herself, implying that, as well as dusty, the dining room was cold.

'So what is it?' Eleanor hadn't meant to ask. She snatched up an orange crayon to make the sun as hot as possible, and busily colouring, she pressed too hard and snapped the crayon. She felt disloyal, but was unclear who or what she had let down.

'Guess! I'm not going to make it easy.' Alice hovered over her drawing of a stick girl with a bunch of flowers. She gripped the pencil like a dart. The figure took up one corner of the paper leaving an expanse of white space. Abruptly putting down her pencil, she sat back in the chair with folded arms. She was smiling with unblinking eyes. Later all Eleanor could think of was that when they had been out in the garden before the rain, Alice had refused to have a staring contest in case it was bad for her eyes. She hadn't told the policeman this.

Four days after this conversation, as Eleanor leaned over to dip into the policeman's paper bag, feeling his fingers through the paper, she heard Alice's voice and saw her face staring up from the sweets.

'Wings off the table!'

It was rude to slouch, she had hissed at Eleanor over lunch before their painting session, darting a look at Mark Ramsay, who had smiled back, which meant he liked her. Up until then Eleanor had been sure her Dad felt sorry for her for having to play with Alice. The shock of realising that along with everyone else, he too liked Alice had made her drop her fork on to the floor. As she reappeared above the line of the tablecloth, she caught the forbidding glare of Judge Henry reading her thoughts. That day Eleanor had realised that, contrary to family tradition, the Judge had no power at all. He could not stop anyone liking Alice.

'Is it about Gina?' Most things Alice talked about ended up with Gina. Eleanor considered it impossible that a secret about Gina would be interesting, but it might be useful.

'No! Warm though.' Alice picked up her pencil again and softly touched the rubber end with her tongue. Pink-red flesh whipped in and out. Alice always finished ice creams after Eleanor, taking small sippy licks to make them last. Her eyes would half close like Crawford's when tucking into a lamb bone, content yet wary.

'I give up.' Eleanor purposefully gave the sun sharp fins: the heat was burning up the fields and evaporating the sea, and scorching the grass on the lawn. She picked light green and brown crayons, making the paper thick and slippery with colour. The rays of light fired like laser beams at the wings of her plane, as she soared into the distance beyond the horizon line, where the earth met the sky. Far away from Alice.

'No. Guess! It's really funny.' Alice made the snuffly noise behind her cupped hands, glancing quickly at the closed dining room door. Eleanor looked too, hoping someone would come, even Gina would do. The house was quiet. Alice tucked her hands under her legs as if they might give her away, she wriggled with suppressed glee, making a show of forcing herself to look serious. Eleanor did not think any of Alice's expressions were real. Alice was always being someone else. She wanted to tell the policeman with the crack in his chin that Alice had pretended all of it. This pretence was odd because Alice wouldn't play spies or spacemen, saying they were not real.

'If it's about my Dad breaking the club house window with the cricket ball, I know, I was there.' Relief made Eleanor exhilarated. It would be all right. 'He doesn't care, a cheque will sort it, I heard him telling my Mum.'

'Cold again! We were all there, how could that be a secret?'

Later Eleanor remembered birds' wings rushing by her ears and then complete stillness before she heard Alice's voice down a long pipe:

'It's about your Mum!' Alice pulled a face pretending the words had slipped out by accident and clapped her hands to scare them off. She leaned on her elbows, resting her witchy chin in her hands, watching Eleanor, with the Judge behind her left shoulder. The table creaked under her weight.

'It's stopped raining.' Eleanor began shovelling up the crayons. Gina was upstairs with Lizzie, she could hear their voices and footsteps through the ceiling. Her father was working in his study and Lucian had gone fishing. Her Mum was in her bedroom lying down.

'Don't you want to know what it is?' Alice snatched up her own drawing and screwed it up, tossing the paper ball back and forth in her hands.

'I said I don't care.'

The crayoned sun stung her cheeks, yet her body was crammed with ice, aching cold spreading into her legs. She couldn't move.

'I'm not letting you go until you answer the question.' Alice rose up from the table. She threw off her cardigan and grasping a wooden ruler, sidled towards the door.

'If it's a secret, that's the thing.' Eleanor was briefly pleased with herself. Originally she had planned to draw a metal frame around the picture to make the edges of the aeroplane window. But now she had packed the grey away. She must not be scared. Outside a watery sun lifted the greenish light of the storm.

'We can go out in the garden now. Or, if you want, you can go home.'

'So is it true? You must know.'

'What do I know?'

'Your Mum tried to kill herself by eating cheese with her medicine!' Alice made a shrill noise and still she paced in front of the closed dining room door, smacking the ruler across her palm in time to her words: 'Is it true?'

Slap. Slap. Slap.

'What do you mean?' Eleanor made the question part of a hearty guffaw. She went on packing up the crayons, drawing out the activity. Light colours at the left, getting darker to the right. Black at the end. Where was the black? She shoved the paper around, and lifted the heavy baize cloth. She must find it, or someone would tread on it and blame her.

'Is it true that your mother would be dead now except Doctor Ramsay saved her life by pumping out the inside of her stomach?'

'No!' Eleanor slammed shut the lid on the crayons and tried to get up, but sank down. She couldn't leave. 'That's stupid. You can't die from cheese. We had some for lunch.'

'Well, that's what my Mum said and she's not stupid.' Alice bit back tears.

'She was wrong.' Eleanor didn't see what Alice had to cry about.

'That's rude. How could she be wrong?'

'She is. That's all.'

'The whole village knows. She said that's why your mother stays in bed. It's called dee-presh-shon.' Alice was speaking faster, and it seemed to Eleanor that Alice's mother – the source of this secret – was in the room too, in step behind her daughter, nodding all the while to show how right she was. 'She tried killing herself by holding her breath until she was dead. That didn't work so she ate cheese and then drank her medicine.'

'She's not always in bed.' Eleanor's hands were limp and dutiful in her lap.

'She's in bed now!' The ruler cleaved the air with a swipe. 'How do you know she's not dead right this minute?'

Eleanor saw the black crayon. It lay inches from Alice's feet. She addressed it in a whisper:

'She's tidying her bedroom. She'll be down soon.'

These were the 'open sesame' words. At the possibility of the approach of Mrs Ramsay, Alice laid down the ruler and said she had to leave; she was already late. She was supposed to be staying for tea under Uncle Jack's tree. Eleanor was not keen to remind Alice of this and willingly watched her go. Alone with the Judge, Eleanor rose unsteadily to her feet and picking up the black crayon she slotted it into the gap in the box.

After Alice had gone Eleanor had run up to her Mum's room. Isabel hated to be disturbed, especially when she had a headache. Eleanor stopped outside the door and, with her ear pressed to the wood, listened.

There was no sound.

Downstairs Lizzie had started dinner, singing lustily to a tinny Tom Jones on her transistor. These were noises in her home that Eleanor loved, but now she required silence. Gina must have gone to muck out her horse and Lucian was still out. There was no sound from her father's study further down the corridor. She inched the doorknob round. With a loud clunk she fell forwards into the room. She had forgotten it was impossible to go into her parents' bedroom quietly, the door was warped and could only be banged shut or shouldered open with a clatter. Her mother complained every time they came down, but nothing that was broken or faulty at the White House was mended unless it brought things to a halt.

'For God's sake. Who's that?' The voice groaned from beneath the bedding. The mound moved slightly.

'Only me.'

'Who's "Only Me"?'

'Elly.' Eleanor just stopped herself from saying 'your daughter'. The Cheese Secret had made her mother a stranger. 'Just came to see if you were ali...if, if, you wanted anything...'

'Can't you all leave me alone, must you all constantly barge in?' Her mother always said this even if she had been left alone for hours. 'First Gina, then...'

'What did Gina want?'

'Oh, Eleanor! What do you want?'

'Do you need a cup of tea or a drink? It's nearly after the Yard Arm.' Their special joke, but her mother groaned and, extracting her hand from under the blanket, flapped feebly at the door.

'It's the afternoon, Elly. Push off!'

Eleanor wandered disconsolately up to the playroom, thumping a rhythm on the banister as she climbed. She swung open the front of the doll's house. It made a snapping sound and stuck half way. Alice said the hinges were rusted and the door was wonky. The dusty furniture had been tossed back into the rooms any old how. She had not touched it since she met Alice. Now she picked up each piece and returned it to the right room. She straightened the tiny bedspread and laid the sitting room rug beside the bed. She hated stepping on the freezing floor in the mornings during winter holidays. She dragged the bed over to the window so the sun would shine on the pillows first thing. Her mother said sunshine made her happy and, when she didn't have headaches, she loved sunbathing best of all.

Eleanor had lied when she told Alice they had eaten cheese for lunch. They had beans and fish fingers. Alice must have realised this because she had eaten lunch with them.

Eleanor had shunted the green sofa against the sitting room wall. In the big house the sofa was in front of the fireplace and was the best place to be in winter apart from by the kitchen stove. Her mother always lay on it when she was out of bed. Eleanor would sprawl on the thick rug in front of the fire and lean back against the sofa as she watched figures dance and leap in the flames. Sometimes her Mum would run spider fingers on the back of Eleanor's neck, tracing messages that made her shrug and duck. Isabel liked to torment. She would nudge Crawford with her foot until he spat at her and blow on the back of Eleanor's head until her skin tingled, while singing made-up songs that made them all laugh uneasily.

Isabel Ramsay had been on the rug the night her family returned from the Lewes fireworks last November. Eleanor had been overjoyed to see her downstairs.

Isabel lay sprawled on her side, an arm across the carpet, and the other bent underneath her in a way that Eleanor thought must give her pins and needles. She didn't get up when they burst in whooping and shouting, pink cheeks stinging from the icy winds. Lucian and Eleanor were jumping like the mad firework that had zipped and dipped and made them giggle for ages after. Gina had been appalled. Her siblings were embarrassing. It was rare for Lucian to side with Eleanor and this had added to her joy.

When she saw her Mum, Eleanor mouthed to the others shut up and did giant hopping steps towards her.

One side of Isabel's face was flushed purple from the fire, which although only glowing, was still boiling hot. Her jumper had pulled up at the back revealing a strip of white flesh and the black strap of her bra. As Eleanor got closer she discovered her Mum wasn't asleep. An eye was open and watched something horrible in the fire without blinking, like one of Crawford's birds. She was about to speak to her when there was a roar like a tornado whirling in from the garden. The living room door crashed against the wall shattering the convex mirror behind. A shower of splinters glittered and flashed in the firelight.

Eleanor could think only of how her father never let anyone near the mirror, which was his dead mother's. He acted like even looking in it wore it out. She had gazed down at the broken glass. It would be impossible to put it back together. Then she was spun off her feet as a great creature blundered past her shouting something about room to breathe. She grabbed at the mantelpiece to keep her balance. It was then she saw the puddle on the floor in front of her Mum's face. A thin thread of sick hung from her lips, from which all the colour had gone.

Her Dad was suddenly there, kneeling down on the floor beside her Mum, but Eleanor knew it was too late. She was dead. Later she would merge the memory of her mother sprawled on the floor with the grainy black and white image of the dying Senator. As her Dad bellowed at the children to get out, Eleanor had wanted to assure him none of them had broken the mirror or done anything to their mother. But before she could form the words an arm went around her, warm hands guiding her away as a soft whispering in her ear said things she couldn't hear properly but that made her feel better.

They had ended up in Gina's bedroom and sat close together on her bed. Gina clasped them both to her in a huddle, and stroked their hair, telling Eleanor not to cry. Until then Eleanor had not realised she was crying, but her cheeks were wet so she let Gina blow her nose with Lucian's handkerchief. She stole a glance at Lucian and saw that he was trembling like Crawford when he used to visit Mrs Jackson. They could hear their Dad calling out their Mum's name so that Eleanor decided she had hidden and he was looking for her. He kept repeating: 'Darling Izzie, it'll be okay now. It'll be okay.'

After what seemed like hours the room filled with blue light going on and off, and they shuffled like a sack race across to the window, and gasped. A huge white van had crashed into their father's brand new Rover. Then they saw it was just parked as close to the door as possible and not actually touching his car. Eleanor had saved up enough for a Red Cross ambulance with a detachable stretcher and doors that opened at the back and at the sides. She had been going to buy it at the weekend. This occurred to her as she stood between her brother and sister, and with a gossamer touch Gina stroked away Eleanor's fringe. Now there would be no weekend.

'An ambulance,' she breathed, then flinched, waiting for Gina to reprimand her.

'It's for Mum.' Gina spoke like their mother, low and certain.

Eleanor was reassured. Gina knew what was happening. They kept out of sight as two men carried a stretcher through the front door beneath them. When the men came back there was a bundle on the stretcher like the Guy earlier that evening. The men loaded it into the back of the ambulance. Then just for a moment Eleanor glimpsed her Mum's face, the eyes looked right at her, before her Dad jumped in and the doors were slammed shut.

'She's not dead.' Lucian stated in his doctor's voice.

'Luke!' Gina pointed at Eleanor, and hugging her tighter, clamped a hand over her ear, which made no difference to what she could hear.

'If she were dead, they would have covered her face. That's all.' Lucian detached himself from his sisters with a shrug.

The children watched impassively as the ambulance followed the circular drive in front of the house and glided out through the gateway. It gathered speed on the lane, and they saw the light flashing, a fallen star moving at speed at ground level, outlining the winding road across the downs to Brighton. Then it plunged into the woods and vanished.

For the first time in their lives the three children had to spend a night alone in the White House because Lizzie was in London until the next day. They had slept in a tangle on top of Gina's bed, their dreams punctuated by the dull booms and stuttering cracks from firework parties echoing over the dark downs. The three children were woken by their father charging into the room the next morning, demanding help with breakfast. It was past ten o'clock, the longest they had ever been allowed to sleep in.

After that everything returned to normal. Their mother came home a week later in new clothes implying she had been shopping. It was dealing with such incidents that taught the Ramsays to treat big things as small things. Her week away became food poisoning. It was not a secret because no one was keeping it.

Eleanor knew that Alice was wrong. No one died from cheese. But it made her admit to herself that she hated Alice. She did not miss her one bit, although at the end of his visit she decided to tell the detective that it was no fun without her.

Her mother smiled as he gave her a sweet so it had been the right thing to say.

On Thursday lunchtime, after the police had left for the day to continue their investigations, Lucian sauntered past Eleanor as she sat cross-legged on the patio at the back of the house ruminatively weeding out blades of grass from between the cracks in the flags, and laying them out in a neat and tidy row. He called out to his father, who was reading *The Lancet* on a camp bed under Uncle Jack's tree:

'Robert Kennedy's dead.'

Eleanor's hand went to her mouth. Her father lowered the magazine just briefly before continuing to read. Eleanor shuddered as Lucian let the side gate bang on his way to the river, whistling a tune on one note. She got to her feet and wandered aimlessly around the side of the house to the meadow.

She walked to the centre and stood in the long grass looking up at the blue cloudless sky, her cheeks warmed by the sun. The handsome Senator in the suit, with brushed hair and squeaky shoes, did not exist any more. Two wasps crawled busily over a rotten apple by her foot. Now the man with the crack in his chin would never save her from drowning.

Eleanor understood with a profundity beyond her nearly nine years that she was truly alone. After that afternoon on the 6th June 1968, this recognition never left her.

Five

On the following Saturday morning, when Alice had been missing for three days, Eleanor had finished a clandestine bowl of cornflakes and was creeping back upstairs when she heard voices coming from the dining room.

She ran nimbly down again. The door was slightly open. This was unusual; another change since Alice went was that doors were mostly shut. Since they had been coming to the White House, Isabel had railed at the creaking doors and windows, left to swing to and fro despite her constant requests to keep them closed, for draughts, she insisted, were definitely responsible for her headaches. After Alice, the White House was quiet.

Eleanor peered in. Her father sat in his chair at the head of the table ready waiting for food. Her mother craned over him from behind perhaps straightening his napkin. Although this in itself was odd, what astonished Eleanor was the way her mother was talking. She was half speaking, half singing like she did with Crawford and her favourite men friends.

'It's boring, darling but it'll soon be over. Like Richard said, it's routine. I think myself that she could simply be trapped in a cupboard here in the house, those children were getting everywhere, I even poked about in the chest freezer.' She gave a strange laugh.

'What would he do?'

Eleanor squinted at her father through the space made by the hinges, as he indicated Judge Henry behind him.

'Oh, Mark!' (Eleanor wished her Dad hadn't mentioned the Judge. It wasn't the way to get her Mum's sympathy.) 'He'd get rid of these damned police, for a start. He was their boss, wasn't he?' Eleanor shut her eyes, but her father only made a mewing noise and put his head in his hands.

Her parents had been closeted in the living room most of the morning, watching Robert Kennedy's funeral on the television. This must have upset her Dad who had lost his twin.

There was a scraping step at the front door and a massive silhouette filled the frosted glass panels. Now accomplished at deception, Eleanor bolted back to the kitchen, then marched out again with stamping steps, before running full tilt up the stairs as someone gave three loud knocks which caused the loft door on the top landing to swing open and smash against the wall. The bangs got quieter and quieter like the ball bearings in a cat's cradle. She knew that now her Dad would never fix the catch and her Mum would be even more cross.

Then Eleanor realised what had really upset her Dad. Chief Inspector Richard Hall had told her mother at the end of their talk yesterday that the police wanted to search the house in case Alice had hidden in a childish prank as he called it. He told her that they had already searched Alice's house and found nothing. Although he kept saying 'Mrs Ramsay', he looked at Eleanor, so that when her mother said she supposed it must be done, Eleanor nodded heartily in agreement. She was Mrs Ramsay. She wished Gina had been there to see.

If things weren't bad enough, for the last few days Eleanor had not been able to find Mrs Jackson's glass amulet. Its disappearance worried her more than what had happened to Alice. She was certain it had last been in her Box of Secrets. This loss was the culmination of a land shift that had altered her perceptions. Wardrobes and wallpaper were different. They were angular and unfriendly, stripped of memory or association. Trees cast menacing shadows across the overgrown lawn and the milk on her cereal that morning had been slightly sour. Nothing was the same.

She had overheard Lizzie telling her mother that the police had opened an Incident Room in the church hall on the high street so today there would be no Bring and Buy sale. Instead most of the village helped in a search across the fields and along the riverbank. Gina and Lucian had been allowed to join in. Gina found a crisp bag that she was told might have a bearing on the case. Lucian hadn't found anything so said the whole thing was a waste of time. At night Eleanor lay watching the creeping shapes on the ceiling made by sweeping headlights and dazzling film lamps. Intermittent rifle-fire of numerous car doors failed to penetrate the cotton wool quiet hanging over the Green. It reminded Eleanor of the muffled stillness inside her father's car as outside he chatted on the busy pavement inches from the closed windows.

All day policemen and journalists consulted in hushed murmurs, perhaps because they knew they were getting in the way of everyday life. A life now deemed precious and lost to an age already passing. Then a reporter would aim a camera lens at the White House windows and, diving to the floor out of sight, Eleanor was her old self.

The house search did not produce Alice, but it did yield a packet of Gauloises in Gina's knicker drawer and a welcome if momentary return to family responsibilities for Mark and Isabel. After administering a telling-off for which neither of them could muster up much remonstrative stamina, Gina was released to make only her second trip to the stables since Alice had hidden. That evening she stormed home in tears and standing in the hall, hurled her riding hat to the floor, where it bounced and rolled on the tiles, as she sliced the air with her crop. Seeing Eleanor strolling out of the kitchen munching on a ham sandwich, Gina had levelled the crop at her and screamed:

'I ab-so-lute-ly hate you!'

Mark had come up behind Gina, car keys jangling, and grabbing her shoulders, he propelled her into the dining room, kicking the door shut behind him. The sandwich turned to sticky dough clogging Eleanor's mouth. What was the matter? There was plenty of ham left, and loads of bread; in fact recently, along with cheese, Gina had stopped eating meat, so what did she care? She swallowed hard and trotted swiftly across to the forbidding dining room door. Squinting into the keyhole through which she could see nothing because of the key, Eleanor listened. Gina was shouting:

'It's not fair. I hate her. She's ruined everything!'

Her father cajoled in a continuous rumble so that Eleanor could not make out separate words. She pulled a face as Gina carried on: '... and she gets away with it!'

The hatred in her voice made Eleanor hiccup on her sandwich.

She backed away from the door and told herself it didn't matter about Gina, because her Dad had proved he was on her side. Whatever happened, Eleanor knew for certain that he loved her. This might make everything bearable. When she had got up the nerve to hear more they were talking calmly, although her Dad sounded like he was putting Gina to sleep as she made baby sounds, which should have been funny, but wasn't.

A chair leg screeched and Eleanor dropped her sandwich. She moved fast, scooping up the scraps of bread, scooting to the kitchen, where she threw them in the bin, scuffling them under a damp wad of rubbish in case she was told off for wasting food with people starving. This made her realise that since Alice went she hadn't been told off at all. As Eleanor retreated to the playroom – now the extent of her world – she wished they would be cross with her. Gina's outburst had been a relief. Since Alice had gone, Eleanor had vanished too.

She settled on the floor and went on with her picture. Despite her gloomy mood, Eleanor was pleased with it. Two small spies creeping through thorny bushes followed by a tall murderer in sunglasses and a denim cap. She drew him, in thick black mixed with streaks of burnt umber and gashes of grey and brown, crawling over leaves and branches like a beetle. The spies were meant to capture the Mill Owner and hand him over to Richard Hall. She put in tumbles of gorse and brambles to rip his clothes and scratch him. Along the top of the paper she added the Tide Mills in the distance, and looming at the forefront, the Mill Owner's house. Then she changed her mind about the thorns and coloured over them. She livened up as

76

she filled the orchard with juicy, ripe pears that she decided the murderer should be allowed to eat because one of them was poisoned by the Chief Spy.

No mention of Gina's explosion was made at supper. Usually Eleanor would have said something, but instead she chewed diligently, her elbows tucked in. Gina did not shout again, Lucian didn't talk about logic and reasoning with cutlery acting the parts. Everyone stared at their plates and munched. As the meal wore on Eleanor propped herself on her elbow, her forehead leaning heavily on her hand, and loudly slurped reluctant spoonfuls of custard. No one told her off.

Isabel had set up camp in the dining room, smoking and talking to visitors, emerging only to take a phone call or get another coffee. The dining room was where Eleanor was asked to go and talk to Richard Hall. Isabel sat beside her, as Richard the Chief Inspector explained how she would be helping them with their enquiries. He was trying to make her feel special. Eleanor was suspicious.

The first time they talked, which was the afternoon after Alice went missing, Richard had asked her to think about playing hide and seek with Alice. He was sure that a clever girl like Eleanor could guess where Alice might be hidden. Eleanor had already informed him it was Alice's turn to look, but he had forgotten. She decided Richard really was bonkers when he asked: 'Elly, do you remember where you hid Alice?'

His mistake made her snigger: as if she could hide Alice! Eleanor imagined her, smooth and white and clean and hard to lift. It was easy to hide from Alice, because she wouldn't look in dirty places. Alice, sharp as a pencil, sat bolt upright, asking impossible questions, always demanding the right answers. Alice was very difficult to hide.

She stopped counting before getting to ten.

Richard the Policeman had rubbed his chin, making Eleanor think of Robert Kennedy, at that point still alive and presumably lying on a hospital bed in America with his head in a bandage. This distracted her so that she jumped when her mother smacked her hand down on the table. Everyone stared at it. Eleanor was sure Richard liked the nails, polished and long, and she hoped he liked the rings, the sparkling diamond, and the gold signet on her mother's little finger that made her father cross because it was from a 'former life'.

'Eleanor, bloody well pay attention. I'm sorry Chief Inspector.' Eleanor knew the man didn't like her mother swearing. His eyes stopped blinking like Alice's. She clutched the sides of her chair as the room bent like the Hall of Mirrors on the Palace Pier. She didn't remember saying anything. She was sure she hadn't. She must have.

In an interlude of truce during tea after the Cheese day, Alice had confessed to Eleanor that she had failed her Underwater Proficiency test and had to be rescued by the instructor from the shallow end. She didn't care that Eleanor had got her life saving certificate and had once swum a mile in a freezing pool covered with dead flies. She said Eleanor shouldn't have pretended to drown by staying under because, she had explained, drowning was not funny. She told her it was rude that Eleanor had waved around in the air the stripey pyjama trousers she had just escaped from, when she finally bobbed to the surface. Eleanor had assured Alice that drowning was like going to sleep.

You close your eyes and let the water go over you. It won't hurt. It's better that you can't swim, you die quicker. Sailors don't learn to swim in case their boat sinks, Luke said.

'Let's hurry this along, shall we, Eleanor?' The chin came closer; unlike the 'Stricken Senator's Chin' it was full of holes and a funny pink colour. 'Where have you hidden Alice?'

'It's not amusing, darling.' Isabel glared at Eleanor. 'You're not normally like this.' Isabel smiled hopelessly at the Chief Inspector. It was obvious that Eleanor was normally like it.

'He said where had I hidden…'

'Be quiet!' Isabel grabbed her by the shoulder, pinching her skin under her shirt, pushing her sharply away and then yanking her closer, so that Eleanor nearly toppled from her chair. 'Just answer Chief Inspector Hall's questions properly. For the last time: this is no time for fun and games.'

Eleanor felt tears well up, like an enemy stalking. She was frightened of the woman with the tin voice and jabbing fingers and now she was frightened of the policeman with the red sweets and the red chin. He had stopped smiling.

'When did you last see Alice?' He had no idea he had asked things before. Eleanor decided that if it was a game she could pretend. She relaxed.

She told the story of the last day. She made the snap decision to put Alice outside the blacksmith's, which was now a garage, at the bend in the lane leading to the White House. Eleanor told only of the first game of hide and seek which they had played in the village on the Sunday afternoon before tea. She pretended they had played it on that last Tuesday afternoon. She could not say the second game had been at the Tide Mills as they shouldn't have been there and although Alice had agreed to come, it had been Eleanor's idea.

It was best not to mention the Tide Mills at all. Eleanor wasn't going to allow Alice to spoil anything.

The detective's face was a gritty mask, as Eleanor elaborately outlined how she had hidden in her den on the edge of the ten-acre field behind the old blacksmith's. It was a secret place that Eleanor didn't think Alice knew about. If Alice had been in the room she would have said Eleanor was lying and told him they were at the Tide Mills not in the village.

'*You know we have to tell, don't you.*'

She would say the game in the village had been on the Sunday and give them accurate times and dates. Alice would have confessed the truth even if it got Eleanor into trouble. She would simper and whimper about how their feet had slipped on the bridge over the millpond and they had nearly drowned. She would say how Eleanor forced her to walk along the crumbling arch over the gigantic wheel underneath. Alice would pop a strawberry sweet between her moist lips and, being allowed to smile, she would assure him that honestly, she had asked Eleanor not to walk there, but Eleanor had forced her to.

It was very good, concluded Eleanor, that Alice was not there.

She did tell the policeman about her special trick, but was annoyed when he wrote it down because it was a secret. It wasn't cheating. She explained how she spied on the person looking, and once they had checked one hiding place and found no one there, she would choose her moment and rush over to hide in it. This way Eleanor could be hiding for days if she wanted to.

She had not done this on Sunday.

Richard Hall noted down that Eleanor Ramsay talked like a boy as she boasted about taking apart dead animals and vaulting across furrows in the triangular field with an old farm cart in one corner. Once she reached the other side she said she had turned back to see if Alice was following her. Chief Inspector Hall prided himself on his ability to be objective, but in this case he was not. He didn't like this child; she wasn't a proper girl or a proper boy. He vaguely blamed it on the mother who was very attractive.

Eleanor did not mention that Alice had cheated in the first game because now she was pretending to the policeman that there had been only one game. In the first game Alice had sneaked a look while she was counting. She did tell him how on the last day Alice had stopped counting too soon.

Eleanor soon found the talks with the policeman boring. So must he, for on the Thursday morning he had suggested they go out and that Eleanor take him to her hiding places. A gang of tall men loped after the diminutive expedition leader, as she marched them up the lane, and showed them her den through a hole in the hedge of the triangular field. She stood back proudly, arms folded as, one by one, they stuck heads into the gap and made 'Ah-yes' noises. In a burst of inspiration she took them to the very petrol pump she had told them Alice had been standing next to when she last saw her. By now Eleanor had forgotten she wasn't telling the truth and waited with hands on hips, while the police measured the exact distance between the spot where Alice had supposedly been standing and the gap in the hedge that led to the hiding place with a wheel on a stick. It was forty-four feet and eight and a half inches. Eleanor had done measuring in the playground, and knew how many inches to a foot and how many yards to a mile if they asked.

Richard had marks on his cheeks like a potato. Eleanor addressed these marks when she answered the question about hearing a car while hiding in the hedge. Patiently she reminded him that she had swapped hiding places so was not hiding in the hedge the whole time. Later she wished she had put in a car. She could have used the one with silver hubcaps that she saw driving on the Thames by the Hammersmith yacht club. She had thought it was a dream until Lucian talked about the car that could go on water one breakfast time. She made up her mind that if Richard asked her about a car again, she would grab the chance to tell him about it.

By Friday, Eleanor had grown used to the questions and could answer them promptly and consistently.

'Why did Alice stop counting?'

'To find me sooner.'

'Is that what you do?'

'No, it's cheating.'

'Where were you when she stopped counting?'

'Hiding in the bushes.'

'What bushes?'

There were no bushes in the triangular field or on the footpath. The bushes were by the Mill. But he accidentally helped her:

'Do you mean the hedge?'

'Yes. I ran very fast across the field and down the zig-zag path to the beach. In the opposite direction to the Mill.' She drew breath and grinned inadvertently. She lost two lives if he guessed about the Tide Mills.

'Why wasn't it fair to stop counting?'

'There was no time to hide. If I hadn't known exactly where to go, I would have been cross.'

'So you were cross with Alice.' He was friendly again.

'No, I didn't 'specially mind. Except I didn't have time to hide.'

'But you *did* hide.'

'Not properly. If I hadn't known about my den...' By now Eleanor knew for certain he had something wrong with his memory. She had a game called Memory that Alice had agreed to play. Each person had to turn up two cards in a go and hope to remember where the other part of a pair was. Alice always knew and always won. When she had gone Eleanor found faint pencil squiggles on the backs of the cards.

'How far did Alice count before she stopped?'

'Five.' He wasn't listening. Eleanor doubted that anyone ever told him off.

'You recall exactly. That's smart.'

'It was meant to be ten, she stopped halfway.'

'Good at maths too!' He made a lopsided smile, with his lips showing his teeth and cracks appeared on his face that made the marks on his cheek move.

'It's likely, isn't it, that you were out of earshot, too far away to hear Alice, and she was in fact still counting, but you could not hear?'

'No. I heard her stop while I was still on the path, I mean... while I was in my den in the hedge. I was only forty-four feet and eight and a half inches away. Sound carries that distance.' If he never remembered anything, they could be there in the dining room forever saying the same thing. He was writing it down, but didn't look at what he had written so it didn't help. Eleanor could put up with it, but she knew her mother would get fed up.

'The point is, you were able to hide, so it didn't matter that Alice stopped counting. No need to get cross, was there?'

'Cheating always matters.'

'It certainly does matter. I expect that made you very angry, didn't it?' The Chief Inspector reached into his pocket and pulled out another bag of sweets, the paper rustled as he spilled them out on to the table between himself and Eleanor and her mother. Eleanor and Isabel stared at the pile. Isabel didn't usually like her children buying penny sweets.

'Have one, Eleanor. What would you like? You choose.'

'Strawberry, please.'

'Yes, of course it's your favourite, you told me. Mrs Ramsay, can I tempt you?' His eyes hovered for a moment on Isabel Ramsay, who had the looks he had never expected to meet in real life. Her mother barely shook her head. Any minute Eleanor hoped she would invent an excuse to go. It would mean they could stop, because her Dad was in Lewes and she had found out that the police couldn't talk to her without one of her parents present. Eleanor spread the wrapping paper out into a square, neat and flat, pressing and smoothing out the folds. Suddenly her mother snatched it away and screwed it up, frowning at her.

'You were saying how cross with Alice you were.' He tilted back in his chair. The chairs had belonged to the Judge and they were supposed to sit sensibly in them.

'It wasn't fair. When she hid, I counted all the way to ten and particularly didn't do it fast to give her time. It was easy to find her because she hid badly.' Eleanor tucked the chew into the back of her cheek, so she could speak clearly. 'Actually, I expect that's why she stopped counting.'

'What do you mean?' The chair creaked.

'She must have wanted to do hiding, she didn't want to wait ages for her turn, because I'm expert at hiding, so she hid anyway. She had loads of time, because I was hiding too. She knew in the end I would look for her.' She pushed out her lips and furrowed her forehead to deliver her diagnosis. 'It is far more fun hiding.'

'Don't you think she was upset after your argument?'

'We didn't have an argument.'

There was silence. Her mother gazed out of the window, the backs of two fingers stroking under her chin over and over again. The next time Eleanor dared to glance at the Chief Inspector he was looking at her mother's fingers. He caught her looking at him and started shuffling his papers, squaring the edges with sharp taps on the table.

'All little girls have fights. I have a daughter the same age as you and she squabbles with her sister all the time. I expect you do! Changes her best friend with the weather!'

'Gina and me do fight sometimes,' Eleanor agreed, moving her hand so that her thumb and forefinger rested on her collarbone like her mother was doing. She tried smiling with the corners of her mouth. She hadn't meant to say that. Her mother would be annoyed later. So would Gina.

'You mean Alice and you fight?' He pushed another strawberry chew towards her. It was at this point Eleanor saw that there were mostly strawberry ones. He did remember some things.

'No, Gina. She's my sister, not Alice.'

'We are talking about your fights with Alice.' He spoke like Lucian fishing out facts. Any minute he might say the Lord's Prayer backwards in Latin without stopping.

'We didn't fight.' Eleanor couldn't say Alice was not a person you had fights with. She wanted to say she wasn't a friend either. When Alice refused to play spaceships, Eleanor could not argue. At least with Gina there were things to say back.

It dawned on her that the Chief Inspector must know about the flower-pressing expedition. All his questions, the sweets, the smiling: everything had been to get her to talk about it. She would not.

She had been so happy when, at tea last Sunday, her Dad had announced they were all going on an expedition after they had finished eating. After only two days Eleanor was at her wit's end with Alice and was even longing for the holiday to be over, which had never happened before. It had turned out that her Dad had been talking to Alice about her flower collection and the reason for the expedition was to find new flowers to add to it. To make things worse, Lucian and Gina were told they didn't need to come. Eleanor had tried to get Gina's attention: if she came Alice would be distracted, but Gina had ignored her frantic signs, probably because Eleanor had egged Lucian into doing the Dance of the Fork with her at tea. Gina had got Alice a fork for her cake then disappeared off to her room without once looking at Eleanor.

The expedition was as nightmarish as Eleanor had expected. Alice had known the names of every flower. She had flitted to and fro like a fairy, then acted like it was private as she crouched down, gripped the flower head between her fingers and confided its name in a whisper to 'Doctor Ramsay', as she called him, though he kept telling her she could say 'Mark'. He then told her the Latin and helped her to pronounce it. Eleanor got crosser as he sliced the stalk with the shiny blade of his sharp knife and slipped the severed flower into a plastic folder for Alice to press.

'Red valerian. Now I love this one, it's sooo pretty.' Alice said she loved every flower they found, in a tinkly voice that Eleanor hadn't heard before.

'*Centranthus ruber.*' Her father was doing Judge Henry. He let Alice use his knife, steadying her hand as they parted the stem from the main plant. Alice was breathing in her sucking-up, wheezy way. Doctor Ramsay knew how to treat Alice like a grownup.

Eleanor snatched up a flint and threw it with all her might. It bounced down the bridleway. Alice shook her head. Her father was too busy fumbling with Alice's flower folders to notice.

Later that night when Alice had gone home and everyone was in the living room, Eleanor had sneaked outside. The sun was going down and it was cooler. Her Dad's study door had been left unlocked, although there was no sign of him so she had hurried in and taken a large envelope from his stationery cupboard. Then armed with her secret penknife she rampaged off down the lane in a private race, charging through the thin gap in the wheat growing in the triangular field. She savagely tore and cut whatever flowers she could find in the hedges and verges. The colours were more vivid now in the gathering twilight and were easy to find. When everyone was in bed, Eleanor sat on the floor of the playroom slapping an example of each flower into an old notebook and belting it in with a bit of sticky tape. She wrote the name in biro followed by jerky printed Latin, got from the battered Collins *Pocket Guide to Wild Flowers* that her Dad had left out on his desk after their outing.

'I've already got a book of flowers, actually,' she had remarked airily after Alice had been in the house about five minutes the next morning. Eleanor had meant to take the book with her to tea at Alice's house later that afternoon when she had planned to produce it like a rabbit out of a hat, catching Alice unawares. But she couldn't wait. As things turned out this was just as well because she wouldn't have got a chance.

'What are you talking about?' Gina trotted into the hall, and executed a *petit jeté* as she reached high up for her riding hat from the shelf above the coat hooks. Alice got there first and thrust it into Gina's arms eagerly. Gina was glaring at her sister and simply put out a hand for it.

'Oh, just pressed flowers. I've been doing them for ages, in my spare time,' replied Eleanor carelessly. 'There's a book I use. It's nothing, just flowers, you know. And some Latin.'

'Have you had a bash on the head, Elly?' Gina had looked at Alice and rolled her eyes. Alice rolled hers too making her head go like a duck. Normally this would have enraged Eleanor but she had been fortified by the pressed flower book, which she produced from under her tee-shirt with a flourish.

The small notebook was swollen and bulging with damp, dying flora. She dumped it on the hall table fully thinking it settled all arguments. For a moment no one moved, obviously taken in by the magnificence of her achievement. Then Alice came over and lifting the warped cardboard cover with just the tips of her fingers, flicked open the front page and stepped back revolted. Gina's interest had passed and she was on her knees rummaging through the shoe rack.

'You haven't pressed them properly.' Alice had rattled the page holding a flower named 'Yellow Toad Flax' in tottering capitals that had stained the paper a nasty brown. 'You can't put them straight in. They need to dry. You need a special book.' She paused for Gina to agree, but Gina was struggling into her boots. As Alice flipped through the notebook, the page heavy with a fistful of Nipplewort (*Lapsana communis*) fell out at her feet. Apparently without realising it, Alice moved her foot, crushing the head of the flower beneath her sandal.

Gina had got up, inches taller in black riding boots, her hat swinging from her arm, and clopped over to give a final verdict.

Eleanor was enraged to smell the scent they had given Isabel. Gina was always stealing things.

'It's a shame to press flowers. They should be left where they are for everyone to enjoy. If we all pulled them up willy-nilly and carted them home there'd be none left. Besides it's a form of murder.' Gina tossed her head and stalked out of the open door, vanishing in a blaze of sunlight like the lady in *Star Trek*. She didn't see Alice gazing at her from the porch until long after she was out of sight.

'Can you think of anything else to tell us, Eleanor?' Richard the Policeman began dropping the sweets back into the bag one by one with precise movements. Isabel and Eleanor followed each sweet. Last of all, he put the lid back on his pen with a click and stabbed it into the breast pocket of his jacket. Eleanor made a mental note to practise this later with Lucian's school blazer.

Was there anything else? She furrowed her brow. There was the old railway line that led from the Mill to the halt where the grain was picked up. There were the remains of the Mill Owner's house, with its empty rooms and flying fireplace. The sand at the end of the beach was dotted here and there with polished pebbles that were engulfed by the incoming tide. But these and other things were secrets she could not tell them. At another of their meetings she did say that when she went down to the beach to see if Alice was there, it was empty, adding quickly that of course she couldn't say for sure. For good measure she emphasised that no cars passed by the triangular field while she was hiding and that she suspected Alice of interfering with her den because it was very tidy.

Eleanor said nothing that helped him find Alice.

Chief Inspector Hall told Eleanor she could go and play, and that they might talk again.

Eleanor's bare legs were stuck to the leather chair, and stung like nettles as she climbed down. She mooched into the garden and sat on the camp bed left under Uncle Jack's tree. She couldn't think what to play. This disconsolate feeling was unfamiliar. Anyone looking down from an upstairs window would have seen a small girl robbed of spirit, thin shoulders bowed under a bewildering weight. The house was at its best in the late afternoon sunshine, its leaded windows were blocks of molten gold and its white stucco translucent.

Eleanor did not think of her stories as lying, they were true to her and she made them true to others too. She had written a piece for Miss Skoda on the summer holidays last year. She had said how she and Isabel found shells on the beach and picked flowers for the sitting room mantelpiece. Miss Skoda said it was wonderful how she had remembered every detail. Miss Skoda did not know that Isabel had been away on one of the trips when she never sent a postcard. She didn't know Isabel hated collecting things like shells and flowers. She didn't know that Isabel hated dawdling and she hated clutter. If she had known, perhaps Miss Skoda would have guessed Eleanor had made it up.

Eleanor often returned to that story about the beach. It made her happy.

Mummy found a shell buried deep down in the sand and washed it clean in the sea until it was pink and white and shiny. She kissed it three times for luck and held it to my ear for me to hear the sea. She said it was a potent spell and to feel the magic. She put it in my pocket and told me to keep it forever.

Eleanor hid the shell in her Box of Secrets.

The story about Alice would be easy to write.

Alice and Eleanor had played hide and seek. It was Eleanor's turn to hide so she had hidden. With the dragons and robbers and magic spells there was plenty to put in. She need not mention the Mill; or the Mill Owner; or what happened if villagers got home late from the pub. She need say nothing about the chatting voices of the workers in the Granary that made her think of pigeons. She would leave out the sharp scream of the seagull and how she knew that Alice had stolen her amulet. None of this made a happy story.

When Eleanor gazed up at the sky laced with speeding wispy clouds, the house appeared to be falling on top of her.

Six

'... six... seven... eight... nine... ten!'

At each count Alice inched further round, taking care to let her hair fall forward so Eleanor wouldn't see her eyes were open. When she was facing the other way, she could see Eleanor running towards the hedge by the triangular cornfield. Alice felt no qualms about looking. It was unfair of Eleanor to choose such difficult hiding places. Alice wouldn't have known where to start if she had not seen which direction she went in. Besides this, she could not admit she hated shutting her eyes, even to sleep. She could not confess the terror that had closed in on her as she counted. After Eleanor had vanished into the hedge there were crackles and snaps like a fight going on in the bushes, and through strands of hair Alice saw the branches sway. Then they stopped and it was quiet. It was always quiet in the country. More than ever she wished they had stayed in Newhaven where even at night there would be dogs calling to each other over the gardens, footsteps on the street and the bleak mooing of the foghorn for the ferry.

The little girl remained in the lane, enervated by heat and immobilised by the misery of playing with someone she didn't like. Eleanor would say she was mad if she started counting again, but Alice could think of no other way to put off looking for her. She knew exactly where to go and she didn't want to find her. Eleanor would be cross to be found so quickly and might even accuse her of cheating. All she wanted was to go home and play with her Sindy dolls who were proper friends.

The sun burned the back of her neck, as she gazed absently at the web of cracks in the ditch: an earthquake for ants. The cracks widened and she realised she was swaying in the intense heat. She slapped the itchy prickles of sweat on her forehead. She was tired and messy which would upset her Mum. How far away her home seemed, even though there were the roofs of the cottages peeping out from behind the trees where the lane bent towards the village, ending with the church. She could walk, one step at a time, towards the beckoning chimneys and find her house. Then she would be safe.

If she balanced on her toes like Gina she could take a beaker down from the kitchen cupboard next to the shelf where her Mum had arranged the cat plates that were a present for Alice's last birthday from her Brighton Nana. Alice could easily reach that high as everyone marvelled that she was tall for her age. She didn't need to get on a chair. The cupboard door would creak, first low then high, as she pushed it shut. The tap would splash and splutter, wetting her face as she turned it up to make a waterfall thundering into the sink. If no one was there she could drink the water in great gulps not caring about cold liquid on her tummy. She had done it before and nothing had happened to her. She would tiptoe into the hallway, and give the barometer a tap to see if it was going to rain so she could stay at home and not go back to the Ramsays'. Then she would run quickly up the steep staircase and hide in her new bedroom. Eleanor would never find her.

It would be the first place that Eleanor would look.

Alice nearly didn't hear the car. At first she thought the soft purring was an aeroplane, then remembering Tufty Club rules, she hurried to the side of the lane, as close to the hedge as she could be, without tipping into the ditch. She stood stiff and still, to face the oncoming traffic and be visible to the driver. A green car shot around the corner and its big silver bumper drove right at her.

She froze. As it got nearer, Alice saw there was plenty of room for it to pass and it was only the way the road looked in the heat that made it seem as if it was coming to run her down. She didn't know if she was pleased that the driver was Doctor Ramsay.

Alice was wary of Eleanor's family. If she had been able to be honest, or had more confidence, she would have recognised dislike but it was a fact in the village that everyone liked the Ramsays. It was impossible for Alice to articulate an opposite feeling even to herself and so she sought other reasons for her dread as she nibbled her Shreddies each morning that half term, before going up to the big house with the tall iron gates to play with Eleanor Ramsay.

It seemed to Alice that the Ramsays were everywhere at once, making loud jokes she didn't understand in funny voices. Back at home, she told herself she would do a funny voice when she next went, but when she was at the White House, she could hardly speak. It was quite impossible to do something that might make Gina laugh or cause Lucian (who she dare not call Luke) to say 'affirmative' in a slow American accent. Alice would croak 'please' and 'thank you' and her cheeks burned as Eleanor's Mum told Eleanor to behave more like Alice in a voice that might have been joking. She expected Eleanor to be angry later, but she never was. In fact Eleanor didn't look at her at all and spoke to the doors and windows beyond which she insisted there were spies and murderers. It made Alice worried that there were things she didn't know, or worse that no one cared about what she did know. Alice had nerved herself up to refuse exploring a jungle that was a settee or fly to the moon in funny plastic chairs that looked as if they had come from the moon in the first place. By the end of two days of playing it seemed impolite to keep saying no, so on that Sunday afternoon, with home time on the horizon, Alice had felt bound to agree to do hide and seek.

As Doctor Ramsay got nearer, Alice considered hiding, but it was too late. The great car slid up to her, filling up the lane, blocking her in. Her face glided to a stop in the reflection of the window, pigtails sticking out like ears in the gleaming glass. Then the window was wound down and inch by inch she jerked out of sight. Eleanor's father leaned across the passenger seat, with his white teeth lined up in neat rows, and his lips stretched back as he strained to hold the window winder. Alice fixed on the long arms, brown and smooth like a woman's, with no hairs. These were doctor's arms. Everything – his very deep voice, his big car and his black sunglasses – were to do with being a doctor. She eyed the outstretched arm. There were some freckles speckling the wrist and twisting blue veins criss-crossed up around the arm, and along the fingers. She imagined them hard to the touch like string. Her own Dad didn't have veins and his arms were thicker and covered in hair that she stroked and patted as he held her tight around the waist and ordered her to climb off his lap, their words a well-worn ritual.

'Hop off now.'

'I can't move!'

'Why not?'

'You know why. You're holding on to me so I can't escape.'

'Stuff and nonsense. Shelves don't put themselves up.'

'Alice!' Doctor Ramsay spoke to the road, like Eleanor did. She looked where he was looking but there was nothing. The strong sunlight made everything wobble. Surreptitiously she steadied herself on his car. The door was burning hot. She let go and rubbed her fingers in her other hand.

'Yes, it is me.' She straightened her dress and put her feet together with ankles touching. She must be on her best behaviour: the doctor was a busy man. His time was precious. Her Mum had said there was no such thing as 'time off' for doctors. Alice pictured Doctor Ramsay, always awake, always curing people with glasses of water and ice-lolly sticks on the tongue like the doctor at her Mum's surgery who wouldn't take out her tonsils because he said they were valuable.

'Do you need a lift? Or are you on some big adventure!' He laughed at an invisible joke. Learning now, quick as a flash, Alice laughed too.

'I'm with Eleanor. We're playing.' She was intrigued at the prospect of riding in his green car. Doctor Ramsay could rescue her from Eleanor. Then Alice's manners got the better of her.

It wasn't fair to leave her hiding. Alice imagined clasping the silver handle, and pulling open the door. It was so close. She'd tell her Dad she had ridden like a princess on the magnificent seats. Through the window came a smell that both scared and lured her: a mix of cigarette smoke, leather and a sharp scent she had smelled on the doctor before. Her mother had said it was aftershave. When she had asked her Dad why he didn't smell like it, he snorted that it was a stupid expense and what was wrong with smelling like a man?

Alice furtively scratched the back of her calf with her foot, balancing perfectly on one leg. The Ramsays scared her. It was not fear like 'murder in the dark' or the fluttering dread of waiting for her turn to read in class. These were bad enough, but she could deal with them. Nor was it the disappointment of a hope shattered as the high jump bar clattered to the ground when she failed to jump three feet, seven inches at the heats for the county championships. The way Alice felt when she saw the Ramsays was worse because the Ramsays were supposed to be great fun.

This was a world where although people talked in English they made no sense, and where they saw nothing wrong with drinking milk straight from the bottle, smoking cigarettes in every room and calling people rude nicknames.

At home, as Alice vigorously brushed the nylon locks on her Sindy dolls before bedtime, she imagined helping Gina with her horse, polishing the tack, carrying her things, mucking out, sweeping up, brushing down. She would hold clever conversations with Lucian, so detailed that she was disorientated to find she was still in her bedroom and not walking through the village on his arm, or helping him catch fish by the river. She whispered to the Sindys that Lucian was in love with her and that every morning she lifted a letter off the mat that implored her to marry him and be the next Mrs Ramsay. She told them he came past her house each night and blew her secret kisses over the dining room table at the Ramsays'. She practised her name in the back of her diary with the Cliff Richard on the cover: 'Alice Ramsay, Alice Ramsay,

Alice Ramsay' in intricate coloured letters with her Christmas felt pens. If she were married to Lucian she wouldn't stay in bed all day like the other Mrs Ramsay.

When she was with the Ramsays, Alice was a standard lamp stuck in the corner, her limbs wooden and her neck stiff, so that easy things like drinking orange juice became difficult and daunting. Lucian never noticed her. He once passed her in the street without returning her tentative greeting. She guessed he didn't remember who she was and was mortified.

It seemed to Alice that Eleanor's family was constantly doing things. They were important people always expected somewhere: opening the fête, captaining the cricket team, winning the gymkhana, climbing trees and walls and driving off in their car with a bang of doors and a tooting horn. With Gina as her sister, Alice would go riding and Gina would stick up for her in squabbles. When he wasn't her husband, Lucian was her brother, getting into fights for her and letting her carry his rods.

The foundation for Alice's dreams about Lucian were built around the day he gave her a bubble gum after they literally bumped into each other in the village store. Lucian stepped backwards on to her foot. She had been nonplussed as he shot out a grubby hand and, opening his fingers, revealed the gum. Bazooka Joe: the neatly wrapped block that smelled sweetly delicious that she never dared to buy. She thanked him properly and accepted it. Instantly she was stunned. Bubble gum would kill her. If she swallowed it, her Mum said it would tangle itself around her intestines until she died. She gasped:

'Thank you very much, Lucian. I really love bubble gum.'

'Yeah, well. I've got lots.' Lucian pushed a pink covered tongue briefly out of his mouth as if there was no such thing as rude.

Alice said she would save it as it was nearly lunchtime. Lucian shrugged and told her that it was up to her. Alice saved it for a day, taking it out after her parents had said 'good night' and closed her bedroom door. At first she was careful to keep it hidden, but then she was worried it would give her away, so sugary-pink smelling with the coloured paper that concealed a shiny comic strip. The bubble gum was a gift from one of Eleanor's demons and she had been tricked into accepting it. Finally Alice couldn't sleep for the guilt. Even if she buried her face under the blankets the heavy sickly smell seeped out from the bottom of her toy cupboard. That morning she had thrown it in the bin, burying it under bits of rubbish to stop it rising to the surface. She could not forget the noise Lucian had made in the road when they came out of the shop. A barking that was not funny, though she had laughed. Alice hadn't known what to do as he staggered backwards with his arms sticking out like a sleep-walker, balancing on the edge of the kerb. At last he had run off without saying goodbye.

Alice laughed when the Ramsays laughed, but never knew why. They made up words for things and spoke in peculiar accents like foreigners. They called her names like 'Alicia' and 'Allegro' and said it was 'splendid' and 'fabulous' that she had moved into the village. When the doctor and Mrs Ramsay left the room, Lucian and Eleanor would chuck sweets or grapes at each other, and dance around calling out rude words. Fruit Salad chews flew like bullets across the lounge, pinging against windows, disappearing under the stained sofa, and once hitting Alice on the side of the head so that she had to laugh louder. She had been miserable when Lizzie told them all to calm down, especially Alice who should know better. Alice had ogled at Lizzie, like a prisoner straining behind a gag, desperately trying to convey with her eyes that it was nothing to do with her.

The Ramsays' house was messy and muddled, and from the first day Alice had felt sorry for the doctor, who must hate it. There was dust on the window seats in the playroom, and piles of books on the floor in the living room. She had thought they were moving out and had started packing. Alice had begun writing her name in the dust, but stopped. Her mother said it was better to leave a room as if she had never been there, with everything put back in its place. The kitchen table had criss-cross scratches all over it because they had no tablecloth. The Ramsays didn't mind about scorches from hot pans or the dents from knives and forks. Her Mum would have been upset for guests to see these marks, but they didn't care. Yet her Mum was surely right, guests did notice dents and had opinions. Alice was a guest and she had noticed them. The Ramsays never bothered with what guests thought. As she had tucked down to sleep the night before, Alice recognised, in a scalping of innocence, that her parents were wrong. This revelation overturned her world.

Alice longed to get into the doctor's car. What stopped her was knowing that Doctor Ramsay might not like her if he was told the truth about her. The afternoon before she had upset his daughter by talking about cheese and now she would be doing it again by leaving Eleanor hiding.

'So, what are you up to?' The doctor jerked the gear stick forwards and backwards and pulled up the handbrake with a clicking sound. Three clicks were enough, her father said, or you ruined the brake. The doctor did loads of clicks and didn't care. The car's noise went deeper. He looked around him, which made Alice look too. If he spotted Eleanor, she wouldn't have to pretend to search for her. Alice was surprised he wasn't in a hurry.

'Where is my daughter, anyway? You two are inseparable. Left you on your own, has she?' He nodded. So it happened to him too. Then he looked Alice full in the face and made a sucking noise on his teeth with his tongue like her Dad did at the end of meals, which her Mum said was a bad example.

There were too many questions at once, Alice didn't know which to answer first. It was so easy to be impolite. She had rehearsed the words: Please, take me home, but now she had said she was playing with Eleanor he wouldn't take her anywhere. He was a doctor and must know she ought to be at home playing in the square of sunlight in the lounge. Sunlight was good for you. The figures grew clearer in the hedge behind the doctor's head. Her Mum making rock cakes and singing 'Please Release Me' through the hatch; her Dad fixing something in the garage, whistling bits of her Mum's tunes out of order till she stopped him:

'The cat sounds better!'

Alice liked the way her Mum and Dad said the same things to each other.

'We're playing hide and seek, it's my turn to look. I don't know where Eleanor is.' She raised her voice. 'She's very good at hiding.'

'I see.' He glanced around again. 'Have you tried all her hidey holes? There's the tree house and the barn. Failing that, you could come back with me and leave her! It's nearly four, isn't that meant to be teatime?' He rolled his eyes like Gina. Alice brightened.

She was about to accept, and then it dawned on her that all along he had been joking. He wouldn't want to give her a lift; indeed he was already preparing to drive away. Five minutes ago she would have been relieved to see him go, but now playing with Eleanor was worse than talking to the doctor, which wasn't so bad after all. As he released the handbrake Alice tried to stop him.

'How is Mrs Ramsay?'

She was horrified to see it was the wrong question. Lines appeared above his eyes as he banged the steering wheel. He turned his head, looking out for Eleanor, or perhaps for Mrs Ramsay. 'As good as ever!' Then he smiled right at her and Alice saw it was all right. After that the conversation went much better and Alice found she had lots of things to tell him and forgot that he was a doctor because he said she should call him Mark. She tried it in bed that night, but it felt like the name of a stranger so she went back to 'Doctor'. She told him about her flower collection and that was when he kindly offered to help her with it, although at the time she hadn't believed he meant it. It seemed there were lots of flowers her parents hadn't told her about. She had forgotten all about Eleanor until Doctor Ramsay exclaimed:

'Good luck finding Elly!' Alice pulled a face to show that she didn't expect to. Really she meant she didn't want to and she was sure now that Doctor Ramsay understood this. He turned on his radio and mimed along to Tom Jones singing 'It's

97

Not Unusual', her Mum's favourite. This time it was fine to laugh. Alice could still hear the music as Doctor Ramsay's car whizzed out of sight round the corner of the lane to the White House. After that she forgot about Lucian. He was childish in comparison to Doctor Ramsay.

Alice shivered. The sun had gone in as dark clouds crept across the sky from the coast. Soon it would rain, like her Dad's barometer had forecast. Doctor Ramsay hadn't mentioned the cheese. She dared to hope Eleanor hadn't told him what she had said, although it was worse not to be told off. Alice would definitely have told her Dad if Eleanor had been mean to her. She heard a rumble of thunder. She should get inside. She decided that next time it was her turn to hide she would slip away. Eleanor would be watching from the hedge so she made a feeble play of looking elsewhere, even checking the ditch in case Eleanor was lying there. Then thinking of Doctor Ramsay and dropping all pretence, Alice trotted up the lane to where she had last seen Eleanor. It was time to end the game.

The branches were knotted together with bindweed and brambles so she couldn't find the hole. She was sure she was being spied on. Alice didn't understand why Eleanor had to spy all the time. She hid behind cupboards, under tables, behind sofas, and wrote down what people said in a notebook. Apart from Gina no one said anything worth recording.

'I can see you,' Alice told the hedge. 'I said, I can see you.' She smiled to cover her discomfort: she had promised herself to be nice to Eleanor after yesterday. She nodded firmly to a twig with three leaves that hid Eleanor's eyes.

The twig didn't move.

'About what I said about your Mum and the cheese.' She spoke to a small bluish beetle that scurried from one leaf to the next on the twig. 'I'm sorry.' The beetle stopped.

Silence.

Alice felt better. It wasn't polite to ignore an apology. Now it was evens. Now Eleanor had upset her in return.

Then Alice saw the hole and made a snap decision. She picked her way down the clumps of grass into the ditch and dragged the branches aside. She ignored the nettles that stung her ankles to come out on all fours in a space between the bushes, completely hidden from the road. By her nose was a wooden crate with French writing on the sides. It was draped with a faded red velvet curtain on which was placed a blotchy canvas cushion. The surprisingly homely feel was emphasised by a mess of comics and two empty bottles of Coke. The ground was carpeted with dried leaves and dry twigs. It was soft and spongy. Alice tentatively turned the cushion over, checking for insects and spiders, rather comforted by its fusty smell. She perched on the homemade seat. Now she had the perfect look out, through a natural window in the hedge. She would see anyone coming down the lane, but no one would see her. Eleanor must have sat here spying while she talked to Doctor Ramsay then got out when she saw Alice coming. Alice reflected that if she had been Eleanor, she would have waited until Alice had left the den and hidden there again. Eleanor would assume that Alice wouldn't come back there.

She would be wrong.

Alice smiled to herself and hugged her knees tightly. She liked her own company and seldom felt lonely. In fact she resented having to play with other children, a resentment that had reached a conscious pitch with Eleanor. But as the minutes wore on, she began to feel lonely. She couldn't dismiss this comfy little hole with its nice things to read. She wished Eleanor would stop hiding, and then they could sit together and spy on people going by. Alice would do the notes because her writing and her spelling were better. She bent down and rearranged the leaves and crushed branches to hide patches of soil and rubbed away at a mark on the box until it went. As she shuffled the comics into a straight pile, Alice made up a story for Eleanor.

There was once a magic cave heaped to the ceiling with treasure where for hundreds of years there had lived a wizard who cast spells on the people of the kingdom. He cured the sick and made miserable people happy. All the children loved him because he treated them like real grownups and cared what they thought. If they were upset then with a whoosh of his wand everything was made better.

Alice was sure Eleanor would like the story and became so absorbed in her narrative that it was a shock to remember that she was an intruder and that Eleanor would be angry to find Alice in her den without permission. She saw that her hands were dirty, and there was a tear in her dress.

Alice scrambled out of the ditch back to the road and ran towards the White House.

Eleanor was by the gates, singing Young Girl loudly with the wrong words and out of tune while slashing the hedge with a stick. Leaves ripped off and flew up in a shower. She was making no attempt to hide and seeing Alice waved the stick above her head like the Red Indian with a tomahawk she had been all yesterday morning. Alice thought Eleanor must be in a bad mood, but as she got nearer she saw that Eleanor was smiling. So she smiled too. They would sit in the garden and have tea. Alice would whisper to her about the wizard and offer to get some pretty material from her Mum to make curtains for the den. They could hang them from the branches, she would show Eleanor how. On another day they might even go back to the Tide Mills. Alice was dizzy with a torrent of bright ideas as she hastened up the lane towards the scruffy little girl dawdling along the hedgerow.

'I gave up hiding as you took so long coming.' Eleanor tossed her stick up in the air.

'Careful, it might hit me.' Alice jumped back as Eleanor failed to catch it and the stick clattered at Alice's feet, just missing her head. Alice's good feelings evaporated.

'Doctor Ramsay said to wash your hands and come in for tea, I just saw him.' Alice was safe because she knew for certain that Eleanor would never talk to Doctor Ramsay about her. If she did, Doctor Ramsay would never believe her because now he was Alice's friend. Alice folded her arms over her chest and stalked past Eleanor up the circular drive to the big front door. Outside the gates Eleanor continued to hurl the stick and after the fourth time to catch it with easy precision.

Seven

When Gina offered Alice a slice of Lizzie's fruit cake she, without thinking, still imbued with courage after her talk with Doctor Ramsay and now excited by the flower-pressing expedition he had promised that they would go on after tea, asked for a fork to eat it with. This had made Lucian and Eleanor hysterical with laughter. They tried to hide it. Alice stopped being hungry as she pretended not to see them gasping for breath. When they finally exploded, they said it was about their cat. She had wished Doctor Ramsay would stop them for after their chat earlier that afternoon she knew he would agree with her about the fork. It would even be all right if Gina gave her a friendly smile, but, one by one, Mrs Ramsay, Gina and finally Doctor Ramsay had gone away. Lucian and Eleanor played hunt the fork, doing mad dances on the lawn, around the table and climbing into the branches of the tree above making crow-noises that sounded like 'fork'. Gina had gone after her mother, striding away in her bright white plimsolls, her hair flying out like a mane. Alice silently pleaded with her to come back. Through brimming eyes, she stared at the fearsome lump of cake on her plate, unable to leave the table without permission even though there was no one to ask or to mind. Gina had actually spoken to Alice when she and her Mum had first met the Ramsays on Friday morning. She had asked her if she liked her new home. Alice wanted to tell Gina how she missed their house in Newhaven, but that she loved her new bedroom and hearing the village shop bell tinkle when a customer opened the door. Instead she had managed no more than a nod.

Alice had sat tight in her chair, hands trapped under sticky bare legs, knees clamped together, holding a smile that made her cheeks ache, as Eleanor and Lucian hurled the stick Eleanor had been thrashing the hedge with earlier back and forth to each other. Everyone had forgotten they were having tea. Alice's slice of cake sat implacably on her plate admonishing her for needing a fork. She wanted to squish it up and scatter the crumbs in the flowerbed. She waited. Cups of tea and half-drunk glasses of orange juice waited with her. Everyone else had been eating with fingers. Broken chunks of cake, a spattering of sultanas and cherry lay on the plates and were scattered on the tablecloth. The Ramsays were messy eaters. Alice's mouth was dry, and she shivered despite the warm sunlight. Her shaking hand would not lift her glass without spilling the juice. She bitterly wished she had gone home earlier while Eleanor was hiding in the hedge. Now the thought of looking for wild flowers was further punishment.

Alice dimly recognised it would be better if she could join in and crawl along the grass like a snake, or swing like a monkey from the tree, but she was a crumpled doll with sticks for arms and legs, and a torn dress clean on that morning.

Doctor Ramsay was coming.

He trod quietly across the grass, his white shirt ballooning out over his jeans, and sank back down into his cane armchair with a loud sigh saying something about Mrs Ramsay having sunstroke. Alice didn't know whether to respond, he wasn't looking at her. Then she reeled in a hot wave of alarm. He had forgotten the fork. She had been relying on it to save her. Now she didn't know what to do about the cake. She should have gone home in his car while she had the chance. It was ruder to have asked than to have eaten with fingers. It had showed up the Ramsays and spoiled their tea party.

Alice pulled her hands out from under her legs and furtively examined them under the table. White and red creases ran across her skin as if she was old. She pretended her thumbs were her friends, curling her fingers into a fist. Two thumbs: two friends. She wasn't alone. Suddenly Gina was back.

Something flashed in her hand. Alice breathed out and thanked her three times which made Doctor Ramsay glance at her with a look of concern. Although Alice had been happy that Gina had brought the fork, she was terribly frightened now of what it might do to Lucian and Eleanor, who were seeing who could throw the stick highest in the air. They could both catch it easily, which made the fork become heavy in her hand and she forgot momentarily how to hold it properly. Without turning round, Gina yelled at them to come back. Alice was impressed when they raced over and collapsed into their chairs. She had come to think of them as untameable animals.

As Alice nibbled her cake in manageable forkfuls, dabbing her mouth with her handkerchief because they had forgotten serviettes, she was hemmed in by fingers. Fingers licked by smacking tongues, fingers picking noses and scratching rude bits, fingers wiped across shorts, flicking sultanas off the table with clicks and taps and dabbling in wet saucers. Eleanor and Lucian got the giggles again. This time Alice joined in until she breathed in crumbs and was nearly sick. Doctor Ramsay rubbed and patted her back and made her sip water from a glass that he held while talking, although she couldn't catch the words. Alice was sorry for Doctor Ramsay and Gina for having to be in the Ramsay family. Afterwards, she told her parents about choking and the kind Doctor Ramsay coming to the rescue. But she didn't mention about the fork. She knew they would have been pleased that she had asked, because it showed the Ramsays she was well brought up. This thought made her hot with shame for good manners shrank to nothing in comparison to playing jazz music on the piano, doing funny voices or curing people. Her mother was no more than a polite and tidy stranger as Alice assured her that yes, she had thanked Doctor Ramsay properly for looking after her and she did realise how lucky she was that he was there.

Eight

When he ruffled her hair, Alice felt a lurch of sickness and closed her eyes. The jelly teddy bear lay patiently: a sacrificial lamb that she must eat limb by limb, sucking slowly, eye by chocolate eye, crunching his sugar teeth and marshmallow ears without mercy. He was her long promised treat for being in the chorus of her school play. But after tea at the Ramsays' followed by her Mum's shepherd's pie, Alice wasn't hungry and she was angry that her mother hadn't expected this and saved it for a better time. Besides Alice had only been in the chorus and it was all over now.

'How's my princess?' He bent over and kissed the top of her head with a loud smacking sound and moved his hand over her scalp in crawly circles. She smiled weakly as he smoothed her hair in case by touching it he had messed it up. Leaning over he examined the bear.

'Is that all for me?' He smacked his lips. She studied the tick-shaped mark on his chin. It showed up more in the afternoons when his face was scratchy. 'Mmmm. Yum, yum.'

'It's not yours.'

She trotted out words. She didn't want jokes today. She didn't want the bear either.

''Course it is.' His finger got ready to pluck out an eye. 'Raspberry, my favourite.'

'It's strawberry.' She was properly cross. 'Have it if you want to.'

'All right, keep your hair on.' He scrabbled it roughly. She imagined him snatching it off like a wig and shied away.

'Alice!' Now her Dad was annoyed. He liked her to be nice. 'What do you say?'

Her mouth went upwards, her lips tightened and she made herself smile. 'You can have some if you like.'

'You know that's not what I meant.' But he was nicer again. 'Sorry.'

'That's better. Don't get spoiled with all these treats. Spending every day with that Doctor Ramsay and his family. Don't get ideas.' Her Dad's voice reminded her of his new car, shiny metal with sharp edges. Only it wasn't really new. Uncle John had owned it first.

Alice couldn't tell him she had already had ideas. She had lost the girl who would have loved a strawberry jelly bear and taken ages to eat it, making each mouthful last. The treat was for the wrong person. Her grandad was coming over from Newhaven later. He would be angry if she left any. He hated waste. Once she had refused to eat her supper when he was visiting because her head ached and her skin tingled. He had shouted so loud that his eyes bulged like gobstoppers. Her Dad had shouted back at him. Alice had sat and listened as her grandad scraped the food off her plate on to his own and ate it with a loud clicking.

She made an investigatory split in the bear's chest with her spoon. It did not cry as she scooped out its heart and slipped it between her lips. She squashed the mixture against the roof of her mouth with her tongue and closing her eyes, willed herself to swallow. She assessed her plate and decided that if she could do the same thing – maybe fifteen times – it would all be over and she could go to bed.

Alice started to eat when she heard her Dad clonk his shoes down on the newspaper in the hall, ready for cleaning. She felt in the pocket of her dress for the jewel. It was still there. She felt better. It was the nicest present she had been given by anyone. Perhaps it was possible for them to be friends. Now she really was a princess. She would keep it secret as she had promised. Already she had planned to hide it in her ice-skating boots at the bottom of her toy cupboard. She was concentrating on ballet now so there was no chance that her Mum would touch her boots.

While he took off his postman shoes, her Dad was whistling a tune she didn't recognise. His whistling normally made her hopeful. Today the long drawn out notes made her sad. She looked round the kitchen, usually so reassuring. It was full of enemies. She gloomily eyed the teacups on the shelves above the sideboard and the row of grinning cat plates propped up behind. The shelves were lined with flowery paper smelling of lemon. The teapot, in its woollen hat with the bobble on top, could read her mind.

'So, did you have a nice day?' Her Dad sat down opposite her. She wished he would go into the lounge and read the evening paper, or out to his lean-to to mend something. Her Mum had popped back to the surgery where she had left her purse. Alice could have had plenty of time to chuck the bear in the rubbish bin. Now her Dad could see right into her head and take out her thoughts with a spoon. She tried to think ordinary things: school…ballet…subjects it would be okay for him to find. Then she remembered the precious glass jewel and closed her mind. The teddy bear would take more than ten swallows. She was sure she had eaten more of its left cheek, but now its whole face was leering at her. If Doctor Ramsay delved inside her head he would discover she had taunted Eleanor about Mrs Ramsay and the medicine. No one knew what Alice was really like. Except for Eleanor who was biding her time.

'Yes, it was a lovely day. Thank you.' This was mostly true.

'Is that all? Where are all your stories? Your Mum said you picked flowers.'

Alice's mouth went dry. 'Yes, we looked for flowers for my collection. Doctor Ramsay helped.'

'Did he? You know your flowers. I expect he was bowled over. Bet you could hold a candle to any of his kids.'

'Eleanor didn't pay attention. Gina knows about flowers, but she was with her horse.' While her Dad was there Alice had to keep eating. She got another spoonful ready and readied herself. He was watching.

'That Eleanor's a bit of a wild one.' Steve Howland looked through his daughter as he considered the truth of his remark. Despite this, he rather liked the girl. She had spirit.

'Mum's asked her to tea tomorrow.'

'Did you bring them home?'

'Who?'

'The flowers you picked. A nice bunch for your Daddy?'

Alice gulped down some jelly and sprawled her arms out around the plate. It was more comfortable than sitting up straight. 'It wasn't like that.' She had been told to chew her food ten times before swallowing, surely that didn't mean jelly. It had gone by chew five.

'Oh-oh, so what was it like? What about what's her name, Lady Muck?' He gave a roar of laughter.

'Mrs Ramsay. I wish you wouldn't, Steve.' Her Mum hurried into the kitchen on an urgent mission. Alice saw that her mother didn't do anything calmly; she was always rushing and going out of control. She grew hot with impatience as her Mum filled the kettle, crashing it down on the stove and waving the gas lighter at it inaccurately so that it took longer to light than it needed to.

'Did you tell Dad about Doctor Ramsay's lesson on photosynthesis? Wasn't he kind to take the time, Steve? So busy and with three of his own. He sat her down and went through it. Normally it's not done until they get to the big school.'

She turned from the stove pointing the gas lighter at Alice, 'Make the most of it, love. You'll have a lovely head start.'

'She said he took them on a jaunt to get flowers!' Steve Howland remained unimpressed.

'Doctor Ramsay works harder than you and I put together.' Kathleen Howland wrapped a tea towel around her hand and pulled open the oven door. Warm air wafted around them.

'You should see the state of their drive, cracks, bumps. Needs seeing to.' Steve judged everyone by the route from the street to their letter box. He gazed fondly at his daughter, she smiled back and collected up some more jelly.

Steve and Kathleen tried not to spoil their only daughter. But at times like this they thought she was perfect. Steve took pleasure in everything his Alice did. He loved the way she held her spoon, daintily like a lady, not in her fist like other children. She was beautiful with her soft eyes, sitting there so straight, with her hair falling down past her shoulders. He often told himself she was the point of his life, the apple of his eye. Despite his sarcasm, he was proud she could go to tea with the Ramsays and be like them. Even if it meant she'd change beyond all recognition he would fight tooth and nail to prevent anything holding her back.

Alice was sure her parents must have heard about her imprisoning Eleanor in the dining room on Saturday. Her Mum would have been astonished and told the doctor it wasn't like Alice to behave unkindly. She would have looked for an explanation, but have been too polite to blame Eleanor. She would have promised to have a quiet word with Alice over tea, perhaps even told Doctor Ramsay about the bear treat and how that would be a good time to choose. She would say Steve would be there to ensure a firm hand, hoping that, as a father himself, Doctor Ramsay would appreciate that. So Alice guessed this was why they were both there, waiting for the right moment. She felt sorry for them. They were so sure there must be a perfectly good explanation. They would say she wasn't naturally mean.

They were wrong.

Alice could not have explained to anyone what had made her torture Eleanor with the Cheese Secret. She couldn't talk about the sniggering, the put on voices, cat hairs, bowls of vegetable soup like sick, and finally the matches in the toilet. Alice could not explain that she hadn't thought Eleanor would mind because she didn't believe Eleanor loved her Mummy as much as Alice loved hers. She had seen no recognisable signs. The Ramsays were not like ordinary people.

'You're clever when it comes to flowers. You've got a gift.' Steve turned to Kathleen for back up, but she was draining potatoes over the sink. 'You could be a florist.'

'Doctor Ramsay said I'd make a great botanist and should get a job at Kew Gardens.'

'Ah well. He should know.' Steve Howland puffed out his cheeks with an explosive sigh.

Alice wanted to tell him about the picture in her head. She could see a face, eyes sparkly like diamonds with trying not to cry. A crayon snapping in her fist as she made the sun bright yellow. The big room with wooden walls was caving in on her. She wished there was someone she could tell the truth to about the sort of girl she really was. She wasn't the Alice everyone thought she was.

After rushing out of the White House last Saturday afternoon, Alice had stuffed her screwed up picture in the bin when she got home. Her Dad could have seen it, if he had looked inside.

Her Mum put a plate with two chops, four potatoes and a map of peas down in front of her Dad. He went off to wash his hands, like he always did exactly when the food was ready. Her Mum tutted at the delay, like she always did. But still she filled his silver tankard with frothing London Pride, his favourite.

'Hurry up with that, Alice.' Mrs Howland flitted from one task to the next without stopping. She began washing the pans, clinking and clattering as she loaded the rack with steaming dishes. Alice saw her chance.

She kept her eyes on her Mum and, stepping around her chair, guided the remains of the bear into the hole at the top of the stove. The rubbish bin was too far away. For a second his face looked at her before it slathered over the unlit coals. Her father returned just as she sat back down.

'What's up, Fannackapans?' Steve was puzzled by Alice's expression. She was gaping at him as if she didn't know him. For a moment he dreaded her growing up more than anything and wanted time to stand still.

'I was taking my plate to be washed.' She glanced down and saw a smear of jelly up to the rim where she had pushed it off and covered it with her hand. She looked at her father, divided now by more than a tea table.

After her Mum and Dad had gone to sleep, Alice crept down and lifted the latch on the kitchen door. She flinched at the loud click of the light switch. Had it woken her parents? There was no movement from above. The lino was cool on her bare feet. All evening she had dreaded her Mum and Dad looking in the stove. She knew that in the height of summer it was very unlikely, but her guilt skewed her judgement. She imagined they knew and as with everything else had agreed to say nothing. Alice was persecuted by their silence. Her crimes were mounting up. She had to show them the person she had become.

She eased open the lid of the stove. Button eyes stared blindly from the coals. She felt into the dark hole and one by one picked up lumps of coal from the sides and laid them over the jelly until the bear was buried. Her hands were soon smeared with sticky black dust. She was about to wash them under the tap when she remembered how the pipes would hiss and clank. She was not allowed to pull the chain at night for this reason. There was a small puddle of water around the plughole, she dabbled her fingers in, rubbing them together and dipping them again until the stains had gone.

She went back to bed, but couldn't sleep. She lay in the dark, thinking of Mrs Ramsay trying to kill herself. Alice had doubted the truth of the story even as she was quizzing Eleanor. Just as she could not imagine Mrs Ramsay going to the toilet, so she couldn't imagine her killing herself. Eleanor had been right, no one could die from cheese.

Nine

It had been arranged that Eleanor would go to tea with Alice on the Monday afternoon. Mrs Howland was up at dawn that morning making sure the house was spotless. She unwrapped the pink china and shooed Alice off the settee to vacuum the cushions. Alice knew Eleanor wouldn't care about clean cushions or eating off the best plates. She hated her mother for her mistake. In despair Alice had set off for the Ramsays' where she was to spend the morning and have lunch. Unlike the other two days, she had to be back in time to get ready for the special tea and Eleanor's arrival at four o'clock.

The Ramsays floated through space: Lucian slid down banisters sideways, Gina did perfect horse jumps and cantered like the Virginian. Eleanor vaulted over walls like a man while Alice walked sensibly round to the gate. Mrs Ramsay floated the most, in a cloud of cigarette smoke, in and out of rooms and across the garden, trailing in flowing robes. Her own parents made everything difficult and Alice was crushed by the weight of their efforts. After her talk with the doctor, she saw the world like a bicycle wheel with the Ramsays at the centre, while her parents were at the end of a long spoke. The home she longed to escape to when she was caught in a Ramsay storm wasn't real. It wasn't where proper things went on. There was no need to wash already clean tablecloths and polish already gleaming cake forks, for no one noticed except her Mum, and she didn't matter.

At the sound of the doorbell her Mum snatched off her apron. Alice stayed in the kitchen, reluctant to see Eleanor. She eyed the table piled high with triangular fish paste sandwiches, jelly, fairy cakes, tall beakers of orange juice, and glittering with the best cutlery. The Ramsays didn't eat this much between them. Through the half open door she saw her Mum greet Eleanor. Never had the cottage looked so dark and small. Eleanor's playroom was bigger than the whole ground floor. She grimaced as Eleanor let her cheek be kissed and, shrugging off her anorak, hung it on one of the hooks, before Alice's Mum could take it.

Alice glared at the table, bright white and stupidly waiting. She wanted to be Gina, wandering in late from horse riding to find a game of hide and seek or Monopoly going on, free to leave or join in if she wished. Gina was the White Witch in her sleigh heaped with furs, making a lashing remark before gliding away. In Alice's house no one interrupted her games, except her Mum to ask her to lay the table or her Dad to take her ice-skating. If she had a friend to stay, she had to play with them. She couldn't go off and read a book like Gina. Alice sat down on the chair reserved for Eleanor and picking up a geometrically folded serviette, twisted it into a ball and scowled at the door.

Last week Alice had believed in God. He was a kindly third parent, rather like her Brighton grandad had been. God was pleased when she did a hundred skips in a row or was pencil monitor for a whole term. He helped her get best marks for her arabesques, a reward for cleaning her mother's china animal collection. She believed that if her Mum was pleased with her, God would be too. He was behind the rare tick in green ink that Mrs Bird, the head mistress at her old Newhaven school, sometimes put beside her teacher's red one, for neat writing or punctuality. Until Alice met the Ramsays, God had kept watch over Alice all the time, taking notes like Eleanor. Now she was certain that, like Father Christmas, God had never ever been there. He was one of the Ramsays' jokes she didn't get, but laughed at until her stomach hurt. He was the stern old Judge whose eyes could see you wherever you hid.

Alice hoped there was not a God to see the fluffy dolls that doubled as covers for the toilet rolls, the toilet brush, the bread bin, hot water bottles, the teapot. Dolls in pink, dolls in blue staring out of every corner, seeing much more than God.

When Eleanor had pointed out that God couldn't be watching everyone at once, Alice had tried to explain:

'He's not like you and me, he sees everything. If he was like us he wouldn't be God.'

'You made that up. Every time I ask how he could do something, like have your dead grandad there with him along with my grandparents and all the other grandpas and grandmas, and heaps of dead people, you say he's special and not like us.' Eleanor was swinging headfirst round and round a railing behind the cricket pavilion. As she returned to a standing position, leaning on the bar, she panted: 'If he is different from us, how come he has a beard and two feet and hands like an ordinary man? He could be your Dad or my Dad. Perhaps he is!' She launched herself over again, legs flying. As she spun round, her head nearly touched the concrete; Alice believed Eleanor would die if one hand slipped, but like everything else Eleanor did that was dirty or dangerous, nothing like that happened.

Alice picked up another serviette and opened it out. As she glowered uncomprehending at the pattern of a sunflower, she remembered Mrs Ramsay saying that Doctor Ramsay was 'playing God' when her Mum had asked her where he was yesterday morning. Her Mum had laughed, but Mrs Ramsay hadn't even smiled. Her Mum didn't understand the Ramsays' jokes either.

It seemed that Alice had found a joke of her own when, just minutes before she mentioned the cheese, she had spotted a box of matches in the Ramsays' downstairs toilet. She had taken Eleanor to see it, chortling loudly all the way, pleased to find something funny at last. How had it got there? Did her parents make fires indoors to keep warm? Eleanor had not laughed.

'Oh that. It's to get rid of the stink after a shit. Feel free to use it.'

Alice was shocked. She couldn't speak as Eleanor drew open the box, picked out a match and struck it. She held the flame up to Alice's face, staring at her with wide eyes, like a wicked witch trying to put her under a spell. The fire had burned right down to her fingers before she tossed it into the toilet. The flame went out with a psst as it hit the water and the blackened wood turned into a live insect swimming around at the bottom. Alice flinched as, with both hands, Eleanor yanked the metal chain above their heads.

The children had peered down like perpetrators of an awful crime, as the water thundered around the toilet sending droplets over the sides. Alice shrank back as splashes landed on the wooden seat. They were the splashes she had previously misunderstood when using the toilet. She had cleaned them up with wads of toilet paper and pinched lips before being prepared to sit down on the yawning wooden seat. The match-insect shot up and down and was still there when the water was quiet. Eleanor made them stand there until the iron cistern had filled so they could try again. They were squashed together in the cramped room smelling of smoke, waiting as the hissing got higher and higher and fizzled to a stop.

As Eleanor pulled the chain a second time, Mrs Ramsay appeared. Alice had thought she'd heard her going out. She had not heard footsteps although she had been listening out. Alice had paid no attention to Eleanor's explanation about the matches. It was one of her stories.

'What are you girls up to?' Mrs Ramsay rubbed the sides of her nose with her hands. Alice started explaining the smell was nothing to do with her, that she had not been to the toilet or set fire to the toilet, but Eleanor was speaking:

'I was showing Alice the matches, so she knows what do to when she does a poo. She was asking.' Eleanor slid the box shut and put it back on the windowsill beside the pile of *Harper's Bazaar* magazines that Alice never touched because of germs.

'Oh, I see.' Mrs Ramsay behaved as if she didn't recognise Alice, but must have for she went on: 'Do go ahead, Alice, just don't be stupid with them.' Alice couldn't get out because Mrs

Ramsay blocked the doorway. 'Elly, come out. Let's leave Alice to do her poo.'

'Oh, I don't do that. I mean, I don't need...' Alice nearly fainted with misery at the way things were turning out. 'I don't need to be in here.' Alice ducked past Mrs Ramsay. Her voice squeaked like one of Lucian's animal characters, but no one laughed. She couldn't say she only went in the mornings after breakfast. She had been told it was rude to talk about toilets.

To Alice's amazement, Eleanor's mother then went into the lavatory and left the door slightly open. They could have seen her on the toilet if they had stayed to look, but Eleanor led the way back to the dining room, far more interested in her stupid picture.

Alice hadn't thought Mrs Ramsay went to the toilet. She was so beautiful it wasn't possible that either she or Doctor Ramsay ever needed to go. She tried not to think of Mrs Ramsay sitting in the spider-webbed room with the cracked walls and the smoky smell. She blushed as, despite herself, she imagined Mrs Ramsay with her knickers down with a snatch of whiteness followed by a darkness impossible to contemplate. Alice had been angry. Eleanor should not have made Mrs Ramsay think she wanted to do *Number Twos* in the middle of the day. Her Mum kept an aerosol of fresh pine trees in their toilet under a Spanish dancer with a wide skirt. Surely her Mum was right? Surely there was a God?

'*I know a secret about you.*'

The effect of her words had been better than she could have hoped for. Alice snatched up the packet of serviettes her mother had left out on the sideboard. She could hear Eleanor chattering on in the hall. Someone called her name, but Alice pretended not to hear. Then she heard Eleanor giggle. She wished her Dad would come home and be on her side. There would be no one on her side if they heard what she had said to Eleanor about Mrs Ramsay. She had only said it because of the matches and the poo.

When they had got back to the dining room table, Alice had sneaked a look at Eleanor as she leaned over her picture.

Her nails had green rims and her hands were always scratched and rough. Her hair needed a proper brush and that day there had been a grey smear across her forehead as well as a bruise on her arm from climbing on to the conservatory roof to fetch a tennis ball earlier in the day. Alice had been relieved when it landed there, the game would be over. But Eleanor had worked her way up the drainpipe, pulling with her hands and pushing with her feet and thrown it down. She never kept still, but must always whizz about. Even in the dining room when they were drawing, Eleanor was bouncing about on her chair. She never walked properly. She had to do cartwheels and handstands. She kept on at Alice to do a handstand, knowing perfectly well that Alice couldn't bear being upside down, not even to have her hair washed.

Alice knew she could draw better than Eleanor, whose pictures made no sense and used up too much crayon. That day the room had been littered with bits of oil pastel and curls of peeling paper torn off to free more crayon. Alice was glad they weren't her crayons. All she could think about after the matches was how to hurt Eleanor.

Eleanor's feet had been tucked up under her and she was very worked up about her picture, which she said was of herself as a pilot in an aeroplane. She didn't even paint properly. She had gone on and on, saying the sun she was drawing was scalding hot, even touching the paper and acting burned. She hadn't answered when Alice asked if it was her best picture.

Now her Mum was showing Eleanor the barometer in the hall. This infuriated Alice, her Dad's barometer was nothing to do with Eleanor. Alice went over to the table and poked the side of the jelly with her finger, and nicking a hole in it, quickly licked her finger.

'I know a secret about you.'

She had stared hard at Eleanor's face, but Eleanor had carried on with her drawing. *Say it again, louder.* Then Eleanor had lied, saying secrets were stupid.

'Not all secrets are stupid.'

'*What is it then?*'

Alice had been worried that Eleanor really wasn't bothered. She had to make her bothered. The jelly was soft and cool, lapping over her fingers.

'*If it was me, I would care about it, because it's a huge secret.*'

She had wanted to pull Eleanor's hair and punch her. Eleanor went on colouring as if she was alone and Alice had gone. Alice might have said her three-year-old cousin could draw better. The sun wasn't that big and Eleanor was a girl so she could not be a pilot.

The kitchen clock struck four. Eleanor had arrived early. Zebedee tipped out into the roundabout clock face four times. Alice had loved the clock when her Dad brought it home. Now she picked up the plate with the cubes of cheese stuck on to wooden sticks, and thought of smashing it into the clock, pushing the cheese into the hole for the characters and gumming up the hands. Instead she tipped them on to the floor. The cheese scattered across the lino. They wouldn't be eating cheese. Her fingers were sticky from the jelly and the plate slipped out of her hands and landed with a thump on top of the bits of cheddar.

Eleanor had tried to pretend she was looking for a black crayon on the floor. Alice had not let her leave the room and enjoyed swishing her ruler like the cruel supply teacher they had last term. For a moment Alice had been happy, then she had seen her own picture. It no longer looked so good, with tiny pencil lines scribbling off the page. She had crumpled the paper into a ball, which she tossed back and forth in her cupped hands as Lucian did with a cricket ball. Eleanor had not dared look for the crayon and with some shock Alice saw Eleanor was trying not to cry. Then Alice wanted to leave and she said she must get home even though she was meant to be staying for tea. There had been no sign of Mrs Ramsay and the toilet door was firmly closed as Alice rushed away, abandoning her favourite pink cardigan to the wolves.

Her Mum and Eleanor had reached the kitchen door. Eleanor was telling her about her cat with the mad name, chatting away as if they were friends, although she had only met her Mum last Friday. Alice envied Eleanor, she did not dare be so friendly with Mrs Ramsay. Then she remembered the doctor and felt better.

Kathleen Howland would later forget what greeted her as she tripped lightly into the kitchen. The scene would be erased as if it had never been. She was very much looking forward to Eleanor Ramsay's reaction to her table display. She loved to see pleasure in children's faces.

She screamed and was distantly aware of stepping backwards heavily on to Eleanor's foot and not saying sorry.

Eleanor peered around from behind Alice's mother and, forgetting her carefully rehearsed manners, swore out loud.

There was food everywhere. Serviettes were shredded and stuck all over the table and the floor, where squelchy stuff lay in soggy mounds. Orange squash had soaked into the tablecloth and dripped slowly on to the lino making a brightly coloured puddle that Eleanor found pleasing. Inching further into the room Eleanor nearly toppled on to the bin. It lay on its side, surrounded by squares of cheese stabbed with sticks pointing this way and that. There were globules of jam everywhere, on the chairs, slithering down the sideboard, even hanging from the ceiling. In the middle sat Alice smattered with red jelly, smeared with chocolate, with her hair decorated with scraps of Victoria sponge.

She leapt up, flinging her hands above her head and standing right on the tips of her toes, she yelled at the top of her voice:

'Surprise!'

Ten

That evening, alone in her room, gazing down the empty lane in the direction of the White House where Doctor Ramsay would be eating supper in his dining room, Alice was determined to be friendly when Eleanor saw her the next day. After her behaviour at the tea table she was frightened by the girl she was turning into. She gave herself one last chance to change back.

As she had helped her bewildered Mum clear up the chaos in the kitchen after Eleanor had been sent home, Alice promised Kathleen Howland faithfully that she would do whatever the Ramsays said and that no, she would never play up strangely again. Her mother couldn't bring herself to use the word 'naughty' about her daughter, usually so well behaved. But 'strangely' was to Alice far worse, because it proved her fears were true. Her Mum was so horrified that she couldn't even be cross. This time Alice knew for certain that her Mum had not told her Dad. It only made things worse.

But he would soon find out. Everyone would. Already people were beginning to see what Alice was really like. As she watched Mrs Carter from the post office come out of her flat above the shop and trot off down the lane in her slingback stilettos towards the station, Alice knew that from now on she must make a real effort to be nice and good or it would be too late.

They didn't meet up until after lunch on the Tuesday because Mrs Howland took Alice into Lewes to get new shoes. When they did, Alice quickly told Eleanor that it was entirely up to her where they went to play because she honestly truly didn't mind what they did. When Eleanor promptly suggested that they go and play hide and seek down at the haunted Tide Mills, Alice, determined to be good, had no choice but to agree.

Part Two

June 1999

Eleven

Isabel was annoyed with Mark. He had taken the lilo because he knew she wanted to lie on it. He had done it to get at her. He hated sunbathing.

There he was, sprawled across the silver plastic, his long legs still muscular and shapely; glistening with sun tan cream and droplets of water. He could have been fifty, not seventy-four. Her friends teased her that it must be like being married to Paul Newman, but better looking. Lucky Isabel, they said.

She hadn't told anyone that she had started to suspect Mark was avoiding her. She believed that communicating this fear would propel it into being. Besides, sometimes she was convinced she was imagining it. Then a brief moment of comfort would be obliterated by her self-knowledge. She was too observant, much too watchful to be mistaken. In the last few months Mark never looked at her when they were talking, his eyes were restless and distant. Indeed right now she could see that Mark was busily paddling the water with his hands to prevent the lilo drifting in her direction. These things were paltry if described on their own, but added together they made Isabel uneasy. The one thing that had always made life tolerable was that they were a team.

She knew it was inconceivable her husband was having an affair, after all he had ignored countless opportunities over the last forty-six years; all those women queuing up in all those waiting rooms over the decades.

The lilo was extremely important to Isabel. It represented a vital comfort that recently, as her body succumbed to its late sixties, eluded her. She would have had it all to herself if Mark had driven into Lewes this morning as he usually did on a Saturday morning. His denying Isabel this crumb of joy infuriated her; not only did he shun her companionship, but he stole her tiny pleasures. To add insult to injury, Isabel's luxury sun lounger, made to order in Florence, had so far failed to arrive. All she had was the lilo and now she didn't even have that.

The lilo was the size of a double mattress and fantastically sturdy, so it didn't fold up like an envelope or tip up unexpectedly if she twitched a toe or turned her head. She could float on it in the pool without getting wet as Mark was doing now. When Gina had brought it over, folded up tight in a deceptively small and childishly colourful zippy bag, Mark had scoffed, consigning it instantly to that place he was too lofty to inhabit: the world of soap operas, chunky holiday fiction, gossip and anything Isabel enjoyed. Mark had declared that Jon had wanted it to use in the pool when he and Gina visited, but as usual had to disguise his materialistic desires as fulsome liberality. It was like Mark to assume that others coveted what he claimed to despise. Then, like a wound he must worry, he would grumble that seeing how extravagantly rich his son-in-law was it was peculiar that he hadn't built Gina a swimming pool. Mark insisted Jon was mean, preferring to use theirs for free. Typically Mark hadn't blamed his eldest daughter for the frivolous present, assuming the idea was her poor husband's, who Mark gleefully found a rich source of jokes. This meant that if for no other reason, Isabel was grateful to her son-in-law for inadvertently diverting her ever more gloomy and restless husband.

Mark remained unimpressed by the fortune Jon had built over the decade through the manufacture of plastic commercial products, mostly grey, although there was a health and safety line that was a jolly yellow. He called him Jon-the-Footrest – usually to his face like a title honourably bestowed – because of the chunky adjustable platforms Jon manufactured for under office desks. It cut no ice with Mark when Jon laboured the point that his success was only due to Mark's wonderful daughter Gina supporting him through thick and thin. Isabel would hear these tipsy speeches, generally made after Sunday lunch, with a sinking heart because they sealed Jon's death warrant. Later Mark would unleash a torrent of cruel wit that luckily Jon appeared to receive as complimentary. Once they had left, Mark would expostulate that it was the last straw for Jon to implicate Gina in his devotion to making mountains of money through flogging roadside grit bins and sand-weighted safety cones. Apart from these, the highly successful Ginaware range included wrist rests, inserts for commodes, baby changing platforms and bucket/wringer combination packs for public spaces. It financed the horse – indeed a whole stable of horses – that Gina's parents had refused to buy her when she was a girl. Isabel would concede that it didn't make her a proud mother to be confronted by Gina's name on a sanitary napkin receptacle (she had picked up the terminology) while hovering over a loo seat in a motorway service station, or negotiating a splatter of spilt salsa sauce guarded by a garish multilingual caution sign near the frozen fish in Sainsbury's. But you had to earn a living somehow and Isabel could think of far worse things a man could do.

Mark was wrong. The lilo had been Gina's idea. She had genuinely expected her father to like it when a lilo was so clearly a more suitable present for Isabel. Yet as Isabel eyed Mark circling on the water, casually regal on his litter of silver plastic, she reflected that after all Gina had been right. He did like his present. Not that Mark would be the one to tell her.

Isabel would watch their children bringing Mark gifts the way Crawford had long ago deposited decapitated rodents on their pillows with doe-eyed expectancy. Mark's grownup children were anxious for a smile, even a nod, as he fastidiously unwrapped them. He always took a long time, careful not to tear the paper, folding it up neatly before turning to the object itself. But as he examined the offering, with a contemplative frown, all they ever got was a gruff thanks drowned out by her own vacuous cries of delight. How much more miserable would they have been if they had seen Mark after they had gone, communing with the Judge, brooding into his whiskey at the dining room table, as he teased out incontrovertible evidence of his children's betrayal in the guise of a Liberty tie or a tan coloured Filofax of the softest Italian leather. The years had turned Mark into a well-dressed King Lear, who read only dissent in his children's pathetic acts of love. Isabel had become adept at spinning a new take on events to render the day-to-day experience that makes up family history palatable. She would hurriedly weave a plausible explanation, even inventing nice things the children had said about Mark to comfort their disgruntled father or vice versa. In her late middle age she had constantly to wield this skill:

'*He was absolutely thrilled with the tie, wears it all the time.*'

'*Gina wanted to get you something special. Isn't that reason enough?*'

Yet Isabel had absorbed Mark's dismal outlook. Perhaps he was right she decided, as Mark gracefully eddied in the middle of the pool, their time was up and their children were waiting in the wings to step into their shoes.

Love had nothing to do with it.

'Mark, I'm getting a drink, do you want one?' He was pretending to be asleep to stop her claiming the lilo. To keep her out. To such pettiness had their lives been distilled.

'Bit early, isn't it?'

'Not for me.' *Fuck you!*

'I'm fine.' With a flick, the lilo glided away.

'When I come back, I want to lie on that,' she warned.

He raised his head in mock surprise at her tone.

'As you like. I have to go anyway.'

Mark must be going to Lewes after all. Despite her dismay Isabel refused to protest because it would be just the response he wanted. He knew perfectly well that Gina and Jon were arriving for lunch any minute, expecting him to be there. Indeed he had arranged it with Gina himself. Recently he had been acting perversely, leaving the house just before supper was served, going to bed early, setting off to the National Hospital in London where he still did consultancy, but instead driving into Brighton or Lewes. Or so he said when she'd told him she had rung the hospital and he wasn't there. He didn't care if he was caught out. Last Monday he had said he was working in his study, but when she had stuck her head round the door to tell him she was going out, he hadn't been there. His car was still on the drive, but there was no sign of him. That afternoon Isabel had suddenly been reminded of herself as a young woman looking for Eleanor who had constantly concealed herself behind curtains, inside cupboards and under beds when she was wanted for anything. And on bad days Isabel's memory would burrow even deeper to another search, one that most of the time she succeeded in forgetting about.

Two weeks ago, as she had stood by Mark's immaculately tidy desk, careful not to touch anything because he laid tiny traps and would know if even a stapler had been moved, Isabel had found herself wondering if Mark was hiding from her. Despite the empty room, she had fancied she could hear breathing and had swept aside the curtain to see if he was standing stock-still behind it.

Isabel had once dreaded that Mark would end up like his father, but she had never really believed it possible. As a young man, Mark had been so different from the grouchy old codger who got pleasure issuing death sentences; she had been confident Mark would always be cheerful and charming. But once they were married things had changed and now Mark was every inch that grouchy old codger. Isabel smiled bitterly at this description as she crossed the garden to get her drink. She had managed the Judge. She would go on managing Mark.

The lawn had been mowed the day before. It was cut close like a carpet and was pleasingly springy under her bare feet. That was one thing: the garden looked the best it ever had.

Flowers were mere pixels in Isabel's grand design. The Mondrian bed, the heady lavender borders, her small patch of wild meadow, and the sculpted busts she had made in her pottery class and mounted on red brick plinths in surprise places all created an enchanted space. She had resisted topiary, to the dismay of Toby, the new young gardener, who had done a course. Hedges were only boundaries, delineating each area and leading the visitor on to the next. A tall beech hedge framed the Rose Garden on one side and on the other, as well as the lawn with Uncle Jack's tree. The swimming pool had been her achievement. She had reclaimed the meadow behind the house, where Gina had planned to graze the horse she never got. Mark hadn't wanted the pool:

'*In this bloody climate, you'll have six days' use each year. It's a crazy expense.*'

'*Six days is better than nothing. It'll be more than that anyway.*'

'*The kids have grown up, what's the point?*'

'*They still like swimming. I like swimming. And we might have grandchildren.*'

Of course he had relented and as with the lilo Mark now used the pool more than anyone. Ten white plastic loungers that Jon had foisted on them were crowded around the edge. A semi-circular set of blue and white tiled steps led into the shallow end. To one side of the pool stood a brick-built barbecue used only when Jon came, sleeves rolled up and tongs rattling at the ready. Mark didn't 'do' barbecues. Large tubs brimming with bright flowers were placed along a gravel path bordered with railway sleepers that wound around the side of the garage to meet the old path along the side of the house, skirted the lawn and led eventually up to the back door.

A trellis, thickly woven with honeysuckle, was meant to screen the garages and Judge's workshop from the pool, but the honeysuckle hadn't yet taken off so Isabel tried to ignore the grimy stucco beyond. Mark had balked at building a brick wall between the pool and the garage and the cost had been too high for Isabel to argue. They had already spent a fortune on CCTV cameras posted high enough to cover the house and the garden. These were filled with real tapes, which Mark indexed and stored downstairs in the basement in a room next to his father's trial transcripts. It had been Isabel's idea, after a burglary ten years ago. Mark had quickly become enthusiastic, constantly checking to confirm the cameras were working and upgrading them regularly. Isabel had come to hate them. Sensors caught the slightest movement and directed the lenses accordingly. They eyed her as she dead-headed roses, cut flowers for the dining room or smoothed sun tan cream in upward strokes along her legs and across her stomach. If she homed in, she could hear the whirr as the camera swivelled, like the Judge's eyes, following her wherever she went. Now Mark could spy on her even when he was in London. The growing library of tapes formed a staccato black and white film diary of the house. Hours and hours of brickwork, portico and lintel interrupted by strobe-puppets jerking through the garden, in and out the doors like characters in a Swiss clock. The only person who watched these interminable silent comedies was Kathleen Howland, the woman in the cottage next door to the village stores, who was still searching for her daughter after some thirty years and who many said had gone mad.

Afterwards, Isabel remembered that Saturday in June 1999 as a terrific convergence of events both cataclysmic and minor. She fixed on the small things like sun loungers and the lilo as lifebuoys in a tumultuous sea.

In a percussive flurry, the telephone bell pealed through the house, the doorknocker banged twice, and far above the attic hatch crashed open, as once again its bent catch gave way. Isabel had just found the cordless handset under a pile of medical journals in the downstairs lavatory and was heading to answer the door when she heard an engine revving right outside the kitchen window, louder and louder. She rushed back to the kitchen, forgetting about the front door and the telephone. Tyres squealed, and as she reached the kitchen door she felt the windows shake as there came a tremendous sound like an avalanche from the direction of the garden, involving glass and wood and metal and climaxing with a splash like a gigantic belly flop. Then there was an eerie stillness.

Isabel answered the phone.

'Mum?'

'Gina? Is that you?'

'Of course it's me. What's going on? I was calling to say we are nearly there but you took so long that now we are here. What the Hell's going on?' It annoyed Mark that Gina and Jon would ring to announce their arrival only seconds in advance, which offered no practical advantage and was always disruptive. He said it was because Jon liked to show off his technology.

Without hanging up, Isabel hurried across the lawn, the telephone in one hand and her drink in the other.

Blinking in the glare of the sunshine, she made no sense of what she saw. The bottom of the garden was in ruins. She could only have been gone five minutes.

For a wild moment she thought a plane had fallen out of the sky. She reached the pool and later had no memory of placing her gin and the telephone down beside her book and sun tan cream.

'Mark?' There was no sign of him. He had gone to Lewes.

Piles of mud had come from nowhere, hundreds of splinters of wood and branches floated in the water and were strewn over the plastic furniture, which of course hadn't moved an inch. Sheets of wet newspaper, a pair of nail scissors, a nail file and a sodden box of man-size tissues were scattered along the side of the pool. Isabel tripped over a face-down copy of the London A to Z at her feet and at the same moment recognised the scissors as her own. She had been manicuring her nails. The street atlas came from Mark's glove box. There was something else, she bent down to read the words 'What to do in an Accident' on the bloated cover of a booklet with a ballpoint pen still clipped to the back cover floating at the edge of the swimming pool. She fleetingly observed that it was considerate to provide an advice manual with the mayhem. Spreading lake-like puddles on the patio reflected a cloudless blue sky. Perhaps it was this image that reminded Isabel about the lilo. She put a hand to her throat as she realised the shiny flaccid heap flopped on a platform of racing-green metal in the centre of the pool was her beloved lilo. There was a rip down its middle. Gradually, it seemed, although it must have been only a split second, Isabel took in the situation. It wasn't a plane or the total collapse of the garage which was now in full view because the trellis was splintered to pieces at her feet. She jolted into action.

'Mark!'

Gina heard her mother's scream from the drive. Instantly she understood that it was all over. She went cold as if the sun had been eclipsed and stared uncomprehending as Jon dashed away up the side path of the house. As he leapt over the gate to the old tradesman's entrance, he bellowed back to Gina over his shoulder:

'Ambulance, police, fire brigade, get the lot!'

Gina fumbled with her new mobile phone, trying to unlock the keypad. She shook it furiously and then held it to her ear. Nothing but the sound of the sea. She glared at it. Where was the bloody asterisk key? She found it. Then flustered, she stabbed at the nought button three times. She had had nightmares like this when no matter how hard she tried, limbs moving in treacle, panic descending, she always dialled the wrong number. The person always died because her agitation woke her up in a shivering sweat before she could save them.

As Gina gave the police her parents' address she passionately wished she had stayed at home. If she had kept indoors then nothing would have happened, because at home it never did.

Isabel skidded down the steps into the shallow end, wading out until the water was around her neck. She took a deep breath and dived down between the car and the tiled wall of the pool, knocking her knee against the bumper and grazing her bare thigh on the back door handle as she felt her way along. She couldn't keep her eyes open for long because the high level of chlorine made them sting. Only that morning she had complained to Mark that he was pouring far too much in. Mark was cavalier about quantities of anything that wasn't medicine.

All the windows were open and already the inside was full of water, but there was not enough room between the car and the side of the pool to allow Isabel to manoeuvre herself into the car or to open the door. She was by the passenger side and she didn't have the breath or the time to get over the bonnet of the car to where Mark was. Besides she wouldn't be able to open the driver's door either. She pulled on the passenger door handle and managed to open it a little, but the gap was too narrow for her to squeeze more than her arm through. There was no way of reaching Mark. By twisting her body sideways she could just strain in through the passenger window. Isabel's fingers were only inches from his leg, if she just could touch him, he might stir into action and help himself. She dared go no further in case she got stuck. Then she ran out of breath and explosively exhaled as she pushed up to the surface. Without waiting to recover, she took another gulp of air and ducked downwards again.

Mark's head was tilted forward, his chin touching his chest, he might have been napping at the wheel. As usual he didn't acknowledge her presence although his hair floated in gentle waves around his head as she flailed towards him creating undulations in the water. He had put on trousers and a blue shirt while she was in the house, and these ballooned at the sides where air bubbles were trapped making him look deformed. His eyes were shut and his cheeks trembled in and out because his mouth hung open and was full of water. How could he breathe with his mouth open? Isabel pushed against the water to slam her hand on the dashboard to get his attention. It made no sound.

There was no point.

Again Isabel screamed Mark's name and a gush of water shot down into her windpipe. She felt strong hands grab her under the arms and suddenly she was being hauled up to the surface, away from Mark. Jon carried her up the wide steps at the end and carefully laid her on a sodden sun lounger where she curled on her side heaving and retching. Barely pausing and still in his precision ironed chinos Jon leapt straight back into the pool. Isabel winced as he overshot and fell against the car.

Action Man.

Later Isabel could only remember that she tried to follow Jon into the water. She had to speak to Mark before Jon did. She would remember that Gina had held on to her and that they had struggled violently in the shallow end as Jon kept bobbing to the surface gasping. Again and again he dived down to the car in a futile effort to pull his father-in-law free and to save his life.

Isabel had no words to explain that she had had to know that Mark had battled frantically to get himself out from the submerged car. She needed to believe he had wanted to stay with her but had got trapped behind the wheel. There was no way of saying any of this because she knew it wasn't true.

Gina had been right; her mother's shrill howl had signalled the end.

After the arrival of the emergency services, the violent attempts to resuscitate Mark on the slippery paving amidst a gaggle of garden furniture and sodden paraphernalia, the eventual removal of his body and the stolid arrival of Lucian from London, demanding the return of his father to life, someone had complained that a huge cardboard box had been dumped right by the front door entirely blocking the porch.

It was Isabel's long-awaited luxury lounger.

Twelve

A lice traced the pattern on the lace curtain, as if trying to find a Braille message assuring her she wasn't alone. She sank back into her chair, the message was prosaic: the lace was in need of a wash. In mounting despair, she looked around the room seeing other things that needed a good scrub, a thorough polish. Her despondency increased, for really the whole flat should be spring-cleaned, but spring had passed, it was a sweltering hot Monday afternoon in June, too hot to move, too hot to think.

Alice's view through the greying curtain was much the same as James Stewart's in *Rear Window*. Rows of windows, mostly like her own screened from prying eyes by net curtains or blinds, filled the frame. But there were still many tenants who were oblivious or unworried about creating a tableau of their lives for all to see. Their windows were flung wide and after dark were brightly lit. For these Alice was grateful. She watched the young mother, who had yesterday had her long black hair cut short, tend her window boxes or pace around the room pacifying her baby. Three windows along and one up was the woman with the iron-grey pudding bowl haircut who Chris said worked in the supermarket on the main road. When she was at home she sat motionless at her desk in the far corner of the room in a pool of angle-poise light working late into the night. Alice had to be careful not to be seen by her, as she would jump up without warning and come to the window where she would stand utterly still for a long time just staring out. Below was a wide concrete yard closed in on opposite sides by the two six-storey Victorian flats in the middle of which stood the new estate office. The other flats cut out most of the traffic noise from the Old Kent Road beyond, but also shut out the evening sunlight and curtailed her view. To her left was a twenty-foot brick wall topped with spikes upon which on her bad days Alice would impale the heads of her enemies. This wall segregated the estate from the Baptist church next door. Now, as on many days, Alice could hear the sound of a packed congregation singing.

'...This is the day the Lord has made, that all may see his love displayed...'

To her right was The World Turned Upside Down from whose juke box Manchester United's song 'Lift It High' mingled discordantly with the strains of the church choir.

Alice was forty, but today she felt eighty.

The lace curtains had soaked up London's grime, the pattern of usually fluffy birds perched in repetition on twisty branches down its length – a design she had chosen more for company than appearance – had wind blown feathers. They too looked tired and old. Alice was an empty barn, with patches of her roof missing. Ravens flapped back and forth, wings smacking against the creaking rafters of her ribs. If she were ill, who would care? But if the ravens abandoned her, would that spell doom?

The obvious answer to the first question was Alice's eighteen-year-old daughter, Chris. Nevertheless the cloud of self pity conjured up by this scenario enveloped Alice in deeper gloom.

On her bad days Alice would picture herself working through the tasks she had set herself in advance of doing them. She would sit as now, in her armchair looking out through the lace at the concrete quadrangle below, and plan her chores and activities, anticipating potential problems and contemplating how to overcome them. So detailed were Alice's mental campaigns that when she came to do the tasks, she performed them perfectly with no extraneous elements or movement. This ruthless efficiency made her impatient when Chris made one small mistake. As a mistake could be that Chris had chosen a different way to achieve the same end, this meant Alice was frequently annoyed with her daughter. Their relationship was fraught with mutual frustration.

Sometimes Alice imagined completed tasks so vividly, she was bewildered to discover the washing basket full or, as in this case, the curtains dirty. Then her sense of control would slip and jerk through clenched fists. Alice had to breathe in and out, in and out until the panic passed, then struggle to her bedroom, brushing the walls for balance and reassurance and tapping the door frame an ever increasing number of set times before she could lie still and regain her composure. That morning she had told Chris she would have to go to the launderette after supper. Chris had been sulky, so that it was almost not worth asking. Except they both knew that Chris had no choice.

'No one understands what it's like not being able to nip down the shops for a pint of milk.'

'No one believes I'm ill because I have a natural bloom to my skin.'

Everyone adored Chris. Chattering voices down the telephone, scribbled school reports and holiday postcards – Wish you had been able to come – told Alice how Chris was kind and always smiling. They all marvelled at how lucky Alice was to have such a clever, thoughtful daughter. Those who came into the flat, the doctor, the woman about agoraphobia, the community dentist, all of them said Chris was like her mother. Alice knew Chris was the spit image of herself so that much was true. She liked the notion that they could be sisters. The doctor had said Alice couldn't be old enough to have such a grownup daughter. Although she had appreciated the comment, she had been anxious in case he was flirting or worse, judging. Alice wished she looked how she felt, because then people might be more sympathetic. She had no respect for the agoraphobic specialist because she had failed to spot the truth about Alice and must therefore be a fake too. Compliments about her wonderful complexion, or the lustre in her hair annoyed Alice because they meant people didn't appreciate how it was for her.

But then Alice went to great pains to ensure they did not.

She imagined people beyond the archway of the flats leading to the Old Kent Road – the extent of her world – admiring Chris for caring for her sick mother. On good days Alice basked in the dreams where they praised her too, disbelieving that she coped with a chronic illness while running a home, being a mother and an expert at invisible mending.

Alice invented faces for the invisible people in her daughter's life most of whom she had never met: teachers, bus conductors, friends and their parents who seldom rang now that Chris was older. There was one mother she had liked who if things had been different might even have been a friend. She was usually smoking when she called which would normally have revolted Alice, but the mellifluous speech punctuated by sucking and puffing was warm and caressing. Alice would see smoke rings rising around the woman's head as she talked, the phone propped on her shoulder, a cigarette in one hand and a cup of coffee in the other. When she had reluctantly to end a conversation with this woman, Alice would briefly be content, then filled with anguish at her fettered state. This was some years ago and now she couldn't think of her name and anyway the woman didn't telephone any more. It was the busy, fussy lady who wanted to take her daughter to France one half term who had riled Alice the most.

'You must be proud, she is so witty, had us in stitches...'

Alice waited for the reason for her call, horrified that this stranger thought she knew her daughter better than Alice did.

'... *I know it will be hard while she is away, is there anyone who could stay with you? It will be lovely for the girls, Chrissie's French will help us all! I can ask for things but once they start rattling back, I'm... Chrissie doesn't know I'm calling, Rachael – my daughter, had her number. I wanted to put my pennyworth...*' Later Alice informed Chris, no, she could not go to France. How could Alice manage for a week by herself? Suppose she fell, suppose she ran out of food?

Suppose.

Chris had said she didn't mind if she stayed at home and Alice convinced herself that Chris hadn't wanted to go. That she had been happy to use her mother's condition as an excuse. But still this was an uncomfortable memory.

This made Alice return to the photograph. Two years ago when she was sixteen, Chris had presented to her mother a framed picture of herself for her birthday. Alice had taken lots of photos of Chris as a little girl. She had lovingly slotted the prints between their mounting corners in a set of albums that made up a brand new history for her daughter. They supplanted the past Alice had been forced to abandon. But none of her photographs so accurately captured her daughter as this one.

Chris was doing a thumbs-up sign. Her hand was partially hiding her face so that the gesture, declaring that everything was all right, dominated the frame. It had been snapped by Emma, Chris's best friend, while on a sailing holiday that this time Alice had agreed to. Chris had posed on the prow of a yacht like a conquering hero, and behind her there was only the sea and the sky. The photograph comforted Alice and she picked it up whenever she was upset or anxious. Chris's laughing smile, the wisps of hair blown out from her face by the sea breeze and the way she looked through, and not directly at the lens, expressed her spirit. Chris was buoyant in the face of adversity. Alice kept her reflections to herself, although she would often tell Chris that the picture was the best present anyone had ever given her.

Late afternoon was Alice's favourite time. She relished the anticipation of Chris's arrival. It was like the start of school holidays. This feeling formed a link to a long lost childhood and she tried to snatch at the fading image of a little girl busily helping her Dad clean shoes on a back step, lining up each shoe to make a straight line of toes.

The little girl was always on her own. The fuzzy figure who was her Dad had gone, perhaps into the house, giving his princess time to make everything right for his inspection.

Alice carefully lifted up the black postman shoes with the metal toe-caps. She folded her rag neatly like her Dad did, and dabbed a corner into the tin of polish.

'*Don't press too hard, you don't need much.*'

The shoe was too heavy to hold in one hand, so she wedged it between her legs as she pummelled the heel with her cloth. After a few minutes she hadn't made much difference. She began to panic. Breathe in. Breathe out.

'*You just put me out of a job!*' He was leaning in the kitchen doorway, slurping a mug of tea her Mum had made.

'*How long have you been there?*'

'*Long enough. Keep going.*' He bent and kissed the top of her head and laughed from deep inside. He smelled of aftershave. No, he smelled of apples and tobacco.

Alice couldn't think what he smelled of. She had only a fragment from which to build her story, which was fading through lack of telling.

Chris would be moody and probably slope off to her bedroom, but still Alice counted down to the sound of her key in the door.

When Alice watched Chris march briskly across the quadrangle each morning, a young confident woman now, she wanted to open the window and call her back.

'*Don't leave me! Take me with you.*'

The words lost power before she could form them, and she let the stranger stride off under the archway to the busy street.

Alice took refuge in blurry memories of a small child skipping or spinning in ballet pumps. No matter what, the innocent schoolgirl who was always top of the class was still safe inside her.

Chris was now twenty minutes late. Alice patted her chest. Chris must have gone off with her friends without telling her. Alice wanted Chris to have friends and in one of her better states she would see her at the centre of a gaggle of girls chatting and giggling, with no responsibilities. But they had an agreement that Chris phoned if she was going to be late. Alice had spent a fortune on Chris's mobile phone.

Alice hated that Chris was so laden down with cares and she longed to protect the little girl who even in summer was pale, her bag full of books, her head full of revision and dreams of a degree at university that would lead to a career in forensic science. Alice would have preferred that Chris wanted to be an artist and paint live creatures rather than take apart dead ones. On bad days Alice felt dissected herself as she tried to ward off the strident, deriding child who daily sucked the life out of her mother, leaving her like a discarded beetle case, turning and shifting listlessly in the draught under the door. On her bad days, Alice's sorry images of herself were never mundane.

'*By the time I was your age…*'

'Were you ever my age? Your story changes every day. One minute you talk about horse riding, the next you say you were scared of them. Which is it today?'

'There was a girl I knew when I was young. She could ride the way you and I walk. I get mixed up between dreams and reality, that's all. I'm not well. It's natural.'

Alice had hoped having a child meant always having someone who would stick up for you and love you come what may. The way Alice had loved her mother. It seemed a minute since Chris was born and she had held her, appalled by the lump of screaming flesh. Then Chris had stopped breathing and a flock of doctors and nurses snatched her away and left Alice alone. When she saw her next, under plastic like a takeaway sandwich, she was overwhelmed by the intensity of her love. This love could exhaust her with its strength and she had known then it would never release her.

Here she was now!

Alice started to tug the lace aside to wave then just in time remembered Chris would pretend not to see her. Instead she twitched the material like the fugitive she was and shrank back into her armchair.

As she watched her daughter return home in the afternoons from school, Alice would know that what she most dreaded had already become reality: Chris had moved on from her. Yet the sight of her nearly grownup daughter living a life in which she could be herself, free of a painful past, always filled Alice with joy.

She believed that this justified everything.

Thirteen

Over time the Old Kent Road had become no more than a stretch of the busy A2, lined with boarded up shops, forgotten patches of scrubland, supermarket car parks, generic takeaways and fly-by-night outlets flogging tired and tawdry goods. The flyover was a brief escape for drivers from the barren road beneath it, which was fogged with choking fumes and overshadowed by high-rise flats whose rows of doors opened on to balconies meant to copy the communal streets they had replaced. Young municipal trees with their spindle trunks encased in protective mesh were planted along the kerbside. Most of the saplings had been twisted and broken, while others had simply died. Many of their cages were crammed to the top with litter; the colourful columns making a pithy statement about inner-city decay.

Far away up in the sky, intermittently blotted by the blazing sun, a passing aeroplane left a white trail of exhaust. There were no clouds, no birds. The noise was continuous: heavy traffic, horns, and the snarl of motorbikes revving off from the pelican lights. The road was busy with people with grim demeanours, their shoulders dragged down by heavy bags or the cares of life. A warm breeze lazily lifted and dropped sweet wrappers and torn sheets of newspaper collecting in the gutters, and brushed hot skin without relief.

A figure was moving in the no-man's land under the flyover: a young woman running fast, unhampered by the rucksack on her back. She ran without apology, her arms pelting the air for balance and speed, as she jumped over a discarded exhaust pipe and swerved out of the way of broken glass. She was dressed in jeans, blue Converse boots and a grey shirt patterned with skyscrapers against a background of wavy lines. Her clothes betrayed an alternative taste, and ensured that she stood out from those around her. In contrast to her dress her hair was conventional, parted at the side and just touching her shoulders. It was soberly immaculate, though thin strands soaked in sweat stuck to her forehead. She was clearly someone who could toe the line if required to.

She vaulted over the central barrier, and hop-hopped with one foot on the kerb and the other on the camber, waiting for a gap in the traffic; then she dashed across the path of a double-decker bus and leapt on to the opposite pavement. By the time the bus shuddered to a halt at the stop twenty yards further on, the young woman had veered off left under the archway of a block of Victorian flats and disappeared.

Chris was eighteen in 1999 and everyone said what a marvellous age it was. She was so lucky to be in the right place at the right time – the turn of the century – with her life before her. Just now, as she sidestepped a wheelie bin that kids had taken for a walk, and tried to catch her breath without inhaling the sour stench of refuse, this luck seemed a long time coming.

She was late and she had to go to the launderette.

Her Mum would say she should have rung if she was going to be late just as Alice had always called her mother. Other times her Mum talked of how the family didn't have a phone so she had to get home on time. Chris usually tolerated these inconsistencies, content to listen to her Mum's bedtime stories of loving relatives, long dead, particularly of the Postman-Dad who let Alice stand on his feet while he took big strides across the living room. As a young child Chris had demanded with gory relish that her Mum tell the tale of the car accident in which her grandparents had died. Alice had been nine. She would say that her life had ended then too. She had only come alive when Chris was born; a point in the story Chris looked forward to. As a young teenager, this tragic incident gave her extra cachet with her friends. No one else had a fatal car crash in their family. During breaks, in response to repeated requests and in a suitably elegiac tone, she would retell her version of the event to a thrilled audience of thirteen-year-olds huddled by the school kitchens.

It had happened outside the Fuller's brewery on the Chiswick Roundabout. Her Mum told her this was ironic because Fuller's brewed London Pride, which was her father's favourite tipple – her mother's word – so he would have enjoyed the coincidence if he had lived. Chris was hungry to learn more about her grandparents, but much to her frustration, her Mum had lost all the photographs or documents just as she lost or forgot many things. Alice would declare that her parents' dying had freed her to carve out her own life without being hampered by the past. This was putting a brave face on it; really all it had done was to make her Mum too frightened to step outside and take part in such a cruel world.

Today had proved her Mum right. Chris wouldn't tell her what had happened; it would only worry her.

Half an hour earlier Chris had squeezed out of a packed tube train at Elephant and Castle. Although it wasn't yet five o'clock, the rush hour was underway and she had filed at the rate of a shuffle along the subway to the exit. Halfway up the passage she heard shouting. She was wedged between two city-suited men, and could see nothing. They wore identical black-framed spectacles and made her think of Gilbert and George. Chris did not exist as they chatted to one another over her head:

'It's some West Indian bloke causing a fracas.'

'What's new?'

'It's all we need.'

The crowd became more congested as people edged across to the left side of the tunnel. By staying on the right Chris was able to break free of Gilbert and George and soon reached the source of the commotion.

A tall black man, a few years older than her, perhaps in his early twenties, was heading in the same direction as herself. He was dressed in jeans, with a loose silk bomber jacket over his tee-shirt, and wore a red baseball cap pulled low over his forehead. Dogging him a few paces behind was a decrepit old man in a filthy parka, the fur around his hood mangled and greasy and his tracksuit trousers ripped and stained. He shambled after the young man with a drunken swaying that was surprisingly efficient. Chris cupped her hand over her nose. He stank of sweaty, unwashed skin laced with alcohol fumes and rotting teeth. His yellowed hair straggled around a swollen face that was the colour and texture of a ripe strawberry. He intoned an incantation of abuse:

'I know your sort. What you looking at? Hey nigger, stop while I'm talking to...'

Chris assumed the young man had decided to tough it out because he could have run away. He repeatedly reached up and adjusted his cap, tipping it down over his eyes and then raising it: a giveaway that he wasn't cool about it. Chris gave a little skip to keep up with him. To her left the crocodile of commuters processed slowly, their eyes firmly elsewhere with the absolute accord of film extras whose role is to be the mute, unseeing crowd.

Chris despised them.

She was trying to come up with the most effective insult, when without warning the black guy whirled around and confronted his chaotic abuser.

The stream of invective and abuse from the depths of the parka ascended to a plaintive whine:

'You can't touch me. I'm a blind old man. You filthy...'

Chris was at one with the man, as with a graceful upward sweep of his leg he hefted a kick at the blind man's chest sending him toppling backwards, his arms raised in clumsy surrender. Chris heard his body thump against the tunnel wall. He slid down to the ground where he sat lifeless, with his head resting against a ripped and peeling poster for the film *A Bug's Life*.

The disembodied litany rambled on without pause:

'Piss off Monkey-man, picking on a defenceless old gentleman minding his own business. Your sort belong in...I said piss off Mo...'

The young man tilted his cap and closed in. He kicked him again, this time hard in the thigh; the impact pushed the tramp a few inches to the right. The voice persisted:

'I'm blind. Help. I'm blind...'

Chris grabbed the young man by the arm. She took him by surprise and so was able to pull him away.

Behind her commuters tensed, terrified of being forced to intervene in a violent situation because of some girl's reckless heroics. She could be knifed; she might get them all killed.

The man was taller than Chris, who at five foot six was not short. Her slight and wiry figure was diminutive against his larger, stronger frame. He could have snapped her ribs like wish bones. She rubbed his arm and leaned against him, pressing her cheek to his chest. She had little time to weave a spell of her own:

'He's scum. Don't get nicked for rubbish like him. He's dog shit on our shoes. He's scum...'

She held her body against his, and made herself a dead weight and in an awkward dance they inched crabwise towards the exit. All the while she repeated the same phrases to let him know that she was on his side. As they reached the foot of the steps, she dared to relax. She turned the man around and keeping behind him talked in a lighter tone now that they were out of earshot of the tramp, as they trudged up the last flight to the street.

'You're worth ten of him...'

When they were on the pavement, without looking back the man broke away from her and darted across the road towards Newington Butts and out of sight. Chris wasn't offended. There was nothing he could have said or done.

Despite the heat, she shivered and a dribble of cold sweat like melting ice ran down between her shoulder blades. She was still holding the copy of the *Evening Standard* she had bought earlier. At some point she had rolled it tightly into a baton and the ink had stained her palm and fingers. She took off her rucksack and stuffed the paper into a side pocket. Then shrugging the bag back on to her shoulders and oblivious of the heat, she too started to run.

As she neared home, keeping under the shadow of the flyover, it occurred to her that if the old man was blind, how had he known the other guy was black?

That morning Alice had announced that Chris must go to the launderette after supper. Chris hated doing the washing there and the chore had grown more onerous over the day so that now, fizzing with adrenalin from the encounter in the underground, she imagined killing her Mum. Not quickly with a gun, but slowly, giving time to explain to her exactly why.

She would tell her in measured tones that she could not forgive Alice for not asking the full name of the Renault car mechanic who Alice had said was Chris's father, so that one day, when Chris wanted a new and better parent, she could find him. All she had to go on was that he was called Gary and specialised in fitting automatic gearboxes. Most days Chris didn't need Gary. She got on with her life, but at night as she clarified her ambitions and formed resolutions it was Gary she told them to.

Chris had left the house that morning without kissing Alice and had run to the bus stop, chased by her mother's snapping hounds. Once in the street, a wet sheet of misery assailed her as she saw her Mum pottering around all day with nothing to do but clean and wait. If a bus hadn't come, Chris would have gone back to her.

She had stared out at Elephant and Castle from the top deck. A man in cycling shorts and a black vest kept pace on a racing bike. The veins on his legs and arms were like thick string. She tried to forget her Mum, but all she could think was that the bus was taking her far away from the woman she loved more than anyone else in the world.

The last time she had been to the launderette was a month ago, when her mother had taken it into her head to do all the bedding and needed two machines; Chris had taken *Pride and Prejudice* with her to read. For once she had done everything correctly, tipped the soap into the right compartment, and she had even found a rogue tee-shirt tangled in a duvet that would have stained the cotton pale blue.

Only when she had settled into a bucket seat and prepared to read, did she realise Jane Austen had gone in with the washing and was now well into the 'agitate' section of the cycle. She cupped her hands to see through the glass. The book was there. Every now and then the spine made a dull thump as it hit the drum.

All week they had picked out snatched words and sentences from their clothes.

'...*"How strange!" cried Elizabeth. "How abominable!"*'

'Next time do the washing yourself!'

'*Her mother only scolded her for being nonsen...*'

This was the worst thing Chris could have said. Both of them knew her Mum couldn't do it herself. Chris believed it must now be years since she had left the flat and had only dim memories of seeing Alice in the open air. Her Mum could get muddled between her dreams and what had really happened. Chris too, would wonder if her memories of being in the park with her Mum were just wishful thinking.

She wanted to go out with her Mum. Perhaps to the park, or they could take a train to the seaside. She might wander around the supermarket picking out treats with her Mum, like other girls did. Some nights she lay awake horrified by the prospect of her Mum dying alone in the pokey flat on the Old Kent Road. If Chris was to see her own dreams of becoming a forensic scientist come true she had to rescue the Alice of the bedtime stories from her rabbit hole and return her to the safety of the riverbank. At other times Chris would be in dread of her mother's hidden self. The sexy monster had had nothing to do with being a Mum.

Chris had seen this monster a few months earlier when she had come home unexpectedly right after lunch. A teacher had been ill and her chemistry lesson was cancelled. She had heard the music from the landing, and assumed it was the people in the flat above with whom Alice had regular run-ins. Chris sighed. Her Mum would have scribbled an embarrassing note and expect her to take it upstairs and wait for a response. Chris had called out in a cheery voice as she shut the front door.

The music was coming from the living room. It was so loud her greeting was drowned out. The door was open three inches and she saw movement in the full-length mirror on the wall in the living room. Her mother had fixed it there to make her feel she had company when she walked towards it. Now it gave Chris a view of the whole room and she was brought up short. Keeping back in the gloom of the darkened hallway, she gaped dumbfounded. Her mother had kicked back the rug, cleared aside furniture and was dancing. Not the sort of dancing Chris would have expected: the clumsy clumping back and forth accompanied by contorted air guitar playing, but proper dancing. Her body was moving in perfect time to 'Rebel Rebel' by David Bowie, a song Chris did not imagine Alice had heard of.

The woman in the mirror spun around, sashayed back and forth, her movements fluid, her timing exact, as she echoed the rhythm of the guitar riff and with consummate understatement mimed the words. She exuded sex and vigour. Chris blushed, and tentatively touched her hot cheek with the back of her hand. She had never had to undergo the agony of seeing a parent lumbering hopelessly to sounds they were too old for. Her mother's agoraphobia had spared her that. This was worse. This was a woman Chris was not meant to see. This woman was a stranger evoking feelings Chris was not meant to feel for her own Mum.

Chris's mouth had gone dry, and feeling sick she had sneaked away. As she ran out of the flat into the street, gulping in the cold winter air to stop herself throwing up, she felt orphaned. Her Mum had abandoned her. As she could not belong with the bold, statuesque woman upstairs, with whom did she belong? Gary in his oil stained overalls was no last resort.

She clattered up the stairs to their flat on the second floor, her thoughts past and present stuck to the dingy walls and appeared half soaked on the staircase, like the washed fragments of *Pride and Prejudice*. She fumbled in her bag for the door key and at last found it swaddled in the tissues her

Mum gave her every Monday. The half-empty packet was her Mum. Whenever Chris pulled a hanky out to blow her nose she was both reassured and annoyed.

She had to lean hard on the door to get it open. Her mother had jammed her brown velvet sausage dog against it. Sometimes the dog stuck, so like now, Chris had to squeeze through the gap. Alice's stuffed emissary greeted her with an expression of lumpy resignation. Not for the first time Chris inwardly fumed at her mother's insistence at using a draught excluder in the height of summer. She complained of being alone, but spent most of her time stopping people getting in.

Chris paused in the hallway. Since the David Bowie nightmare, she'd been entering with trepidation. She also savoured the illusion of being on her own. How different this flat would be if it were hers. She had never been alone in it.

The short corridor had no windows and depended on one of its five doors being open for light. They were always shut. Chris sniffed. The hall smelled of air freshener and washing and was pleasantly cool despite the heat outside. It was a relief now, but in the winter the hall was a place to avoid. There was no central heating. That was Stage Three of the modernisation of the Victorian estate. Stage Two had been security doors and a bench manacled to the estate office with a dedication plate to a dead councillor around which the information: '*WP liKEs it up thE aRsE*' had been carved. Also included in Stage Two was a brick trough of dusty soil now populated with browned-eared shrubs and dotted with colour from drinks cans and food packaging. Stage One had been the Norwegian double glazed windows that could be cleaned on both sides without ladders or risk of death by falling. The third stage was on hold because the housing association had run out of money.

Chris tossed her bag on to her narrow single bed, registering with a stab of fury that it had been made. Now it was a pretend bed, with no creases or folds, a series of straight lines like a prison. Her mother always tucked the duvet in at the sides. How many times had she asked her not to?

'*Mum! No one tucks in a duvet!*'

'It's neater, otherwise it'll slip off the bed.'

'How? Is the bed on a slope?'

'Why do you have to contradict? You have to have the last word.'

'No, you always have the last word.'

'See what I mean?'

Now Chris snatched at the duvet and wrenched it out from the wall. Discarded and rejected clothes had been folded in reproachful piles on her desk, covering papers and pens.

Chris lay down, her arms outstretched.

After a bit she felt between the wall and the mattress and hauled up a square of crocheted wool and clamped it to her nose. Contentment crept through her like a paper slowly catching fire, licking and lapping: spreading heat. The room was hers again. Her mother had knitted the small pink blanket for her cot. She sniffed it, breathing right in. A kind of peace descended.

The walls were dark red with shiny black skirting. Chris had done the gloss four years ago when she was supposed to be doing her French homework. Nothing had been greater than her buzzing excitement as she left the shop with the tin of paint, a brush and the bottle of turpentine secreted in her bag. Chris had paid for everything with money from her Saturday job at the library. Her Mum had brushes and cleaning fluids, she was an expert on decorating and home improvement. But she would not have let Chris use her brushes, even if she cleaned them thoroughly afterwards. As it turned out, the borrowing of brushes might have been a small crime in comparison with the much larger one of painting her skirting boards black.

Streaks of cold tea had dribbled down the woodchip wallpaper, mingling with black paint. Even years later, Chris still found flakes of china tucked into the edges of the carpet. She liked this, preferring to think of her bedroom as a preserved crime scene. The next day she had bought her mother a new mug. It seemed her Mum, normally so fiercely tidy, always had to make a mess when she was cross.

It had been worth it. Now Chris knew every inch of her bedroom, the places where there were cracks and indentations and ominous bulges. She had painted like the bloke in the shop had advised, following the grain of the wood in rhythmic sweeps. Now though Chris regretted the black. But she kept this secret from Alice.

'You're late. Was the traffic bad, darling?'

'Same as usual.'

'The sun has left the quadrangle.'

'*Do you have to use that pretentious word. Yard. It's a crappy old yard.*'

'So what?' she retorted and too late berated herself; despite the launderette, they might have a nice evening. Chris repeated her usual resolution.

'*I will be nice. I will be kind. Just do as you're told.*'

Leaning against her Mum's big old armchair, she glanced out of the window at the shaded yard. She wanted to see her Mum laughing with her own friends in some crowded restaurant or sipping a glass of wine in a pub garden decked out with lanterns like other people's mothers did. Sometimes when Alice tapped her feet to a tune on the radio, Chris spied the girl in the stories, who skipped and pranced and wore her hair in bunches. More recently she was reminded of the woman in the mirror.

At two in the morning, listening to the flat flexing its limbs: the whimsical trilling of the fridge, groaning water pipes, and the other indefinable sounds of her home, Chris would whisper a wish to the darkness that one day her Mum would be able to go outside and feel the warm sun on her face. She would turn Alice into the carefree girl she was before her parents were killed. She would restore that happy child spinning a figure-of-eight on the ice rink watched by proud parents up in the stands. Then Chris would hear her Mum cough through the thin wall and despair that she would ever get better.

'How was your day?'

'I've made you *bœuf en daube*. With extra wine the way you like it.'

Chris loved her Mum's cooking; it was their private language. Alice didn't cook according to the seasons, but by mood or priority. She had defrosted the fridge, and was working through the contents and then gave her dishes fancy names enunciating the French with guttural enthusiasm. This was a joke they shared. Alice had spent three days over the dish. Chris was impressed that Alice was expert at cooking without going anywhere. She never picked up flavours and smells or ate other people's food and swapped recipes and tips.

This flash of good feeling prompted Chris to bring on another high spot in her Mum's day. She went to get the newspaper.

'Hey Mum, you sit and read. Let me set the table and serve up. Then we can do the crossword.'

'I'll take you up on that.' Alice started out of her chair to hug her daughter, but she had gone.

Chris opened the kitchen door and entered a world where only good things happened. The rich herby smell laced with garlic triggered another burst of love for Alice. As she lifted the lid from the pan and stirred the reddish-brown mixture, Chris called to the living room in a chirpy voice:

'Mind you the news is weird. Some doctor bloke drove his car into a swimming pool and drowned himself at the weekend. Probably killed a patient and couldn't admit it! There's a great photo.'

There was no reply, but Chris was too preoccupied choosing especially tender pieces of meat for her mother to notice.

The kitchen was warm and bright. The surfaces were gleaming. It could have doubled as an operating theatre. No mistakes were made here. No crimes either. Her Mum rarely left traces of herself in a room, wiping down cupboards and polishing handles after cooking. She left no chance for mould to grow anywhere.

Alice had put out a tray with plates and cutlery so there wasn't much for Chris to do. She was surprised her mother had let her serve the food. Alice liked recognition and presenting her culinary feats was part of the ceremony.

Chris handled the ladle Alice had put out with clinical care, lifting out meat and vegetables without splashing. She made sure to give her mother a bit more potato and lots of juice. She hummed to herself as she lowered the brimming plate on to the tray. She would come back for her own. She manoeuvred with care, concentrating on each step, keeping the gravy from slopping as she walked back through.

'Mum, this looks delic...'

Chris staggered backwards as Alice shoved against her. The plate slithered across the tray. Chris tried to get her balance, but couldn't stop gravy and bits of meat splashing to the floor. The room vibrated as Alice slammed the door behind her.

The settee was still warm where her Mum had been. Chris plonked the tray on the floor and sat motionless. At her feet the rug was a limp animal with gashes of gravy for open wounds. What had she done now?

After about ten minutes she went into the kitchen and filled the washing up bowl with soapy water. The gravy disappeared as she scrubbed. Then she took the tray with the rest of her mother's supper back to the kitchen, tipped the food back in the pot and washed the plate. Her own plate had not been used. She put the lid back on the casserole dish and switched off the light. She had no appetite.

The *Evening Standard* was on the settee. She looked at the picture of a car hanging from a crane over a swimming pool of some posh country mansion. When she had scanned the paper earlier before getting off the tube, Chris had found the picture funny despite the story. It was a surreal sight. She considered whether her mother was going mad. She would not know how to check, for she was used to her odd ways. Alice would touch five things on entering a room and talk to her draught excluder dog as if he was real. The estate didn't allow proper pets. On good days Chris even loved Alice more for these eccentricities. The doctor said her Mum was marvellous, coping so well in the circumstances. What would he have said about her tonight? Her Mum had ruined the evening for no reason.

She read the story properly. It put off doing anything about Alice.

An internationally acclaimed Parkinson's Disease specialist was found drowned in his swimming pool on Saturday. Police can find no reason to explain why Professor Mark Ramsay drove his car into the swimming pool of his Sussex home. Despite brave efforts by his 66-year-old wife Isabel and son-in-law Jonathan Cross (46) they were unable to free him from the submerged car. Professor Ramsay, who would have been 74 in November, was pronounced dead at the scene. Lucian Ramsay (42), a pharmacist at Charing Cross Hospital in London, said his father had been looking forward to his birthday. 'He categorically would not have taken his life. My mother said he fought to escape. He adored his family. He had every reason to live.' Police are running checks on the 31-year-old Rover. Professor Darius Meeching, a colleague at the National Hospital in Queen Square where Professor Ramsay still worked, said the loss to the UK's knowledge of Parkinson's was immeasurable...

Chris didn't know anyone with Parkinson's Disease but swiftly concluded it was obviously suicide and that the son was kidding himself. Children knew less about their parents than anyone. Although she could be sure that Gary would never kill himself using a car.

Chris admitted that the professor was okay looking for an old man, with no grey hair and a dimple in his chin. She remembered her Mum saying newspapers always had pictures of dead people smiling to show they had been nice when they were alive and to make readers care that they were dead. Apparently the professor had everything, good looks, a successful career, children and a wife described as a 'glamorous sixties socialite'. Chris reflected that, even dead, Mark Ramsay looked happier than she was at that moment. Wealth might not bring happiness, but it provided better places to kill yourself or be miserable in.

Whatever his son said, Chris guessed something must have upset the old professor. Parents were unpredictable. Not that she knew about fathers. Her father would be unlikely to ruin a perfectly good car in order to kill himself. She remembered the man in the subway and closing her eyes, she felt the warmth of his tense body against hers. Her body's memory was better than her own. Chris could not remember what the man had looked like. Only then did she realise that she had not seen his face.

She left the paper on the glass coffee table. Her Mum might still read it. She would be better tomorrow.

Fourteen

Isabel climbed out of bed as soon as Gina had left the room. Her whole body was stiff after the business in the pool and when she stood up her temple throbbed. It was a relief to be alone as long as she knew it wouldn't last. She had read somewhere that people felt closer to death after both their parents had died, when the buffers shielding them from mortality were removed. Her own parents had died when she was too young to remember them so she had never had that feeling. She felt it now. With Mark's death Isabel had been shunted forward in the queue, suddenly old, a widow, a dowager.

Her turn next.

Isabel's arms ached as she drew back the curtains and leaned out of the open window into the warm dusk. A pale square of light from the kitchen was like a sheet spread over the grass in the growing gloom. The ghostly outlines of the table and empty chairs under the willow tree were both emblems of the past and finger-posts to a bleak future. The thick bushes and the trees that were now grown as tall as the house rustled in the late evening breeze. She stared hard, but no amount of looking changed anything. Mark was not there now.

There were voices, distant enough for her to feel held in a private silence. Did other people have these thoughts, inconsequential, yet integral to one's self? In a drunken conversation after making love before they were married she and Mark had once confided their most trivial experiences to each other. They discovered for instance that they touched the end of a biscuit with their tongues after biting, to stop crumbs dropping. Tiny expediencies they had seldom acknowledged since, yet she had believed those shared assumptions were always there. Now it was all over.

The intruders had gone for the day. All afternoon there had been a policeman posted at the gate. He was back there after thirty years. His presence should form a direct link to a lost time, as a blanket of snow can level changes to a landscape, and precipitate the recall of forgotten events. But Isabel felt only disintegration and heavy limbs. A hand clasped her waist. She opened her eyes and preparing her face, gave in to its pressure, turning round ready to speak; she must sound patient and try not to snap at him.

There was no one there except the half-drunk glass of water on Mark's bedside table and his reading specs.

Now only the children were left in the house. She could hear them through the window, talking in hushed conspiracy downstairs, presumably the kitchen. They would have formed a committee around the table, drinking cocoa made by Lucian who had the sensible answer for everything. Lovely, dependable Lucian: boiling the milk to precisely the right temperature, lining up the cups like soldiers, dispensing the exact measurement of powder. He would leave enough milk for the morning in case the milkman failed to deliver. It had never happened yet. Lucian the Pharmacist spent his life working through a computerised list of instructions and descriptions. Isabel had always languidly assumed his work was limited to doling out pills and potions into receptacles; pouring powder into delicate sachets from larger packets, dripping from small bottles on to spoons, slipping syringes into plastic bags, coaxing blobs on to petri-dishes, and tweezering on to microscope slides. All day long, he transferred something to somewhere else, when he had wanted terribly to be a doctor. Isabel knew her son had grown up into a disappointed man. She despised him for his blinkered ambition, so inappropriate for a boy who might have been artistic and created works that changed the world. Isabel sometimes found the sight of her son, so imperturbably stoical in the face of his substituted life, quite unbearable.

She was livid with Mark for leaving the police entirely to her, literally leaving them. She had told them she had been lying in the sun reading, and even described how the heat was somewhat mitigated by a refreshing cool wind and how her blue and white umbrella positioned to the left of her lounger shaded her face and book while allowing the rest of her to tan. Police liked detail.

'Oh, and it was factor fifteen, in an orange squeezy thingy. No idea what's happened to it. I'm sure I had it outside. Mark was lying on my lilo which my daughter, this one here, my eldest, gave to me last year.'

She turned to Gina for confirmation. They needed corroboration. Statements backed with hard evidence:

'It was last year, wasn't it? Or the year before?'

'It doesn't matter, Mum. They don't care about the lilo.' Gina had glowered at her toes. She blamed it all on Isabel, of course. Even today it was not Mark's fault.

'We went to the Caribbean the year before, so yes, it was last July.' Gina's commitment to accuracy got the better of her.

Gina had gone to the hospital with Mark's body, hovering possessively close as they zipped him up in a shiny black body bag and loaded him on to the gurney before wheeling him round the side of the house to the drive. Absurdly the wheels rattling over on the gravel reminded Isabel of a supermarket trolley and she had stifled a shout of laughter. She had expected Gina to be squeamish – as a girl she had been unable to contemplate her dead hamster – but she had been devout in her attention to her drowned father. She had even tried to make Isabel come in the ambulance too.

'I'm not ill. There's nothing the doctors can do for either of us, me or your father.' She had already disowned him.

'You've had a shock, they could sedate you.'

'A large gin could do that.' Isabel was shapeless in Jon's gigantic pullover and Gina's jodhpurs, which hung loosely on her thin legs. None of them had thought of going upstairs for her clothes, but had grabbed what they could find in Jon's car. Her hair had dried in clumps but now there was no Mark to care. Or so she had said to Jon when he offered to find her a brush. She could see the dismay in her son-in-law's chlorinated eyes, and knew that he saw Isabel's abandonment of her appearance as a sign of madness. Perhaps it was. It was a long time since she had lived in the real world.

Finally Isabel had upset Gina over the sun lounger. Her eldest child had never been good at relaxing.

'What are you doing?' Isabel had found Gina in the hall filling out a label on the side of the cardboard box containing the luxury lounger.

'I'm sorting this out. It's not like anyone will want it.' Gina gave the cardboard a thump.

'I want it. I've been waiting absolutely ages for it. It's come from Italy.'

'Isn't there enough to deal with? Police, forms, questions; a frightful mess?' Gina continued to write, then she looked up and spat out: 'There's going to be a post mortem.'

'What's going on?' For a brief moment, it was Mark. Isabel had never properly noticed how much Lucian resembled him. Had the quality of likeness changed now there was only Lucian?

'Nothing.' Gina had screwed up the address label and stood close beside the box.

'We have to be a team on this one.' Lucian was brisk.

'On what one? No we fucking don't.' Isabel had snapped. 'We just have to get through without ballsing up.' Her children instantly became a team.

'I'll get scissors.' Gina had moved towards the kitchen, but Lucian produced a blade from the key ring in his pocket and slid it precisely along the rim of the box.

'Where do you want this? It's um, rather busy at the pool.' He grinned quickly and for a second she had back her young son.

'Oh, stick it out the back. I can lie on the lawn at least.'

Gina had elbowed Lucian out of the way and set to unpacking the bed and studying the cleaning instructions.

In the hours after his death Isabel had been intent that Mark's death should not stop her living as he had during life. But he was stopping her. Isabel's lifestyle was being raked over and awarded marks. She wasn't doing very well. She had told the police:

'I went inside for some orange juice and when I came out my husband had gone.' Gina had been beside her on the swinging Jack and Jill seat with frilly blue and white canopy a little way from the pool. The police had wanted to interview Isabel in the house, but she had said she couldn't bear to be indoors on such a sunny day. Gina was holding her arm in a show of emotional support although it was Gina who needed it, so Isabel held her hand. The double seat swung if they moved only slightly so this arrangement kept them stable if nothing else.

'So was that your husband's gin and tonic by the side of the pool?' The young man knew it wasn't. Isabel was glad she had made him sit on a stool at their feet.

'It was lunchtime, my daughter was due any minute.' At this she had felt Gina stiffen as if unwilling to be implicated and Isabel became momentarily flustered.

'Did I say orange? No the gin was mine.' Silly old bag, he was thinking. Out of the corner of her eye, Isabel caught Gina biting her cheek, doing that dreadful face, pulling her mouth across like rubber. She already had lines around her mouth and now it might make her look unreliable. Isabel only just stopped herself from slapping Gina's hand. The seat swayed, making the policeman teeter backwards to avoid being kicked.

'Mark drinks whiskey,' she added for good measure. Mark was not getting off scot-free.

'So Mark had been drinking?' The young man was sure of himself. He had soon dropped 'Professor Ramsay', no doubt the result of communication training. Use first names to make them feel at ease. Isabel remembered the detective talking to Eleanor when Alice Howland went missing. He had been deferentially polite, and never gave away what he was thinking. Perhaps he had been cleverer than she had given him credit for. He had never found Alice so he wasn't that clever. She wondered if he was dead too, policemen died young, they worked such terrible hours.

She had roused herself:

'No, my husband said it was too early.' She hadn't meant to say that and quickly offered: 'He was driving into Lewes. He never drinks if he's driving.'

Drank. She wasn't in denial. She knew Mark had gone and was not kidding herself, saying 'we' because she couldn't bear 'I', but it was too soon for past tense and besides she needed Mark to be in this with her. Later she caught a young constable – a boy – looking at her. She knew the expression, and felt a frisson of triumph that she could still inspire that look in the opposite sex.

'Was he in a funny mood recently? Low, distracted, uncommunicative?'

'Oh yes, always!'

'Mum's joking.' Gina squeezed her arm. 'You're in shock, Mum. Is this okay? They can stop for now.'

Isabel thought of Eleanor over thirty years ago, refusing to take Richard Thingummy's questions seriously. Perhaps she was entering her second childhood.

'Mark was the same as ever. There was nothing different about him.' But there had been. Suddenly she knew what it had been like; Mark had behaved as if he was being hunted.

'Is there anything special about today? The 6th of June, is that significant?'

'Not remotely.' She held his gaze. What could she say? There was no sense in mentioning Robert Kennedy, then they really would think she was mad.

'You had no idea he was going to do this?'

'Are we assuming he knew he was going to do it?' she had replied archly.

The interview by the side of the pool was punctuated by a bubbling sound that might have been relaxing had it been a water feature. It was the car shifting in the water. Actually it was a water feature. She had snorted with sudden laughter, startling the police and making Gina squirm, which in turn rocked the swing seat and unsettled the policeman.

'You think your husband accidentally drove his car into the swimming pool?' The man would have been openly sarcastic if death and status hadn't been involved.

'Of course.' She thrust out a long jodhpured leg. The policeman flinched. 'He was on the lilo when I left the garden. He had to hurry, to get to Lewes and be back in time for lunch.'

'Strange time to choose to go out, with guests due any minute, wouldn't you agree?'

'They weren't guests, they were family. We don't stand on ceremony.'

'How long were you in the house, Mrs Ramsay?'

Gina was watching her.

'How long does it take to make a gin and tonic?'

The policeman had raised his eyebrows in a 'you tell me' way, probably relieved his own mother didn't drink gin in the day.

'Minutes, I suppose, I don't know, maybe five, maybe ten? I took my time, I had no...'

She stopped mid-sentence. She could read his mind: '*Strange woman, not shed a tear, drinks at all hours, lies about it, keeps laughing at odd moments. The minute she's out the way, husband slams his car into the pool and drowns and she doesn't bat an eyelid.*' Isabel was crying inside but that didn't count. She wanted to go back to lying in the sun with Mark doing graceful circles on the lilo. She wasn't ready for this phase of her life.

Now she trailed across to their bed and, finding Jon's jumper folded on Mark's side, hauled it over her head and rolling up the sleeves, prepared to go downstairs. She didn't want to be on her own any more. There would be enough time for that.

Fifteen

Just as Isabel had guessed, her children and their partners were in a tight group around the kitchen table vainly trying to weigh up the consequences of what Jon had dubbed with transparent enthusiasm 'a total fuck up'. It was not that Jon lacked feeling, he had always been intent on gaining the admiration of his father-in-law, but he was at his most congruent full tilt in a crisis. This was his chance, now they would see him come into his own. The pity was that the one Ramsay he most wanted to impress was dead. In the hours after Mark was taken to hospital, everyone had vied for supremacy in practical prowess as lists were drawn up and then ripped up, and scenarios of the future were described and dismissed. Everything led back to the big question: what had really happened?

'I doubt very much it was an accident.' Jon had forgotten the emotional implications, so carried away was he with vaunting specialist knowledge and infinite capability. 'There might have been time to get out of the car, if the windows were up. But he had wound them down. Besides what was he doing there? He'd had to drive out of his way to be in the pool.'

'Of course it was an accident. That's not up for debate.' This from Lucian. 'It's summer, do you drive with the windows up in this heat?'

'Well, I've got air-con so...'

'That old car was knackered and Dad was tired, he works harder than you and I put together.' He glared at Jon who failing to heed the beady scowl cantered on happily.

'Hey, but you know, the great thing is that those camera tapes will tell us. Funny how we all banged on at the old man about them, and now he's been proved right. We'll have the whole thing on film. I'll tell the police first thing tomorrow.' Jon persisted in referring to Mark Ramsay as 'the old man', thinking it made him sound rakish and one of the family.

'That film is none of their business. Besides, let me be the judge.'

Then Caroline, Lucian's girlfriend who had never felt the precarious nature of her relationship with him more than now, and spurred on by Jon's seeming disregard for Lucian's authority, chose this moment to mention Mrs Ramsay's 'problems'. Alliances solidified. Lucian and Gina closed ranks and closed down the discussion.

The two out-laws made mumbled exits:

'Check the garden, lock up the house, run baths...'

Soon after this Isabel appeared in the doorway. Her wispy and hesitant demeanour, one hand on her stomach, the other on the door jamb, brought their whispered conspiracy to a stop just as a little girl's unwanted presence had done in the same room years before. Lucian screeched back his chair as he leapt up to pour his mother the last of the cocoa from the pan on the Rayburn into the mug that Gina snatched up off the dish rack.

After Isabel had returned to her bedroom with her drink, unable after all to bear the company of her children, Lucian and Gina stayed sitting at the table like statues keeping vigil in stony bewilderment, as the sun set on the last day in this world that included their father.

Sixteen

When Chris had opened the bedroom door, Alice snapped shut her eyes, and pretended to be asleep until at last she heard her go away. Chris had not gone to the launderette, but Alice could hardly blame her. Her behaviour earlier that evening would have seemed peculiar, and in the morning she must make up for it. Alice lay on her back and tuned into the sounds of the building. The creaks, hisses, bangs and whines orchestrated the lives of residents as they did her own. The woman upstairs had gone to the lavatory five minutes ago. She had heard the intermittent trickling followed by a rushing of the waste pipes in the wall behind her head. Alice hated having such intimate knowledge of her neighbours, although perversely her distaste provoked a prurient obsession with these secret existences and she would listen out for them. Alice was the possessor of facts that no one else knew.

Then she heard Chris's radio: a thin chattering interrupted by music emerging into a track she recognised, 'London Calling' by The Clash. She had once remarked that she liked it. Perhaps Chris would remember this and might now be thinking fondly of her. Alice wanted the music to do the work of reconciliation for her. It was unlikely. Finally there was nothing but thoughts inside the gothic Victorian tenement as it fell into uneasy night silence.

At one o'clock it was safe to get up.

Alice shrugged on her dressing gown, a size too big: a peril of mail order. Her feet fished around in the dark for slippers. Amber light from the lamppost in the quadrangle gave the living room an uncanny appearance, filtering out vitality, memories; all specificity. Alice crept in with the spatial unfamiliarity of a visitor.

She saw immediately that the casserole stain had vanished, and kneeling down she ruefully touched the damp rug in front of the fire. The gas fire was where she always heard the voices. This was how Alice knew they were real. If they had been inside her head, they would be everywhere.

At first she had assumed it was a television in one of the other flats. But then getting so close to the blue and orange flames that her cheek stung, she had worked out that they came from behind the heater and were too unruly and spasmodic to be scripted. Arguing. Shouting. Soothing tones of making up. There was a child crying, a voice that might be a man interrupting. Sometimes the voices weren't talking to each other, but speaking in isolation, like a bedtime story or a stern lecture and then the boy or girl laughing or perhaps crying. Alice rarely caught actual words although she was certain they were speaking in English from the inflections. If Alice did hear words, like *exceptional, beautiful, special*, they were like her own thoughts.

Alice hadn't yet told Chris about the voices but did wonder if she had heard them too. Chris would be matter of fact and say they'd come from next door. But there was a stairwell on the other side of the chimney and the voices were constant, not those of passers by. At other times she liked to imagine they were the inhabitants of the world inside the mirror. Now she put out her hand and touched the wall above the fire. Perhaps they had been trapped inside the wall. Was she hearing their ghosts forever calling, pleading, destined never to be heard or believed? Perhaps it was the people who had lived here a hundred years before. Or was it that all rooms were busy with the palimpsest natter of past conversations that the living were mostly too preoccupied to hear? Mostly Alice couldn't think of the place beyond the gas fire as a brick tomb. She preferred it to be a room with pools of lamplight and filled with easy companionship. There were no voices tonight.

Alice had not got up to hear the voices; grabbing the newspaper she settled on the sofa, and less cautious, switched on the light.

The White House had been at its best in the summer: draped in laburnum and lilac, lattice windows flung wide, hanging baskets shapeless with so many frowsy blooms. But in the photograph the line of the diving board led the eye away from this backdrop to a large green car hanging from a crane over the water.

The word suicide was not used in the article. Lucian Ramsay insisted his father was happy. Mark Ramsay loved his family. She frowned at the gas fire; did loving people make you happy? It seemed that he had rammed his car through a fence into a swimming pool. She knew he was a strong swimmer. He had taught all his children to swim. All the Ramsays knew how to get out of their pyjamas and up to the surface in less than a minute. Alice had always been mocking. She had asked Eleanor what the point of it was. If you were in bed, why would you be likely to drown? She had argued that getting out of daytime clothes would be more realistic. Alice thought this now.

She knew how to escape from a car underwater. She had heard Dave Allen explaining it on the radio. She knew to wait until the car was almost full of water and the pressure inside the same as the pressure outside, then push open the door and swim out. Simple.

Suddenly Alice heard a voice. This time she was certain it was a girl. She was like a conspirator, hissing out words. Alice hitched up the sleeve of her dressing gown and wrapped smartly on the wall. Three times. '*Knock three times on the ceiling if you want me...*' The voice stopped.

It wasn't until Alice was back in bed that she found she was hugging the newspaper to her chest. She didn't let go and during the remainder of the night was partially woken by crackling as she turned over. Never asleep, yet not properly awake, her thoughts were tall and thin like evening shadows.

They would look for her again. Mark Ramsay's death would have reminded them about her. Now more than ever it was important to stay hidden. But if she didn't want to feel forever a fugitive she must take matters into her own hands. In the middle of this, she fell into fitful sleep.

When she awoke in the morning, Alice decided that despite the risks she would go to Mark Ramsay's funeral.

Seventeen

Kathleen nearly lost her in Marks and Spencer's. She was cross with herself, there was no excuse, she had been distracted for the pettiest of reasons. Spitting muttered admonishments she scoured the store. The sign had been practically waving to get her attention.

Everything 60% off!

Kathleen looked this way and that. Now she saw that the sales notice had been a test, thrown like a smoke bomb into her path, luring her to be taken in and lose the little girl. One glance at the blouses on the rack, their silky tendrils cool to the touch, and she had been caught in the spell. She had been doing so well, snaking adroitly between islands of clothes carousels, and towers of crockery, and CD racks. Now, she looked desperately about her for long fair hair and that bouncy step that had always put them in mind of a pony.

Always helpful, always cheerful; never in a bad mood. Always.

The shop was busy with rush-hour adults pushing and shoving, and amidst all this the child had vanished. Kathleen should not have taken her eye off her for a second. Normally she was so good. But today her heart was not in it. Indeed for once it wasn't her reason for being in the store. She had made herself go out, if only for Doctor Ramsay's sake, he had always been so encouraging about not giving up.

Kathleen had learnt to ignore what wasn't important. She blinked, trying to read a placard suspended from the ceiling by thin wire, but couldn't make out the words. She ought to get her eyes seen to but there was no time. Each morning was taken up with preparations and making sure she left the house with everything she needed for the day. In all this she had neglected herself. Her sight was a vital tool of the trade. She could not afford to ignore it.

Practise by walking down the street, fixing your focus on a point in the distance. Anything will do: a postbox, a leaf. Begin with objects yards ahead, then move on to further away. It would be ideal to begin with a flat place, perhaps the horizon where the earth meets the sky or lines converge. The vanishing point. At no time let your attention stray. If your point of focus is a leaf, do not look anywhere else until you are upon that leaf. You will find this harder than you expect. Small things will conspire to distract you. You will distract yourself. You are your worst enemy.

The blouse was too good to miss. Reduced by so much and with one in her size. Clothes usually went by the board, there was never time to buy things. Kathleen was size ten now. How her younger size-twelve-self would have envied her.

No one envied her.

Kathleen ran the material through her middle finger and wedding ring finger. It was so soft, like butterfly wings, soft like the snippet of baby hair in her locket. Then she lifted the blouse from the rail and held it away from herself. She had to provide her own objective view. She had no shopping companion.

It would look lovely on you, Mum. Try it on.

The buttons were as delicate as shell, although they would be too fiddly for her. The slate blue was her shade: the colour of her eyes a teacher had once said. She had a skirt and an old navy pair of trousers it would go very well with. Surely, at sixty-four she wasn't too old. The shirt might make her feel young. This put Kathleen off; she had a fear of becoming a grotesque parody of herself thirty years ago. When she put on her make-up she sometimes had to quell the urge to trace the cracks on her face with her eyeliner pencil. Stark, black curves, implacable dashes would criss-cross her face, then she would colour the jagged shapes inside the lines with bright red lipstick and green mascara to make a component face held together by her determination to get through each day.

She must be alive when Alice came back.

It was at this point, the blouse scrunched up soft against her face, that Kathleen had remembered the girl. Where had she gone? Darting forward, she changed her mind and stepped back down the aisle she had come along. Which way? Her tufted head pecking back and forth, her slate blue eyes trained to the honed skill of a store detective.

The little girl was nowhere to be seen.

She shoved the shirt back on the rack, and hurried in the direction she had last seen her.

When you have nothing to go on, rely on logic.

Kathleen had learnt to bank on predictable behaviour. If the girl had doubled back then she would never find her. All the time she grumbled childlike substitutions for swearing. *Flip. Sugar. Drat! Fool! Idiot!* Tissue-wrapped words kept along with the carefully cleaned toys arranged in greeting for the wanderer returned.

How could she have let herself be side-tracked? It was out of character. The second time in two days.

Doctor Ramsay's death had set her back.

Kathleen's battery was draining away. Sometimes as she followed the pre-ordained paths, the red biro routes she plotted out in her *A to Z* each morning, she agreed with the newspaper readers, the train travellers, brick dusted builders and ungenerous housewives who all judged her delusional. Yet they would be there to shout and throw eggs in her name if there was a grey-blanket covered culprit to whisk from car to courthouse.

With no body, there was no culprit. Perhaps, just perhaps, no crime.

As Kathleen pushed past a group of women examining a maypole of bras, she caught her ankle on a buggy parked between nightwear and swimwear. The child had pulled one of the nightdresses over itself, and was hiding patiently, waiting for its mother to find it under the lacy tent. Kathleen caught hold of the buggy's rubber handle to stop herself toppling on to it and the mother tore stormy-faced out of the scrum, bras dangling like exotic fronds, as the toddler – nightie snatched off with magician swiftness to reveal a boy – embarked on an obligatory howl. There was no time to explain, so holding her bag to her chest, Kathleen ploughed on to the food section. It was her last hope. The girl could already have left the shop.

There she was.

Kathleen stopped and gathered her breath. A girl of about eight was standing on one leg by the prepared salads, singing peacefully to herself. Her blonde hair was newly washed and beautifully brushed. It was much too short. Her dress was a lovely pink, but spoiled by a thick stripe of black that went like a sash over her back and over her shoulder. Sidling closer, Kathleen could see it was just a giant tee-shirt and looked cheap. Her black sandals had thick soles like bricks and were too high for her age. They were really quite ugly. If Kathleen had been with her when she chose them she could have talked her out of buying them.

If you want to have pretty feet when you're older, look after them now.

She drew nearer to the girl. There were tattoos on her wrists. She supposed they would wash off, no one was allowed to tattoo an eight-year-old. These days they could make them so life-like. She would tell her, tattoos were for fat old men.

'Tut tut.'

The little girl whirled around, whipping her hands away from the bags of watercress with which she had been idly playing shops. She stared up at Kathleen.

She had freckles on her nose and her mouth was wrong, too wide, too mocking. There was no recognition in the defensive glance, only puzzlement and worse: fear.

She was not Alice. Nothing could make her Alice.

Kathleen stepped into the space made by the girl, who had dashed off to become a limpet on her mother's trolley and was wheeled away with kicking heels. Kathleen picked up the bag of watercress the girl had dropped and joined the nearest queue. She would soak her feet in a bowl of water with Friars Balsam when she got home, and sip a lovely hot cup of tea.

For The Best Mum in the whole world with lots and lots of love from your Alice.

With extra sugar as today she was more tired than usual.

A young man leaning on the rail of his heaped trolley noted the elderly woman lost in a zipped up waterproof clutching a bag of salad with both hands, like a kid with a prize. The idea of his Gran shopping on her own, her list lost along with her direction, flitted like Reuters ticker-tape across his busy mind. It was a humiliating fate for the fantastic woman who twenty-five years ago had plunged into teeming traffic to snatch up a runaway three-year-old from the wheels of a bus. Her newspaper photo was framed in his mother's kitchen. *'The Have-A-Go-Granny'*. As the thought-tape fell in coils among the rich pickings of his hectic life, it conjured up his brushed, tightly-coated, clean-eared self teetering on the kerbside for her to return and take hold of his hand. He straightened up and shifting the heavy trolley aside, motioned the old woman through. To his astonishment, she assumed he was telling her off and hesitated before making sense of his gesture. A packet of watercress shuddered its way up the belt to the cashier. They both stared at it as if tacitly agreeing that even her shopping testified against her. He wanted to cry as she handed the cashier her money, the coins dipped for from a chunky leather purse. As he watched, her right hand began to shake while she waited for her receipt and shopping. Suddenly she stretched forward and lifted up one of the boxes of meringue nests he had stacked next to three chardonnays for the price of two. Surely she wasn't going to nick it?

'They love these, don't they! My Alice can eat a whole box, you have to keep an eye, don't you.'

'Ah. Yes. Way too much sugar, but for a birthday...' He breathed as she replaced the box exactly where she had found it, handling it cautiously as if it were a pet mouse.

'I make my own. Once Steve got me the Kenwood, there was no going back! No use with a hand whisk, you can't get the stiff peaks.'

'I don't do desserts. My Gran...' Later he had no idea why he felt the need to introduce his dead grandmother into the conversation: perhaps she was his passport to credibility. A woman of the same species.

The old woman wasn't listening, she retrieved her shopping and melted out of his vision as he was forced to dive into the frenzy of keeping up with the cashier and defend his personal challenge that they never had to wait for his money.

Months later the man would linger over a picture in the *Independent on Sunday*, unsure why the old woman's face was familiar, before shaking out the business section and moving on.

When she got home Kathleen stuffed the watercress in the salad compartment of the fridge. She didn't eat watercress. Not being an adventurous salad maker she stuck to the islands of lettuce, a spoonful of cold baked beans, a halved tomato and small blob of salad cream she had always made for Alice. She frequently came home with unwanted purchases bought to mask disappointment or explain strange behaviour.

Kathleen Howland was aware that people thought her unbalanced. Children in the village treated her warily, even adults who knew her well avoided her if they could, crossing streets, or leaving shops when they saw her coming. She helped them by looking away as they pretended to have forgotten something, patting pockets, rootling in bags, in exaggerated mimes before excusing themselves. She saw through these charades and wanted to assure them it was fine. She might do the same if things were different. If, as the saying went, the boot was on the other foot. She had read about women like herself in the papers so she knew she wasn't alone.

Finally Kathleen did not care what anyone thought and this was one thing that was better than before. Now she could do what she liked without worrying if it was the right way, the right colour or the right accent. She was beyond right and wrong. Her life sentence had set her free.

She shut her ears to the chorus of public opinion of gaping mouths and simple minds.

Move on, it's what she would have wanted. Start a campaign. Work for a charity. Change the world so that it doesn't happen to other mothers.

Kathleen would start by explaining, if she had the chance, that she knew quite well that Alice was not eight any more. Alice had been missing for thirty-one years and four days. Kathleen would be the first to agree that to stalk a little girl through a shopping precinct because she looked like Alice, was the action of an unbalanced mind.

Two months after Alice disappeared in June 1968, Kathleen had been sure she would find it impossible to survive in a world without her. There were no floors or supporting walls. With no meal times or baths to run, no clothes to wash and iron, no school bag to pack or spelling tests to take, daily life had collapsed. She could not carry on without gravity, with the clocks stilled as time slipped stealthily past uncleaned windows, leaving only dust as proof of progress.

Kathleen did not see Alice all the time. She did not follow every child who might be Alice. For example, she no longer hung around outside the school or sat in the spectators' gallery at the local swimming pool where there were plenty of young girls laughing and shouting. Alice didn't like swimming. She loved school, but Kathleen knew the staff would ring if she came back. They had rung Kathleen at the surgery when Alice broke her arm. Teachers could tell when children weren't right even when the children themselves made no fuss. She trusted them with her child. Alice had not cried with her green stick fracture; not wanting to miss maths, she had sat for two hours white with the pain. As a girl, Kathleen would have welcomed any excuse to miss maths. She had admired her daughter's stoic efficiency, her easy intelligence and had stood helpless listening as Alice instructed her teacher how much food to give the fish – relinquishing her post of Pet Monitor – her face pinched and white as she clasped her limp arm. In that moment Kathleen had seen the woman Alice would one day be: a cleverer, calmer, more competent adult than herself. It was an exciting, yet disturbing, vision and Kathleen had been deliriously happy when Alice burst into tears that evening and asked for hot chocolate Nesquik. As she watched Alice take sniffing sips she had secretly welcomed her small daughter back.

It was that little girl Kathleen was determined to find. Somewhere, in a competent adult living out her life, the little girl who was Alice must exist.

Alice would have been forty on the 25th of March. Seventy-five days ago, Kathleen knew exactly, she didn't delude herself.

Over three decades on and Kathleen had refined her search. She now looked for an essence with edges polished smooth by time and embellished with wistful properties, like generosity and limitless kindness. Kathleen knew the girls she was trailing would not be Alice. She had seen their faces, heard their voices, yet the way a girl would skip along beside her Mummy or put her arms out against the wind could be enough to bring Alice back. Then Alice's soul would gain clarity and Kathleen would feel the back of her neck tingle and be convinced she was near. Once she had gone to the bottom of the stairs and called up to Alice in the empty cottage:

'Can't you give me a sign?' The lights fused. She had been unafraid of the darkness, she was no longer alone. If he had been alive, Steve would have questioned why a soul would signal its presence through the electricity circuit just as once he had refused to apply for a transfer on the basis that she was convinced someone had died in the cottage. But perhaps her deep feeling of unease had been the premonition of a terrible event just around the corner, not divining of the past.

The quality of 'missing' had altered; Alice's presence in the cottage had become another prop for alleviating the pain of her absence. It managed Kathleen's grief and fought her conscious desire to die.

Kathleen Howland's life had changed again the day, eight years earlier, when she collapsed in Boots in Canterbury, falling against a life-size cut-out of a woman gaily brandishing a deodorant. As she went down Kathleen's eyes conveyed apology to the brightly smiling image. Her chest refused to breathe. Later she tried to explain it was less a blacking out, more of a greying, a steady diminishment of sight and sound. She had been rushed to hospital. After many white-coated questions they told her what she already knew because she had seen the same symptoms in her mother. She was diagnosed with Parkinson's Disease. She confessed that the tremor in her hand had been going on for over a year. As she lay on a trolley bed while they tapped her arm for blood, Steve's sheet white face appeared like the moon between hospital curtains glaring accusingly at her. This too was her fault.

That day, Alice had got away.

After that, Kathleen had been forced to recognise her limits and adapt her methods. For some time there had been plenty of time between tablets, when she was almost herself, but had to be mindful of her energy. Too much excitement and she trembled visibly, jerking involuntarily and attracting attention. Then she developed low blood pressure in the mornings, and had to lie still, her feet propped on pillows until she could rise without feeling faint. They gave her steroids, but these drained her of potassium and she had an angina attack. This time no one turned up in Accident and Emergency to claim her. She told them there was no 'Next of Kin'. After they cut back on the steroids, Kathleen's symptoms got worse, and she couldn't go until the mid-morning. She was informed that her Parkinson's was advancing fast.

One night five years earlier, as Kathleen was writing up her activities for that day, she had flipped back through her notebook and was upset to see how her handwriting had changed: it was tighter, smaller and crabbed, only just decipherable. Like an old woman's. Except that she was not yet out of her fifties.

Time was not on her side.

In the first months after he died in the summer of 1992, Kathleen would see Steve in the street too. She didn't try to follow him, knowing how much it would annoy him. Steve was a private man whose feelings were his own business. She kept in the shadow of an awning as he stared in at the window of a hardware shop or strolled out towards the fields to merge with the sky. Although she had let Steve go, she missed him. She had howled like a wounded dog with its stomach ripped wide open to reveal a mash of ribs and spleen. She was scared of the noise, a giving birth sound that was death. Nothing could stop it as it rose up, rushing out of her, to roar about her ears like a typhoon. Steve had left without saying goodbye or leaving a note. His dying had been a subtle creeping away, a sick animal first curled irritably in a corner, then one day the corner was empty.

With Steve dead, Kathleen was alone with the loss of Alice. She was by herself with the knowledge of what it was to have a way of life wiped out, one sunny afternoon. The police had informed her that her precious little child was missing and all they could offer her in return was a nice warming cup of tea with extra sugar in.

The isolation was her choice: she had resisted joining groups or answering sympathy letters. She had passed up the chance of conversations with other bereaved parents or with a counsellor that might have sanitised her state. To utter barely formed fears and possibilities gave them the credibility of fact. Kathleen preferred the fluidity of fiction.

In June 1968 there had been Steve. Without speaking, they had clung to each other, sheltering in a shared language. Then, as hours and days slipped by unacknowledged, they had let go finger by finger until they were awkward strangers sharing a kitchen, hovering with polite reticence to use the bathroom. Then Steve left Kathleen by herself to hold the creaking, ticking quiet of the cottage in hands clumsy with tremor. Gradually as the palpability of his absence waned, Kathleen gave herself up to an undertow of relief: it was easier to look for Alice alone.

When Alice went missing, they had been besieged by reporters. Kathleen had welcomed them, grateful for their interest, confident they could help. Her numb disbelief was awakened by the flow of words; the flickering phantoms of her home and her daughter on the new Radio Rentals television were an impression of life. She had grasped at every opportunity to talk and keep talking.

Steve sat in Alice's bedroom, in the chair he used for bedtime stories, holding the book they had been reading when she vanished. It was *Alice in Wonderland*, Alice's favourite. He opened and shut it, a thumb inserted at the place they had left off – 'A Caucus Race and a Long Tale' – rubbing the words perhaps to make them vanish too. He only came downstairs if the police asked to speak to him. He would have nothing to do with the journalists. After a while he did not even talk to Kathleen, but retreated into silence. She understood, for silence was where Alice was.

Kathleen wondered how her husband would have coped if Alice had gone missing today. The media interest had been less then, or perhaps it was just not so polished. Having learnt the importance of what was called the 'oxygen of publicity', she now regretted that Robert Kennedy had been shot dead in the same week and that there had been riots at some university in Paris in the days after. She had learnt the importance of keeping the story in readers' minds. She knew that it was the public that caught criminals, or found missing people, hardly ever the police. People soon forgot. One missing child becomes another missing child: their fresh faces forever smiling in spotless school uniform generic as sheep.

As the weeks went by and there was no sign of Alice, the aftermath of the death of Kennedy and the American election eclipsed the disappearance of a small girl in Sussex. In return, Kathleen forgot about most of the journalists. She did keep the newspapers, although she could not bear to read them. She had been frightened by the lack of intimacy in the black and white picture of her daughter in the papers. Alice's face was made up of hundreds of dots. Her daughter had become a story like the ones Kathleen had read many times while drinking coffee and taking the weight off her feet. The same portrait had been in pride of place on top of the television since Alice brought it home from school the previous September, but in the newspaper it made Alice unfamiliar. Kathleen had stacked the newspapers in a cardboard box and got Steve to put it in the loft. He wanted to throw them away, but however alienating they were, she said it was like throwing away Alice. Kathleen didn't tell Steve that she hoped one day, perhaps when Alice was about thirty, around the same age as Kathleen had been then, she would haul them down and show them to her. Then they would fall about at the pictures of Kathleen and Steve, in his postman's cap with his stiff old-fashioned face. They would not talk about how awful it had been, but just how long ago it was. It would be a past life and they would be relieved that like in fairy stories, everything was 'happy ever after'. Outside, Alice's children would be playing with their grandad in the sandpit, and he would be explaining to them that he had made it for his princess in the olden days.

But thirty-one years and four days later Alice had not come back. Thirty had passed and this year Alice would have been forty. The papers were still in the loft, probably turned to ash by mice and moths, and Steve was dead of a broken heart at the age of fifty-eight.

One reporter had stayed in Kathleen's memory. Jackie Masters looked twenty, with blue eyes and fair hair. Over the years Kathleen had looked out for her name, but had never seen it. Until recently Jackie Masters had vanished as completely as her daughter.

At the time she had been very present. Arriving with a big 'Hullo!', she would march in treating the cottage as her home: filling the kettle, mashing the tea, getting out the milk bottle and flicking off the foil top with such confidence. The place was her own. Kathleen had relinquished everything, her home, her habits; her life. Jackie learnt which cup Kathleen preferred, and washed up and dried and wiped down the draining board. Kathleen found she could talk to Jackie without crying, and say exactly what she meant. The words came out right, not like when she was with the police or with neighbours, when she was unable to speak or move. Jackie could nearly have been Alice's big sister, she tossed her hair in the same way and, like Alice, she had come top in her schoolwork and had wanted to be a ballet dancer but was too small. They discussed the length of Alice's hair, would it look good up, did she have a boyfriend? (Kathleen had not liked the question. No.) Which Beatle did she like best? Or did Alice prefer the Monkees? As they chatted Kathleen could hear Alice in her bedroom upstairs, small feet mousing about as she dressed up her dolls or rearranged her glass animals. Jackie was encouraging when Kathleen confessed she had started leaving the porch lamp on and the back door unlocked at night so Alice could get in. She told Jackie that when they were coming home after dark from her father's in Newhaven, she would insist on putting the light on before they left, so that it would be shining if Alice turned up while they were out. Alice had called the light the 'beacon'. Until then they hadn't known she knew the word. Steve had put this down to the Ramsays who he didn't like. Remembering this stopped Kathleen telling Jackie. She had wanted her to like Steve, although he never came down when she was there.

'Such a grownup word for a little girl, she must have been good at reading.' Jackie Masters had written '*beacon*' in her notebook as if it was a new word to her too.

Oh she was. She loved her books. She always came top at spelling. She knew so many words.

Alice would know the beacon was a message for her. Kathleen had assured Jackie that Alice would come round to the back. They never used the front door except for special occasions. Although of course, her return would be a special occasion.

One night Kathleen took Jackie to the kitchen door and pointed timidly at the packet of sandwiches placed next to the empty milk bottles and yoghurt jars. In case Alice was hungry, she explained. Strawberry jam, her favourite. It had felt wonderful making them, she had whispered not wanting Steve to hear. He would say sandwiches were going too far. She had almost been her old self as she laid the slices out on the board exactly square, then smeared a thin layer of butter on each one. You see she doesn't like too much, but she likes jam right to the crust. She doesn't like the crust, but she must have it, for her teeth. Jackie had squeezed her hand and given such a nice smile. She had no children of her own yet, but said she understood exactly.

Alice liked Robertson's Jam, and was collecting golliwog tokens. Kathleen had helped her send off for a brooch the Tuesday she went missing. Jackie was writing busily as Kathleen recalled Alice skipping and jumping next door to the village stores to post the tokens. Kathleen leaned on the gate, to wait for her, just as excited. Years later, Kathleen still ran this scene like a film. Sometimes it had a different ending, where Alice came home in the evening, hungry and so full of things to tell her, sliding on to a chair at the kitchen table going on and on, like a canary let out of its cage.

After lunch Alice had gone off to play with Eleanor Ramsay; Kathleen had not watched her leave and try as she might, she could not think what the last words Alice had said to her were, however many times Jackie asked.

The golliwog brooch had arrived two weeks after Alice disappeared. Jackie was there and opened the envelope self-addressed in Alice's pretty writing to save Kathleen. Jackie had behaved like a child, clapping her hands and exclaiming 'What a surprise!'

'Oh, she'll love this.' By now they had both forgotten that Jackie had never met Alice. Jackie had become a family friend who Alice would be so pleased to find waiting for her when she came home.

'When she comes back, I'll give it to her.'

'Yes, make things normal again as fast as you can.' Jackie was wise before her time.

Kathleen had forgotten that Steve was in the house as she told Jackie how she spread out her treats, the sandwiches, switching on the beacon, changing the sheets on Alice's bed, preparing her school bag for the new term; different tasks spread throughout each day.

'That's lovely.' Jackie had sighed, as she noted everything down.

Jackie had a way of listening, she looked right at Kathleen, letting her know that what she said mattered above everything.

It had been a mistake to put the sandwiches in a paper bag.

One morning a fox or a cat ripped it open and ate most of the contents. Kathleen had gone round the garden picking up the last scraps of bread, soil had stuck to the jam and the bag was in shreds with strips of sticky paper all over the grass. Steve had been angry. Had she gone off her head? It was when he read about the food left outside his back door by his wife in his Sunday paper that Steve stopped speaking to her.

For some weeks Kathleen worried that Steve had upset Jackie because she didn't come round. Kathleen kept lifting the receiver of their new telephone to check if it was working, or if the other people on the party line were making a call; this would explain why Jackie hadn't rung. In the end she dialled the number Jackie had given her. She had said to ring if something occurred to her or of course if she just wanted a chat. After Kathleen explained who she was and that she only wanted to say 'Hello' and that no, there was nothing new to say, the man on the other end went away. He came back to say Jackie was out. Kathleen hated to be a nuisance and as she was rather scared of the telephone, she didn't call again. However, even without Jackie there, Kathleen continued to talk to her. She told her how she was each day, she chatted to her as she cooked, cleaned and tidied. At first Steve would come in to see who she was talking to.

Just thinking out loud.

Kathleen couldn't have said when this invisible listener stopped being Jackie and became Alice. Perhaps when Alice reached the age of her missing friend. Perhaps she had always been Alice. Certainly for as long as Kathleen could remember she had been talking to the wise and competent woman she had glimpsed on the evening of the green stick fracture. There was now a reason for getting up in the morning. Kathleen had someone who wanted to know how she spent her day and she must have something to tell her.

Steve never approved of her searching for Alice. He was a man who called a spade a spade. Once a thing is done it's done. He wouldn't talk about Alice and eventually stopped going into her bedroom. He had never had a daughter. This meant they had truly lost the greatest thing they shared. Once she had overheard him telling the landlady in a bed and breakfast in Wales that no he didn't have children, he hadn't wanted them. After that they didn't go on holiday.

One night Kathleen had woken up alone in the bed. She got up, not turning on the light, finding her dressing gown and slippers with the dexterity of a person used to sneaking around in the dark. Steve was talking.

Someone was with him.

She had to steady herself as she reached the top of the stairs. Like Alice, Kathleen knew to avoid the creaky step, but feeling ill with hope she hardly dared admit to, she had had to cling to the banister to prevent herself pitching headfirst. Halfway down she stopped to listen to the murmuring from the living room.

Steve was speaking to Alice. How she had cherished that voice he used – caressing and wondering – describing a miracle to Alice. The voice that had made her love Steve even more after Alice was born. Kathleen would gaze contentedly as her young husband led Alice along the edge of the beach at Newhaven or bent down with her to look for tiny creatures in the pools of shallow water at the foot of the cliffs. At barely two years old Alice could imitate his words. *Caterpillar. Grasshopper. Spider.*

It was years since she had heard that voice.

Kathleen nearly screamed. *Alice is back!*

She had been right all along when she asserted Alice was alive and not buried in some hastily dug grave like everyone privately thought. Steve was a father again.

Daddy.

She had run down the rest of the stairs, and then as she touched the doorknob something made her stop in her tracks. Steve wasn't saying anything.

There was no one else talking. Then she heard it.

The silence was broken by a low moaning like the wind. She knew the sound. Steve was crying but Alice wasn't comforting him. She would have tried to make him better the way she had when she was just three and Steve's father had died suddenly of a heart attack. He had been briefly enchanted out of grief as his little princess reached up with a tea towel, and pushed through his criss-crossed fingers to dab at his face. Kathleen had prided herself on not being jealous of the way he looked at Alice. She had assured her sister that she didn't mind that Steve never saw anyone else if Alice was there. She loved the Steve that doted on his daughter.

'Daddy. Please don't cry.'

So why wasn't she handing him a towel now?

Then she heard him:

'Alice. Where are you? My little Alice...'

Kathleen had rushed back upstairs. She lay rigidly, wide-awake for the rest of the night. Steve didn't return to bed and he left for the sorting office without coming to wake her with a cup of tea. When he had clicked shut the front door, quietly so as not to disturb her, it struck Kathleen that he hadn't brought her a cup of tea in bed for a long time.

After that Kathleen understood that they were lost to each other. They had taken bits of Alice away into separate places to examine and treasure. If Alice had come home she would have found it occupied by two people who didn't know each other.

So when Steve died Kathleen was no more alone than she had been before. She also had the comfort of knowing that for Steve at least, the gnawing pain was over.

Thirty-one years and four days later Kathleen still kept the kitchen door unlocked with the beacon burning brightly, although she no longer tried to work out what had happened to Alice. She had gone over so many possibilities for years and had exhausted them. Was she abducted? Did she run away? Did she bang her head and lose her memory and wander off into the house of another family who took her in and brought her up as their own? Had Alice been imprisoned in someone's basement and over time become attached to her kidnappers like Patty Hearst? Kathleen didn't dwell long on the option of murder. She had read that statistically it was the most likely. She now knew that most abducted children are killed within hours of their kidnap, for few people want to be caught holding a child captive. She knew that whatever the police said, after a fortnight they are looking for a body. They keep that to themselves. She had also read that the more time that passes the less chance there is that the child will be found alive. Over time the clues grow fewer and the trail gets colder.

Nowadays she noticed there were big rewards from newspapers and celebrities appeal for missing children to come home, assuring them they are not in trouble. Their favourite music is played on the radio and later, if there is a funeral, it is piped over loud speakers to silent crowds. Hollow-eyed parents, like herself and Steve, stare into the camera begging their child to come home, pleading with their child to come back, or with an anonymous abductor to release them. Kathleen would snatch hungrily at the snippets of these shattered lives to add something to her own jig-sawed world.

Now that Doctor Ramsay had drowned, life would change again.

Kathleen had never told anyone how important the doctor was to her. (To Kathleen he would always be Doctor Ramsay.) It would have confirmed opinions that she was not stable. Doctor Ramsay had been kind to her after Alice went. He had told her to keep hope alive and said something about hope being a flame of life. She should have written it down. He continued to make an effort with her, going out of his way to speak to her if they met in the village. Kathleen guessed that some people only talked to her because they saw that he did. He had never treated her as if she was mad. Years ago he had become an expert on her illness, although neither of them discussed this coincidence. Of course he wasn't her doctor, he was far too important, but he always asked how she was and really seemed to want to know. Kathleen took any comment Doctor Ramsay made about health seriously. The Ramsays had sent flowers when Steve died. She knew they were really from Doctor Ramsay.

Doctor Ramsay had volunteered to join the line of men in the second search at the Tide Mills. Half the village had taken part in the first one, but for this one they wanted only men. When she heard this, Kathleen had passed out. She had guessed it was because they expected to find her body. She had urged the Chief Inspector not to bother. Alice never went there, Kathleen had told her it was too dangerous. Then Steve had pulled her up off the floor and together with the detective helped her on to the settee:

'Let them get on with their job.'

'I was only putting them right.'

'They don't need putting right.'

'She never went there.'

'Yes, she did.' Steve was steely and brutal.

'What do you mean?'

'She went there last Saturday with that Eleanor Ramsay.'

'But she was last seen on Tuesday afternoon in the lane near the Ramsays' house.' Kathleen robotically spoke in a newspaper phrase.

'So, it means she knew about the place.' He had kept close to her, perhaps already concerned that the police should guess how disturbed she was. Maybe he thought they would try less hard to find Alice if they thought her mother was unbalanced. Or was it that he worried that seeing this, the police might blame Kathleen, as Steve already blamed her, for their daughter's vanishing?

'She went the day after you first took her to meet those Ramsays.'

'Alice would have told me.'

'She told me.'

'She what? Did you tell her off?' Kathleen had hoped that Steve was nice to her. Her anguish for every harsh word either of them had ever said to Alice, however mild, was still unbearable now, decades later.

His face had gone strange, twisted, tight. He wasn't Steve.

'I was never cross with her.'

'On the last day, she promised me to behave.' She could only repeat: 'They played hide and seek by the White House. Chief Inspector Hall told us that Eleanor said…'

'Like I said, let them get on with it.'

That was when Kathleen had learnt that Alice had been closer to Steve than she was to her. For the first time since Alice was born, Kathleen had minded about the strong unspoken love they shared. Only in life is the heart a bottomless pit. Alice's love was now finite and Kathleen wanted more than half her share of it.

With the doctor dead, Kathleen assumed she would get no more tapes. So she had lost another chance of finding Alice. He had delivered them to her every Saturday on his way to Lewes when he would also collect last week's batch. She had the tapes ready by the door in a plastic bag. He never came in and they always went through the same routine:

'Here's another week's worth. You keeping well?'

'Can't complain. I've put these back in date order and rewound them. How are you?'

'Tired and I do complain, but no one listens!'

'You must treat yourself properly.' Kathleen didn't like to delay him, he was still a busy man. 'Perhaps I'll see you next week then.' She never liked to presume.

'Same time same place!'

Doctor Ramsay never asked if she had found anything on the tapes. He was too sensitive. He trusted her to tell him. Whatever she said he would believe her.

She knew this for a fact.

The tapes recorded all the comings and goings at the White House. Initially Kathleen had ignored anything that was outside the remit of her search. She was poised, intent, because this might be the week when Alice would materialise: a sneaking image skipping past the pool, dodging out of sight of the windows, cutting across the garden on her way back home.

But Kathleen had observed that the Ramsays had a lot of visitors. She could not help becoming familiar with the man who came to see Isabel for several months on Wednesday afternoons when Kathleen knew the doctor was in London. But she didn't notice the day he stopped appearing on the film. Kathleen tried to forget most of what she saw because she respected the Ramsays' privacy; she was looking for Alice, everything else that went on was irrelevant. Yet despite herself, Kathleen got to know all the routines of the house. The video counter recorded the times of arrival of those who delivered: groceries, chemicals for the pool, furniture and of course the post. In the early tapes Kathleen would see the figure of Steve going up and returning down the drive, the film making him look like a character in the Woodentops. Then Kathleen would have to wind back and look more closely. This was a Steve she had never known, after he left the house in the mornings. In the past she hadn't needed to know this other Steve for she had her own one. But as she watched the blurred black and white figure jerk across the screen over and over again, she felt miserable in a new way to the constant ache of Alice. This out-of-focus monochrome image was all she had. When Steve died the figure changed. First there was a relief postman, an elderly man, who would pause on the path to smell the lavender and here and there to dead head a flower, and then the permanent replacement – a woman young enough to be Kathleen's daughter, who didn't look in the least like Alice.

Kathleen had begun by taking notes, partly to help her concentration, but as her Parkinson's got worse, her writing became harder to read, and it was harder to write. So she gave up and kept no notes on her thoughts about the woman who she saw lingering behind the Judge's shed every Friday morning when Doctor Ramsay was out and which, Kathleen also knew, was the gardener's day off. She didn't mention her for a long time because the woman always had her back to the camera and, besides, the film quality was very poor. Kathleen didn't want to risk her relationship with Doctor Ramsay by bothering him with stupid fancies until she was absolutely sure.

Last Saturday Doctor Ramsay hadn't appeared. Kathleen waited in, confident that he would come. He was so reliable. She hadn't liked to ring, they didn't have that kind of relationship. The tapes were a big favour. Perhaps after what she had told him he had decided to stop letting her see them.

Perhaps he had decided to use the same tape, erasing the previous week's worth. Kathleen had tried not to panic. She relied on the tapes.

Kathleen had not believed Iris when she told her, and she had wanted to get out of the shop. She wished she had not gone there, perhaps if she had stayed at home, she could have prevented his death. But she had gone for precisely that reason, worried as the time went on and Doctor Ramsay did not come. If there was anything to know, she had known that Iris would know it. As she struggled back and pushed open the front door, which these days she used all the time, she had caught her foot on the bag of videos still by the hat stand in the hall. Now Kathleen would have to find a way of returning them that wasn't rude.

Doctor Ramsay's death made Kathleen think again about Alice. If he could die, with his big smile and his sparkly eyes, perhaps Alice could die too. She wouldn't believe village rumours that the doctor had killed himself. He was a doctor; he gave life. She didn't go out all of the Sunday. But on the Monday morning she remembered what he had said about the flame of hope and when she felt well enough she ventured next door to the stores and bought a sympathy card for Isabel Ramsay. She had planned to send roses too, until Iris informed her they had specifically said no flowers.

Since Alice vanished Kathleen didn't go to funerals, but she decided she would make an exception for Doctor Ramsay, as she had for Steve. She would buy herself a new outfit especially. So this was why on the Monday afternoon following Mark Ramsay's death, Kathleen was in Marks and Spencer.

That night Kathleen told Alice what she was doing, certain she would approve. Alice had liked Doctor Ramsay. Kathleen would always be grateful to him, because busy as he was, in those last few days that Alice spent with his family, Doctor Ramsay had given up some of his precious time to her.

Eighteen

Alice leaned her forehead against the front door and counted down from ten. Somewhere, perhaps on a quiz programme, she had heard that the Russians considered it good luck to sit for a moment on their travelling bags before embarking on a journey, and contemplate the expedition ahead. Today she needed all the luck she could get.

...four, three, two. One.

The door made no sound as she opened it. Once on the landing she used the key to close it. She was taking no chances.

She had planned her journey, calculating travelling time, including delays and unforeseen events. Two weeks ago, when she had decided to go to the funeral, Alice had lain awake mentally mapping out the churchyard, working out where she would stand during the burial. She couldn't risk going into the church. She must be vigilant and not make assumptions about people's focus of attention being on the coffin. There would be interest in a stranger.

She was not a stranger.

She would make sure to blend in, and meet any glance without looking away, as that attracted more suspicion. She would stay by the bank of nettles under the oak tree where the graveyard dipped away towards the downs. If necessary she could nip over the wall there. When it was all over, she would hurry away and come home. She had been taken aback to see the square-headed detective, grizzled with age and frustration, on the evening news. Of course, very quickly the media had made the connection with Doctor Ramsay and June 1968. Richard Hall ought to have been dead, but these men never let unsolved cases go. The police saw funerals as an opportunity, and from his interview the other night she knew he was still looking for Alice. She would have to be extremely careful.

She had been shocked to see the photographs of the two girls in the papers. She had not followed the story from an adult's perspective before and it jolted her to see how many people were involved in the search. It had been the biggest manhunt on record. A gruesome record that Alice was sure would be broken one day.

She had felt winded when she read the Punch and Judy roll-call of participants: the Hanging Judge, the Kind Doctor turned Dead Professor, the Jackie Onassis look-alike, the Reckless Tomboy and the Innocent Schoolgirl who liked playing with dolls and might have been a ballet dancer if one day she hadn't vanished off the face of the earth. Her eyes swam with tears as Alice read of the loving Dad who had died of grief. And last of all: long shot footage of Kathleen Howland combing the beach with a metal detector in the eighties, and more recently trawling through a black and white CCTV tape, or patrolling the Churchill Square shopping centre in Brighton while daily eroded by Parkinson's Disease. Alice had folded up the paper unable to read more. The papers made the story seem real.

The press had got a perfect summer story.

Charbury had not changed. On the BBC news the reporter had broadcast from beside the red telephone box where Eleanor had called Gina, pretending to be a boy that Gina fancied, with the deep and panting voice she used for singing '*I was born under a wandering star.*' She had sounded stupid, rasping into the phone, that he was desperately in love with Gina and had to see her at once. How could she have thought Gina would be taken in?

I will kill you! Gina had promised in a matter of fact voice when they got home. She had been taken in. She told Alice and Eleanor that the boy's mother had just died of cancer, which ruined the joke. Then the report had cut from the Ram Inn, bathed in sunshine, to pan out over undulating countryside – a natural home to Shredded Wheat or butter adverts – where cows pranced in unison upon green, green fields and people laughed in ceaseless mirth and slipped farm-fresh strawberries between white, white teeth.

Paradise. Lost.

Alice tried to tackle the ironing as the voices went on about what a lovely man Doctor Ramsay was.

How did they know?

Later she had cut out the articles about Professor Ramsay from the papers and spread them out on the living room table.

Alice had thought all the games Eleanor wanted to play were silly. She didn't approve of pretending.

Just before Chris was due home, Alice gathered up the cuttings and shoved them under her pillow in an old envelope. She had become practised at flourishing sewing materials or watercolour sketches as alibi activities to avoid suspicion of her secret self. She couldn't afford to arouse the attention of her ever-curious daughter. Alice had already pushed the bounds of normality by asking Chris to get three different newspapers for several days in a row. There hadn't been that much coverage; the Ramsays were no longer important. Out of habit she still peered out through the lace, but he wasn't there crouching behind a wheelie bin or sitting in the snug at the World Turned Upside Down. As she leaned against the front door, preparing after so long to leave the flat, she reflected that now she need never look to see if he was there. Now he would never come again.

Finally in *The Independent* she had found what she was looking for:

> *Ramsay, Mark Henry. Died at his home 6th June 1999, missed by Isabel, Gina, Lucian and Eleanor. Funeral 11.30am, Monday 28th June St Andrew's Church, Charbury, East Sussex. No Flowers. All donations to the Parkinson's Disease Society.*

The date of the funeral rang a bell. Alice had simply written the number: '11' in her diary. She did not need the address. The service was well timed; she could be home by the afternoon. It was just possible that Chris would return early; now that she had finished her exams she came and went as she pleased. That was a risk Alice had to take.

The funeral would be a huge risk, but now Alice was used to pretending, so wedded to her fabrications she mistook them for reality. Now a real event had interrupted her complex weavings.

As Alice reached the ground floor and trod lightly past the door of the last flat, a latch clicked. In a second the door would open.

It was over.

She prepared herself for the neighbour's amazement that the recluse-lady from upstairs was out and about, for the supposition that she had escaped. *Call her daughter, call an ambulance*. Alice had time to run, but she couldn't move. Then she realised the door hadn't opened. Instead, someone had double locked it from the inside. Footsteps receded.

As she was going to step out into the quadrangle, Alice saw Jane arriving for work. She couldn't believe her stupidity: how had she not considered Jane?

One morning last November Alice had been gazing listlessly out of the window when her attention was caught by a woman striding towards the estate office. The woman was smartly dressed, in a dusky blue suit, and carried a slim brown leather briefcase. She looked too well heeled to be one of the housing association's tenants and Alice watched keenly as she put her case on the ground while she jangled through a large bunch of keys to open the door.

Suddenly and quite inexplicably the woman looked up at Alice's window. Alice was astounded and jumped back from the glass bashing her hip against the dining table. She had been seen through the curtain.

The next morning Alice had waited for the woman to arrive. Once again, with her brandished keys catching the winter sunlight, the woman – Alice had realised she was the new estate manager – glanced at Alice's window and this time she smiled and made a slight movement with her hand that could have been a wave.

By the end of the week, against her better judgement, Alice was waving back and even dreading the end of the working day, once her favourite time, when the manager would go home leaving the office dark and empty.

When a Christmas card was put through her door, Alice had found out the woman's name was Jane. Alice thought the name suited her. Nevertheless the card disturbed her. It was too informal, presuming too much. Alice didn't want to place Jane in the midst of life and she couldn't afford to be placed there herself. She had stared at the card, trying to guess what Jane's second name might be. There must have been a letter of introduction when she took over from the dowdy man with dandruff shoulders and plastic shoes who had always behaved with Alice as if he doubted her. Alice had probably thrown the letter away unopened. She avoided the post. This propelled her into the admission that she knew nothing about Jane. Everything she knew she had made up. Alice didn't want to think of Jane having a life beyond the archway; beyond her control.

She had chucked the card in the bin.

Halfway through the morning Alice had found a reason to retrieve it. Just as she was about to toss her used tea bag away, she pretended to spot the card as if thrown there by someone else, propped against a crushed milk carton. She lifted it out and wiped it down with the dishcloth. Then she read the message properly:

'*Have a lovely Christmas with your daughter. Perhaps in the New Year we could meet for coffee in the office. I could come and fetch you, if you liked. Best wishes Jane.*'

Alice analysed the words. She appreciated the fact that Jane hadn't said 'my office' which would have put her off. She must know about the agoraphobia, but she was tactful. This disturbed Alice who tried so hard to be private. She decided not to reply. She would not go for coffee. There was always the chance that he had got to Jane. It made perfect sense as a first step. He would guess how to get to her.

One January morning Jane didn't turn up. After she had been absent four days, and just as Alice was weighing up the consequences of calling the head office of the housing association with a query about her rent, a postcard arrived from an island in Greece.

'*Taken the flu bug with me! But being ill in Athens beats being ill in Bermondsey! See you soon, all best Jane.*'

Alice had tucked the card into the frame of her pin board under the brochure for a new Chinese takeaway.

A week later on the morning when Alice had guessed that Jane would return to work her anticipation had reached a ringing pitch of visceral anxiety.

Chris had mixed feelings of relief and dismay when Alice wasn't at the window to wave her off, but stayed at her dressing table, laboriously applying make-up as if she did so every morning. As she saw her mother soften the blotches of blusher with upward flicks of face powder Chris had hung about seriously considering staying off school to look after her until Alice got annoyed and shooed her out.

Alice was at the window long before nine.

When Jane didn't appear, Alice began to worry that she had been wrong about the date. It was twenty past nine and the office remained shut with the blinds down. Alice grew angry, and abandoning caution she went away to find the number of head office. This meant she nearly missed her. She was carrying her briefcase under her arm, already getting her keys out of her coat pocket by the time Alice returned to the window with the telephone directory under her arm. Jane had a suntan. Alice dropped the book and in a burst of excitement was about to pull back the lace curtains and wave to her. She had unlocked the window in advance because today she had planned to pluck up the courage to lean out and suggest she came down to the office and accept Jane's offer of coffee. She couldn't let him rule her life. But as Alice took hold of the lace she had heard a distant tune: a crude snatch of Mozart playing on a child's toy. She let the curtain drop and getting well back out of sight checked the quadrangle. There was no one else there. Then

Jane fished into her bag and pulled out a mobile phone. Alice wasn't used to mobiles. She never had need of one. She had bought Chris one for security reasons, but had been annoyed when it became a way for people to bypass her when they communicated with her daughter. Few of Chris's friends called on the home telephone any more. Because of this Alice viewed mobile phones with antagonism. Her body had turned to sand as she saw Jane laughing and smiling, her head cocked to one side, wedging the handset on her shoulder while she opened the office door. She had not looked up at the window for Alice. The door swung shut behind her with a bang.

Later that morning Alice's own telephone had rung. Jane had invited her to coffee. Again she offered to fetch her. She did know about the agoraphobia, it was in Alice's tenant file. No, it wasn't common knowledge. Everything was on a 'need to know' basis. It was simply that Alice had been marked down as requiring help leaving the flat in case of fire. At first Alice had refused, she was still smarting from the phone incident, which she had taken as a personal slight. Then she had pulled herself together. Jane had sounded genuine. Her allusion to the housing association's confidentiality policy must mean Jane hadn't been talking about her. Perhaps she could trust her.

The estate office was only about twenty steps outside the flat. She told Jane she could manage the distance by herself, but made sure to sound sufficiently hesitant. She would check that the coast was clear beforehand so there was surely no risk.

After she replaced the receiver, Alice imagined Jane's rich, deep voice and reflected that talking to her had been easy; they might have known each other a long time.

After that the two women met in the office about twice a week. Alice hadn't told Chris. She couldn't think how to. She was ambivalent about a friendship with Jane. It was dangerous to get close to anyone. If she confessed to Chris about leaving the flat to see Jane it would commit her to continuing. At the moment she could stop at any time. If Chris knew, she would try to make Alice go out with her too and she might even guess that Alice wasn't agoraphobic at all.

When Alice read about what happened to Doctor Ramsay, Jane was the only person she had to talk to about it. But she must keep silent. If anything, his death confirmed that she had been right to keep her distance. In the end, because she was sure Jane would see something was wrong, Alice said her uncle had died, but that she hadn't seen him since she was eighteen; he lived in New Zealand so she wasn't grieving. Jane behaved, as she always did, with sensitivity and kindness. Then Alice worried that Jane would mention it to Chris who knew there was no uncle and would say so. So she had to tell Jane to keep quiet because Chris hated talking about death. It was getting complicated; Alice began to wish she had stayed in her living room.

Despite all the deception and fabrication, Alice was herself with Jane. After so many years, she had forgotten her real self.

So when Alice saw Jane outside the office a moment before she was about to step outside the flat, she was furious with herself. Only a few minutes longer upstairs and she would have been there if Jane had rung. She could have given herself an alibi, should she need one. She could have said she was ill and would be asleep all day and so would not answer the telephone. She ought to go back and call Jane now, but there wasn't time. Now Jane would be worried if she rang and got no answer. When she had made her meticulous plans Alice had not included Jane because she belonged in a different part of her life. Now it was too late.

Alice felt her way in semi-darkness down the last flight of steps to the basement and heaved open the back door. She was in a concreted area across which was slung a line of colourless washing. This sign of life took her by surprise. Someone might come out at any minute. Alice ran over to the door in the high wall she had seen from her bedroom; once upon a time it had run along the railway tracks but now it bordered an industrial park. She tugged desperately at the bolt. It was rusty and wouldn't budge. After hitting it several times, she shifted it and, rubbing her bruised palm, plunged into a filthy alley, littered with syringes, used condoms, beer cans and crisp bags and slippery with dog shit and vomit. The bolt had held the door shut so now she had to leave it ajar. She felt guilty – the washing might get stolen – then it dawned on her that this was her only way back as she couldn't use the front entrance. Alice had not planned her return journey. She had to hope the owner of the washing wouldn't notice.

The alley came out on the main road. Alice was blasted by the heat and the sound of traffic thundering down off the flyover on to the Old Kent Road. She shuddered at the engines roaring, gears grinding, coughs of exhaust, blaring horns; and shrank from the gigantic tyres of articulated lorries that could crush a life in moments and missed her by inches. She retreated to a convenience store with windows protected by metal grills. The shop had been a general store when she was last on the street years before. Then its produce had been displayed in abundance on the pavement, with more goods on show easily visible through the gleaming glass. Now piles of packets and tins bricked up the windows that were in turn behind the grill so she couldn't see inside the shop. Alice nearly gave up and longed to scuttle back to the sanctuary of what now seemed like home. Maybe after staying indoors for so long she actually did have agoraphobia. She sat down on a yellow plastic grit bin to get her breath. The words *Another day in Paradise* had been sprayed through a template several times on its side partially hiding the manufacturer's name and telephone number. *-inaware 01273 622*. Shading her eyes, she could see the archway to the flats a few yards down the street and was overwhelmed with exhilaration that at last she was on this side of it. She was free.

Although she had lied about her health, there had been a genuine reason for staying in the flat. Alice began to imagine that just possibly today's expedition might mark a change to her life. Today might let her draw a line under her stolen past.

With renewed determination Alice stepped out into the road, and flagged down a taxi to take her to Victoria station. As she slid into the corner of the cab, out of sight of the driver's mirror, the years Alice had had to bury began to surface and she remembered what was special about the 28th June.

Today was Eleanor Ramsay's fortieth birthday.

Nineteen

Kathleen had been disappointed not to get an invitation to Doctor Ramsay's funeral, but was not surprised. The only Ramsay likely to think of her was Mark Ramsay himself. Although only family and close friends were allowed to attend the service, Iris had said that most of Charbury would turn out to watch the cortège and see him buried. Kathleen was sure there would be no harm in going up to the church to pay her respects.

She was the first to arrive at the churchyard, having left her cottage an hour early to be sure of getting somewhere to sit. She found a bench about thirty yards from the gravesite. From here she could see the whole length of the path up to the church but she would not be conspicuous. Iris had also informed her that the hearse would start from the White House and go at walking pace along the main street as it had for the old Judge and every Ramsay before him. Iris had shooed her two Persian cats out to the back of the shop and bustled around the counter to confide in Kathleen's ear that Isabel Ramsay had been keen to avoid fuss; rumour had it that she had wanted a cremation, but she couldn't argue with Ramsay tradition. Iris had been strident in her defence of Doctor Ramsay's right to a proper send off, but Kathleen privately felt sorry for Isabel. She too knew that Mark Ramsay would not have wanted so much bother. When Steve died, her sister had organised his funeral. Kathleen had not known where to begin and had even considered going away until it was all over, while knowing that such an idea was impossible.

The organist was practising scales, which made Kathleen anxious; he was cutting it fine if he wasn't perfect by now. She didn't want Isabel to be offended by a wrong note; today would be hard enough for her. Kathleen was also uncomfortable with the position of the bench she had chosen. Perhaps after all it was too prominent. She didn't want the Ramsays to think she was drawing attention to their omission of her name from the guest list. The day was heating up and, unlike the other seats, this one wasn't in the shade. But the other benches would give her no view at all, so there was no choice but to stay here.

Then more people began to drift into the graveyard and soon Kathleen was less obvious. The ones who had invitations held them conspicuously and took up sentry positions around the church door entrance, their expressions stern and distant. She didn't recognise any of them and guessed they were friends and colleagues from Doctor Ramsay's London life; the women in discreet black hats, the men in funeral suits that didn't look hired or years out of date. This group showed no interest in their surroundings and, seeming to Kathleen cold and aloof, struck her as the opposite to Doctor Ramsay. If he had been here, he would have made everyone talk to each other regardless of who they were. But of course if he were here then no one else would be.

There were many people who Kathleen didn't know. Whole families, making a day of it, milled up the path through the lych gate, while locals used the side entrance. A gang of youths tumbled over the wall at the back, initially laughing and joking. Then they were quiet as they formed a tight bunch on a rise near the old rowan tree, cowed by the gravestones, the sonorous tones of the organ and the sombre dress of the gathering crowd. Then she saw them; the kind who wrote her long rambling letters supposedly to help but really as cries for help. They were the pilgrims come to be healed by the kind doctor who even in death could provide solace. Men and women, their movements erratic, some clutching carrier bags, some dressed in dark corduroy jackets or trousers, worn overcoats and puffa jackets inappropriate for summer.

Kathleen reflected that in their own way they would be genuine mourners.

Of course there were the reporters, behaving with self-conscious discretion, some laden with recording machines, others wielding cameras with long lenses. Kathleen prayed without hope that no one would recognise her. She could not talk about Doctor Ramsay, today of all days. A group of middle-aged men, who looked like councillors and bank managers, stood to attention under the yew trees, shuffling their feet, with their hands behind their backs. While other people, mostly women, had settled on the grass or had perched on larger tombstones, making a show of brushing off invisible leaves before lowering themselves with exaggerated care. Everyone kept a respectful distance. Soon Kathleen reckoned there were over a hundred and fifty people.

Then over the cemetery wall she saw movement far up the lane. A black hearse followed by five limousines and a straggle of cars had appeared from over the rise and was passing the village shop and her cottage before processing down the hill towards them. It was escorted on foot by Harry Norton in a top hat, the funeral director who had been one of Steve's coffin bearers. Both Harry and the tall car behind him appeared to shimmer and warp in the heat, making the sombre procession look ethereal. For what seemed like an age, the cortège seemed to get no nearer and Harry was pacing on a giant grey conveyor belt that moved in the opposite direction to the steady pace of his black boots. Then the hearse was outside the church gates.

It was greeted by an uncanny hush. No one spoke or moved. Kathleen's right hand began to tremble violently and she stilled it with her other. Her drugs were wearing off with the upset of it all. Luckily she had thought to bring a container of water with an emergency tablet already dissolved and, trying to make no noise, she fumbled for it in her bag. It nearly spilt as she unscrewed the top with ineffectual fingers. Finally she managed to swig the medicine down, dabbing the crumbly white sediment from her lips with her hanky. She mustn't spoil things by being ill.

For a moment the ceremony was halted as the guests climbed out of the cars and assembled into line, hanging back for the family who had not yet emerged from the first limousine. The eerie quiet was interrupted by just the odd cough, or the clearing of a throat, thumps of car doors closing and the crunch of leather shoes on the shingle path. Kathleen did not take her eyes off the coffin. It was majestic and like Doctor Ramsay, beyond question. Mark Ramsay had been a tall man, an athlete in his youth, so she had expected it to be large, but it was very big indeed. She felt a flash of love for the man who had been so good to her daughter, so good to her, and who she would genuinely miss.

In the face of this loss, Kathleen found it mild compensation to see that Lucian was so like his father. The clock was wound back thirty years as she studied the strapping, dark haired man walking behind his father's coffin with Isabel Ramsay on his arm. Isabel was smaller than Kathleen remembered, and moved stiffly. Kathleen felt no satisfaction at seeing that she was not the only person ageing. Then she recalled Iris describing how Mrs Ramsay had bruised her leg trying to rescue Mark Ramsay from his car. It was at least a year since Kathleen had last seen Isabel, who seldom came into the village.

Gina Ramsay looked beautiful. Kathleen had a soft spot for Gina because she had been Alice's favourite, although Kathleen had been drawn to Eleanor who had such a lovely nature. Iris had said Gina had taken her father's death very badly.

'She cried like a baby, I heard. It's her that's organised it all. Just goes to show, it doesn't matter what age you are, when your Dad goes, or your Mum, it hurts as if you was a little girl again.' Then Iris had stopped and floundered around for another subject. Kathleen had got used to people's dismay at uttering anything that hinted at Alice. They did not realise that for Kathleen, everything was to do with Alice.

As the Ramsays filed into the church under the shadow of the porch, Kathleen was consoled once again by thinking that Alice had not had to mourn her parents. Her child had been saved that pain.

But unlike Doctor Ramsay, there had been no funeral for Alice.

Steve had stopped believing in God after Alice went, but Kathleen had found excuses for God's actions and looked harder than ever for the good in everything and everyone. Doctor Ramsay's quiet kindnesses had shored up her faltering faith. Kathleen shut her eyes and relaxed as the warm sun played gently on her stiffened features, willing the dopamine to give her back some life and, with it, hope. The doors and windows of the church were open and as the service began, the mourners outside were able to hear the service:

I am the resurrection and the life, saith the Lord;
he that believeth in me, though he were dead,
yet shall he live;
and whosoever liveth and believeth in me shall
never die.

It was only when the Ramsay family was trooping out of the graveyard, after the coffin had been lowered into the ground, that Kathleen caught sight of Eleanor about ten yards away. Eleanor was looking right at her. She must have been watching her for some time. Kathleen hoped she hadn't appeared to ignore her and been assumed rude. Her Parkinson's could make her seem distant, as her face refused to smile, or words were uttered with sharpness in her determined effort to get them out. Now Kathleen struggled to her feet buoyed up at the prospect of speaking to Eleanor. But by the time she felt steady enough to walk, Eleanor had gone. She must want to be alone. Kathleen didn't feel offended by this; she expected that for all the Ramsays she was the last person they wanted to see. That was why they hadn't asked her to the funeral. When Alice vanished it had been awful for the Ramsays too.

'Hello Mrs Howland.' The voice made her jump.

She would have known him anywhere, although he had filled out and looked like he drank too much, but perhaps he was just the outdoors type.

'Chief Inspector Hall.'

She couldn't think what to say. She wasn't pleased to see him.

'Rick, please.' He took her hand in both of his like an old friend. 'I wondered if you'd come.' Then he too had nothing to say. The words: Have you found my daughter yet? hung between them. He let go of her hand.

'Have you spoken to the family?' Kathleen hoped he had left them alone.

'Only a nod to Mrs Ramsay. Not sure she recognised me, but there we are...' For a fleeting moment he looked disapproving, reminding Kathleen of the reason she hadn't liked him. He had not been nice about Eleanor when she was a little girl, once comparing her unfavourably with Alice, assuming it would please her. He would have gone further if she had encouraged him, but she had stopped him. Kathleen said nothing as he stepped away from her and let himself be carried along with the queue of people heading for the lane.

It was then she saw her.

Kathleen lurched forward, her hand fluttered towards the back of the bench to catch herself. She missed it and toppled against a man and a woman cutting across the grassy plots to the path. The woman caught her by the arm and held on to her. She looked impatient but when she spoke her voice was concerned as she asked Kathleen if she was all right. Recovering, Kathleen tried to laugh it off, but her mouth wouldn't move and her reply was incoherent. The couple helped her around to the front of the seat and stood over her as she sank down. Kathleen was so distracted that it was all she could do to be polite to them. They were in the way. She needed to get to her and they were blocking her view. She summoned up all her energy to urge them to leave her. Eventually she convinced them that she was fine and with thinly disguised relief they went.

The sunlight was so strong it was hard to make anything out in the glare. Kathleen scoured the churchyard. She was still there. She was standing on her own by the church wall bending over to read an inscription on one of the headstones behind the buttress. Her hair fell forward across her face the way it had when she had first spotted her. It was why it took a while to recognise her. She stood out from the other women because she was wearing trousers. Kathleen kept her eyes on her as she shakily made her way over the clumpy ground, between the graves, her fingers brushing worn limestone and cool marble for balance as every step brought her closer. This time she wouldn't let anything distract her. Kathleen's progress was painfully slow and she dreaded losing her because she had to keep checking where she put her feet for fear of tripping. Any minute she would mingle with the crowd and vanish for a second time. There was nothing Kathleen could do to stop her, she couldn't risk drawing attention to either of them by waving.

She had tipped her sunglasses up on to the top of her head as she examined the worn lettering on the headstone and didn't look up as Kathleen approached, her shoes catching slightly on the gravel.

'Hello.' Kathleen was surprised at the strength in her voice.

The woman stared at her.

'It is you, isn't it?' It wasn't a question, Kathleen was certain. The last time she had seen her was in black and white, but it had been enough to know for sure.

'Mrs Howland.' She avoided looking at Kathleen.

'Oh, don't call me that. It's Kath, please.'

Kathleen took a couple of steps nearer and then she could see her properly. A fine mesh had been thrown over her face making it puckered and lined. There were dark bags under her eyes and tiny red marks flecked her grainy cheeks, which sagged, softening her jaw line. Thick grooves on each side of her mouth appeared to pull it down at the corners despite her efforts at a bright smile that did not extend to her eyes. Her blonde hair was dry and brittle and dark at the roots.

Jackie Masters must be about fifty-five, but she looked older. 'How are you, love?' Kathleen touched Jackie's sleeve.

'I shouldn't have come. But I couldn't resist...' Jackie abruptly adjusted her glasses back over her eyes and retreated a couple of steps towards the gate. Kathleen gave a slight nod.

'I'm sure he would have been glad.' If only the dead could know how much they were cared for in life. Kathleen started to tell her about Doctor Ramsay's CCTV film but Jackie interrupted:

'Oh, I didn't...' Jackie tailed off suddenly curt. 'Actually, I'm in a tearing hurry as always.'

Just as Jackie raised a peremptory hand in farewell, she hesitated and Kathleen was looking at the young woman who she had last seen in her kitchen three decades earlier, fussing with a dishcloth over the draining board. Jackie relented and said:

'I'll ring.'

This time Kathleen knew enough to understand that Jackie would never ring. But now she didn't need her to. It was a chapter closed. What she had seen in the film was none of her business.

Kathleen turned to the gravestone Jackie had been reading. There was nothing special about it. A man called Leonard had died aged eighty-one, two years after Alice had gone missing. The inscription read that he was reunited with his wife who had 'fallen asleep' over forty years before him. The name rang a bell, but as with so many things, Kathleen couldn't place it.

She was tired and could do with falling asleep herself. She leaned against the warm buttress and waited until everyone had left and she was alone, listening once more to the organist, and shutting her eyes to better hear the bell tolling for the doctor. Then before her drugs wore off and her feet already beginning to stick to the ground, she made her way out to the lane.

If Kathleen had trusted her balance enough to turn round and look behind her, she would have seen an inconspicuous figure in dark clothes climbing over the low wall under the oak tree, and then keeping their head down, make off across the triangular field towards the station.

Twenty

Eventually, far off in the future, Chris would come to think of Tuesday 29th June as the start of her new life. But most of the day had been the same as any other. The only difference was that she had to go home on foot because two cars had collided under the Eurostar Bridge at Waterloo and traffic was snarled up right to the Old Kent Road. She had jogged most of the way, passing eight stationary buses as she raced along. Carbon monoxide fumes made her eyes smart and every few paces she slapped dribbles of sweat from her cheeks and forehead. She invented tricks and games with herself to ward off the distance, dividing the route into gaps between lampposts and the numbers of idling cars as she dodged between them. She promised herself the manageable target of 'just to that office furniture shop', 'only around this bend' and 'seven steps times three into the subway and up again'. At last she reached the archway to the flats, spurred on by the promise of an imminent cold shower.

As Chris unlocked the door, the cool passageway was almost reviving and for once she didn't bemoan the lack of light in the flat. She faintly registered the ease with which the door opened. There was no draught excluder.

'I'm back!' She swung her bag on to her bed and had the usual brief inner tussle: bathroom or living room. Pushing back a sweat-soaked fringe Chris went to her mother.

The living room was empty.

Chris frowned at the armchair and clasped her hands in quelled disappointment. Alice must be ill. She hurried down the passage and paused outside her Mum's door. No sound as she turned the handle.

She gasped.

The curtains were tied back and the window was open. This in itself was extraordinary; her Mum kept her bedroom window shut, disturbed by any noise, with the curtains closed because the view of the storage units depressed her. When Chris was small, there had been a disused goods station on what had been a railway line from London to Dover. Chris could just remember how the orange-pink of the setting sun picked out the castellated roof canopy, and how she had imagined making up a bunch from the wild flowers widening the cracks on the deserted platforms.

Her Mum had said it reminded her of a place she had once been to when she was a child, but the way she told it made Chris think it was one of her made-up stories. They had sat at her dressing table imagining the trains waiting at the platforms. Sometimes her Mum would press a finger to Chris's lips and, cosy conspirators, they would pretend to hear the sneezing of a far off steam engine.

Then the station was pulled down. They couldn't bear to watch as the great stone ball pendulumed into the sides, and slabs of wall tumbled away from twisting metal supports in huge clouds of dust. Soon in its place there was a warehouse of corrugated aluminium that gave the bedrooms a thin, insistent light. The silver cladding with its featureless surface had no magic to offer. Now, as Chris scanned the stunted view, somewhere on the industrial estate beyond the warehouse she could hear voices. Men were shouting to each other, a lone instruction reaching her above the scrambled sound of a distant transistor radio:

'...find the hole, and pump it with mastic...'

Her Mum's bed was unmade, a corner of the duvet flung back; she must have got up in a hurry. Chris became aware of the bedside clock ticking and heard a quick succession of car horns from the street on the other side of the building.

There was no sign of her Mum.

Although she knew she was alone, Chris checked every room, banging doors open and shut, kicking up the mats as she stormed up and down the passage in rising distress. Now she was looking for a note, a clue, any sign. If her Mum had got ill surely someone would have tried to call her, at the school, on her mobile? Why hadn't a neighbour appeared at the front door to tell her? Chris dashed back to her bedroom, and shook her bag until everything was on the floor. She checked her mobile. The battery was charged. There were no missed calls, no messages.

Chris gravitated back to her Mum's bedroom. With her hands on her hips, she took stock as she willed the room to yield an explanation. The objects around her had acquired a vibrancy emphasising the emptiness. Alice's procession of Russian pottery animals on the dressing table mocked Chris. The tortoise was in the lead, speaking for her Mum's belief in the strength of the apparently least able. The glass fronted box holding a tableau depicting a sea-battered groyne with a seagull stuck on the third strut and string coiled around the base of the second, was testimony to her Mum's model making abilities. She had made it for Chris ten years earlier, and it had returned to her, not so much rejected as reclaimed. This was flanked by a London bus commemorating the Silver Jubilee, a red paint-chipped Citroën DS 19, and a 1930s model of the Eiffel Tower. Chris lifted up the mouse-size, furry cat dressed in knitted pantaloons and sniffed it. Her Mum.

Never before had Chris come home to an empty flat. Her Mum was scared of the traffic, and of crowds. She had once said she was terrified of the height of the sky. She hadn't been out for years. Now, when her Mum had needed Chris's help, she wasn't there for her. Chris slid to the floor, still holding the cat to her nose. She leaned against her Mum's bed and stared at the wall, following the meandering line of a crease in the wallpaper until it petered out halfway up.

She should call the police and the local hospitals, but this was too drastic, it would make all the fear-pricking possibilities real. What did she and her Mum have to do with police? The reassuring familiarity of the bedroom had to be proof that things were normal? What did this peaceful room, with its picture by Wintz, of a village street leading to the sea, have to do with an intensive care unit, or worse, the hygienic silence of a morgue? Chris knelt over the bed and buried her face in the cotton. After a few minutes she slipped her hand under the pillow, groping for respite from her mounting dread in her Mum's bedding.

Mum!

Where are you?

Chris realised that all her life she had known this moment would come. Sometimes she had wished for it to happen. To come home and find her Mum gone and herself released. Even in sleep, the idea was there, in the repeated images of rooms without doors. She burrowed into the bed clawing in anguish and atonement. The pillow smelt of the cream her Mum used and faintly, her perfume, so familiar it made her stomach uncoil.

There was something under the pillow.

Chris pulled out a padded envelope. It was addressed to herself, which made no sense. Then she recognised it as the envelope that had come with the copy of *To the Lighthouse* she had ordered off the internet a couple of weeks ago on the recommendation of her English teacher. Her Mum must have got it out of the dustbin. Her bloody mother was always in her wake, righting and retrieving things, getting her own way.

Not always.

Inside was a wad of cuttings. Chris saw they were from the newspapers her mother had recently asked her to buy. A creeping foreboding came over her. The stories were all about the Parkinson's Disease specialist who had killed himself. She felt a clutch of terror and her insides became sand. Her mother was ill. She was at the hospital.

She was already dead.

Chris sat down on her Mum's bed. Something stuck to her palm. She peeled it off. It was a return ticket to a place called Charbury, dated yesterday. The words meant nothing. It had been clipped. Chris tried to think of anything her Mum had done recently that might show that she was ill. She knew nothing about Parkinson's Disease.

She became a ruthless detective, as she speed-read through the articles, some nine or ten in all once she had unfolded them. She went back to her bedroom and got a pen and notepad. She worked quickly to subdue her panic. Chris had always taken refuge in her work. Her talent for meticulous research and examination of the most insignificant clues would one day soon bear unwelcome fruit. Now she recorded the names that came up most often, although she didn't think them important as proof her mother had something seriously wrong with her. At this point she dare leave nothing out.

Mark Ramsay, Isabel Ramsay, Jon Cross, Gina Cross...

Then she reached a cutting about a little girl who went missing in June 1968 and had never been found. Much later Chris described this moment as an epiphany. It seemed that time stopped still, there were no more noises outside, and the text before her eyes was subordinate to the pictures it conveyed to her. She heard her mother's story-telling voice as she read:

The missing girl's name was Alice, and if she had lived she would have been forty on the 25th of March 1999. This year. But one afternoon in June 1968 she had disappeared while playing hide and seek with a friend and had not been seen since. The article said that nowadays DNA would probably solve the thirty-year-old mystery, but no body had ever been found. Apart from a tramp who had been seen in the vicinity and was found drowned in the River Ouse a few days later, there had been no solid leads. Now it was a cold case.

Chris had made her mother's card, using magazines, cutting up old birthday and Christmas cards, bits of newspaper and packaging to create a collage based around the numbers of her age. Alice had never liked celebrating her birthday, so she had been especially sulky about forty. Her birthday was on the 25th of March.

Chris didn't hear the front door so she was nearly sick with shock when a voice called out 'Goodbye' to someone outside on the landing.

It was her mother.

Chris sprang to life. She shovelled the papers back into the envelope, tearing some, creasing others then pushed it back under the pillow. As she was getting up off the bed, her foot catching in the duvet and ripping the material, she saw the train ticket on the carpet. She slipped it into her jeans pocket just as Alice shut the door and crossed the hall to Chris's bedroom. Chris beat out the indentation where she had been sitting, and forgetting the original unkempt bed, straightened the duvet. She leapt to the door. An expression of agitation can easily be translated into concern.

'Where have you been? I've been really worried.' It sounded like a lie.

'I went down to the estate office!'

Alice made only a hollow attempt to express her sense of achievement about a phobia miraculously vanquished. Rendered cunning and so playing for time, Chris was determined to show no surprise. Alice would expect her to believe anything she told her, and clearly didn't think she needed to make an effort. Now that she was watchful, Chris could tell the excuse was feeble, her Mum's manner too relaxed.

Chris had been robbed of the life she had taken for granted only fifteen minutes earlier. Already the existence in which Alice's announcement would have made Chris euphoric was a foreign land. Now she didn't have any connection with the new Alice in the hallway confidently clinking door keys she had supposedly never used before and smiling like a mental patient.

Alice kicked the door shut behind her, oblivious of the bang. Chris felt no happiness at this joyful new being; lost and found. She was winded by a treachery without precedent. Yet her mind was busy and already a plan was forming. Until that moment, she hadn't known what it was to truly hate someone.

Twenty-One

C hris walked round the side of the station and set off down the lane in the direction signposted to Charbury. She was the only person in the street. The absolute stillness was unsettling. She was further perturbed to find the village was oddly familiar. She knew it in the way she remembered places during dreams, with no association, just a tremulous familiarity. This must be because of the pictures in the newspaper articles she had found yesterday.

The lane was lined on both sides by detached cottages or larger houses, behind manicured gardens some fronted by neat hedges, or low whitewashed walls. Chris stopped by the steps of one house to examine a selection of blue plastic strawberry punnets and milk crates in which were jumbled weird looking vegetables, oversized cucumbers, misshapen potatoes. A pint mug had a label stuck on it offering 'flowers for fifty pence'. These must have sold out, for now there were no flowers and the glass was filled with nasty brown water. A felt-penned notice next to an empty tray for duck eggs read 'Egg Boxes Are Welcome'. Chris wondered dubiously whether this welcome would be extended to long-lost relatives. She regretted her spontaneous decision to find Kathleen Howland and tell her that her daughter was alive and living under an assumed name in London. It had initially been prompted by the desire to punish Alice. Now she was ashamed of this; she should have been thinking what it was like to be Kathleen, scared all these years that her daughter had been murdered.

Now that she was in Charbury Chris didn't feel equal to the task she had set herself.

At several points in her journey she had considered turning back, overcome by the violence of her mood, the temerity of her idea; everything. But then she had contemplated the prospect of going back to Alice and behaving as if everything was normal, and this was even worse. Her mother had left her with no choice. There was no one else to talk to. Chris was more cut off from her friends for she couldn't tell them any of this. Her mother had always said action spoke louder than words. So now she was taking action that would speak bloody loud. She was capable of anything; she would put everything right.

The village could not have changed much since Alice's childhood; there were few signs of the twentieth century. Gaping stone faces above doorways, the diamond patterns in the brickwork were like the deepest patterns of life, Chris knew them without words; they were within her. This must be *déjà vu*. Chris halted in the middle of the road.

She had been here with Alice.

Until she found the cuttings, Chris had paid scant attention to the story about the professor. She had always been unforgiving about suicide, arguing with her friends that it was a cruel thing to do to people you loved. She had shouted at Emma for saying it was fair enough if you were very unhappy. Chris had been unable to confess to Emma her morbid fear of coming home to her Mum's body suspended from the drying rack pulley wheel over the bath. She would have been horrified to know that her friends had guessed as much.

As the train left London, Chris had peered out of the railway carriage's dirty windows at a shantytown of car breaker and rolling stock yards, disused offices and factories with broken windows. Even the flourishing bursts of buddleia growing between the buildings were unnatural and ugly. The Escher-tangle of viaducts and bridges, the boarded-up arches, some patched with corrugated iron, reminded Chris of the constructions she had made as a child, piling on extensions, roofing in enclosures with coasters, playing cards, and bits

215

of cereal packet to make a warren that covered the carpet. Lying on her front, Chris would peep inside, longing to enter these labyrinths. Then it was bedtime and she was never allowed to keep them and would have to dismantle them and tidy everything away. On the train it occurred to Chris that grownups were no different, their buildings were haphazard, created without care, extensions added at random with no concern for design or beauty and then left neglected and forgotten. They were not told to clear them away before bedtime. Maybe that was the thing about growing up, you could create whatever mess you liked.

Her journey to Victoria station had been jaundiced with crazed examples of humanity. All the commuters were paltry and mean, raddled and reptilian, clammy and lantern-jawed. She could see why Alice wouldn't go out.

Except it wasn't true, Alice had been out of the flat many times. She had gone to the man's funeral the day before yesterday, the train ticket proved that. Chris had been scared of how murderous she felt. Yet underneath still, like an Achilles heel, was the insidious threat to this new will power: Chris could not help speculating wistfully about what her Mum might be doing at that moment, sitting by herself in the living room, spying on the neighbours in the windows of the other flats and making up lives for them because she didn't have one of her own.

The train had rumbled above ragged strips of back gardens, many devoured by geometric conservatories with matching patios and dotted with primary coloured children's slides and swings, others by piles of tyres and rusting shapes heaped amidst a confetti of litter. Shaking off the city's suburbia – a mishmash of less coveted Victorian housing, and new-build cul-de-sacs – the train had left London behind. At last clattering out of the tunnel that cut through the South Downs, her carriage had been flooded with sunlight as it raced through lush green pastures, alongside a river lit by dancing darts of light.

Chris had jumped down on to the platform into a place where nothing had been left to chance or erected with cold pragmatism. She was incredulous to see immaculate hanging baskets and octagonal tubs on a station platform.

She had been the only person to get off at Charbury and there was no ticket collector. She had faltered yet again as the train receded to a flat shape and vanished under the bridge, leaving her with an unremitting click replacing the clunkety-clunk of the carriages. The clicking had grown louder as she became aware of it, hesitating and entirely bereft on the deserted platform in the baking heat. For a ridiculous moment Chris had assumed it was her heartbeat. Two enormous digital clocks hung from the canopies. The time on both was identical and completely wrong: ten past eleven when it had been nearly one. Nothing was as it seemed or as it should be.

As she had paused outside the shuttered booking office unconsciously seeking some small interaction, it dawned on Chris that Alice would never have killed herself. All along she had only been concerned with concealment. Chris had to reassess every part of her life. Alice was not agoraphobic; she didn't go out because she was hiding. Her parents had not been killed in a car crash on the Great West Road in Chiswick. It made a joke out of Chris's conviction, while peeping through the wrought iron gates of the brewery, that her grandparents were present. There had never been anyone who loved her keeping watch over her. All the time Alice's real mother was living in a cottage miles away in some village and her Dad had died only eight years ago, thinking his daughter was dead and never knowing he had a grand-daughter who would have loved him.

For some insane reason, Alice had fooled everyone.

Chris was crushed by the weight of the pretend years, she was overwhelmed by layers of fake memory, made-up names and made-up places. Her past was quicksand into which solid events like birthdays and Christmas, happy stories of her Mum's early childhood, of her own childhood and every cherished assumption had sunk without trace. She couldn't even trust her own experience. As the fables that had moulded her were swallowed in eternal stasis, Chris was a blank page. The terrible enormity of Alice's deception and its far, far-reaching repercussions had made it impossible for Chris to be near Alice. It was a deception beyond her imaginings. Now she knew that there were more chilling ways of absenting yourself from those who love you than committing suicide.

A young woman who survived by taking action, Chris was doing the only thing open to her. She would find Alice's mother and put everything straight.

At Lewes where she had changed trains, Chris had bought a map covering Newhaven to Eastbourne, but now saw she wouldn't need it. It would be easy to find Alice's cottage. She could already see the church spire with its perky cockerel weathervane, over grey slate rooftops and a clump of silvery, green trees at the bend in the road. Halfway down the lane she spotted a sign attached to a lamp-post for the post office and church. Nothing was left to chance. She had noted down that the cottage was next to the post office from a newspaper interview with Kathleen Howland. There was a big chance that Mrs Howland wouldn't be in, the article had described how she went out regularly searching for her missing daughter. Over the years she had been to all the cities in Britain, sticking posters to tree trunks and on to walls and lamp-posts, getting them displayed in shop windows, and tirelessly handing them to shoppers in malls and high streets up and down the country.

Missing. Can you help?

Chris recalled the words with mounting anger. Alice could have helped.

Mrs Howland had scoured districts in London, ridden the Circle line in both directions, even struck up conversation with beggars in the streets. The reporter had hinted that her searching was indiscriminate, driven by Mrs Howland's certainty, *'call it a mother's instinct'* that Alice was alive. She would not rest until she found her. It was clear to Chris that the man who had written the story thought Alice Howland was dead and Mrs Howland in need of medical help.

Alice was not dead.

An *Evening Argus* headline outside the village stores declared *'Death Crash: Car was Flying'*. There were more flowering tubs outside the shop, Chris was hemmed in by flowers, fresh and sweet smelling. She had never seen so much trouble taken in a street before. She crossed the road and went up to the shop window. Now that she was here, she was cowed by what she was about to do and keen to put off arriving. It had been the hardest thing Chris had ever achieved, to smile, to help with tea, and to appear to share in Alice's supposed triumph in leaving the flat for the first time in at least ten years. It was only later in bed, her body thrilling with inchoate fury at her Mum's betrayal, that Chris reached her decision. Indeed it was less of a decision than a viciously inspired impulse for revenge.

Now Chris was the one who knew the facts. Now she knew more than Alice. Except that once she was here in the village where Alice had lived, she was overawed by the mundane actuality of the deserted lane, the tidy cottages and of Charbury Stores with its adverts for first day covers and a jaunty poster for the summer fête. Chris pressed her nose to the glass to read the postcards slotted in a plastic holder dangling from a rubber sucker. The items advertised were eclectic and eccentric: a motorised mobility buggy with waterproof shopping basket for £900, hardly used; piano lessons at £10 per half hour; domestic help required for six and a half hours at £40 plus travel expenses; purple bunk beds hardly used.

An elderly woman with a florid complexion emphasised by her sixties-style make-up, tightly clad in a bright blue overall, bustled out of the shop and shut the door behind her making the bell inside jangle discordantly. She stopped in surprise when she saw Chris:

'Oooh! Did you want something, dear? Post office counter's shut, but anything else?'

'No, that is…'

'Only I'm closing for lunch. Back in an hour, but if you're quick…'

Chris cast around for something trivial to explain her presence. Whatever she came up with would inconvenience the postmistress who was moving away from the door. All Chris could think of were the bunk beds.

'I'm fine, thank you. Just looking.' The cliché fitted her new counterfeit self.

The woman appeared satisfied and muttering words that sounded to Chris like *'two Russians flats'* vanished around the corner of the building. Chris put her hands to her cheeks. She had so nearly given herself away. One of the articles had said that since Alice Howland had disappeared, the village had been 'overrun' by the media and sightseers, many with teddy bears and other stuffed animals, on anniversaries, on Alice's birthday, when Mr Howland had died; or when another child went missing. So the villagers were less friendly to outsiders, they no longer welcomed them as allies in the search for Alice. They guarded their privacy, and were frustrated by invasions from as far away as America and Australia.

Would Mrs Howland guess her connection to Alice? Chris knew she looked like Alice. She had been proud of this when she was little; with no other family, at least she belonged with her Mum. When she became a teenager the idea had horrified her. Did she too have that grim expression and do that stupid thing with her mouth when she was thinking? Did she roll a sweet wrapper into a tight ball between two praying mantis hands? Chris wanted to break the news to Kathleen in her own time and not have her uncanny resemblance to the missing girl do it for her. Although she was twice the age that Alice had been when she went missing, still Mrs Howland might see her little daughter in her. Chris was the only person who knew Alice's hair had darkened and was cut into a short bob that didn't suit her. She was the only person who knew that Alice was smaller than might have been expected, since one of the articles had said she was tall for her age. Chris was the only person who knew what Alice looked like now.

She sensed a holding of breath in the air and glanced up and down the lane. It was lunchtime in the middle of the week, which could explain why there was no one around. Few cars were parked, which added to the timeless impression. An old motor scooter by the kerb was padlocked to a bucket of set concrete. So they did expect some crime here.

Apart from Charbury Stores there were only houses on this stretch of the lane. Chris knew from the map that the road went past the church. It was a village, but she would have expected to see at least one person driving or perhaps walking from the station. Chris began to suspect she was being observed, but all the windows were blank. She thought of Alice behind her lace curtains but the image had no substance. She didn't know Alice, so she couldn't imagine her.

Still feigning interest in the cards in the post office window, Chris turned furtively to look at the cottage next door. It was a compact little house on two levels with sash windows, one up, one down, to the right of the front door. There was yet another hanging basket outside the door, but this one was full of dead stuff, pale withered fronds fringing the rim, the chain rusting. In contrast, the privet hedge was trimmed so neatly that individual leaves were not apparent. As this blended in with the one next door, Chris guessed the neighbours had lumped it in with theirs. The cottage was at the end of a terrace of four. Chris remembered from her notes that they had been workers' houses, part of an estate owned in the nineteenth century by the Ramsay family, and now almost all of them sold off. All the doors were painted green. Chris had read that the Ramsays still owned a large house just outside the village, with about ten acres of the original land. She had also read that the friend Alice had been playing with that afternoon was called Eleanor Ramsay, and was the youngest daughter of the dead professor.

Chris panicked. She didn't have a number. This might be the wrong house. It might be the one at the other end of the terrace, or it might be none of them. She had trusted her memory, reluctant to write too much down in case Alice caught her. She shut her eyes. The house in the picture had been to the right of the shop.

It was a hot summer's day in 1968 and Chris was Alice hurrying home from her brilliant game of hide and seek, tired, contented and ready for tea. As she pushed open the warped, wooden gate and tried unsuccessfully to latch it back, she imagined skipping up to the front door, or up the side path to go in through the kitchen as she had read Alice usually did. She could call out: 'I'm back!' to her Mum and Dad. Chris had scribbled down that Alice's Dad had died of a broken heart, which was a bit far-fetched. Chris didn't know what having a father was like. She doubted Gary would die of a broken heart, or that he even had one. Her mother had said she didn't know much about him, just as she had hardly known her own father. As if the fact that she had done without a Dad meant that Chris should do so too without complaining. Alice's deprivations always had to be greater than her daughter's. When Chris questioned her about the man who had got her pregnant, Alice would shrug her shoulders and explain it away: the sex with different men, drunk at parties, a bathroom floor, a bed piled with coats. What's in a name? The main thing was she had been happy at the time. So Chris could be happy too. Besides she had been young, it was easy to make mistakes when you were too young to know better.

Everyone made mistakes.

Chris would stop her Mum, furious at Alice's stupidity for letting facts escape, and not bothering to find out more about the man who she had known for about an hour at a party, but who Chris would not know for the rest of her life. At eighteen Chris already knew better. Now it occurred to her that perhaps the man on the bathroom floor was made up too. After all why had Alice disappeared when she was nine? What had she been doing all those years? Who was she hiding from? Chris was dizzy with questions. There was too much she was scared to know.

The scrap of grass in front of the house had dried yellow. Weeds had forced their way between the terracotta bricks on the path and around a cracked pot of woody lavender and thistles. The paint on the front door and on the soffits under the eaves was peeling and there were tiles missing from the roof. Alice could have kept it looking lovely if she had cared to. As Chris hesitated before lifting the doorknocker she was surprised that a house in Charbury was allowed to be so neglected; the locals must disapprove. She supposed Mrs Howland was excused.

Chris gave two tentative taps, she would go home if there was no reply. She was sure now there wouldn't be. The house showed no sign of life. As she waited, flicking back her hair, and very nervous, switching her bag to her other shoulder, she hoped Mrs Howland was out.

From inside the house came a muffled ringing, Chris became nervous as the ringing grew louder and louder. The sound came from her bag. She rummaged furiously in every compartment before finding her mobile in the outside pocket.

'Chris, is that you?' Her mother always asked the same question, which Chris took as an admonition that she was not with her since it would obviously be her. Now she added a more sinister interpretation. Alice could not afford to have her daughter roam free doing what she pleased. She would probably have liked to have prevented her leaving the flat at all.

'Of course it is,' Chris snapped.

'Where are you?'

There was a noise on the other side of the door, a scuffling, a sliding of bolts. The door creaked open. Chris was looking down, the phone clamped to her ear and first saw sensible shoes with light coloured soles, fixed with velcro straps, then a creased trouser leg hanging loosely around a thin bony ankle.

'I can't talk now.'

'What do you mean? Just tell me where you are.'

She was guided inside. She had no sense of walking. Objects floated past her, as a hand lightly caressed her shoulder. A dark wooden hat stand laden with garments – a red anorak, a man's trilby, a walking stick, a plastic mac, a canvas shopping bag. She was Alice tumbling down the rabbit hole to Wonderland, a barometer pointing to *Rain* floated by, followed by a print of a dewy-eyed boy in a straw hat, hands in the pocket of baggy trousers. A gas meter screwed to a thick board above a doorway looked like a school metal work exercise. Chris hissed into the mouthpiece:

'I'm with your mother!'

She snapped shut the telephone and turned it off. She was confronted by a tan sofa facing an upright chair with wooden arms. On a hearse-like television with spindly legs a framed photograph of Alice Howland smiled right at her. Chris recognised the smile only too well.

'Sit down. Can I get you tea, a glass of water? Here, let me take your jacket, you must be sweltering.'

Chris allowed herself to be led to the sofa, which received her with a sigh.

'A cup of tea would be nice.' She remembered her manners. '...but please don't go to any trouble. Can I help?'

'You've taken the trouble to come all this way, it's the least I can do.'

As the woman walked out of the room Chris noticed she didn't pick her feet up properly, which would have annoyed Alice, who constantly nagged Chris about her posture. The backs of Mrs Howland's heels dragged on the carpet and for a moment, in the doorway, she acted like she had forgotten something. Chris expected her to turn round and she put on a bright face in readiness, but then Mrs Howland continued with a more confident step and soon Chris heard the roar of a boiling kettle and the clinking of tea things.

The room was dim, its small windows were covered by net curtains. Despite the scrubby front garden the room was tidy and a smell of polish lingered in the air, so it must have been cleaned recently. Chris noticed that the carpet was worn around the sofa and the chair and in a path out of the door. She hoped it was the same carpet that Alice would have played on, and then recalled something about her mother playing on floorboards and complaining it hurt her knees. Perhaps they had thought putting carpet down would entice her back.

There were no books, newspapers, or even a clump of knitting in the room. No evidence of how Mrs Howland spent her time. A silver tankard had been placed on one side of a tiled mantelpiece and above, ranged along the wall too high and too far to the left, were three bronze plates embossed with ships in full sail. On the other side was a remote control for the television, the size of a brick. The room could have belonged to anyone.

But pride of place was given to the photograph. Chris shifted along the sofa and examined it. It was taken slightly from the side, with a fake backdrop of the sea and the sky behind it, still effective in black and white. A flick of fringe nearly reached one thin eyebrow, otherwise her hair was in two plaits held by elastic an inch from the ends. The plaits just reached her shoulders. She wore a cardigan and under this the brilliant white collar of her shirt was marginally too big for her, leaving a shadow at the back of her neck and increasing the appearance of frailty. She had never grown into it.

Yes she had.

Chris rushed over to help as Kathleen Howland came back carrying a tray. She was moving more easily than before, and without effort placed the tray on the sideboard. As she handed Chris a cup and saucer her hand shook, making the crockery rattle dangerously. Chris took it off her before the tea was spilt, and mumbled a mixture of thanks and helpless protest, as Mrs Howland lifted out a folding table from behind the armchair and set it up beside the settee.

As the two women sipped tea and nibbled on homemade fairy cakes topped with lemon icing, they looked at each other properly for the first time.

'So, what can I tell you?'

'I had to come. Once I knew. I had no choice.' Chris blurted out the words.

'Did you?' Mrs Howland dabbed at her mouth with her serviette. Chris had forgotten about hers and picked it up, at once putting it down again without unfolding it.

'I used to think it must be interesting doing what you do, meeting people, writing down what they say. Hearing their stories. Every day is different. But you all say it's a job like any other. You could stay at home, but you wouldn't get paid. So here you are!'

'Oh, no I didn't mean...'

'Don't worry, I understand.' But she didn't.

Chris shook her head impatiently as Mrs Howland offered her another cake.

'I'm more thick skinned than they think. Also dear, let's be honest, I need the publicity.' She spoke in a quieter voice, almost a whisper: 'I don't want people forgetting. There's a chance someone will read what any of you write, and, I don't know, listen to their conscience and come clean.'

Chris scalded the roof of her mouth as she gulped her tea. Mrs Howland had been expecting her. She had assumed Chris was a journalist doing a piece on Alice. She didn't know she was an eighteen-year-old who had come without her mother's permission. Any minute now the real journalist would turn up and she would be exposed. The gushing scene that featured herself as the rescuer, the restorer, evaporated. Her own hand began to shake and she hastily put down the cup in case Mrs Howland thought she was making fun of her.

'So, you'll want to see her room? We kept it the same.'

'I ought to be goi...'

The words trailed off because Chris had no intention of leaving. She would see the room, then tell Mrs Howland the truth and they could be out of the house before the real journalist arrived. She traipsed behind Mrs Howland up a steep dark stairway. Her shame at her duplicity increased as she saw Alice, running up and down these stairs, waiting on the landing outside her parents' bedroom door in her new Brownies outfit or to wake them up on Christmas morning. Chris had adopted the stories Alice had told her and made them her own memories. Her mother had done what good liars do: she had kept as much to the truth as possible. So she had said her Dad was a postman and Chris knew the weight of his huge postman's cap as the peak slipped over her eyes. Her arms ached, and her stomach swooped as they swung her high into the air between them with a *one-two-whoaaghgh!*

Chris had no better idea than Kathleen Howland what had happened to Alice after she failed to return home that afternoon. But she did know where to find her.

Alice's mother didn't open the bedroom door immediately and from the way she hesitated Chris thought for a wild second that there was someone in the room. She steeled herself in readiness. Then Mrs Howland let the door swing slowly open and stood aside.

Chris recoiled. 'You go first.'

'No dear, it's better if you do. It's not a big room.'

Chris practically stormed in to show Mrs Howland she wasn't afraid.

The room was indeed small. There was just enough space for a child's dressing table with a chair, a built-in cupboard and the bed. A beam of sunshine, thick with motes of dust, slanted across the faded candlewick bedspread and a white fluffy rug beside the bed. On the other side of the alcove to the cupboard was a set of shelves on which books – Enid Blyton, *Winnie-the-Pooh*, *Alice in Wonderland* and another called *Ballet Shoes* – were stacked neatly. On the shelf above were three Sindy dolls, propped up against the wall in symmetry. They looked brand new, but had been in her Mum's stories so couldn't be. Chris nearly made a sound as she spied the neat parade of shoes: brown sandals with crepe soles, silk ballet pumps, small Wellington boots, yellow woollen slippers with ladybird buttons. Two top shelves were empty. Alice had not stayed long enough to fill them.

There were no pictures on the walls, the dressing table was bare save for an ebony hairbrush and matching hand mirror that were unlikely possessions for an eight-year-old. Chris was disappointed: the room yielded no secrets. The things in it looked new, so obviously bought recently and never used. She realised that what she had most dreaded and most wanted were clues, a trail of signs that would link her to the Alice she had grown up with. Yet if Chris had believed in ghosts, or indeed had believed Alice was dead, she would have been convinced the house was haunted, for Alice's presence filled the room.

'What's in the cupboard?' She adopted the blunt curiosity of a reporter. One more minute and she would tell Mrs Howland the truth.

'I'll show you.' She was used to showing people around her house, anticipating their questions, managing their responses. She tried twice to raise herself off the soft bed where she had been sitting, then with the air of a confident owner, sure of the verdict of the potential buyer, she opened the cupboard doors. Lavender talc clouded into the room and made Chris sneeze four times in quick succession.

'Bless you.' Mrs Howland had a kindly voice. So far Chris could see no resemblance between this calm, sensible woman and the neurotic obsessive described in the articles. 'Sorry about that. The powder keeps the must at bay. Funnily enough I got that tip from dear Doctor Ramsay. Doctors have to deal with a lot of unpleasant odours, of course.'

Chris nodded sagely as she gazed at the open cupboard. It was crammed with clothes. At the bottom were plastic bags out of which Chris could see folded garments peeping: jumpers, tee-shirts, some with labels still attached. At the top was a charnel house of soft toys, beige, fawn and brown.

'Most of this is new,' Chris exclaimed, before she could stop herself.

'I see things she'd like, dresses she'd look so pretty in, tops and such. I can't resist them.'

The cupboard, packed with toys and clothes, was a shrine to a well-dressed, well-loved child. Chris recognised a shirt identical to the one she had worn about six years ago. Her mother had got it out of her catalogues. As a child Chris had learnt to submit to keeping things because they fitted, for it was she who would have to take them to the post office if they were too big, too small or just too horrible. Nowadays, she bought her own clothes, scouring charity shops or spending hours in Red or Dead, and dressing just how she wanted. Chris had always suspected that Alice bought her the clothes she would have liked to wear herself. Here was the living proof. A whole bloody wardrobe awaited her.

'There's something you should know...' But Mrs Howland was speaking:

'It's not that I don't know how it looks. I know she's gone. I like, just for a little while, to feel what it's like to choose something for my daughter. I get such pleasure, you know, well you will know. The cashier thinks I have a little girl, and so we can share the experience. Now I tell them she is a grandchild, a godchild. I'm too old to be her mother. Just to stroke the cloth and agree how hardwearing the cotton is, shake our heads at the scrapes they get into. I let myself be that person for a little while.'

'My Mum still gets cross if I stain my clothes, she still treats me like a kid,' Chris replied without thinking as she knelt before the mound of plastic bags.

'The sales people are happy to go along with you. They only say what you want to hear. They are meant to make the customer comfortable, so that we enjoy what they call the buying process. I did a course on selling, for a job in Hanningtons, oh, this was years ago. Before Steve died. My back couldn't take the standing...besides I didn't like leaving the house empty every day.'

'Did Alice wear any of these clothes?'

'All the things on this side.' Mrs Howland seemed anxious to prove the truth behind what Chris could see was only a stage set. 'The skirt I found in Exeter, and the blouse too, we went there when Alice was six. This cardigan was hers too. She loved pink.' Mrs Howland shook her head as she straightened the limp woollen sleeve. Then rousing herself: 'I don't keep all the new things. I take them to charity. Or return them, saying it's wrong on her or doesn't fit. They understand, children grow quickly, and they're so fussy these days.' Kathleen sat down heavily on the bed. Her tablet was wearing off. She would take another one after the girl had gone. She wanted her to leave now, but she owed her a proper time for coming all this way. But then there would be another visitor. Kathleen was alone a lot less than people knew.

She didn't tell the girl that Steve had broken the mirror in Alice's dressing table.

'That's seven years bad luck.' She didn't get cross with him often, just that one time.

'We've had our share, what's another ruddy seven years?'

Kathleen clasped her hands to prevent the girl seeing the tremor.

'I know she's dead.'

Chris was beside her.

'Dead? No, she's…'

'After all this time, I don't kid myself. If she were alive, she would have come back, wouldn't she? I don't really think she's stuck at nine years old. People think I'm not quite the full… If Alice were alive she'd be a grown woman. She could come home if she wanted. Even if she treated me as a stranger, she'd have to at least visit.'

Chris hadn't thought of that. Why hadn't Alice come home?

'You told the papers you knew she was alive!' This was another betrayal. Chris was out of her depth; nothing was going according to plan. She should have told Alice to come herself instead of being so intent on getting all the glory. Mrs Howland wouldn't believe Alice was alive. She must get a lot of weirdos knocking on her door claiming to have seen her daughter.

'Papers print what they like. Besides, I say different things on different days. Depends on my mood. Since Alice went, I get asked all the time how I am coping. I say whatever comes into my head.' Mrs Howland clicked shut the cupboard with a gesture of finality.

Chris longed to stay in the bedroom, to lie on the bed and read one of the books and listen to the seagulls.

She had expected they would return to the living room. Perhaps they would have another cup of tea, but Mrs Howland stopped in the hallway.

It was time to go.

'You didn't have a coat, did you?' She stroked the collar of a girl's anorak on the coat stand absently.

'Just a jacket.' Chris lifted it down because Mrs Howland wasn't listening.

'Forgive me saying so, but you are young. You seem…'

'I'm eighteen.'

'You're not a journalist, are you?' How did she ever think she could fool this wise old woman? Chris flushed crimson.

She had treated Kathleen in just the way her Mum had treated Chris; as a pawn for her own ends.

Long, blonde hair. Blue eyes. Thin legs. Tall. Skin pale as a ghost.

Alive and living in South London.

Before Mrs Howland could speak, Chris heard herself speak:

'I want you to come to London with me. I know where...'

Her head was in a vice and the breath was being squeezed out of her. Everything was convex and then concave. Chris smelled the sea and saw the word:

Alice.

Then everything went black.

Twenty-Two

Isabel lazily stroked more sun tan cream into her ankles and up her calves, rubbing it in with lingering strokes, noting with satisfaction how smooth her skin was, with no surface veins, which would be remarkable in a woman of over fifty let alone sixty. This comforting observation was straight away eclipsed by the sharp pains in her thigh and at the base of her spine as she stretched. She could not get Mark's car out of her mind for long. Sunbathing helped. As she submitted to the heat, the watery image would be evaporated by the scorching sun, but every time she moved, her leg hurt and there it was again as if she was under water, her lungs bursting, groping desperately towards Mark.

Shifting about on the wonderfully soft mattress of her new lounger, Isabel applied circles of cream around her eyes with Impressionist dabs and kneaded it into her neck, wiping away the wrinkles. Finished. For a fraction of a second she was calm and content. Then an engulfing wave washed off the good feeling, leaving her old and shivering. She set the bottle on the table, next to her book, radio and empty coffee mug. Was the rest of her life going to be like this? One long to-do list marked off by a series of ticks.

Spots of sunlight flashed on the surface of the freshly filled pool: yellow and gold segments like exotic fish whose progress Isabel tried to follow across the rippling surface until they vanished. She had heard somewhere that gazing at sunshine on water made you happy. Something to do with serotonin, but she hadn't listened to the medical bit.

Perhaps she did feel a bit better.

Isabel tried to build on this tenuous impression. They were almost back to normal, the pool had been restored, and she had got through the funeral. Now she might believe that nothing had happened. It was a Wednesday afternoon when Mark was usually in London. She told herself he would be home tonight as usual.

Only recently the garden and the house had been teeming with strangers. After the frenzy of trying to save Mark was over and they had driven off with his body, it seemed to Isabel a more measured, calmer crowd took over.

First more police: some in white jump suits like spacemen. One was a woman, which had irritated Isabel, who was more conventional than she preferred to think. They had told her that only when they had completed their measuring and photographing and questioning, could the car be taken out of the pool. Until then it had lain there, bubbling away like a hookah. Isabel had been frantic to right everything to how it had been before Mark drowned. But she had lost the impetus to do it herself. She had bullied Lucian to get on to Mr Bunting and his son to come and clean the pool right away. Lucian had argued, unconsciously imitating the police, which before she might have enjoyed.

'They will be impeded by the presence of a motor vehicle.'

'You can be such a prat!' Isabel found giving her children unconditional love exhausting. 'They'll have lots of bookings at this time of year, we need to get in or it won't happen. I'm not looking at this cesspool for the rest of the year.'

'Do we actually need the pool?' Now Lucian was Mark without the good bits.

'I've called them. The police say that the car's going this afternoon. Mr Bunting will be here in the morning at eight and the fence people on Saturday. Everything will be ready in time for Dad's funeral.'

Gina was carrying a tray of tea out to the white overalls and didn't stop.

233

As the car was winched out of the pool Isabel had stood beside Gina to watch. She identified all the colours of the rainbow, and was saddened rather than outraged at the streams of oily water cascading out of the quarter lights. The bonnet tilted upwards and the car was once more inching up the steep hills of family holidays, as they all sang out in anthemic glee *Breathe in, don't move. First one to speak has to get out and walk!* The radiator grill flashed as it caught the sun: a paean to Mark's polishing.

Mark would have understood Gina's need to witness everything. He too would have been rapping out instructions, warning them to treat his car with care. Shielding her eyes from the sun's glare, Isabel had gazed up at her husband's most coveted possession dangling uselessly. A twisting shadow darkened the patio, the car revolved slowly before swinging away from the pool as the crane chugged past the garage and up the drive. Although Mark's body had been removed, Isabel didn't feel he had gone until the crane disappeared round the bend in the lane. She walked back to the house, keeping pace with Gina, neither of them able to speak.

In lots of ways, Isabel reflected, as she let the sun take her over, Lucian and Gina were like herself; they got other people doing things, whether it was compensation for a faulty service, getting a price down or organising a funeral. Isabel twitched a hand to bat away the image of Lucian gazing forlornly at her whenever she was impatient with him. He was too sensitive. He and Eleanor were like Mark in that respect. Gina was made of sterner stuff. Mark had said it was apt that after marrying Jon, Gina took his name to become Gina Cross, because she so often was. But Mark had been crosser, that she wasn't Gina Ramsay any more. He had taken her decision to change her name as a snub.

Of course he had been right.

When they were little, Isabel had felt powerless when her children bickered and had always relied on Mark to sort them out. Then she had hated to see their faces, white and staring, as he shouted and stamped. Each word was a bullet fired with precision, while Mark appeared to thrill with an electric current. She would feel she had let them down.

She had let them down.

No, it was Mark who had let them all down. Isabel closed her eyes.

Mark's death, a phrase that she wasn't ready to use, was like a power cut. Although it is easy to grasp the fact of no electricity, in practice it is still a surprise when no light comes on or the kettle fails to boil at the click of a switch. It is the last straw when the television stays blank at the wand-wave of the remote. As Isabel lay on her treasured luxury lounger, she reflected on the yawning future.

That morning she had walked around the side of the house, past the thick bushes of fuchsia and hydrangeas that grew beneath the study and dining room windows, gingerly raising branches, even checking in the old outhouse by the pantry. She had stopped quickly when she realised she was searching for Alice as she had when the girl first went missing.

If she had told them, the family would have called it the Raleigh complex, named after Gina's stolen bicycle which was cut from its chain outside the Chiswick open air swimming pool when Gina was nine. The police had said it would be local kids having a lark and to keep a look out for it. After that, the whole family stopped to examine every chipped blue bike they came across, looking for the tell-tale dabs of mismatched paint on the cross bar. This habit haunted them for years, long after Gina could have ridden the bike had it been recovered. Now Isabel was doing the same thing, except Alice's worth hadn't diminished in the same way as a battered old bike. Her mother, at least, would want her.

At the time Isabel had been desperate to prove that Alice had got herself trapped somewhere. Houses were complicated structures, she had insisted, particularly this one. Alice could be anywhere. She had never told Mark that she had encouraged the police to search their house. There would, she had assured Richard Hall, be a good explanation. She suggested they try the basement.

'It's a warren down there, lots of little rooms, great place to hide.'

Isabel had made repeated journeys into the cavernous basement herself and, careful not to be heard by anyone above, called out to Alice. She was cajoling, tempting, luring: *Don't be frightened; we're not in the least annoyed with you.* The police had been down there the day before, but Isabel had suspected that Alice would have been too scared to respond to men she didn't know, however kind they appeared to be. You had to gain the trust of a girl like that. Then she would do anything for you.

But years went by and still Alice had not been found.

More than once, Isabel had sneaked off through the orchard to the Judge's disused workshop – now filled with bikes, old lawn mowers, tins of paint and bits of broken garden furniture – and cupping her hands, peered through its grimy windows. In the cobwebbed interior, the disused contents kept their counsel.

One evening when Mark was in his study, she made up her mind to tell the police about her dream. It was five years since Alice had gone missing and she had just watched a programme about the Kennedy shooting, which had happened the day after Alice disappeared. After some flicking back and forth she found Detective Inspector Hall's number in the back of her 1968 diary. Making sure she wouldn't be interrupted, she started dialling the number. Then common sense had prevailed. How absurd to tell them about a dream. They would section her. Instead she went down to the basement and methodically searched it yet again. As she moved aside boxes and shelving units, felt her way through the cold dank cellar where the ice had once been stored, she whispered Alice's name, as she often did when she was on her own.

Even after so many years Isabel could not stop looking for Alice although now, more than ever, she was terrified of finding her.

Isabel wriggled her toes, and lay so that her body was aligned, as she had learnt at her transcendental meditation class.

She breathed in and out with her palm on her abdomen. While doing this exercise she was supposed to recite the personal mantra given to her by her teacher. For maximum effect she was meant to keep it secret and not share it with anyone else. But these days unless Isabel wrote things down or told other people she forgot them. She had quickly forgotten her mantra and was unwilling to confess this. Instead she would recite as many titles of Thomas Hardy novels as she could remember. This worked just as well. Although the effort of recalling them made her tense, it did at least take her mind off things.

Today the temperature was ideal: a breeze had got up, so it was not too hot, but warm enough to let go. Isabel did find it extraordinary that the sun could shine and that she could feel its warmth while Mark was lying buried under a mound of cold soil up by the church. She closed her eyes, not daring to think what else was possible.

She was aroused from the first driftings of a dream in which she was lying in Mark's arms, cushioned on his shoulder, by the sound of familiar footsteps.

She was in the car Mark used to drive before they got married and started a family. He was young with bristly short-back-and-sides, and eyes that glittered. His white coat with the stethoscope slung around his neck was too safe an image for a man who she had discovered was so unsafe. She tried to grab his leather-clad hand but it slipped away leaving her with a floppy glove. His scent faded as she struggled to reach him, to rest her hand on his thigh; to attract him. But his attention was on the road; he was gripping the wheel of his sports car, a laughing mouth refusing to say where they were going. White teeth bared, lips taut like a fox. She cried out, but made no sound.

The dream had dwindled and Isabel was awake.

The footsteps stopped. Already smiling, already knowing, Isabel opened her eyes and reached out her hands to greet Eleanor, her favourite child.

Twenty-Three

Alice's mother helped Chris on to the settee. She was now the stronger of the two as she snatched up cushions and tucked them in behind her, plumping them smartly, easing her backwards with the economic efficiency of a nurse. A warm dry hand stroked Chris's forehead, tidying back her hair, brushing her cheek. Chris blinked as her eyes stung with sudden tears; it was just how her Mum would have been. She couldn't think of that now. She gave in as her legs were gently lifted, so that she was lying full length on the settee, her feet propped on another cushion. If only she could stay here. The village was no longer a science-fiction nightmare; she wanted to live here and start again. But of course once she was better she would have to go. When she had gone Mrs Howland wouldn't care because she would have Alice.

'Have a few sips.'

As she took the cup and saucer Chris noticed there was no trace of the earlier shake and that Alice's mother walked without catching her heels on the carpet.

'What happened?' Chris gave a groan.

Alice would have the right to stay as long as she liked. Her mother would be newly alive. Upstairs a fluffy hot water bottle would once again warm the immaculate bed. On an impulse Chris decided it could not happen. She wouldn't tell Kathleen Howland about Alice and she wouldn't tell Alice where she was. She too could start a new life, with a new name and story and see how Alice liked it. Mrs Howland would be her new mother.

Chris could be Alice. She could fill her space and stay with this kindly woman, who was after all her grandmother, lulled by the cluck-tock-cluck of the old clock on the mantelpiece. There was nothing to stop her. She needed a mother and this mother needed a daughter. This was the 'grandma' she had gone looking for outside Fuller's Brewery.

Chris could not know that she was one of a long line of women, and some men, who, claiming reasons of research or detection, had come to Alice's cottage wanting to occupy the vacant role of the nine-year-old child. If only for an hour. There had been many 'orphans' drawn like magnets to this mother going spare. With the callous vigour of the cheated and betrayed, Chris reasoned that if a life could be invented for her, populated with phantoms she had been taught to love like kindred spirits, she could take a loving mother and hot sugary tea and make up a new life for herself.

'You fainted, that's what happened. Down like a nine-pin. Lucky you didn't hit your head.'

'I'm sorry.'

'Don't be daft. It's the heat. Abroad apparently they have thick walls and tiled floors. That's better, you're looking more yourself now.'

Chris sipped the tea and settled further into the cushions. Already she loved this woman with soft hands, adorned only with a gold band on the wedding finger, who talked with quiet confidence. When she had brought in the tea, she had sat on a footstool next to the settee, her hands gathered around her knees like a girl.

'You came out with something a bit odd before you keeled over.' Alice's Mum took the empty teacup off Chris and set it on the coffee table. 'About going to London.'

Chris could say she felt ill again, but this would mean more pretending. Despite the perfectly placed cushions and caring attendance, Mrs Howland was going through the motions. She was not Chris's mother, nor did she want to be. No amount of fainting would change that. Chris would have to make her come to the flat and let her see Alice for herself.

In her bafflement at Alice's terrible deceit, Chris had viewed Mrs Howland as no more than a catalyst, a prompter of events that would blast apart Alice's world in the way Alice had shattered her own. Her trip to the eerily deserted village baking in hot sunshine and her arrival at a dark cottage had been for Chris part of a plot to make her Mum very sorry. She had been so intent on knocking down the tower of cards that her mother had painstakingly erected that she hadn't taken on board the stark truth that there is no knowing how people will react.

'It is a bit much. The heat.' Chris didn't know what to do next. 'The bedroom...the dolls.'

'You're not the first. They think I don't know how it looks, but it's not possible to be normal. No parent should outlive their child. It's normality turned on its head.'

'I think I've found...' Chris heaved herself into a sitting position. She would sort this thing out and put everything back in its place. She could do that, no problem.

'Found what, dear?'

It was the second time she had asked the question.

'It's best you come with me and see for yourself.'

'Now? To London?'

'I'll explain when we get there.'

Kathleen got up unsteadily.

'I'd have to book a bed and breakfast. There was a good one in Hammersmith.'

Already Kathleen was arranging the expedition with no trace of indecision. She thought nothing of getting on a train and being in a different city by nightfall. No one understood that for her nowhere was home, so it didn't matter where she was. It was a relief to be kept busy. All these years the one thing she had learnt was to keep an open mind and trust that anything was possible. She would go wherever this young girl wanted to take her.

Kathleen's practical willingness emphasised the flimsiness of Chris's own intentions.

'Hammersmith is miles away. You could stay with us.'

'Who is *us*, dear?' Alice's mother was rifling through her purse, a bus pass between her lips as she flicked through the credit card section, zipping and snapping, opening and shutting compartments.

'Me. And…my Mum.'

'Your Mum?' Kathleen looked up. 'Have you asked her?' She looked at Chris as an adult checks the story of a child, respectful yet doubting.

'She won't mind. She'll be pleased.' Chris nodded firmly. Everyone would be pleased.

On the train down, Chris had watched a little girl sobbing and being mopped up by her Mum and decided that nothing was certain. The child believed that her mother was protection against the world. Just as Chris had once assumed her own Mum was, until at three years old she had first seen her cry. She had not explained why she was crying, and would not stop. Chris got her tissues and patted her shoulders, repeating, 'there, there', but she had gone hollow inside and after that she had not felt safe.

The mother on the train was troubled and tired, and embarrassed that her daughter was wailing loudly in a quiet railway carriage. Earlier Chris had helped her load a suitcase on to the rack above their heads. The shared effort hadn't opened up further interaction. Chris hated knowing that the child's sense of safety was an illusion. Yesterday she had discovered that all certainty was illusionary.

Once thought, she could not unthink it.

'I'll be ready in two ticks, my bag is packed, just need to check I've got my pills, water, bits and bobs.'

Chris wandered to the window.

A blue Range Rover was parking outside the cottage. Its glass reflected the sun, so she couldn't see the occupants. A door opened slowly, sending a lighthouse beam around the living room. Chris went up to the pane, interested now to see who would get out. So far the village had been devoid of life.

Two women emerged, one from each side of the car. Although they were dressed differently, and one had short hair, the other shoulder length, there was a similarity that contributed to an impression of choreographed symmetry. The woman nearer the cottage had her back turned as she bent back inside the car and then, standing up, she slung a handbag on to her shoulder. The other woman held a bulky plastic bag in her arms. The doors slammed shut at the same time, and the woman who had been driving strode around the bonnet, a hand trailing over it as if staying an animal. As she came into view something fell out of the carrier bag on to the road. Chris stepped closer to the glass. It was a video tape. The woman who had been driving fumbled for it, and finally picked it up. Both women paused and examined it briefly. Then the woman with the short hair and the handbag turned to face the cottage and this stopped being a play in which Chris had no part.

The woman was Alice.

Her companion lifted the latch on the gate. Chris bounded across the room to get to the door before they rang the bell. Already they were coming up the path. In the hall, she collided with Mrs Howland, nearly knocking her over.

'What's the matter?'

'I was going to tell you…'

'Calm down, you'll be ill again.' Mrs Howland was in slow motion. Chris held on to the wall as the hallway reeled and dipped.

A shadow fell across the porthole of moulded glass in the door and the barometer needle trembled on Fair as the knocker thundered down.

Already Mrs Howland was far away as Chris pitched forward trying to stop her getting to the door. Too late. The front door opened with a deafening creak over which Chris was shouting. Later she wasn't sure she had made any sound at all.

'It's Alice. I've found Alice!'

Sunlight flooded the hallway. In the glare, two figures on the doorstep loomed – shapes with no features. Chris was helpless as Kathleen stepped forward and all the while in the background, a voice was talking.

'*Mrs Howland, we've brought Dad's camera tapes. Quite a collection, over two weeks' worth, but what with...*'

Kathleen Howland gave a cry, of pain or joy, Chris couldn't tell, and grabbed Alice's hands, grasping them, intertwining them, and jigging them up and down. She drew the other woman in too, pulling them to her.

'It's Eleanor Ramsay! And Gina too. How thoughtful of you both, with all that's happened...oh, come in, come in! You can meet my new friend.'

Kathleen ushered the Ramsay sisters into the living room. There was no one there. The young woman whose name she had already forgotten had vanished. Kathleen wasn't surprised. She was almost used to it. They got what they came for and went.

Nevertheless she was disappointed. This girl had seemed so different.

Twenty-Four

Chris wasted valuable seconds fumbling with the back door key before realising it was already unlocked. A raised step tripped her up and she tumbled out into the garden sending a plastic box, like the one she used to take to school for her lunch, spinning over the path, white bread spilling. She dashed down the path between the cottage and the post office, and stopped at the corner of the cottage. The front door was shut, but the car was still outside. Chris bowed her head, then taking a deep breath, hands shielding her face, she ran out down the path and, leaving the gate swinging, she set off up the lane.

The pavement rushed beneath her, cracks passing faster and faster as she quickened her pace up the hill. Her lungs were bursting, sweat soaking her shirt, but still she kept going.

Since Chris had discovered the articles under her mother's pillow, her landscape had been demolished. It was years since that morning when she had banged out of the flat without saying goodbye to the woman who was supposed to be her Mum and supposed to be called Alice. Hours and minutes had dragged, shot forward, wound back, and now in a benign country churchyard on a warm summer's afternoon, they halted altogether.

Storming between the plots, tripping on the uneven ground, Chris was an agitated figure to anyone who might see her.

There was someone.

She caught a movement by the corner of the churchyard. In this horror-film village Chris hadn't reckoned on meeting anyone. There was a woman, maybe not much older than herself, standing in the dappled shadow of a silver ash. She hadn't seen Chris. She was looking at a grave and writing, supporting a notebook with one hand, her blonde hair falling forward. At first Chris assumed she was some mourner come to spend quiet time with her loved one. She must have made a sound because the woman looked up and saw her. She snapped shut her book, dropped her pen in the bag slung on her shoulder and marched swiftly over the grass back to the path. As she came towards Chris, a smile already prepared, Chris saw she was much older than her hair and clothes had made her think. Not actually old, but worn-out looking. Chris was also taken aback by her expression. Far from behaving as if Chris had interrupted a precious moment, she was embarrassed and the quick nod of greeting as she hurried by was apologetic.

After the woman had left the churchyard, Chris decided to find out which grave had so interested her.

She was not prepared for what she found. The grave was recent, a long low mound of soil flecked with bits of white chalk with nothing else to distinguish it, no flowers or messages of love. The thick clods of earth were rudimentary and raw while a makeshift wooden cross at its head undermined the permanency of the place and the significance of the grave itself. Chris imagined the body buried below, it probably still had eyes, and a lolling tongue turned colourless by death lying inert in its mouth. She read the name on the metal strip screwed to the wood.

Mark Henry Ramsay
20th November 1925 – 6th June 1999
The Dead Professor.

Chris knew nothing remarkable about this man except the bizarre way he had died. The mass of this ignorance, literally a body of uncharted facts, lured her closer. What had the woman been writing? Who was she? This man might have given her answers. He might have consoled her. They might have consoled each other. But she had arrived too late.

Mark Ramsay's grave was but a marker for the magnificent marble headstone with forbidding lead lettering that stood next to it. The marble was pristine, unblemished by the years, which Chris calculated dated from when the first name was carved on it – Rosamund Ramsay – in 1934. The shiny stone contrasted with the state of the grave itself, a rampant weed bed entirely merging with the surrounding grass. The neglect was callous. Yet the leaden words said that Mrs Ramsay and her husband Judge Henry Ramsay, who had died in 1958 and was buried beside her, were 'greatly missed by their children, Virginia and Mark'.

Chris was familiar with graveyards. Before they'd graduated to pubs, she and her friends would sit on a bench in the cemetery behind the school, passing round Red Bull and vodka in a plastic toothmug and spinning preferred realities. Pock-marked angels with spread wings cast gravity on teenage sagacity, as they made up torrid lives for the dead surrounding them from scant tombstone information. One woman had lost her husband in the First World War and all her sons in the Second. Another had ten children and died aged thirty-eight. There had been no words engraved for Pauline Davies who had died aged twenty-one in 1972, just the glazed image of a happy face, with a dreadful hair-do. They had let this pass as they searched for signs of her impending doom in Pauline's too-red lips and bright brown eyes, looking for what made her different and would ensure their own immortality. There had been no clue except the awful hairstyle. The group would straggle on by, eager to put death behind them.

Chris had always gleaned reassurance from the brevity of the words on the headstones. People were born, they were related to other people and then they died. The facts of life.

Now she sat down on a bench beside the Ramsay plot and from a comparatively safe distance stared at the graves, willing them to yield their secrets. She felt a tickling on her cheek and reaching up to scratch it, her fingers came away wet; she was crying, maybe that was why the lady with the notebook had been weird with her.

The sun was dropping down behind the downs, and Judge Ramsay's headstone cast a long shadow across his scrubby plot. Between the inches that separated Mark Ramsay from his parents there were over forty years. The child who had 'greatly missed' his father was now dead himself, with his own children to miss him. Or not. Where were the years? Were they in the rustling leaves of the ash, the chunks of soil, the lichen-covered stone? Were they around her now, the hundreds of minutes experienced, the birthdays, the family holidays or Sunday lunches? Moments like this, when sitting still she could hear the engines and gears of all the lived lives? The woman who wasn't Alice had said there was no Heaven and Chris had thought this idea reasonable. But what happened to all the seconds that amounted to a life?

'That's your grandfather.'

The whispering voice made Chris start. Then with a rush of delight and relief she put out her hands. Her Mum was here. The next instant white heat urged her to smash Alice to pieces.

'What do you want?'

'I came to find you.' Her reply was addressed to the freshly dug grave. She was holding a twig in one hand and flicked it over the fingers of her other hand, leaves fluttering and tearing.

'Well, you found me. So piss off!' Chris was tugged with vicious insecurity at the sight of her Mum, baffled and vulnerable, looking with such desolation at the flimsy cross. There was no one to step out of a crowd and save Chris from kicking, stamping and smashing her mother's face into silence with a chunk of flint.

'Haven't you seen a grave before?'

'Not this one.'

'Couldn't even be arsed to get a proper headstone. Like that ugly bastard of a mausoleum.' She waved impotent arms at Judge Ramsay's tombstone. 'Is that false too? Going to take it away as soon as I've gone, are you?'

'Apparently it's being carved, this is temporary. And the ground has to settle.' Eleanor had not meant to point out Chris's ignorance and reveal her knowledge of the Ramsays' affairs. 'Oh, Chris.' She turned to her, not bothering to dash away the tears that trickled down her cheeks. 'He's your grandfather!'

'Whatever. Until the next lie.'

'I know you're cross.' Eleanor could see that Chris sniffed insincerity in her clumsy choice of words. Sometimes the truth didn't speak for itself.

'I don't think you do.' Now Chris too addressed Mark Ramsay's grave.

'I never meant to hurt you. Quite the reverse.'

"Quite the reverse' oh, lah de dah. She's got new words to go with the new name. Who do you think you are to lecture me!' Chris gulped for air and added with self-conscious triumph: 'In fact who do you think you are? Does anyone know? Or was it just me you lied to?'

'Chris, please...' Eleanor couldn't sound as upset as she felt. She had grown too adept at being someone else.

'It's only stupid-git-features here, who thought her Mum was Alice Kennedy, the Agoraphobic of Bermondsey...doh! So who are you today? Elea-nor-Ram-say!' She put on an upper class intonation, as she spat out the syllables.

Eleanor shrank back, unable to disguise her fear of her own daughter. Chris realised with a jolt that she couldn't remember when she had last seen her Mum out of doors. Eleanor was dazzled by the sunlight. Chris pictured her Mum behind the partial screen of the lace curtains or with her kindly features softened by the light of the gas fire. She was still holding the strange handbag that had confused Chris earlier. She was an indecisive figure, the dainty handbag incongruous because Eleanor wasn't collected enough or tidy enough for its understated elegance.

Eleanor's legs were unsteady and her attempts to hide this were pathetic. Of course, her Mum was frightened to be outside. It must be torture to her to be so exposed.

No, that was another story. Yet anger briefly ebbed as Chris saw her Mum did genuinely seem to be upset. She would part her hair, numbering the different coloured flecks – brown, gold, blonde, no silver at all.

You'll never be old to me.

'I will go if you want me to. I could wait for you at the station.'

'Where did you get that?' Chris spoke evenly.

'What?'

'You heard.' Nasty now.

'My mother...Isabel Ramsay gave it to me, just now. Your grandmother.' A futile placation. The bag incriminated her. She couldn't tell her daughter she had accepted it only because she had seen that Isabel hadn't known what to do with her. She couldn't explain that it had touched her that her mother had tried so hard to make a maternal gesture. Neither of them had been able to talk properly because they never had.

She had not told Isabel she had only come to fetch her daughter, after which she was going to leave again. Her mother had been so happy to see her, so that when she hadn't found Chris at the White House, Eleanor had lost volition and had submitted to Isabel's uncharacteristic stream of hyperbolic chatter that had culminated in the handbag. Isabel had snatched it off a pile of jumble in the utility room and thrust it into her hands. None of this could she explain to Chris.

Chris knew Eleanor tossed in the word 'grandmother' as stale bread to a duck and had noted her mother's snap decision to stand her ground as Chris advanced towards her. She didn't even flinch as Chris tore the bag off her, wrenched it open, ripping the gold clasp from the flap, and tipped it upside-down. The contents spilled on to the grass. Chris's arm described an arc as she prepared to smash the bag down on her mother's head, but at the last moment she hurled it over the top of the gravestones. It smashed through the branches, and in a shower of leaves landed in the wheat field behind the churchyard wall.

Her mother didn't react and Chris was afraid of the blatant misery in her face. There was no satisfaction in defeating the defeated.

Who was this well-spoken stranger?

'So are you just going to stand there?' Chris demanded.

Eleanor scuffed a toe in the ground, kicking up dust.

'I hate the bloody thing anyway.' Eleanor did not sound convincing. After so long doing a good imitation of Alice, she had forgotten how to do herself.

'Yet, you were happy to be given handouts by Mummy, and forget about me. Go there a lot do you, while I'm at school, or doing the shopping or the washing.'

'It was for you.'

'You got a stupid cast-off from your mother for me?'

'No, I mean all of it. The going into hiding and changing my name. It was all for you.' Eleanor regretted the trite words – too Alice. Except there was no Alice.

Chris sat up unnaturally straight on the bench, the muscles in her temples and jaw twitching. Eleanor desperately wanted to comfort her. She was moved by her child's valiant effort to be unaffected. Chris had been thrown into the situation by her own mother.

Eleanor was stunned by what she had done. It had been a minute-by-minute thing with extraordinary consequences. With a dull and crushing recognition like a glimpse of death, Eleanor saw she had lost the right to Chris's love the day she went to the Tide Mills with Alice. The soon-to-be-nine-year-old was too young to know she was stepping into Hell.

'Let me get this right. I'm on a train going to Alice Howland's mother to tell her that her missing girl was very much alive and living near the Elephant and Castle, and you're sneaking out and running back to your real mother when she's meant to be dead in a car crash!' She finished with a strangled shout: 'You were never Alice! You're a liar. You fucking bitch!' Chris had only ever spoken to Alice this way in her head. How good it would be to go back to the time when the only problem she'd had was how to tell her Mum that she'd had sex with a supply teacher and not had a period for five weeks. How innocent she had been to think that the arrival of her period signalled the end to her worries.

'That's not right,' her mother protested.

Chris snapped her head round and Eleanor froze.

Chris looked down at the clutter of objects scattered in the rough grass. She loved them for the picture of Alice they eloquently portrayed. A nail file, a packet of tissues, a used foil of aspirins half hidden by a blue plastic packet with 'Handy Shopper' printed in slanting writing. Her diary had landed half open, its spine broken by the fall. Chris had given it to her for Christmas. She must have grabbed all this stuff before leaving, as usual thinking of every eventuality. Chris hadn't thought of buying her a handbag, because she never went out.

They both knew Alice wanted the bag. They both saw Alice leaning over, pulling it up, and methodically replacing her things. Tidying up. She would want to check if the clasp could be saved and give the leather a buff with a tissue.

Eleanor didn't care. The bag was too small and ladylike to hold anything useful.

They both knew that if Alice got the bag sorted, they could go back to Bermondsey and carry on as before.

But there was no such person as Alice.

'So how was it then?'

'When I rang you, you said you were with my mother. You have no idea what that did.' Eleanor stole a furtive glance at Chris and emboldened by her stony silence continued:

'I didn't think of Mrs Howland. I assumed you were with Isabel Ramsay, I came to get you.'

'So how come your name is Alice?' Chris's voice quavered.

'People change their names. It's normal.' As soon as she heard the words, Eleanor saw her mistake. Unless she told the truth without excuses or expecting sympathy, Chris would go. Already it was probably too late.

'Don't patronise me!' Chris was on her feet. 'I know people change their names! What I want to know is why you did. You changed your whole life, don't tell me that's 'normal'. You pretended to be a missing schoolgirl and lied to me, your own child. That's if I am yours.' She held up her hand. 'There's *nothing* you can say. I thought my grandparents died in a car accident. Me and Emma even went to that brewery where you said they were killed and put flowers there. I've always thought you were all the family I had.'

'She wasn't just a schoolgirl. Nobody knew what Alice was really like.' Eleanor was talking to herself. 'She could be so cruel.'

'I don't care about Alice.' Chris stalked over to her mother, and coming up close like the boys in the playground, she jabbed her hard on the chest.

'You were my Mum. Have you ever thought of that?' She pushed her roughly. 'You've taken my whole life away by pretending to be a girl you didn't even like?' Her speech was blurred with sobbing. 'And you call that being a mother? You're mental.'

Chris was breathing through her teeth, a gulping hissing.

'Chrissie, I have nothing in my life other than you. You're the point of it.'

'I'm so grateful!' Chris punctuated the exclamation with another push, rougher this time, even though she guessed her Mum was telling the truth. She saw her wince, then hide it. Her Mum would stand there taking it. Chris punched her hard on the shoulder, knocking her backwards.

'Why?' Her voice was low and grating.

'What do you mean?' Eleanor would not cry. She knew what Chris meant.

'Why did you call yourself Alice?'

A small plane buzzed high overhead, and on the other side of the church a car engine purred into a rev as it drove up the lane; there was the bass boom of a snatch of 'Baby One More Time'. The village was coming to life, but neither woman noticed.

'I've done my best to make it up to Alice.'

'Make up for what?'

Eleanor stepped away and with her back to Chris she gazed far into the distance at the point where the downs became the sky where she wished she could be:

'For killing her.'

Twenty-Five

Kathleen was worn out. She had been astounded to find the Ramsay sisters on her doorstep. People said children were resilient and being young they didn't feel things. Kathleen had always doubted this. Alice had been very sensitive.

Eleanor Ramsay had barely spoken and, with a shake of her head, had refused tea when her sister had just accepted, which made Gina change her mind. The girls had looked no more at ease with each other than they had when Kathleen had first met them that fateful summer. When Kathleen told them that a young lady who had said she was a reporter had turned out to be yet another sightseer, Gina had said she was appalled and wanted to call the police, while Eleanor had said nothing. Then just as Kathleen was reassuring Gina that she didn't think the girl had meant any harm, Eleanor had announced she had to leave and fled the house before Gina could go with her. It was a long time since Kathleen had recalled the suspicion that the detective had confided to her in the garden where Steve couldn't overhear. After the Ramsays had left it came back to her clearly.

She hadn't cared for Detective Inspector Hall and for this reason made more effort with him. He was like a cat, drawn to her because he sensed her dislike. Most people took Steve to one side if they had something unpleasant to talk about, like the search of their cottage or of the Tide Mills and the day they dragged the river. They supposed Steve was the stronger one and could absorb bad news. But after a while Richard Hall realised this wasn't the case, or maybe he preferred to talk to Kathleen.

He led her out into the little garden, guiding her with a cupped hand on her elbow, which she had resented for its suggestion that she had lost so much she couldn't walk unaided. Over time Kathleen came to see that this insistent protection was more complicated. While Isabel Ramsay intrigued and disturbed him, Kathleen Howland was Richard Hall's ideal woman. In the first few days after Alice's disappearance, she too was bathed in an innocence that over time, as she failed to fit people's expectations of a grieving mother, eroded. At the time her maternal mimings with her arms flailing in an empty embrace, made sense to him.

Like Jackie Masters, he said he had understood about the sandwiches and the freshly ironed nightie on the freshly washed pillow.

As their feet sank into the soft soil around Steve's vegetable plot, Richard Hall's proximity, so close she could sniff waves of minty breath, revolted Kathleen. She remembered noticing that one of the canes for the runner beans had snapped under the weight of the plant and thinking she must tell Steve. Then in the same thought she had known not to bother. Steve had lost his love for the garden and let his plants and flowers run wild or die. He too had broken under the weight.

'I don't know how to say this.'

'What?'

'I don't like the attitude of the youngest Ramsay girl.' He seemed to suppose Kathleen shared his contempt for the Ramsay family and their privilege. Once upon a time this privilege would have earned them automatic respect from men like Richard Hall.

'Eleanor Ramsay?'

'Her story doesn't add up. She isn't one bit bothered by any of this. I gather she's a handful at the best of times, but now she's too clever by halves. The idea beggars belief, but we have to keep our minds open.'

'What idea?'

'I'm giving mileage to the theory that this Eleanor had a bit of a run in with Alice and things got out of hand.'

'For pity's sake, don't waste your time bothering Eleanor Ramsay. What you're really saying is my Alice is dead.' She had been frightened by her words.

'I'm just trying to keep you up to date with the investigation. I wanted you to be the first to know.' He had bent down and fiddled with the runner beans, using a nearby cane to lend support to the broken one and tying them together with a bit of loose twine that he found lying on the grass. Richard Hall was free to do this; he still had both his daughters.

'Eleanor's upset.' She had tried to be nice. He was only doing his job; they had to leave no stone unturned.

'I didn't want you to hear it from anyone else. I know reporters hang around you. If you want me to get rid of that young woman...'

'They're only trying to help. ' At the time she had believed Jackie Masters really was a friend. 'They're no different to you, Inspector.' Then, for he had looked hurt by this, she had let him lead her back into the house and make her a cup of tea.

So after the Ramsay girls had left as suddenly as they had arrived, Kathleen had sat motionless in Steve's armchair raking up old memories. The dopamine had drained away and she had to wait for the tablet to give her some movement again. Her 'off' times, when along with the dopamine, her serotonin levels plummeted, were her bleakest. She was overcome by an eerie stillness that froze her features and all hope. As far as Kathleen knew, Richard Hall had dropped his suspicions of Eleanor. The main suspect had become the tramp whose body was found tangled in the river weeds under the bridge near Southease by the police divers.

Seeing her today, Kathleen wondered if Eleanor had known more then she had told the police.

So later that evening when someone knocked on her door, Kathleen only struggled to her feet to answer because she guessed it must be Eleanor returning.

But it wasn't.

This time she didn't offer refreshment. Jackie knew where to find the tea things.

They sat on either side of the fire, Jackie in Kathleen's chair and Kathleen in Steve's. Jackie gripped her notebook like an insurance salesman.

She was businesslike:

'After all this time, I think we both know she's not coming back.'

'Eleanor?' Kathleen's mind was still on the Ramsay sisters.

'Alice.'

'Oh.' Kathleen's body began to tremble and she held her right hand tightly in her left. Jackie noted this down. She was like an artist doing a quick sketch, darting looks at her subject before scribbling busily.

'It's certain that Alice is dead. I wanted you to be the first to know.'

Why did they always say this? What difference did it make if she were the second person to know?

Kathleen was floating; her feet were sliding out from under her, pulling her down towards the floor. She needed an emergency tablet, but couldn't move.

Doctor Ramsay had advised her to take care of herself.

Her face had stiffened to a mask, and her skin colour drained to a pasty grey as, in her head, Kathleen called out to Eleanor. She knew why Eleanor had gone. She must go after her. But her feet were lead and with Jackie here, she could not go anywhere.

Jackie Masters drew a perfectly straight line in her notebook and tapped the page peremptorily with her silver pen:

'I've been doing some digging. I know who killed Alice.'

At the same moment, Kathleen realised that so did she.

Twenty-Six

The Judge's tombstone dwarfed his son's makeshift cross. The bench was now in shade, but it had not cooled down, the eiderdown air was still and heavy. Eleanor was in the dock, knees together, humble, before the stark lettering.

'How did you kill her?' For the moment her anger had gone, leaving a silt of bewilderment. It didn't even matter who her mother was. These doubts were the luxuries of a lost life. Her mother's confession had extinguished any glimmer of hope.

'I can't remember.'

'You must remember.'

'I hid. There was counting. Alice cheated.'

'She cheated?' Her Mum was mad, she ought to be kind to her. 'If you can't remember anything, how do you know you killed her? Why would you?'

'She said terrible things.'

'So you killed her?' Chris would tame the word. *Kill time, kill off the germs, stop it, you're killing me, kill two birds.* She could keep meaning at bay and save her Mum. Last week Chris wouldn't have thought her Mum could murder anyone. But now…

'She was an innocent schoolgirl. Always in a good mood, always willing and always top of everything. I worked it out. If Alice was so good, I must be bad because I was the opposite of her. She sneered at me and said everything I cared about was rubbish. She said my Dad didn't love me.'

'She said those things?'

'Maybe I made it all up.'

As she talked Eleanor's mouth relaxed, her lips were fuller and wider, the lines around them smoothed away; she was no longer Alice. Chris supposed her confession had relieved her of a burden. She forced herself to listen:

After the night of the smashed mirror when her Mum went off in the ambulance, Eleanor had invented a new story. Her real parents were a poor couple living in Friston Forest who had left her on a blanket in the car park when she was a baby. They wanted her to have a better life than they could give her. They took pleasure in seeing her grow up from a distance. They kept watch as she went to the sweet shop to buy bubble gum or played secretly at the Tide Mills. This meant Eleanor was never alone because the kind couple – the woman a spit image of Mrs Jackson – were always there, they would even take her back if things got too much.

After Alice had gone, her parents really were the strangers who had found her on the rug deep in the forest. They became silent and separate and stern except at night when she heard their voices talking long after their bedtime. Then as everyone finally went to sleep there would be the banging and knocking as Alice sneaked back from hiding. But only Eleanor saw her.

One night Eleanor had crept to the window to find Alice on the other side of the pane. She was on the sill trying to shelter from the fine rain, tapping with scratchy nails to be let in. Alice was like the lady in the bit from *Wuthering Heights* that Gina had once read to her and Lucian to stop them pestering her. It was pitch black outside, but Alice was lit up like the Christmas tree angel with a light bulb stuffed up her skirts.

Alice had menaced Eleanor with secrets that made Eleanor's eyes prick with tiny needles. She had tried to make Eleanor cry.

That bruise on your mother's neck is a love-bite. Like a vampire.

Your Dad said I was the daughter he wished you had been.

Still in the dream, Eleanor had been disappointed to see Alice carried in through the front door of the doll's house in

Mr Howland's hairy arms. She hoped she had gone for good. Eleanor was in the doll's house. The front was open so that the windows were suspended in mid-air like the fireplace at the Tide Mills. Mr Howland had cuddled Alice like a doll. She had been bath-time-cosy in a rabbit dressing gown and fluffy slippers. Alice was completely dry, which Eleanor thought was strange because it was pouring outside. Eleanor felt a cold draught as Alice sneaked up on to the green sofa beside her. While the grownups were in the kitchen making cocoa, she explained in a fast whisper how she was sorry for cheating. She had learnt her lesson. From now on they could play whatever game Eleanor suggested and she would pretend it was real. Eleanor told her it was too late. Alice had used up her last life.

'I can't hear you?'

Alice's voice had been like a radio, with the volume getting quieter. Yet she was still sitting beside her making Eleanor as cold as ice.

She had nearly gone. Finally, like the Cheshire cat, there was just her mouth, smiling like a good girl.

'The Mill Owner. You were right about him. I didn't believe you.' The Alice-mouth had no voice. Eleanor had to lip read.

'He doesn't exist. I made him up. He's dead in the churchyard. He died of Apo-plex-ey on a train from Seaford.' Eleanor had yelled, but the ears had faded away long ago.

In the morning, Alice was still missing and Eleanor's Dad was furious when she told him Alice had come back in the night. She showed him the marks on the bedroom window frame as proof. But he accused her of making them herself. Eleanor had not confessed that when she had tonsillitis last year, she had tried to carve her name in the wood with her penknife. But he had known. She wanted him to understand that the point was Alice had come back. She had thought he would be pleased.

Long days crawled by, stretching into weeks and soon years were laid down like paving slabs with no secret animals or messages scratched in the stone. Alice never returned and after a while she wasn't mentioned in the Ramsay household.

Aged sixteen, Eleanor was expelled from her expensive central London school for stealing a teacher's purse. Her last year of education was at a crammer in Kensington where to everyone's incredulity she got three 'A' levels. She was befriended by one of the teachers, a man with corkscrew hair whose boyfriend was an oboist in the Covent Garden Orchestra. She bunked off lessons to go to rehearsals of operas and ballets, lounging in the stalls of the empty auditorium, knees propped up on the seat in front, munching sweets and desultorily revising *The Duchess of Malfi* with an usher's torch in the boring bits.

When she was not much older than Chris was now, Eleanor had sex with a boy called Gary on the bathroom floor of a squat in Shepherd's Bush. He was head mechanic at the local Renault garage and she had fancied him because he looked like Paul Weller. Eleanor told him she was engaged when he asked to see her again. She never told him she was pregnant.

By the time she had the baby – a girl she called Chris after the oboist who she had loved more than anyone – Eleanor was getting flashbacks. Her memories were like dreams and at first she could dismiss them. But they began to make too much sense. Eleanor had seen Alice near the halt at the Tide Mills and was outraged that she wasn't looking for her. She would get her.

She told Chris that as the unbidden pictures came more often, she hadn't been able to go on seeing her family. She had found a room in Holloway. At twenty-one, Eleanor had inherited a trust fund set up by Judge Henry for his heirs and this small allowance was paid straight into her account. This income coincided with giving birth to Chris. So as the truth of what happened on that June day was pieced together out of the fragments of a sunsoaked past, Eleanor changed her name to Alice Kennedy after the Senator with the dimple in his chin who had been shot the day after Alice vanished, and with her small baby, she too disappeared.

'I took away her life. If I became Alice, she would not be dead.'

'You didn't actually think you were her, did you?' Chris had thought her Mum was intelligent, despite her illness. 'An eight-year-old might just believe it, if they were a bit bonkers, but you were a grownup. Mrs Howland was searching for her, you hadn't brought her back at all. What did your parents say?'

'I was Alice. They weren't my parents. Until today I hadn't seen my mother since you were a baby.' Eleanor appeared just to register this, she went on with less energy: 'I had to be punished.'

'So we should all be grateful.' Chris snorted.

Eleanor had found the flat in Bermondsey and, keeping her address a secret, cut herself off from everyone she knew. This wasn't difficult; after Alice vanished, she only had one friend – the oboist – and she assumed he wouldn't miss her.

'You have never known Eleanor Ramsay. You knew Alice Kennedy. You made Alice real.'

'But how real did it make me?'

'You're my daughter. I love you more than anyone. That's all that matters.'

'You think?'

'You said that an eight-year-old would have thought it possible to become someone else. I was eight when I became Alice. Everyone wanted me to be Alice. No one wanted Eleanor. Mrs Howland was stunned after Alice went. Not eating, not talking, and then she got this obsession about seeing me. She livened up. No one could talk her out of it. So I had to go there a week after Alice went.'

The day before the Ramsays were to go home to London, Mark Ramsay came to tell Eleanor that Alice's parents wanted her to come to tea. He had stomped into the playroom more like a doctor than her Dad and stood over her. She was shielded from him by the open frontage of the doll's house. They avoided looking at each other. One huge foot was planted against the drawing room window, trampling on the fuzzy felt lawn. It snapped off the window sill, and when he lifted his foot the green material stuck to the sole of his shoe and ripped away. Before Alice vanished Eleanor would have protested, even pushing him, directing his attention to her sign: *Keep off the Grass.* She had rubbed the felt in a pile of grass cuttings behind the garage so it smelled real. But as her Dad had not spoken properly to her for days, she decided not to make things worse by pointing out the rule about the grass. Alice would have said it was because Eleanor was bad. She said bad things happened to bad people.

Who are you to tell him off? He's a doctor; he knows best.
I don't know, who am I?

Doctor Ramsay took Eleanor to the Howlands' cottage for tea. Neither of them said a word on the very short journey from the White House to the tidy cottage by the village stores. Eleanor had sat in enforced primness in the back, Jeremy Fisher-feet dangling over the leather seat. Although she was alone, Eleanor sat where she always sat when the family went anywhere, in the middle. Gina and Lucian had the window places, Gina because she got car sick, and Lucian because he was going to be a doctor. Usually if she went anywhere without the rest of them, Eleanor would clamber gleefully over to one of the windows, wind the glass down and stick her face into the wind. That day she kept quite still like a good girl and waited to arrive with clean hands and an unclear conscience. She could see her Dad's eyes in the driving mirror. They flicked back and forth like a cat as he reversed the car round at the front of the White House then roared out of the gates. Then they whizzed up the hill to where Alice lived.

Everyone became bothered about Eleanor before she left for the tea. Her mother had brushed her hair so hard she made her eyes sting and she sneezed five times, which made her brush harder. She had to put on the disgusting fairy dress they had made her wear to a recent wedding. It scratched under the arms. Gina had been instructed to lend her black, patent leather shoes with poppers. Gina could no longer fit into them, but normally she never let anyone else wear her shoes even when she couldn't wear them herself. She had done so only on the whispered condition that Eleanor kept them clean. This was the first time Gina had properly spoken to her since her furious return from the stables.

'How can I get them dirty? Is their house muddy?' Eleanor had forgotten to whisper back, so her mother heard and snapped:

'Eleanor! This is not a joke.'

Eleanor had not been joking. She had given up making jokes.

Instead she shouted things inside her head so they could not guess where it came from. All the while she sat neatly with her mouth tight shut. She would not look over at the kitchen clock, where instead of the hands telling the time there was Alice's white face smiling virtuously.

The Howlands were waiting on the doorstep as the car drew up. She had expected them to be cross like everyone else and glumly assumed she was going to be told off about Alice. They were like two matching vases placed on each side of the front door with hands clasped together and to her surprise they acted pleased to see her. Suddenly Eleanor knew they were the couple who had left her in Friston Forest. These people were her proper parents and seeing that she was unhappy, they had claimed her back. She felt a rush of joy that was like the start of crying and the start of Christmas all at once.

She grabbed the fruit cake Lizzie had baked – that she was to say was her present – from the front seat, and trotted up the path holding it out in front of her like one of the three kings bearing a gift. This image was so vivid to Eleanor she had to resist dragging each foot the way the boys who played the kings in the play did. It was giving in to an impulse such as this that always got her into trouble.

Instead of answering her when she said 'Hello Mr Howland', as she had been told to, Alice's Dad, who Eleanor rather liked, did a strange clucking thing with his throat, and pulled a funny face with his mouth halfway up his face. She laughed – he was good at faces – but glancing back saw her own father's face darkly forbidding and stopped as if he had slapped her.

Her father was staring at Mr and Mrs Howland, who he obviously thought were frightening creatures. For a minute Eleanor expected him to scream with terror because cords stood out on his neck like they did to people about to be murdered in scary films. She prepared her fingers to block her ears.

Later, she decided she had made this bit up.

'Come in, Eleanor, tea's all ready.' Mrs Howland bent towards her and putting out a hand, stroked the top of her head with short sharp pats the way boring guests did with Crawford. 'And you too, Doctor Ramsay. Stay. The more the merrier!'

The two men stood with the gate between them looking back at the little girl in the immaculate party dress as she skipped obediently into the house holding hands with the nice woman. They watched Mrs Howland as she snatched up the role of mother and hostess with eager fervency.

Eleanor pinpointed that moment on the doorstep as the sloughing off of her life and the first steps towards resurrecting Alice. As she unwittingly took part in a crude rehearsal for a reunion that could never be, she had decided to make it come true. She would be Alice living her life somewhere in the world, just as Mrs Howland came to hope she was. Yet even Eleanor was impotent to undo a tragedy. She had read enough fairy stories to know that an evil deed once done cannot be undone. Eleanor's childish chatter that day could only be one of the cruelties of everyday life.

Both men were unequal to their parts, they could only stand helplessly until Doctor Ramsay snapped into action, talking like a telegram.

'Have work to do. Back to London tomorrow. All go!' He promised to be back in an hour.

Steve Howland leaned on the gate as the doctor's car roared away, tyres screeching. He had not said a word and stayed where he was looking down the street in the direction that Alice had walked that last afternoon. He had thoughts he could not share, crude inventions about what had happened that Kath would be right to dismiss as jealous and even rude.

So he said nothing. At last his wife called him inside to join in the tea with Doctor Ramsay's daughter.

Eleanor was disappointed that, unlike the other time she had visited, Mr Howland did nothing during the tea without Mrs Howland prompting him. She had been looking forward to another tour of the tools in his garage and the go on his soldering iron he had promised her the time before to make up for Alice spoiling the tea.

She had pattered after Mrs Howland into the kitchen with wary steps, mindful of this first visit. Suppose Alice had been hiding brilliantly and had planned the tea as another surprise. Then she reminded herself that Alice reappearing could not happen. She relaxed at the sight of the neat, empty kitchen. Of course there would be no chocolate covered Alice lying in wait. This meant Eleanor had the opportunity to see the room properly and she admired the six plates propped up on shelves above the fridge. There were cat faces on them, a fluffy ginger with flourishing whiskers made her think of Crawford, so she told Mrs Howland about her cat and her visits to Mrs Jackson. The table was hidden beneath plates of cakes and jelly with a gigantic jug of orange squash right in the middle. Eleanor gaped at the mountain of food and swallowed. This time, she had no appetite. She was pushed firmly towards the chair that Alice had been sitting on when they found her coated all over with food that day.

'Would you like some of your own cake, dear?'

'No, that's for you, thank you.' Then remembering her lines. 'It's a present from me.'

'Aren't you lovely!'

It was finally growing cooler in the graveyard. The sun had left it altogether, but neither woman noticed as Eleanor recalled that she had forced herself to eat a large number of cakes and two bowlfuls of jelly, only by thinking of one mouthful at a time, chewing then swallowing, chew-swallow, chew-swallow. The trick was not to look at what was on her plate. This became her approach to life. A minute at a time and don't look down.

When she left, Mrs Howland gave her the Crawford plate. This was a nice surprise, for although Mrs Howland had smiled and nodded as she talked, Eleanor had been sure she was not listening. Nor was Mr Howland because he nodded in the wrong places and mostly never spoke at all. Mrs Howland made him wrap the plate in newspaper, and then because he went into a trance she took over. There was a gap on the shelf where the plate had been. Eleanor saw Alice's father notice this too.

As they got to the door, Mrs Howland rushed upstairs. Eleanor stayed in the hall with Mr Howland. She had tried smiling up at him, but he was like her clockwork sparrow and couldn't strut or peck without Mrs Howland to work him. He had tapped at the barometer, which was pointed at *Rain* and Eleanor was just thinking that this was her chance to mention the soldering iron, when Mrs Howland came down again. She had held out her fist to Eleanor and then splayed out her hand to reveal a small purse. It was Alice's purse. It had her name inside. She had tried to write all of it but had done 'Alice' in such big letters that there was only room for an 'H' and an 'o', which Eleanor had thought made her sound more jolly than she was. It was brown leather, patterned with gold spirals laced with blue and maroon flowers. Inside there were two threepenny bits.

'Don't give her that.' Mr Howland had stopped examining the barometer.

'She should have it.'

'No. When she comes...' He ran his hand down his face as if a different face would be there when he had finished, like the conjuror at Christmas.

Mrs Howland had hold of Eleanor's hand and she pressed the purse into it. 'Don't be spending it on sweets, especially bubble gum. That's very bad for you.' She had stopped smiling, and was looking at her closely. Eleanor wanted to get away.

She slipped the purse into the pocket in her dress meant for tissues and dashed down the path to the car at the gate. Her father was sitting stiffly at the wheel like Parker in

Thunderbirds and didn't look round when Eleanor got into the back. She hadn't thanked Alice's Mum and Dad or said goodbye. She had forgotten they were her real parents and now it was too late. She only just remembered to look back to wave as she was driven away. The cottage door was shut. Eleanor was only eight, but with perfect understanding she divined it wasn't Eleanor Ramsay that the Howlands had invited to tea, but Alice. From now on it would always be Alice.

Once Eleanor turned into Alice she tried to blot out Eleanor and what she had done or failed to do.

'He knew though, didn't he?' Chris tripped over to Mark Ramsay's grave. She stood unsteadily beside the mound. 'He couldn't bear what you'd done any longer and so he killed himself.' Chris grabbed a handful of the soil and cupped it in her hands the way she made snowballs. They had done this together. She had made a snowman in the park with her Mum, she was sure of it. Until now she had totally forgotten this.

A moped puttered past on the lane and on the other side of the church a gate squeaked, followed by the clink of the latch.

'It was an accident. '

'There's no such thing as an accident.'

'Please come home.'

'You're mad. We can't go home. It's all over; can't you see that? You've smashed things up for me as well as you. You're sick and you need help but you have had all you're getting from me.'

'What are you going to do?'

'She's going to come back with me.' The voice was reedy but firm.

Kathleen Howland was on the path a few yards away. Her frailty augmented her aura of command.

When Jackie Masters had left, Kathleen had sat still in Steve's chair looking at the empty grate. This time there was no offer of sugary tea; no attempt to shield her from exactly how it was.

Kathleen tilted her head and there was Alice's photograph on the television. As the evening closed in and the living room grew dim, Alice's eyes and nose, her pigtails and the painted seascape background faded to shades of grey. But for Kathleen her bright and cheerful smile remained just the same.

And at that moment Kathleen saw what she could do.

Part Three

August to December 1999

Twenty-Seven

On a warm sunny afternoon at the end of August, Kathleen eased open the window in Alice's bedroom and surveyed the street below. Cars were parked bumper to bumper: there had been a fête on the green that afternoon and the lane was still busy with people – laconic couples, darting children, hot and tired parents were straggling along the pavement leading to the station, most licking ice creams or pecking at toffee apples while lugging spoils and homemade produce from which the magic had already faded.

The curtain brushed against her face as she drew back in, she gathered it up; the material was beginning to wear. Perhaps now she would get new ones.

That morning she had pulled their suitcases down from the top of the wardrobe in the bedroom. After Steve died, Kathleen used the smaller case for her trips but as her Parkinson's progressed even this was becoming too heavy. She had told Chris she kept it packed with essentials so that she could leave at short notice, as she had done on the morning Steve took her to the hospital to give birth to Alice. He hadn't stayed for her birth. In those days he was on the docks at Newhaven and lost pay if he didn't work. Kathleen emptied everything on to her bed and dragged the cases through to Alice's bedroom.

That morning she had popped next door to the stores to see if Iris had any cardboard boxes. Iris could find only two, including one for toilet rolls for which she apologised, but really no, it didn't matter what had been in them. What mattered was what she planned to fill them with. Kathleen knew Iris wanted to ask what the boxes were for, and if it had been anyone else Iris would have. Kathleen told her anyway.

'I have a young friend coming to live with me. Eleanor Ramsay's girl, Christine. The one that's been visiting, she's gone home to get her things.' Kathleen cheered as the information took on life with the telling.

'Eleanor Ramsay! There's a name to conjure with. I always wondered what happened to her. She simply vanis...haven't seen her for years. Doctor Ramsay never mentioned a little girl.'

'I'm clearing out...I'm preparing the guest bedroom.' There, now she had said it.

Iris was trying to fit sweets into the counter display, she was jamming Munchies and Mars Bars into too tight a space and had bent two of the packets, but in her determination to prolong their chat she hadn't noticed.

'Didn't go to her poor Dad's funeral, which between you and me...' Iris continued gruffly. She had developed a trick of not finishing sentences, so that other people completed them, giving her more information. Kathleen knew this, but unlike most, preferred to indulge her. Iris Carter meant no harm.

'Oh, she did go.' Kathleen gathered up the boxes, fitting one inside the other. 'Eleanor would do anything for her parents.' This idea passed like an aeroplane crossing the sun, the brief lack of light a fleeting insight, a momentary chill. Then she added, 'Christine's just the same as her mother. She's a good girl.'

Kathleen had stayed longer than she intended to show that she was like other customers and could sit on the chair by the rack of postcards nursing a mug of tea and petting the Persian cats with the best of them.

After Jackie had told her about the CCTV footage, explaining in formal tones that had frightened Kathleen before she took in the impact of the words themselves, Kathleen had been shattered. She wouldn't have believed her. But she had seen the evidence for herself. It had made no sense until now.

As she had made her way unsteadily up to the church, her hands brushing and clutching at any surface for support to keep herself from falling, she knew that Jackie was right. Kathleen had sent Doctor Ramsay to his death. She had broken his trust. Ever mindful of his family's need for privacy, he had lent her the tapes on the unspoken agreement that she was looking for one thing and would ignore the rest. But she had taken note of everything. Perhaps not literally, but only because her hands refused to write. She had looked out for the woman who was Jackie Masters, not because she looked like Alice, but because she was curious about her. Kathleen had spied on the Ramsays and then acted on her information. But it wasn't for this indiscretion that she would never be able to forgive herself. It was for all the times she had shut her eyes and ears to the unpleasant in favour of a Wonderland of nice clean hands, lovely manners and unchipped tea things.

Kathleen was glad that at least Steve had not lived to know the truth.

Steve had known all along.

She unlatched the church gate and leaned on it briefly to get her balance. As she shut it behind her and strode without support towards Mark Ramsay's grave she was clear. She would take Chris home with her. If in any way she had failed her daughter, she did have a chance to save another child's life.

Now, Kathleen imagined Chris filling the cupboard with her clothes, and the house with her bright chatter. She hadn't expected to feel so elated at the prospect. Eleanor was unhappy about it, but accepted it. Kathleen had told Chris her mother was not a killer. She had promised Eleanor that for the while, she wouldn't say more.

People would assume Chris was her substitute for Alice. They would be right. Yet no one would replace Alice. Kathleen had learnt that time was not a healer, it only clarified the loss. Now she knew nothing could bring her cherished little girl back.

She worked quickly, packing the cases and the boxes with the contents of the shelves and most of the toy cupboard. She had already got rid of the new clothes and since the day Chris had first appeared on her doorstep, Kathleen had bought nothing else in Alice's name. She stuffed the rest in bin bags and stacked the bags and cases on the landing. As she worked, a cacophony of inner voices squawked in protest, disapproving and reproving. The heap of possessions didn't amount to much. But then nine years was not much of a life.

Chris was coming back at lunchtime the next day. Preparing the room had taken Kathleen over three hours. The sheets were not dirty, but she remade the bed because it must be made for Chris, not for Alice who would never need it. While she had been staying, Chris had insisted on sleeping on the settee in the living room. When she returned it would be different. Kathleen laid a sprig of lavender under her pillow and as a finishing touch placed a vase of wild flowers by her bed – scabious, buttercups and sow-thistle – a taste of real countryside for a girl escaping from London.

A life for a life.

Through the open casement came the twitter and squabble of birds bustling on the guttering, and the jingle of the shop bell. When they had moved in, Kathleen had been so happy and those sounds, which she hadn't noticed for years, had orchestrated her happiness. Perhaps they would again.

She needed dopamine; sorting out the room had used up her resources. Although Kathleen accommodated the disease, she would not give in to it. In the last few weeks her Parkinson's had accelerated, flaying her outer layer, exposing raw flesh to the elements and making her anxious about the simplest things. When the effect of the drugs wore off she was engulfed in a terrible sadness and time shrank so that it was only yesterday since Alice had vanished and she had raked through her mind for a clue everyone had missed. Take the 'c' out of Alice and replace it with a 'v'. She had played this spelling swap in the hospital after Alice was born. Then everything had been alive, everything was Alice.

She had stripped the room of Alice's belongings and of the clothes that had never belonged. Kathleen had so often stood in this room imploring Alice to give her a sign that she was present. Downstairs the telephone began to ring. It would be Jackie Masters. Kathleen hadn't answered her calls and she wouldn't today. Through the floor she heard the monotone voice leaving another message. Jackie would not give up, but she dared not sound frustrated.

Kathleen was the blackmailer now.

Just as Kathleen was about to go down to get her supper, she spotted something glinting on the carpet by the bed. She got down on her knees. It was a round lump of green glass, thick as a pebble, smooth on two sides. It looked like a jewel, the deep green enriched by the sunlight. It must have been in the cupboard. She had heard a thud as she hauled out Alice's skating boots. Kathleen raised herself on to the bed and sat with the glass in her palm. It was cold and weighty. There was one tiny air bubble that only enhanced its perfection. Kathleen didn't recognise it. As she closed her hand around it she felt her anxiety leave, and more than at any other time she had been in Alice's bedroom, this was the sign she had asked for. Alice was with her; she would never leave home again.

Kathleen placed the glass on the lace doily spread out on the bedside table, where it looked just right. She would give it to Chris as a welcome present. She knew that Chris would treasure it. She would tell Chris that it would bring her luck.

As she unsteadily descended the stairs it occurred to Kathleen she had kept very little to remind herself of Alice; no school reports, no books, no toys. All that Alice had owned was bagged up on the landing or shoved in the rubbish bin; except for her pink cardigan and some photographs. Kathleen had been ruthless. This made her pause on the last stair. Steve was standing by the barometer, tapping the glass with indirect admonishment. If Alice had stayed, Kathleen wouldn't have kept all her things. Now Alice would be grown up and living in a house of her own. She would have other possessions, more fitting for a forty-year-old. The room would have been a guestroom for when Alice and her family came to stay. Alice was beside Kathleen, always approving; urging her lovely old Mum onwards.

Once Kathleen was by the front door her feet refused to move. She could hear the tweeting of her tablet timer by the cooker, but she was stuck fast to the floor. At last, only by steadying herself on Alice's arm, she was able to make big strides and reach the kitchen. As she shakily placed a yellow tablet on her tongue and swallowed water with drainpipe imprecision, Kathleen told Alice she had been thinking about what Chris liked to eat. Alice agreed that Kathleen would have to ask Chris to help her cook, for these days she found it harder to prepare food.

They both wanted Chris to feel entirely at home.

Twenty-Eight

At the end of November, Kathleen told Chris that Eleanor had asked to see her. So far Chris had refused to have anything to do with her mother; but this time Kathleen asked her to meet her. Eleanor turned up on the doorstep in a new fancy wax jacket and swathed in a huge wool scarf, and announced she was taking Chris to the Tide Mills.

They hadn't seen each other since Chris had gone to live with Kathleen. Eleanor had been shocked by Chris's hostility. She had hoped that her acquiescence would herald a change of heart. Over the years she had become so used to her Alice-self, that the enormity of her deception was reduced in her mind to mere dressing up. She was Alice, and being Alice hurt no one. Or so she had believed. But Chris refused to link arms or look at Eleanor and stomped up the lane a pace behind her.

Eleanor had been staggered when Chris went to live with Kathleen Howland. It was a terrible punishment. She endured it because she decided it was the punishment. Being Alice was the rehearsal. To atone fully she must lose her own daughter. It was tempting to see it as Kathleen's revenge, but she knew that Kathleen had not looked for someone to blame. Like Eleanor, she blamed only herself. Kathleen had respected Eleanor's wishes and said nothing to Chris, so in return Eleanor had to take her advice – give it time – and leave Chris alone.

Eleanor was confounded: Chris had changed completely. She was taller, quieter; a steadfastly separate being who vigorously resisted Eleanor's feeble attempts to draw her into the Ramsay family. She was prepared, however, to go with her to the Tide Mills.

Trotting and skipping like a young girl, Eleanor led Chris out of the village, scrambling through a hedge when there was a perfectly good gate and running helter-skelter across a stubbly field. Chris was imperturbable as Eleanor leapt over a stile; she followed with deliberate reluctance, determined to provide a sober contrast to her mother's strangely skittish state. Soon she had no choice but to caper beside her, for Eleanor grasped her hand and Chris was pulled and tugged along over a pot-holed lane that ended at a six-foot-high wall, topped by rounded bricks coated in yellow and white lichen. There were holes where the wall had crumbled, creating windows with a vista of gnarled fruit trees. Assuming the authority of a tour guide, Eleanor explained that the trees were the remains of a pear orchard. This was the garden of the Mill Owner who had run the thriving mill, its hours dictated by the tides, in the mid-nineteenth century. Over a hundred people had once lived here, at one point making flour for the British army during the Napoleonic wars. Most of the houses were demolished during the Second World War to stop the Germans using them for cover, but a whole section of the big house had survived until the late sixties.

'You must remember me telling you about the crane with the massive metal ball that swung back and forth, smashing into the walls? Like the one we saw from my bedroom when they knocked down the Bricklayer's Arms station? I saw it here first. The noise was deafening. It was a fantastic sight, but I was devastated when I came back straight after breakfast the next morning and found everything reduced to rubble. I hadn't stopped to think what would happen in the end.'

'What's new?'

Chris snatched away her hand.

Eleanor leaned on the makeshift sill of a hole in the wall, talking fast as she described the row of workers' cottages beyond the orchard; the blacksmith's, the carpenter's shop. In a minute she would show Chris the last remaining millpond and then the railway track that carried the grain away from the Granary to the halt on the main line. They had passed it on their way down, now reduced to a stranded platform, marooned in a thick tangle of nettles and hawthorn. They had waited by the crossing on the branch line. Eleanor had made Chris listen out to be sure there was no train, although the line was grown over and there hadn't been a train since the 1930s. She had got very excited by an ancient signboard covered in graffiti, and had insisted on spending ages working out the word *Bongville* behind the staccato scrawl. She said the name had been painted on the sign in the sixties, and that Alice had said it was rude, but Eleanor couldn't see why. Nor could she now. Chris couldn't either, but said nothing. So far, she thought coming down here was a waste of time, but Kathleen had pleaded with her to make an effort to get to know her real mother. For once, Chris decided, Kathleen was wrong. Eleanor Ramsay was an embarrassing and pathetic middle-aged woman.

They came across a narrow path overshadowed by the high wall, and had to pick their way over the uneven ground, moving branches out of the way to avoid being slashed across the face. They tripped up on the remains of a fire glittering with bent and crushed drinks cans. Later, as they had to avoid twists of shit-stained tissue, Chris could see nothing secret about this place. Despite her intransigence she was disappointed. They emerged into a clearing that Eleanor told her had been the back garden of the Mill Owner's house and was where she had once planted a secret flowerbed. There was no sign of Eleanor's garden. All her nasturtiums had gone.

Then the flinty path gave way to a two-foot square section of terracotta tiles surrounded by a tide of coarse grass and moss. Suddenly Eleanor was on the ground scrabbling at the soil, tearing up clumps of turf, ripping away long tresses of ivy to reveal more tiles.

'This was the kitchen in the big house. I once dissected a dead cat near here. You would've been in your element. It was a great place to find dead animals. The entrance hall had these brilliant diamond shaped tiles in a really complicated black and

279

white pattern, oh in fact, like the ones on the ground floor at the White House. I'll show you.'

'No way. I'm not going.'

'They must be somewhere under those bushes over there.' Eleanor talked in bursts as with the sharp edge of a flint she cut away a section of moss and then buffed the exposed tile with the spit-wetted heel of her palm. Chris lost patience and nudged her shoulder; the task was pointless. Now the tiles would be nicked.

'No they won't. No one comes here but me. Help me; who cares about a bit of dirt.'

Chris hung back.

'Come on! Don't be like that.'

Chris got down beside Eleanor and sulkily snapped off a couple of blades of grass. Then, making a bit more effort, she lifted off a whole tussock of coarse grass to reveal three tiles at once. Despite herself Chris was triumphant, and grabbing a stone she used it to saw away the moss and sever the thick ivy stems. She had spent most of her life wishing her Mum would do things outside with her and now she was. Soon they had cleared another square foot. It really looked like a floor.

'This'll take all afternoon, there's lots to show you.' Eleanor flung down her flint: 'I'll come another day to finish it. I want you to see my cottage. Where I carved my name.'

Eleanor paused at the bottom of a steep slope. She stroked Chris's sleeve briefly, but Chris shook her off. 'I told the police we played near my house and that I last saw Alice in the lane, just before the bend.'

'So?'

'We were here. Just over this hill is where she was counting.'

They climbed up a steep incline, helped by steps cut into the chalk. Over time these had lost definition, and it was hard to get a foothold, so that they had to use gorse branches to keep their balance.

'This goes to the beach.' Eleanor's febrile chatter infuriated Chris whose own past had been demolished by a swinging ball. Her mother was only intent on justifying her lies, and crushing

Chris's own memories under the weight of more of her stories. Chris wished she hadn't come.

They got to the top and were brought up short by a metal fence that ended in jagged spikes exactly like the one at the back of their flat in Bermondsey. They gripped the bars while they got their breath and stared uncomprehending through them to a huge aluminium structure with vast orange and wood panels clamped to its side. A Sainsbury's Superstore. Chris recognised it as the one she shopped in with Kathleen every Friday morning. A man in a forklift truck, moving with the erratic swivelling of a dodgem car, was unloading a tower of boxes from a lorry. In the distance they could hear smashing glass from the bottle banks in the car park. The discordant sound orchestrated Eleanor's shock. A landscape had been wiped away. The crumbling flint wall at the bottom of the hill and a few kitchen floor tiles were all that was left of the Tide Mills.

Eleanor clutched the railings.

'I left Alice counting over there to the left of that doorway. It's impossible to be sure exactly where.'

'There's a salad bar there now.'

The path continued along the side of the fence. The place where Alice had last been seen had vanished too. Alice might never have existed.

'This is the hill I ran down to hide.' Eleanor spoke as if in a trance. 'I hid in those bushes halfway down on the right. I found his handkerchief on the path. I said I got it off the ironing pile. I didn't tell the police it was Dad's.' Eleanor put her hand to her mouth.

Chris felt sick. It was the first time she had referred to the dead professor as 'Dad' since she stopped being Alice.

'You said you lied to the police about where you hid. Why was anyone searching here?' Chris stared dubiously at the bushes lining the slope down to the sea. A child would be cut to shreds hiding in there. They would risk breaking their neck falling down the sharp drop on to the shingle. She scanned the beach wistfully as a cold sharp wind blew the hair away from her face. On one side the stretch of shingle was enclosed by a chalk outcrop and at the far end by a huge pile of boulders near to which a group of young blokes were playing Frisbee. There had been a girl at her school who had refused to see her Mum after she walked out on her Dad. Chris had thought she could never cut herself off from hers. Now this is what she planned to do. As soon as she could, she would make an excuse and go.

'Why couldn't you just tell the truth?' Chris asked gruffly. *No, don't answer that.*

'I would have got in trouble for coming here. I said we played near the house. Alice hadn't wanted to. She always did what she was told. But oddly that afternoon she said we could do whatever I wanted. I should have realised she was up to something; she had never been so eager to please before.'

Eleanor stepped off the track and thrust her way through a mass of thick brambles down the steep hill. After a few feet she stopped and looked out towards the sea, behaving like the last surviving explorer on a desert island, scanning the horizon for a rescue ship. Then she turned back to the hillside and indicated the dense shrubland.

'I hid somewhere over there. It's so changed. It's grown so much.' She wasn't talking to Chris. 'I heard footsteps. I didn't dare look in case I gave myself away.'

'So where exactly did you kill her and what did you do with her body?' Chris was humouring her now. She hadn't worked out which was worse; to have killed someone or be so mad that you thought you had.

'I can't remember.'

Chris hated that she still loved her. She had hoped staying with Kathleen would break the suffocating connection. But when Eleanor had arrived at the cottage that morning, Kathleen had been kind to her so Chris had felt obliged to be the same. Kathleen had told Chris a lot about Eleanor. How she had been so much fun as a child, making everyone laugh, and so imaginative. Never a dull moment.

'I once found myself wishing my Alice would be more like her. She was such a free spirit. But in the end she was fine as she was. I did feel sorry for Eleanor because she was called naughty when really she was just different. I think she meant well.'

Chris marvelled at how Kathleen could be so saintly about a child who had killed her daughter. None of it made sense. Kathleen had stopped Chris going to the police, or even to the doctor's. Although she had grown very fond of Kathleen in only a short time, Chris was now sure Kathleen too was lying.

There was only one way to find out the truth.

'Okay, I'll come to your house.' She was careful to be casual because her Mum would change her mind if she guessed the real reason. 'See them all and that...'

Eleanor contemplated the sea. It was tourist brochure blue. A strip of mirrored sand glistened between the straggling strata of wet pebbles and the encroaching water. She would like to have stripped off and dived into it. Closing her eyes as the cold water stopped her heart.

Who was the man in white trousers talking to a little girl? They were too far away for her to see their faces. Eleanor couldn't get to them that way, because the tide was coming in and would quickly cut her off. Already it had washed away their footprints. Their voices were lost in the crashing waves. They had only been a trick of the light. When she next looked the beach was empty.

'Did you hear me?' Chris expected her at least to be grateful.

'Come for Sunday lunch. I'll get everyone over. Or is it too...'

'No, it's fine. Get them all.' She would need to observe the whole family.

Chris let Eleanor trail off down the path. Her coat was open, her shirt coming out of her jeans and her hair was sticking up at angles. She hadn't been taking care of herself. Yet, in the jaunty step, the nimble hopping across ruts and stones, Chris saw again the woman she had glimpsed dancing to David Bowie. Once upon a time she had wished she could have a mother like this woman leaping and jumping through bushes to the beach. Now it was too late.

283

Eleanor loped over the loose shingle and flopped down at the foot of the cliff. She had been sure she could bring Chris round if she would agree to meet her. Today's journey had not been wasted. She shut her eyes and listened to the ceaseless whoosh and hush of the incoming tide. That sound had come through the open windows in the evenings as, tucked in by Lizzie and waiting for her Mum to come upstairs and kiss her good night, Eleanor would drift off to sleep lulled by its rhythm. It would still be there when they had all gone home after the holidays. It was there the day Alice went missing.

Isabel hadn't come. When her Dad crept into the room, Eleanor had pretended to be asleep.

'I brought you here when you were a baby. Isabel persuaded me to.'

'What, right here on the beach?'

'Yes, you and me and my mother. An odd little party. Then my Dad turned up. Isabel had said he was in London. Now I think she was telling the truth. She was as appalled as me. He carried you down to the shoreline to show you the sea.'

'Did we come by train?' *Did you walk with me in your arms down the quiet road to the church?*

'Yes. Then we left. They didn't stop me. It was you they wanted. To be touched by innocence.'

'Was that the last time you saw him?' Chris went cold. Eleanor was crying. Not in her usual way with sobs and loud sniffs, but silently, rubbing her nose with the back of her hand like a kid. If Chris ran now, she'd have a head start.

But Eleanor would know where to find her. There would be no more hiding.

'I saw him in London about ten years ago. He was following me. I dodged down an alleyway. He came into the alley, but I was behind a dustbin. He could easily have found me, but he'd never have thought I was hiding from him. So he went away. I didn't come out of that stinking passage for an hour. After that I never went out.'

'Did you think he was going to hand you over to the police? After all, he didn't at the time.'

Eleanor sat up and dried her face with the flat of her hands. She looked tired and beleaguered, yet there was more life in her features than Chris had seen before. She could imagine Eleanor as a young girl rampaging through the countryside bareback on an imaginary horse. Except that she was frightened of horses.

In another life Chris could have been happy here too.

'As each day went by, you and I were building up a new past.'

'How could you be so stupid?' Chris was angry with herself for still wanting to soothe her and stop her crying. 'I've never been real. Even today you only wanted me here to listen to your stories and let you off the hook.'

'That's not true.' But it was. Eleanor had never bothered to find out the second name of the boy in the bathroom, because he meant nothing to her. Yet he was Chris's father. Now he too had vanished and with him the Renault garage where he had worked, demolished to make way for executive flats while Chris was still a baby. Eleanor had robbed Chris of her own story and substituted only fantasies and phantoms.

'I have always been me with you.'

'That's not true.'

'I always loved you.'

'You don't know what love is. You're off your head!'

'Don't be like this.' Eleanor got up and came towards her.

Chris backed away and rushed back up the hill. At the top she looked back and saw the silver roof of Sainsbury's twinkling in the wintery sunshine where the Tide Mills had once been. For a moment Chris thought it possible Eleanor had been real with her. Then she dismissed the idea. Tomorrow she would worm her way into the Ramsay family. Eleanor wasn't the only one who could play spies.

Chris would do what Eleanor had avoided doing.

She would find Alice.

Twenty-Nine

Chris had stumbled on to the scene of a murder. The body had been removed, but all around the room were signs of a fierce fight for life before it was snuffed out. There were broken toys, half a chair on its side, books flung across the room to land in sprawling heaps, some with torn covers and twisted spines. The contents of a board game were strewn across the floorboards. Then she pulled herself together – two glasses of wine had got the better of her – it was only the rough and tumble of a long abandoned playroom.

The doll's house was in the centre of the room.

It loomed now, as it had dominated the stories her Mum told her long ago, quietly thrilling with concealed knowledge of past events and vanished inhabitants. Lingering in the doorway, the chatter of her mother's 'gas-fire-voices' jogged Chris's memory with broken sentences and stifled cries. She felt nauseous, and to recover herself fixed her attention on the two tall chimneys at each end of the roof of the house.

Images from her deserted life swapped in and out like lenses in an eyesight test. Chris saw in quick succession her bedroom window, the shadow of the light shade on the ceiling like a static sundial, the dips and folds of her mother's duvet, and the hawkish lace-curtain birds that, like everything else, her mother had given names to. When Chris was small, the bedtime stories were punctual, each night at six-thirty, because Eleanor believed structure and routine were all. This had become an enchanted time they both had loved.

Whose memories were they?

Each new lens brought the doll's house into sharper focus so that it became obvious to Chris that this was the room where she was meant to end up. Her diligent detective work of the last five weeks would end here tonight.

It was 31st December 1999, the last night of the twentieth century, and many months since Chris had discovered the truth about Eleanor and had met her real family, the Ramsays. She was living with Kathleen Howland, sleeping in the room that was once Alice's but was now hers. Having passed her 'A' levels, she had begun a forensic science degree at Sussex University. Doctor Ramsay's grand-daughter was at her calmest when staying late at the lab examining the different types of insects that feed on corpses. Eleanor was still in their flat, but she would have to move out because she was now a wealthy woman and the housing estate was for tenants on little or no incomes. Besides the flat was no longer home.

Without any explanation, Mark Ramsay had left his youngest child the White House, which Isabel was to hold in trust for her, as well as a share of his estate. He had left Chris the doll's house; a pecuniary legacy, again with no explanation, to the grand-daughter he had only once held in his arms. Chris was glad he was dead and she didn't have to deal with him along with the other Ramsays. She wasn't grateful for his gift. She was suspicious. There must be strings attached that would one day become clear. This was confirmed by the lack of surprise expressed by any of the family, who had been horrified when Eleanor had offered to make the White House over to all of them or pass it to her mother. No one wanted either house. Chris thought her mother might as well have been offering to share blood money with them and, intrigued, stepped up her visits. Eleanor thought Chris was becoming reconciled to her new family after all. This in turn encouraged Eleanor to soften towards them too.

Eleanor spent little time in the flat. After years of being cooped up like a prisoner she could not bear to stay indoors longer than was necessary. She had to be out and she had to keep moving. She left early each morning to tramp miles through London, never returning until the evening. She would cross and re-cross the Thames, pausing on Hammersmith Bridge by a plaque in memory of a man drowned one Christmas in the freezing waters below while rescuing another man. She would climb the steps of Hungerford Bridge and wait in the gloom for a smile without a face that she now saw only in her dreams. Often she veered impulsively down side streets, hurrying as if chased, down alleyways, into subways, cutting corners off palatial Victorian squares to emerge on to busy rushing streets. She strode along the Euston Road, and faltered on Eversholt Street at the point where one day a woman would be killed trying to stop thieves stealing her handbag. She stayed at the kerbside through several traffic light changes on a corner of Wood Lane, where a woman cyclist had been crushed by an articulated lorry. She trudged through the oozing green river mud that slimed the shoreline at the Bell Steps in Hammersmith, where on Lady Diana Spencer's wedding day a young mother had been murdered and her killer not found. Eleanor stepped on pavements trodden yesterday by people who were dead today or would die tomorrow in a distracted bid to join up the dots and become whole.

Each night she traced the day's route in her *London A to Z* with a red biro. Soon she had covered most of the pages with the crouching creature shapes of her journeys, each one a fine thread leading through a dark forest. She would open the book at random and retrace the ink line of a day's route. As her pen flitted along each high road, detoured around each crescent, or moved with precision down a broad tree-lined avenue, she recalled her walking thoughts: the weather, the passers by. Eleanor's life was recorded in the London street atlas. It was her secret diary written in a code that was impossible for others to crack. Until one evening, forced into the Underground by a flash storm, Eleanor would accidentally leave it on a westbound District Line train, where it would be found by someone with a mind like her own.

On Fridays, Eleanor would came back early to catch Jane before she left the estate office. Jane made bearable the teeming, screaming traffic along Newington Butts and the urine-scented lift in Wood Green shopping centre. A good genie, there to make the most modest of wishes come true. Jane hadn't cared if Alice was Eleanor. She liked her whoever she was.

During the day, Eleanor imbued her private London with her unarticulated hopes of their new friendship. After Alice vanished, Eleanor had found it impossible to keep up her existing friendships and, burdened with secrets, made few new ones. When she had absented herself from her old life, she cut off all contact with the people she knew. Now she was terrified she had forgotten how to have a friend of any kind.

As her pen completed the shape of each day and ended back at the Old Kent Road, Eleanor would dare imagine that their cups of coffee in the estate office, and more recently glasses of wine after work in her flat, were inching her back to sanity. She knew Chris had been right. She must be mad.

At weekends Eleanor returned to Isabel at the White House. The two women watched television, cooked elaborate meals and shopped in Brighton. In between, they played end-to-end games of Scrabble and Racing Demon.

After the trip to the Tide Mills, Chris was willing to go to the White House but, to Eleanor's disappointment, would insist on returning to Kathleen's cottage at night. To everyone's astonishment, Chris embarked on riding lessons with Gina. She agreed to learn to drive with Gina's husband, who her new grandmother called 'Jon-the-Footrest' without humour or apology. Chris planned to save for a car and take Kathleen out for day trips. Kathleen no longer searched for Alice. She stopped watching the tapes. Chris knew there was something Kathleen hadn't told her.

It was only that morning, when Kathleen had brought her a cup of tea and stayed sitting on the side of her bed while she drank it, that Chris had found out what.

Until tonight, despite her secret intention to find out the truth about Alice, Chris had never explored the White House. She had become immersed in university work and when she visited she preferred to stay in the warm kitchen with her Aunt Gina, with whom she had formed a bond that puzzled them both. This was the first proper opportunity Chris had had to examine the room that had been her mother's childhood sanctuary. Besides, she had tired of the Millennium Eve party her grandmother had impulsively decided to hold and craved some quiet.

She was diminished by the implacable walls of the model house topped with its brutish chimneys. She blanched, with the same sinking feeling as once when she had to wait for the Queen, being driven down Museum Street in a glass-topped car with a crest on the front, preceded by a fanfare of outriders blowing whistles. Chris had stood on the kerb, spare-parted by such significance. The doll's house was as grand, proud and sure as royalty. And like the Queen, Chris knew its face intimately although she had never seen it before.

She moved in a circle away from the house, edging towards the salt-streaked windows, the back of her neck crawling like sifting sand. As an old woman, when it was too late to change anything, she would think back to this last night of 1999, the detail still sharp, and identify it as the last point when she might have turned back and left everything alone. Then she would remind herself that it was already too late.

It was the largest doll's house Chris had ever seen, over four feet high and as deep. A mass of boxes jumbled to the brim with toys, wooden bricks, a plastic truncheon, cricket bats, tennis rackets, tennis balls, footballs, straggling dressing-up clothes nudged at the house walls. A bicycle wheel with a flat tyre had been propped against a sagging space hopper with a rip in the side; broken spokes had caught under the eaves of the house, lifting up part of the roof. Circles of plastic from an old Spirograph set littered the floor. A child's black patent leather court shoe poked toes first from beneath a crate filled with scratched and dented cars, bits of Lego and racing green Meccano. Shelves piled with books and games climbed the alcoves by the fireplace. A tired one-eyed bear with moth-eaten fur had retreated to the top shelf with an Action Man, khaki legs doubled up to his chin, collapsed on the bear's lap. They were crumpled refugees from a happier land. The broken and tawdry state of the toys and books, sprinkled with a shading of dust and scattered with dead leaves (how did they get there Chris wondered), signalled not a room abandoned by children since grown up, but the debris of a childhood dumped without notice.

Chris felt uneasy. She was sure no one had seen her leave the party, but she was equally convinced she wasn't alone. She scanned the room, her head pounding with rising panic. There was nowhere to hide. No curtains on the windows. No furniture to creep under. It was the alcohol.

She backed into the windowsill. Daunted by the stillness, she was fearful of making a sound, and from the spurious safety of the wide seat she studied the replica of the White House. The 'real' house was her family home, although she wouldn't admit kinship. Peace after the noise downstairs was like the intense presence of someone holding their breath and keeping very still. Chris wished she hadn't come upstairs. The doll's house glared back at her, its sharp lintels and gaping windows arched and callous.

The Ramsays never stopped talking, declaiming their opinions on food and cars, in brash tones, glugging wine into glasses, breaking into songs from musicals – *Oliver!*, *The Sound of Music* – with Lucian conducting and Eleanor singing the loudest. They kept conversation going with a myriad of petty subjects; their words leapt and jumped like fish in a net, slippery and shiny, a mass of possibility. It seemed to Chris, armed with the perspicacity of the young adult, that not much moved on: each time she went there they said and did much the same things. At meals she was put next to her mother, yet despite their lavish attentions she remained an outsider. Chris thought it peculiar that neither Mark Ramsay's death, nor the fact that her mother hadn't been back there for years, was ever discussed. Mark Ramsay's inquest had returned a verdict of 'death by misadventure', because, coupled with the fact that he had no history of depression, the master cylinder in his Rover had failed and this would have disabled the brakes. Chris dared not say what she thought about it to Eleanor because until today Kathleen wouldn't discuss it.

Now she knew why.

Chris was fascinated by her Uncle Lucian, who would spring out of his seat and dash away to open wine, shine glasses with a cloth, and clatter around in the cutlery drawer for a bottle opener. Her Aunt Gina was trapped in a loveless marriage, so Chris felt a bit sorry for her. Lucian should be good looking, but he wasn't, his nose was too large and his chin too prominent, yet he compelled the eye. Jon-the-Footrest, in pink socks and garish bow tie to make him more exciting, actually was attractive, his features even and clear; but Chris found his looks instantly forgettable.

In the Ramsay world Chris was a determined foreigner who had unwillingly picked up the basic language but refused to learn the idioms and colloquialisms to enable her to understand it. She made only feeble bids to decipher signals. She didn't want to belong. She realised that they must think she fitted in when she observed how the Ramsays were with true outsiders. They closed ranks and despite snapping each other's heads off and betraying no signs of affection to one another, they did look after each other. It was with solicitous care that Lucian gave Gina a glass of wine or Eleanor followed Isabel into the dining room bearing an enormous dish of mashed potato, a tea towel slung on her shoulder in a way that declared: we do it this way and nothing will stop us.

That night a breeze from the garden had flickered the flames in the giant candle holder at the centre of the table, the low light making the group seem to converge and conferring on them an impression of camp fire camaraderie that found echo in the boisterous chatter. Chris looked askance as they lapsed into votive silence while Isabel plunged her ladle into a steaming cauldron of Boeuf en Daube. Each Ramsay sniffed the air appreciatively as she released the rich smell of herbs and garlic laced with red wine that whirled Chris back to the flat in the Old Kent Road.

Home.

She was sickened. So it was an old family recipe. The rush of love was saturated with betrayal. Her appetite was deadened as she studied her mother brimming with wit and chat that must be further signs of mental illness. Chris had seen only too clearly that Eleanor was more at home here than she had been with her, and hardened her heart. Bit by bit the Ramsays had hauled Eleanor back in. With a stab of jealousy Chris imagined the juices, whose subtle flavours they were all going mad about, slicking the dining room walls and dribbling down the face of the dead Judge and oozing between triangles of shattered china and a smashed existence.

As she chewed and swallowed, chewed and swallowed, Chris issued a silent warning: when she had finished with them, there would be nothing but bones.

If she gave in and reached out to her Mum, maybe accepted a drink, or asked for more potato, Eleanor would have her back. Sometimes Chris considered it might be worth it if only to prove she was the grand puppeteer nimbly twitching her mother's strings. But she resisted, knowing it would only make her misery worse.

Now she knew what she had to do.

The Ramsays did not extend their brand of affection to 'Jon-the-Footrest'. Chris felt oblique sympathy for Gina's husband, despite the incredibly stupid things he came out with. She winced at his ponderous explanations of boring subjects (load bearing beams, hi-fi speakers, or his earnest and sonorously dull deeds for the Rotary Club). She perceived that despite his ever-busy efforts, Jon would stay an outsider. He talked and laughed as loudly as the Ramsays, but in the wrong places. He fussed around his wife, when it was obvious Gina hated fuss of any kind. He shadowed her with outstretched coats, or staggered after her in garish weekend jackets, weighed down with huge new gifts for the kitchen, when Chris knew Gina hated cooking. He drove too fast up the drive with horn-tooting panache in a churn of gravel, the chrome on his Lexus gleaming. As he whistled his train-signal arrival, the family sighed and braced themselves.

The Ramsays guffawed at jokes that flitted as invisible moths around the room, every word brushed by fluttering wings of private meaning. As Chris spied on Jon over a skyline of wine bottles and candles at the dinner table, she divined with a wash of sadness from the way he sat forward humming 'Always Look On The Bright Side Of Life' under his breath, that he too knew the family would never accept him. She felt his anguish, as she knew full well the Ramsays couldn't be dismissed as irrelevant.

She worked out that the Ramsays dealt with the big things by devoting themselves to the small things. In this way they had dealt with Mark Ramsay, who although dead was not gone. His presence was more pervasive than that of the Judge. Mark Ramsay wasn't just in the dining room, he was everywhere. Chris guessed that everything they did was done in the way Mark Ramsay would have approved.

She sat with her knees under her chin on the windowsill in the playroom. It was deep enough to curl up in with a cushion and a book, but solid vertical bars clamped to the outside wall rudely extinguished this idea. She gazed out into the darkness. A thick swirling fog had enveloped the house earlier that evening, turning the newly arrived guests into spectres gliding out of the inky darkness with freezing wispy trails clinging to their clothes. Now she could see nothing except her own ghostly reflection. She remembered watching scary films with her Mum at home. They would be cuddled up on the sofa and protest in fake terror when someone excused themselves from the brightly lit room and went off alone with a candle down a corridor lined with suits of armour and wood panelling. No wonder they ended up strangled in a cupboard or sprawled over a roll top desk with a knife in their back. Her Mum joked that the music always gave it away and the change in tempo should have warned them. Now Chris had done the same. Here she was alone, in a cold dark room at the top of a creaky old mansion. She could have stayed at the party with her Kathleen and her Mum. Perhaps by now she had been missed, perhaps downstairs her Mum was asking where she was.

Beneath her feet a Turkish carpet, ruckled and shredding, was spread over black painted floorboards. Wallpaper, probably once chosen with excitement and optimism, drooped limp and peeling, and was patterned with brown stains edged with lines like the gradient marks on a map. The design of flowers intertwining in vertical rows had all but gone, the original colour was impossible to tell. Between the skirting board and the floor was a gap wide enough for a child to slip its hand in. Chris fleetingly thought it a good place to secrete a diary, letters, private thoughts. She should check it. Puffing out a wistful sigh, she breathed in a smell of damp, and shivered.

She smacked her hands together and marched with 'coming-to-get-you' purpose over to the doll's house.

Getting warm...

She hurled away the bicycle wheel and kicked the space hopper; it flumped on to the rug and with a hiss resumed its exhausted pose. Shoving up her sleeves, she heaved aside crates and boxes, clearing a space on each side of the house. She insinuated herself between the wall and the house, easing the house further out into the room. It snagged on the carpet and there was a ripping sound. She had torn some threads on the Turkish rug. Who would mind?

She grudgingly admired fine detail on the model house, the tiny lion above the porch, and unable to resist, crouched down to peep through the windows into rooms with doorways offering a partial view of dim passages. Cutting through the centre of the house like a spinal cord was a replica of the intricately constructed staircase that wound up to the top of the real house, complete with the banister snaking atop spindly balustrades. Minute gold stair rods gripped thick carpet. Leaning in closer, unwilling to open the front and lose the illusion, Chris saw that the pile on the stair carpet had been flattened by a heavy or constant tread. Eleanor had been right, people really had lived here.

The house was nailed to a sheet of hardboard streaked at the front with scraps of felt that speared between islands of dried glue. This was all that was left of the lawn that Mark

Ramsay had accidentally destroyed. A detective verifying personal statements as fact, Chris also noted the missing dining room windowsill. It was all exactly as her Mum had described. Chris had never seriously believed such a house could exist. It was a toy within a toy, reducing her to a doll.

Finger-sized dolls dressed in clumps of velvet and cotton – the material stiffened with globules of glue – lay strewn in the rooms like victims of a gassing. There was one in the dining room and three on a bed in the room that had once been Gina's. Only the lady doll had 'died naturally' and was covered with a blanket in the master bedroom that in real life overlooked the lawn with the willow tree.

Chris went through the house with forensic care. The miniature playroom had the same wallpaper as its life-size counterpart, which turned out to be eggshell blue with pink flowers clustered around dark leaves. This version of the playroom was furnished with only a cradle, three marbles – giant glass spheres – next to the fireplace and a set of crudely made books, each on a different alcove shelf. There was the same number of shelves as in real life. Chris was daunted by the acute replication; she almost expected to see a tiny version of herself. Then it came to her. There was no doll's house in the tiny playroom. This Judge, who was meant to be so clever, had missed an opportunity.

Eleanor had said the doll's house was a friend, tucked away at the top of the White House, far from her family. She had hated to leave it behind when she went back to London. Chris frowned as a gust of anger swept up her lost chances, the hours she might have spent here, the games she might have played in this room as a little girl herself. She despaired of ever losing the stomach-fizzing fury at Alice's deception (she could not consistently think of her as Eleanor).

She didn't notice swelling and fading of the noise as a door opened and closed two flights below and she jumped as a shadowy figure appeared in the doorway.

'Kathleen was wondering where you were. She said to come and find you.'

Chris got up from the window seat and brushed herself down. 'You found me.'

Her mother strode over to the other window and, cupping her hands to cut out the electric light, peered down into the night. She thumped on the bars:

'These were put in by the Judge's father in the nineteenth century, well over a hundred years ago.' She gave the bars a sharp tug as if she might loosen them. 'His eldest son fell out of this window and crashed down on to those flags when he was only seven.'

'Did he die?'

'Oh yes.' She spoke with the satisfaction of someone who can't be faulted on their facts, and added: 'Not immediately.'

Chris went across to her. 'Listen.' She shook her arm. 'I know you didn't kill her.'

'The swimming pool wasn't there then, of course. That's new.'

'Did you hear me?'

'You're hurting me!' Eleanor shrugged her off. 'Just leave it, Chris.'

'Why? Is that what you'd prefer?'

'It's too long ago.'

'You don't think you killed her and then forgot. There's no way you'd be normal, well, quite normal. You'd be mad with guilt and unable to live with yourself or to face Kathleen. Or me.'

'And you think I'm not.'

The fog thinned for a moment and Chris could just see the flagstones on the broad path along the edge of the lawn. It was a dizzying drop. She thought of the little boy pitching out and somersaulting to his death. 'So you wanted to kill her. You've got imagination and reality mixed up.'

'I hated her.'

'Kathleen said there was a tramp. They found him drowned up the road from here...'

'Stop it.' Eleanor unscrewed the latch on the window and with all her strength pushed it up about six inches. They were

297

shocked by freezing air and coughed as ribbons of fog drifted into the room, catching their throats. Eleanor squatted down and stuck her nose through the gap, holding on to the bars. The ground floor rooms cast a pale light over the grass. She could just make out Uncle Jack's willow in the middle of the lawn where they used to have tea. It had grown to the size of a giant umbrella. She had never been clear as a child whether Uncle Jack was actually buried under it. She had not wanted to ask, because she would have been upset if he wasn't. It had been fantastic to have tea on top of a real live corpse. Gina had remarked that they never sat under Uncle Jack's tree after Eleanor stopped coming. She had said this to Eleanor like an acquaintance, polite and friendly, not as an admission of affection, it was just how it was once they built the pool.

'There are no bars on the windows of the playroom in the doll's house.'

'What?' Her mother was like a kid going off in all directions; this happened all the time now she was Eleanor and not Alice.

'The Judge was anal about making an exact copy of the house. He got hold of the architect's plans to get dimensions right, and took loads of photos. He drew quite good sketches. He made one mistake. He forgot the bars.'

'Maybe they weren't there then.'

'I told you, they were put in after the Judge's brother was killed, when he – the Judge – would have been about six. They were close in age. The bars were there.'

Knowing her mother was changing the subject, yet unable to resist verifying the accuracy of what she had said, Chris trooped obediently over to the doll's house. There were no bars on any of the windows.

'Dad pointed it out to the Judge; he thought it was the test. There was always a test to pass; everything had to be earned. Instead his father was furious and nearly hit him, Mum told us.'

'He got cross over some stupid bars?'

'They were evidence that the Judge wasn't perfect. Strangely the Judge had made the same mistake as his parents when they turned this room into a playroom. He forgot the bars. Mum always said the missing bars in the doll's house windows revealed that the Judge wanted his brother dead. He inherited everything including the house. When she wanted to wind Dad up, Mum only had to bring up the playroom bars. She'd say the Judge left them out as his confession of murder.'

'That's far fetched.'

'Most murders are.'

Neither of them spoke.

'I know who you're protecting.'

Eleanor gave a hoarse laugh. 'I don't give a toss about the Judge.'

'I'm going to find Alice.'

'If Scotland Yard couldn't, how can you?'

'They didn't know what to look for.'

Chris snatched a random paperback from one of the shelves and tapped it. 'The clues are in here, or here, or here.' She waved at the shelves. 'Messages and answers are staring us in the face. We know about obvious clues like using plants, chemicals and insects to determine time of death and all that. But what about the other stuff that's going on in people's lives, that policemen with rigid ideas and closed minds would never think of? The questions they never asked and the places they never looked in because of their assumptions. Your Mum was right, the bars tell us a story all right. They are absent in the doll's house for a reason.'

Eleanor took the book from Chris, handling it delicately. She turned it over. She knew what it was: *The Young Detectives* by R.J. McGregor. She didn't remember the author although she had read and re-read the book many times. The story was a memory more vivid than life, as for Eleanor most stories had always been.

'This was brilliant,' she breathed. 'Mrs Skoda read it to our class when I was seven, but the summer term finished before she got to the end. I bought it in the holidays with my birthday money and read it tucked up in that chair one rainy afternoon.' She went over and, as if in illustration of her eight-year-old self, settled down in a dirty brown armchair by the fireplace that Chris hadn't noticed before.

As she flicked through the dusty yellowed pages it all became clear.

'There was a secret passage in a window seat, just like those ones under the windows. You had to open and shut the window in a certain way to release the catch on the seat.' Chris was staring at the doll's house and didn't appear to be listening. Eleanor continued to herself:

'I tried it with these seats, but the lids are stuck fast.'

Eleanor dropped the book on to the floor. The story had got mixed up in her mind with real life.

'What's the matter?'

'I'm tired, that's all.' Someone was standing close to Eleanor's chair but Chris would only repeat that she'd gone mad if she told her. 'Let's go, or they'll be coming to get us. It's eleven-fifteen already.'

'Why did he leave me this?' Chris waved a hand at the doll's house.

'I imagine he wanted a child to have it. Even a grownup one.'

'But Gina might have children.'

Eleanor shook her head. 'She won't. He knew that.'

'Why, is she sterile?' Chris thought of Gina, who only seemed to cheer up in front of a horse.

'No.'

Eleanor dragged open the front of the doll's house. It was coated in thick dust. A bird had got into the playroom, there were splashes of dried droppings along the roof of the house and down its front. She marched her fingers down the top passageway lined with minute oak panels and stopped at the top of the stairs. She could get no further. She had once tried and got her arm stuck. Gina had grazed it as she pulled it out. Eleanor's face loomed into the bedroom where she and Gina had slept until she had to move because Gina grew older and too grumpy to share.

'*Warmer…*'

'Do you know where Alice is?' Chris's voice was harsh behind her.

Eleanor pushed her hand in as far as she could go and tapped the wood panelling on the landing. It made a hollow sound.

'Hot!'

But then so did all the walls in the doll's house. Eleanor shut the frontage sharply and got to her feet.

'You know who killed her, don't you.'

'I think so.'

Eleanor was aware of a different kind of silence. There was no bird song, no scratching at the windows or creaking floorboards, only an uncanny quiet, final as death enveloping the dimly lit room. The sense of a presence other than themselves had quietly evaporated. Through the open window came the smell of wood smoke. Cedarwood. Eleanor's favourite…once upon a time.

Eleanor was afraid. Her daughter had an expression on her face that Eleanor couldn't fathom, that she had only ever seen once before on a human being. That time she had managed to get away. She wouldn't get a second chance.

She had no more lives left.

'So, who was it?' She would make her Mum say the name.

'It's a long story. Some of it may not be true.'

'Let me be the judge of that.'

'It starts that Tuesday afternoon in the main street of the Tide Mills. I took you there. It's where the Sainsbury's…'

'Yes, yes, go on.' Chris leaned against the space hopper and shut her eyes, the way she had always done when her Mum told one of her stories. It made them more real.

Thirty

It seemed to Alice that her voice was fading away. When she spoke, each number came out soft and flutey, and she imagined herself as a distant pigeon and not a girl at all. The heat was making her feel queasy and as she squinted in the direction in which Eleanor had rushed off, she seemed to float above the chalky path for it heaved and swelled at her feet.

'One... two... three... four... five...'

Everything went black.

Enormous hands clamped over her eyes, and soft firm fingers pressed into her eye sockets making the darkness fleck with bright red arrows. As Alice tried to scream, one hand moved down her face to her mouth shutting it. This meant she could see again.

'It's okay, Alice. It's me.' Hot words whispered in her ear and the hands turned her to face him. Even with her eyes open, Alice still saw dancing darts, like sparklers. He had his back to the sun so she couldn't see his face. But by now she was relaxed. She knew who he was.

Doctor Ramsay crouched down to Alice's level, one knee on the stony path that had once been the Tide Mill's busy main street, resting his elbow on his other knee. For a moment Alice imagined he was going to propose like the prince in Cinderella. She flinched as he stretched out and brushed a strand of hair from her cheek, whipped out his handkerchief, and went through the motions of dusting her down. She tried to stand stock still throughout; it annoyed her Mum when she wriggled during hair brushing.

'Did I frighten you?'

'Not really. Perhaps at first, until I saw it was you.' She grinned. She was pleased to see him. He spidered around on his haunches so that the sun shone properly on his face. Now Alice could see fine drops of water on his forehead and she wanted to reach and wipe them away in return. The sun was beating down on their heads, no wonder he was sweating. But just as this idea was forming, Doctor Ramsay did it himself, mopping his hankie across his face as if in a hurry.

'I'm sorry. I didn't mean to upset you. I wanted to catch you before you finished counting and dashed off. I suppose you've been roped into playing hide and seek again, have you?' The doctor looked quickly back up the path towards the outhouses and the last remaining cottage. There was no movement from the remains of the Mill Owner's house, the ruins were choked by ivy and nettles. Tall straggling blackberry bushes had obliterated the once flourishing pear orchard. Alice knew Eleanor wasn't hiding there. She nearly told Doctor Ramsay this, but she was grateful for his help. She had guessed he understood how horrible it was playing games with Eleanor.

'It's my turn to look. I don't know where to start, Eleanor has so many secret places. And really we're not supposed to be here anyway.'

Instantly Alice knew she shouldn't have pointed this out, she was assuming too much too soon. Doctor Ramsay might not really be her friend. Eleanor might have sent him as a spy to test whether Alice was a traitor. Eleanor had made it clear that treachery was a terrible crime.

'You're quite right, it is dangerous here. What if one of you fell and hurt yourself? Who would be there to help? People tend not to come here, the locals think it's haunted.' He guffawed, his head going back, so that Alice could see down his throat.

Doctor Ramsay thought ghosts were stupid. This changed everything. Alice's Mum insisted that their old cottage was haunted and had kept on at her Dad to ask the Post Office to find them another place to live. He had stayed up one night in the living room with all the lights off to prove to her it wasn't. No ghost had appeared, but she had said ghosts didn't show themselves to everyone. Now Alice laughed loudly too. Of course ghosts were stupid.

Only stupid people believed in ghosts.

'This is Eleanor's best place.' Now he would know she was a traitor. She flushed, already she had broken the morning's resolution to be 'specially nice to Eleanor.

'It would be. It's full of insects, dead animals, hazardous places to climb and fall out of and secret hidey-holes. But what do you think, or didn't you get a say?'

'I think it's a bit scary. My Mum says you get all sorts these days.'

'Your Mum is right. You do indeed. Come on, I'll take you away from here.'

These were the words that Alice had been dreaming of hearing Doctor Ramsay say. She had relived their encounter in the lane two days before, picturing his long brown arm resting along the sill of the car door with his fingers only inches from her nose while his other hand tapped on the steering wheel. The fantasy always ended with his suggestion that she come for a ride in his gleaming new car. The narrative had developed at quite a pace over a short time, from being a simple offer to drive Alice the short distance to her parents' cottage to a more ambitious journey. Doctor Ramsay would whisk her to London: they would visit the Zoo and then go on to Madame Tussaud's, where they had waxworks of the Royal Family and the Beatles. After a short while she would be his wife and make him happier than Mrs Ramsay did, who she had heard her Mum describe as a trial.

Her friend Jean at the Newhaven school had said the waxworks were like actual people. She had told Alice that she had asked a policeman in the entrance what time it closed and he hadn't answered because he was made of wax. Alice had known that she would never be fooled as to whether a man was real or not.

Or maybe Doctor Ramsay would show her the big house he had in London. Alice had never known anyone with two houses. Her Mum had said the Ramsays were very important in London and had parties full of famous people that got reported in the papers. Eleanor was dismissive when Alice quizzed her. She preferred to talk about crane flies, cats and marbles. So Alice had been none the wiser. Doctor Ramsay would take her on a tour of all the sights. There was nothing she wanted more than to run away with him and leave Eleanor behind. Alice had to face facts; he would only take her home. She dared not hope for more.

For the first time since playing with Eleanor, Alice didn't want to go home. The little cottage next to the post office was no longer a safe haven. Cracks and doubts had appeared on its perfect surface. Now the thought of her Mum and Dad and the way they lived made Alice uncomfortable.

'I'm supposed to be with Eleanor. I'm not expected back until tea time.'

'Oh, I see.' He stuck out his lower lip and shrugged his shoulders. It was all up to Alice. Only she could take away his disappointment.

Alice was dumbfounded. She had never been in charge of a grownup before. The experience was terrifying and exhilarating. What should she do? She must not let this chance slip away. It was like Eleanor's complicated rules. Alice had three lives and after saying 'no' to Doctor Ramsay a second time, she would have one life left. Perhaps she might not get a third go. He might not ask her again. His rules might be stricter than Eleanor's and include fewer lives. She would never go with him to London, they would never see the glasshouses in Kew Gardens or the River Thames at the bottom of his road. Doctor Ramsay was going to leave her alone on this boiling hot path in the middle of nowhere searching for his daughter forever. Or worse he would dump her outside her boring house and never see her again. Alice made a snap decision:

'Maybe it wouldn't matter if we did go. Eleanor usually goes off by herself when she does hiding anyway. She has a lot of dens, and forgets we're playing.' She didn't want to sound cross with Eleanor so quickly added: 'I don't mind. She has a lot to do.' Alice didn't pause to consider that Eleanor had never actually abandoned her during a game of hide and seek.

'I'm afraid that's the nature of the beast.' Doctor Ramsay had cheered up. 'Okay, let's not give her another thought. She'll make her own way home when she's ready. Let's give her a dose of her own medicine and hide too. I bet we can hide even better.' Doctor Ramsay had become like Lucian, boyish and excitable. Alice watched in amazement…

'I know a secret place that Eleanor has never seen. It's ages until tea, shall I show you?'

'But Eleanor knows all the secret holes.'

'Not this one, she doesn't. I promise you.' Doctor Ramsay put out his hand to her. 'Cross my heart?'

Without hesitation, and by now brimming over with joy, Alice grasped it. She couldn't believe how things had turned out. She had made the doctor better.

'Now, the quickest way is down here, but it's very steep with lots of loose bits of chalk, so keep your eyes peeled. We'll be very quiet in case Madam is spying. Stay close to me.'

'But this is the way Eleanor went.' Too late Alice remembered that she wasn't supposed to know. 'I think.'

'Be very quiet. We don't want her to hear us,' he whispered. 'And I mean, if she appears, I'm only taking you home. She can't be cross.'

Mark Ramsay and Alice descended sideways down the steep winding track between the thick bushes of gorse and blackberry. They passed only a few feet from where Eleanor was crouching, deep in the undergrowth. As she heard their footsteps she shut her eyes and held her breath. But as they went by, she dared to lift a branch to see where Alice was going. What she saw made no sense.

She slumped back against a bush, settling into its armchair comfort, shifting until the springy branches finally stopped poking into her back. She didn't know what to do now.

One, two, one, two.

She told herself the steps had surely been one person walking, and this is what she would later tell the policeman. She also said she had kept her eyes tight shut so she hadn't actually seen Alice. If Detective Inspector Hall had realised that Eleanor was lying to him about hiding in a hedge by the lane, he might have guessed she was making up other things too. As it was, although he didn't trust the scruffy little girl who was more like a boy, he had nothing concrete to go on.

Eleanor's ears were pounding and to stop the sound she scrubbed at her hair and shifted about. After a few moments it dawned on her that there was no point in hiding. Alice wasn't looking for her any more. That much had been clear. She came to her senses; there was no time to waste.

Thrusting aside brambles, she slithered along the floor of the leafy tunnel on her stomach until she reached the path. She stood for a moment, unsure whether to go down or up. Either way she risked being seen. Did it matter?

Then movement to her left caught her eye. There was a white shape like a giant flower on one of the bushes some yards back up the path to the Tide Mills. As she got nearer she saw it was a giant butterfly fluttering hopelessly in dying throes, too weak to disentangle itself from the blackberry thorns. Eleanor stumbled towards it, tripping on chips of chalk and nearly falling; her feet had pins and needles from sitting for so long.

The butterfly was a white handkerchief. She pulled it off and put it to her nose. The familiar sharp tang turned her stomach. There was embroidery on one corner, and Eleanor knew without looking what the letters were. The handkerchief might have been a coded instruction because it galvanised her into action. She knew what she had to do. In Eleanor's mind she was doing it to save her mother's life. In reality Isabel, at that moment curled in a light doze on her bed, was in no danger.

Eleanor plunged back into the dense bushes on her hands and knees, pushing deep through the small tunnels in the undergrowth. To prevent herself from hurtling down the steep slope, she held tight to the stronger branches and skidded downwards. Eleanor was reckless as thorns ripped at her skin.

Soon bright beads of blood dotted the scratches. After a few minutes of shoving along, with her face close to the dry baked earth, she came out into blinding sunlight. She was yards from a sheer drop of about six feet down to the beach. Efficiently she scootered backwards on her bottom, then rolled on to her stomach and inched over the edge feet first, feeling for toeholds. There was one, but as she trusted her weight to it and searched for the next one, it gave way in a spray of chalk. She shot down and crash-landed on to the shingle, bruising her knee and jarring her ankles.

She heaved herself into a sitting position, relishing the pain as part of the massive task of slaying the monster. Her palms were stinging. She fought the urge to cry without being able to articulate what had made her miserable. It was what had always made her miserable. At the time, she thought she was alone with her pain, but over thirty years later she would see, without words being exchanged, that Gina had also suffered. What might have unified the sisters, drove a wedge between them. They stopped inviting friends to stay if the friends had not already stopped wanting to come. Eleanor had always thought Gina was okay; she had her horses.

She wiped her forehead with the handkerchief and frantically cast around as she tried to recapture the heady feeling of one of her imaginative games. But she could not. This game was real.

The beach was enclosed by a chalky outcrop at one end and a pile of rocks at the other, that few people ever climbed. When the policeman asked her to recall details of that day, Eleanor had assured him the beach was empty. A rusting boat, slouching dark and sulky against the sky, interrupted a stretch of pebbles that dropped in terraces to a thin slip of wet sand at the shoreline. She told him that it was a cloudless day full of colours – yellow, blue and red – and didn't mention seeing anyone. But by then she had said they had been playing hide and seek in the lane, so it would have made no sense to mention the beach. Eleanor would say she'd gone to the Tide Mills after Alice had been missing for about an hour. She told the police she had decided to look everywhere since Alice wasn't in the usual places.

This meant of course that Eleanor couldn't tell the policeman that the beach was the last place she had seen Alice alive, nor could she tell him that Alice had not been alone.

Doctor Ramsay took Alice along the sand where it was wet but the ground was firm. The seawater frothed up close to their feet. She wanted to suggest they go higher up where the sand was dry and there was no chance of getting wet. But he knew what he was doing. Glancing back she noticed that the sea was already where they had been walking, and the lapping water had washed away their footprints.

He told her that soon the tide would come in and the old ship they had passed, with its hull stuck deep in the shingle, would vanish because water would pour in through the portholes and engulf it. He said they were getting out just in time. Alice hoped that Eleanor hadn't chosen to hide inside and this made her enquire:

'What about Eleanor?' She was worried. It was wonderful to be free of playing daft games, but even Doctor Ramsay had said the Tide Mills was dangerous and so although Eleanor could swim in pyjamas she might not be safe.

'Oh, she'll be fine. It's you I'm concerned about.' He let go of her hand for a moment to stroke the back of her neck. His fingers were warm and they tickled up and down the way the nice post office lady's did. Her Dad would have been rougher. Once again, Alice unconsciously compared her parents with the Ramsays and was frustrated with her Mum and Dad for falling far short of them.

They reached the steep mountain of rocks at the far end of the beach and Alice was dismayed at the prospect of climbing them. Jagged boulders with sharp corners and few places to hold on to piled high against the sky. Doctor Ramsay would expect her to be as nimble as his daughter. Her mouth was parched and the hot sun pressed down on her head, burning the back of her neck where his hand had been.

309

'This is where I carry you. Let yourself go limp.'

Doctor Ramsay came towards her and, putting his hands underneath her armpits and clasping her tightly, he hoisted Alice up easily into the air like a rag doll. She hung over his shoulder, her head dangling downwards, her arms swinging, nervous of touching him. She could only think of her skirt riding up and blush at the awkwardness of being so close to him as his hand gripped her thigh.

'Hold on to me, it'll be easier then,' he gasped.

Alice dared to place her arms around his neck and then to clasp his hips with her knees. She began to relax as it became clear that he wouldn't drop her on to the rocks and let her get hurt. He jumped quickly and easily back and forth as he found a way up that wasn't obvious from the beach. When they got near to the top she dared to lift her head and look around.

In the distance, on the bushy hillside that led to the Tide Mills, just where there was a chalky ridge that dropped to the beach, she was sure she saw a figure. It was hard to focus and the person melted into the background when she tried to make it out.

'Don't move, we'll lose balance,' Doctor Ramsay gasped.

She held him tighter. If the movement on the hill had been Eleanor watching, then this was Alice's moment of triumph.

Once they were on the other side of the rocks, he lowered Alice down with great care, making sure that her skirt was straight and that her hair was spread out around her shoulders.

'Not far now. But we must make sure no one sees us, so be ready to hide if I tell you and keep very, very quiet.' Alice was overjoyed. This game, although similar to most of Eleanor's as it involved spies and hiding, was much more fun.

They made their way along a track beside the flint wall that marked the northern boundary of the Tide Mills village and was parallel to the railway line. Most of the wall had crumbled away and was only about a foot high, but in stretches it was still the original six feet, topped with rounded terracotta bricks. With the tall brambles on the other side of the track, at these points they were in a cool damp tunnel. They had to walk in single file because the foliage had encroached up on the path to the wall. Doctor Ramsay went in front and every now and then he would pause to hitch branches up, so that they didn't flick in Alice's face or lash her knees the way they had when she had been out with Eleanor. Her Mum was right. He was kind and thoughtful.

If the wall had been lower, they would have seen the tramp before he saw them. As it was, ducking around a tangle of branches they almost fell over him.

He was worse than in Eleanor's descriptions of him, which at the time Alice had assumed she'd invented. He was exactly like one of Eleanor's monsters. He was taller than Doctor Ramsay, with clothes so filthy and ragged that Alice couldn't make out where they began or ended or what colour they had ever been. His head and face were covered in matted hair: long grey straggling strands fuzzed around his shoulders and were draped over a bald patch on his head, not like hair at all. He was blocking their path, with his flies undone, peeing against the wall. Alice had only ever seen a man doing this once before when she had accidentally gone into the toilet when her Dad was there. But he had had his back to her and they had never talked about it. The tramp was practically facing them and Alice stared at the arc of bright yellow liquid splashing against the flints and running in a rapid stream over the ground towards their feet.

'What the Hell do you think you're doing?' Doctor Ramsay's voice was no longer kind. Alice shrank back as the two men confronted each other. The tramp didn't move until he had finished, his eyes on Alice throughout. Alice had expected him to be frightened but he started to laugh, his cracked lips curling back over blackened stumps.

'Get out of the way, you bastard.'

When Alice's Dad got really cross he went red, which until this minute Alice had thought was the most frightening it was possible to be. To her dismay, the tramp carried on wheezing. He turned from the wall, shaking something in his hand as he

311

advanced on them, all the while talking in a long growl that didn't make sense. Doctor Ramsay gave him a shove in the chest that sent him reeling against the wall and he sank in a heap into the nasty liquid puddling at their feet. He didn't move or speak. Grasping Alice's hand in his, Doctor Ramsay guided her past what now looked like an old Guy waiting for a bonfire. Alice noticed with relief as she stepped around him that he had stopped smiling. Soon they had left the tramp behind, and there was no one but them on the path.

'Are you all right, Alice?' Doctor Ramsay was irritated and not so nice.

'Ye-es.'

'Now we do really have to be careful that no one else sees us. We don't want that happening again, do we?' Alice presumed from this that the tramp had been her fault and nodded firmly. She didn't know what else to do to make amends except to go on being herself, which he had seemed to like before.

Mark Ramsay was leading Alice back to Charbury along a route that few people had used because it went only to the White House. Because of this, it would be a couple of days before the police got round to searching it. By the time they did, the tramp had gone.

Ahead they could see the high garden wall of the White House. Then Doctor Ramsay stepped off the path and pushed his way through some bushes.

'Come this way.'

He brought her to a rusting gate in the garden wall. It was cloaked in tangles of thick green ivy. Alice was astonished. As she came nearer, she saw that the wrought iron depicted an idyllic rural scene with all the animals of the countryside. At the base of a spreading tree she spotted a badger, and a hedgehog, while up in its branches was a tiny wren and a goldfinch. Doctor Ramsay bent down to her and made her follow very carefully the direction of his pointing finger.

'No, up a bit, D'you see? To the right of the butterfly.'

Right at the top, looking out at the hills that formed the curve of the gate was a little man crouched over an easel.

'He's fixed forever painting the landscape. Look carefully. What he is painting hasn't changed over the last two hundred years.' Doctor Ramsay straightened up. 'Let me show you properly.' Very gently, making sure her dress was straight, he lifted her high up, past the level of the gate, past his shoulders so that she was looking down on to the top of his head. Then she looked beyond the gate, at the thick canopy of the trees. There was a hole not much bigger than a dinner plate through which Alice could see the downs veined with white streaks of chalk exactly like the shapes wrought into the gate. Sloping light green grass was spotted with darker green blobs for trees. Doctor Ramsay lowered Alice back to the ground.

'It's the most beautiful thing I've ever seen.' She sighed. Invested with Eleanor's imaginative powers, Alice knew the gate was the entrance to a magic land visible only to those with the password. Doctor Ramsay's next words proved her right:

'This is the secret way into my garden. I have the only key.'

He slipped his hand into his trouser pocket and brandished a bright silver key. Alice came closer to him as, still smiling into her eyes, he inserted it in the lock. It turned easily and the gate swung open. He ushered Alice through. They were in a small clearing, sheltered from the blazing sunlight by the tall trees growing around the edges of the garden. It was cool and damp and quiet except for the occasional echoing chirrup of a blackbird far above them. There was a rustle – a baby rabbit broke cover and hopped quickly off into the undergrowth. Alice was overjoyed; she had stepped into *Bambi*. Doctor Ramsay had transformed her life.

'I'd like to live here for ever and ever,' she confided to him.

'Be as quiet as a mouse. I know you can.' He was being nice again.

They tiptoed around the tree trunks following a zig-zag route. Beneath their feet the ground was soft. It was carpeted with pine needles, chips of bark and spongy moss all draped in snaking tendrils of ivy that had crawled around the base of the trees.

A heavy scent made Alice drowsy and filled her with a rush of optimism. She gave in to a succession of happy associations: building a snowman with her Mum and Dad; piggy backs on her Dad's shoulders; making fairy cakes with her Mum on a cold winter afternoon. And most of all: the flower expedition with Doctor Ramsay.

Then she saw it. It was the most exquisite rose she had ever seen. A brilliant white, it reminded her of a giant snowball. Even her Dad didn't grow such big ones. Doctor Ramsay pulled the branch with the rose down towards her and standing on her toes, Alice buried her face deep into it.

'*Boule de neige*,' he murmured in her ear.

'Snowball,' Alice returned promptly. She had come top in French last year. Suddenly she knew she wasn't a bad girl after all. She closed her eyes. The rose's petals were cool and firm on her cheeks like a cat's ear. She filled her lungs with the insistent smell as she imagined it really was a snowball, cold and thirst quenching on this boiling hot day.

As she opened her eyes, she gasped. There were roses all around them, great nodding white flowers like beacons in the dark, secret place where Alice was positive that Eleanor had never been. Their branches intertwined with the ivy to form an impenetrable wall of foliage; untrimmed and untamed. This was a proper garden.

Alice saw where they were. Up until now, being with Doctor Ramsay had shed a different light over everything, rendering it strange and exciting. Now Alice recognised the Ramsays' lawn, although she had never seen it from this angle before. To their right was the willow tree where she had sat through several horrible tea times, and beyond that the gate to the river where Lucian tried in vain to catch fish. The house was on their left, and now Alice could acknowledge its close resemblance to Eleanor's dirty old doll's house. Now that she had Doctor Ramsay, Alice could admit to herself that she was jealous of the doll's house. She had never seen anything so magnificent. So when Eleanor had proudly explained that it was exactly the same as the real White House, Alice had assumed an air of indifference. So she had never fully appreciated that it was indeed a precise replica. Now as she stared up at the solid grand house, three floors high not including the attics above, standing proudly on a sprawling lawn, it seemed less forbidding. With Doctor Ramsay there beside her, the White House was nothing but a toy.

'Thank you very much for bringing me to your secret place. It's the best I've ever been to.'

'Oh, this isn't it. Just wait and see. There's more.'

Alice gazed up at the windows. Apart from the ones on the top floor with the bars, which she knew were the playroom, all the windows were open. Then Alice saw that the middle window on the second floor was shut, with the curtains closed. Alice guessed this was Mrs Ramsay's bedroom and assumed she must be having one of her lie-downs. As they were about to venture out across the lawn, Doctor Ramsay put his hand on Alice's shoulder, keeping her still. Not that she would have gone anywhere without him. Lucian was running out of the back door and was struggling across the lawn hampered by all his fishing equipment. The Ramsays were always in a hurry.

Not all of them.

Lucian's rod caught between his ankles. He tripped and fell headlong on to the grass. Alice heard him swear as he picked himself up and readjusted his knapsack and her cheeks went red. She marvelled that she could ever have wanted to marry him. His face was pink from sitting out on the riverbank in the sun all day and he had untidy hair sticking up like Eleanor's. If she had been with him when they met the tramp he wouldn't have saved her. Because this occurred to her, Alice resisted going over to him when he fell.

Instead, Alice crept closer to Doctor Ramsay, breathing in his lovely smelling aftershave and clean clothes mixed in with rose petals.

'Okay, the coast's clear.'

As they skirted the lawn, following a path made of red bricks like the ones at the Tide Mills, Alice was sure she saw the curtains of Mrs Ramsay's window move. She didn't want to have to be polite to Mrs Ramsay and for the game to be over so she pretended not to have seen it.

They hurried down some slippery mossy steps at the side of the house that were also new to Alice, who was beginning to realise she had seen very little of the White House until now. Eleanor clearly didn't know as many secret places as her father. Eleanor's power to upset Alice was diminishing. Abandoning all her good intentions, Alice imagined scoffing at all Eleanor's games and suggestions. Alice could hardly wait to see Eleanor so that she could tell her about all the things and places she didn't know. But then she knew she would keep quiet. This adventure would be a secret she shared with Doctor Ramsay.

The steps led to a dark basement. The door had been open and they ended up in a small room with shelves packed with boxes with dates written on them. Alice could make out the words on one box as they went past: 'Edith Barwick Murder 1931' was printed in thick black lettering.

She shivered, and Doctor Ramsay noticed. He noticed everything.

'Are you cold?'

'Not really. It's not very nice in here. Is this your secret place?'

'No. Everyone knows about this, it's where my father's files are stored. These are the transcripts of trials and all the related papers for his cases. Gory reading. Not for you, Alice.'

'Was it your father who was the Judge in the dining room?'

'Well done. That's right. He taught me a lot.'

They were in a paved tunnel with a curving brick ceiling. His voice sounded hollow. There were doors all along the walls on both sides. Alice thought how if they hid down here, no one would ever find them. One of the doors was open and she caught a glimpse of a long low freezer and vaguely remembered Lizzie, the Ramsays' housekeeper, warning Eleanor never to think of hiding in the freezer or she would end up as stiff as a board.

Doctor Ramsay was whispering again, 'We're going to go upstairs, if we meet anyone, you must say you felt ill and that I found you in the road and brought you back, okay?'

'But Eleanor knows we were at the Tide Mills.' Alice knew as soon as she had spoken that she shouldn't have pointed out to Doctor Ramsay that he was asking her to lie. But he wasn't. It was part of the game, and in games it was all right to make things up. He read her thoughts.

'We have a secret to keep, don't we?'

'Yes,' she replied and nodded.

'It's you I'm thinking of. It would be a shame to have things spoiled.'

He eased open the basement door and pulled a face as it creaked noisily. They waited. The only sound was the dull click-click of the grandfather clock near the front door. Alice could see the black and white tiles on the floor that had reminded her of the chessboard in her favourite book. Gina's riding boots were missing from the rack by the front door. Alice was disappointed because Gina was the one person she was prepared to share Doctor Ramsay with. In fact Gina would make it even more fun. Turning to her left, Alice saw that they were outside the downstairs toilet where Eleanor had made her look stupid by talking about poo. The door was open and she could see the big box of matches on the windowsill. The memory of that afternoon made her cheeks tingle with a horrid mixture of dread and shame. No wonder she hadn't noticed the basement door before. Now she was glad they had left Eleanor to whatever terrible dangers the Tide Mills had in store for her. Alice held her breath as, step for step, she walked beside Doctor Ramsay up the wide staircase. He put one hand on her back to stop her falling backwards the way she had once seen him do with Mrs Ramsay.

They reached the landing. There was a settee on it, perhaps for people who got tired while climbing the stairs. Alice had previously thought how she would like to sit on it when she had been trailing after Eleanor on the way to the playroom. She would have preferred to stay here unnoticed noting the comings and goings in the house. This wish applied to most things. Alice dreamed of simply observing without having to take part and to always come top.

The second floor was much darker because the walls were panelled with wood almost black with age. There were two corridors, one going off to the left and the other to the right, and more stairs going on up to the floor with the playroom and finally to the attics where the maids had slept long ago. Alice would have been disappointed had they been going to the playroom. He must know there was nothing secret about it. But she felt a swoop of joy as Doctor Ramsay, his finger on his lips, guided her over to the closed door that Eleanor had told her was his study. It had always been locked before. Alice knew that Eleanor didn't have a key as she had once tried the door, although she also knew that Eleanor had been in there. But this time would be different. Alice would be entering at Doctor Ramsay's invitation. Her heart pounded in her thin chest as he produced yet another key from his magic trouser pocket and quietly opened the door.

Alice's first impression was that the room was extremely bright. After the dark landing, the sunlight hurt her eyes. She hovered by the door, unsure what to do. The room was as daunting to her as Doctor Ramsay had once been. It was the private territory of an important and imposing person, even if that person had become less awe-inspiring and pulled faces like a little boy. An enormous desk stood at an angle near the window. Taking a few steps further into the room, Alice was delighted to see the book with the names of flowers that Doctor Ramsay had used for their flower pressing expedition two days earlier. It lay open on the blotting paper pad. Doctor Ramsay might be planning another expedition. Perhaps they could plan it together now.

Apart from Newhaven Library, Alice had never seen so many books in one room. The alcove to the left of the fireplace was filled with books as was the wall opposite this. There were even books on a shelf above the door. Lots had leather covers and gold or silver writing on the spines like in the reference library. Alice was used to the odd paperback and magazines stacked in neat piles on the sideboard.

'I like reading too,' she offered brightly.

'I'm sure you do, you're exceptional in many ways. Come and sit down.'

Facing the window was a very big brown leather settee with studded buttons. Alice had seen it before. There was one in the doll's house just like it. This excited her. Alice's oblique familiarity with the exact copy of this room in miniature contributed to her impression of everything being enormous. She fleetingly imagined telling her Mum later how she had been like the other Alice. She would say she had been in Wonderland and was small enough to fit in the palm of a hand and be held up for Doctor Ramsay's inspection. Doctor Ramsay indicated the settee and with trepidation Alice perched on the edge.

'There, are you comfortable?' The leather was cool and smooth on her bare legs.

'This is a nice place.' She didn't want to hurt him by telling him his study wasn't at all secret. Eleanor had been inside lots of times to get books. Thinking of Eleanor brought Alice down to earth and she began to fret about the time. She couldn't see a clock and Doctor Ramsay wasn't wearing a watch. She didn't want to be late home, not after the bad behaviour with Eleanor's special tea the afternoon before, and now having left Eleanor on her own. She could see no way to broach the subject of going, since she had just got there. She put on a smiling face and pointedly looked about her.

'Welcome to my lair!'

He sat beside her, pushing himself into the other corner so that he could look at her properly. One leg was crooked on the settee, his knee nudging hers.

'I hide in here to escape the chaos. It's nice to have your company. I don't really like being on my own. You're a beautiful girl, Alice. Rather special, so it's a pleasure to have you.' He talked in the hushed voice he had on when reciting the Latin names of flowers. Alice's skin was getting itchy from where his trousers were rubbing up against her, but she dared not move. Doctor Ramsay craned forward and once again stroked her hair away from her face. It made Alice apologetic. She was mortified to think she needed tidying up and that

319

Doctor Ramsay had noticed and minded. She sat up, shifting away from him, causing him to do the same.

'What's the matter?' He was concerned, perhaps even nervous, which Alice thought strange. Maybe he wished she would leave and didn't know how to suggest it.

'I ought to be going. Thank you for having me. It's a lovely secret hidey-hole. I like it very much.' When Alice had imagined being with Doctor Ramsay, she had pictured herself having loads of interesting things to tell him and original comments to make about anything he showed her. Instead, here she was, like one of Eleanor's abandoned dolls plonked on a huge settee, her feet only just reaching the carpet, with nothing to say. She was prickling with heat and unable to see properly because the hot sun flooding through the open window shone full in her face.

Eleanor would still be searching for her at the Tide Mills. Her Mum would be worrying about where Alice had got to. Doctor Ramsay had seemed an escape from playing with Eleanor, but he wasn't. Tomorrow he would go back to being a doctor and Alice would have to see Eleanor for three more days. She wanted to go home. Even Doctor Ramsay was disappointing. He had promised a secret but there was no secret. Alice saw with a perception beyond her years that Doctor Ramsay was ordinary. She had been right all along. There were no real magic places. There was no Wonderland.

She would have to lie and say she had been ill and Doctor Ramsay had taken her to his study. She had never lied to her Mum. Maybe Doctor Ramsay himself already judged that Alice was a bad girl for agreeing to come with him and leaving Eleanor. Perhaps he had been doing the Traitor Test after all. Alice slid off the settee and stood up, tugging at her dress. Doctor Ramsay had locked the door when they came in. She would have to ask him to open it.

'Oh, you can't go. I haven't shown you my secret place.' He stood in front of her, his hands on his hips. He was frowning now, his eyes looking at something behind her, above her head.

'I thought this was it,' Alice retorted. In the distance she heard the grandfather clock strike four times. Four o'clock. The time she had told her Mum she would come home.

'Oh no wonder you're cross with me!'

'I'm not cro...'

'What I have to show you is far more special.' Doctor Ramsay didn't move. They might have been the waxworks Alice had hoped he would take her to see.

Alice was astonished by his expression. He was looking directly at her. He was frightened. Alice took a step nearer to the door.

'If I'm late my Mum will kill me.' The words tumbled out. 'I want to go home.'

He had her by the hand, strong fingers closed down on her thin wrist, not like before, which she had liked, but squeezing so tight that it made her eyes smart as he pulled her over to him. He began to shake her arm as if it didn't belong to her while staring wildly at the thin flapping thing.

'Just do as I say.' Alice had heard him speak like that to Eleanor during the flower picking expedition and she had refused to pay proper attention. Eleanor had ignored him and gone running off by herself. There was nowhere for Alice to run. He was blocking the way to the locked door. He grasped her shoulders and spun her around to face the fireplace. All Alice could think in those last moments was that there would be bruises on her arms and that she would have to lie about them too.

They were walking towards the wood-panelled wall, keeping close together, the way her father used to march with Alice standing on top of his big black postman shoes.

Clump. Clump. Clump. Moving without moving.

She was going to bang straight into the wall. Then he leaned over her head and gave the carved wooden rose by the side of the fireplace a thump with the flat of his palm. This action made no sense to Alice, but then nor did what happened next.

The panelling began to slide. It swung inwards, like a revolving door. Then it shuddered to a halt leaving a low doorway through which came a guff of chill air that smelled like the tramp.

Doctor Ramsay pushed Alice through the dark entrance. Once inside he pushed the wall back the way it had come. At the same moment as it clicked back into place, a dusty bulb dangling from the ceiling on a long wire came on so that they were just able to see.

It was a very small space, about six feet square with a lower ceiling than the room they had left behind. In one corner was an old lumpy armchair. Beside the chair was a pile of notebooks and paper. A bottle of whiskey stood next to a glass that had fallen on its side. It was much like Eleanor's den in the hedge but not as homely. Alice had no wish to make this den into a proper home.

As she got used to the dull light, Alice saw that a bundle in the far right-hand corner was a pile of clothes that looked like someone had got undressed quickly without hanging anything up. It made her think of the tramp after Doctor Ramsay had knocked him over. She staggered slightly as Doctor Ramsay loosened his grip on her and let her go. She leaned on the wall to stop herself falling.

Then she saw her cardigan.

She had been sure she had left it at the White House, but when she asked, no one had seen it. Doctor Ramsay had even said he would make sure to keep a special eye out for it and she had been pleased. He had offered to lend her his jacket for the flower expedition. Alice had suspected that Eleanor had stolen it. She knew she was lying when she said she didn't know where it was. She had looked guilty. Afterwards Alice had felt bad for making it obvious she suspected Eleanor because she knew her Mum would be ashamed of her for even thinking such a bad thing of a new friend. Especially one of the Ramsays. But once again her Mum was wrong. The Ramsays did steal things. 'I don't like it here.' Something prevented Alice from mentioning the cardigan.

'No one knows about my den.'

'I want to go home.'

'You've only just got here. You wanted to come. It was your idea.' He had the little boy's voice again, but this time Alice didn't want to make him better.

'That's not true.' Alice pulled away as he tried to take her hand. She caught the whiskey bottle which tipped over. The top hadn't been screwed on and liquid welled out over the floor, soaking the clothes. She dived forward and snatched up her cardigan.

Then as her eyes grew accustomed to the light Alice saw the passage beyond the bundle of clothes. It was beyond the darkest part of the chamber. There was another way out.

'Calm down.' Mark Ramsay wasn't calm. He kept wiping his hands on his trousers. He appeared unable to make sense of how things had turned out and keen to make friends again. Once again he tried to touch her. It was obvious he only meant to calm Alice down while he found the catch to open the wall. He was sure there was still time to explain the mistake and take her home. That was definitely still possible.

But unexpectedly Alice made a lunge for the passage and Mark knew she could escape that way. At the end of the passage was another secret door. This only opened from the inside on to the landing. It was cleverly constructed to form part of the wooden panelling. Only Mark Ramsay knew it was there. All Alice would have to do was turn the knob and she would be free. It dawned on Mark what he had done. Alice running away from him was the worst thing she could do. He grappled fiercely with her. He held her. But she slipped away leaving only her cardigan. The whiskey-soaked wool that only last night he had clutched to his face with thoughts of such tenderness spelled his doom. He flew after her and halfway down the passage caught her and dragged her back by her lovely hair into the priest's hole.

Alice stared up into his face uncomprehending as he smiled weakly at her. Her last impression was that he was trying to ask her a question but she couldn't speak. As Doctor Ramsay's hands closed around her neck, it seemed to Alice that the light bulb in the ceiling went out.

Thirty-One

The playroom had become bitterly cold. Wind rustled the trees and bushes in the garden and rattled the window frames. The centre light flickered, in time to these sudden gusts. Far away, downstairs in the hall, the grandfather clock chimed three-quarters of the hour – fifteen minutes to go before midnight.

'How long have you known?' Chris cleared her throat.

'Until tonight, not properly. Or maybe I've always known.'

'What do you mean?'

'My friends never said anything. But they would giggle or blush if he was near, or far worse, I saw their fear. In the end they didn't come. So there was only Alice. It was the same for Gina, although we never acknowledged it. In those days there was no word for it. Now I've come back they don't mention I was away.'

'Why didn't you tell the police?'

'Report my own father? For doing what? No one would have believed me. I didn't believe it.'

'Couldn't you tell your Mum, or your brother and sister?'

'They don't want the truth. They want just to get through life relatively unscathed. I couldn't destroy my family's fragile existence on the basis of vague hints and imaginings. His terrible act had threatened to do that. My mother made sure we all got back to normal. She was a great believer in structure and routine.'

'You lied to me.'

'I tried to keep you out of it. Stupid. I had relied on you never finding out. When you did, I said what came into my head. I took the blame like I always had. I had to keep my mother safe too. That's all we've ever done. He did too. Until the end when he couldn't face her. Isabel's an old woman now. It's too late for her.'

'Do you think she knows?'

'She doesn't want to know. But it might explain the headaches.' Eleanor got off the window seat. 'Besides if the truth had come out imagine what it would've done to Kathleen? She worshipped him. She's a sick woman.'

'You know nothing about Kath. How could all of you let her suffer all these years? For the sake of the reputation of the Ramsay family, you let another family be destroyed.'

'I was a child remember?' Eleanor went across to the doll's house and stood beside it in the wavering lamplight, dwarfed by its magnitude.

'So that lets you off?'

'No. Of course it doesn't. That's why I became Alice. It was all I could think to do. Crazy, I know. But none of this bloody mess is sane.'

Suddenly Chris understood her Mum's bizarre behaviour. After all she hadn't gone to the police when her Mum had confessed to a murder. It wasn't that simple.

'I knew he had taken her. I saw them through the bushes. Then I glimpsed them way off in the distance on the beach. I tried to catch up. If I had, he wouldn't have been able to say anything. He would've had to take us both home. I could have stopped him.'

'Probably not. He would have pretended to be furious with you about taking Alice to the Tide Mills. He would have said you couldn't be trusted and sent you packing. In front of Alice you would have had to do as you were told. He was your Dad.' Chris found she didn't hate her Mum any more. Not for being trapped in a flat with fake agoraphobia, not for being Alice; for lying to her daughter. Not for protecting a murderer. All of it made sense. She might have done the same.

'I couldn't get down to the beach. The tide was coming in. So I rushed back up the path and through the Tide Mills village. Halfway down the street I collided with an old man. The Bobby Charlton tramp. He caught hold of me and dragged me towards the workman's cottage: my secret den. He was bleeding from the nose and shouting at me, but it was hard to make him out. Something about being attacked by a madman. I screamed and he let me go and staggered off. No one heard. All I thought was that Alice and my Dad had left me to die. Alice had been happy to leave me there by myself.'

'She had no choice. If he said it was okay, then how could she argue?'

'I wanted to have one friend who dared stand up to him.' Eleanor dragged her foot over the rug, kicking out the wrinkles. 'When I got back to the house, my Mum was asleep. I belted along the passage to my Dad's study. The door was open but the room was empty. Dad and Alice were nowhere to be seen. I decided I had made the whole thing up. I couldn't say about the tramp as I wasn't supposed to be at the Tide Mills. I wanted to. I still hoped that if my Dad knew what had happened he would have felt guilty for leaving me.' She turned to the doll's house and slowly eased open the great frontage. It creaked on its hinges. 'So I showed the police his handkerchief. I said I had got it off the ironing pile. I had used it to wipe the blood from the bramble scratches on my leg. The handkerchief told Dad that I knew.'

'There's something I haven't told you.' Chris bent down and addressed the bars:

'That reporter, Jackie Masters, asked to do an interview with Doctor Ramsay last year. She was drinking, she wasn't getting any work. She needed money. It was going to be an anniversary piece, looking at where people in the case were now. He told her to get lost. Without him, she wouldn't have been able to get others to co-operate, especially Kath. She decided to have revenge. She found out he'd never been interviewed by the police. At the time, the press had assumed Doctor Ramsay had an alibi. In fact the police had considered him above suspicion because he was a highly respected doctor. People like him wouldn't kidnap children. She went through the evidence files and the cuttings. It didn't take her long to find what she needed.' Chris shut the window and sat down on the window seat, facing Eleanor:

'Doctor Ramsay had handed in Alice's cardigan. He claimed to have found it in the lane near to Eleanor's den. This played a big part in falsely placing Alice there at the time of her disappearance. It backed up your story.'

'Alice was convinced I had stolen that cardigan.'

'Jackie checked the accounts of what Alice was wearing that day. There was no mention of a pink cardigan. It was too hot. She had on a yellow dress. She also knew that Kathleen would never have put pink and yellow together. You had said in one of your interviews that Alice had left her cardigan behind in the dining room after drawing one afternoon. She hadn't worn it since. Richard Hall didn't pick up on this. He was focusing on you because he found you weird. No one suspected Doctor Ramsay.' Chris sighed. 'If only they had.'

She came over to the doll's house; both women knelt in front of it, like children solemnly preparing to play.

'Jackie wasn't thinking of a good story by this time. She had a better plan. She began to blackmail Doctor Ramsay. He was easy. The cardigan stuff wouldn't have been enough, but he was guilty and scared. It seems all she had to do was lie and say she had a witness who had seen him with Alice and he caved in. So every week she went to that old shed in the garden at the White House and collected a parcel of money hidden under the ivy at the back. He knew it was the one place the family never went. No one saw her. If they had, it wouldn't have mattered; they had agreed Jackie would say she worked with him. Nothing he did was questioned. Nothing was questioned. He could at least depend on that. Besides it didn't matter what Isabel thought. She would never do anything. They forgot the CCTV. Or rather that the only person who watched those films was someone who would recognise Jackie Masters and wonder what she was doing there.'

Chris watched her mother's fingers begin the walk up the carpeted stairs from the hall to the first landing. She continued in a lower voice:

'It took time for Kathleen to place the woman she saw on the film. Then one day she did. On the Saturday when he came to swap the tapes she plucked up her courage and told Doctor Ramsay. She didn't like to admit she noticed what went on at the White House. She was so grateful that he gave her the chance to look for Alice by seeing the tapes. When he said he didn't know anything about Jackie Masters she accepted what he told her. After that Doctor Ramsay changed the meeting place with Jackie, but this didn't help him. He must have brooded all that last week. It was harder to face Kathleen. He was caught between these two women, one so innocent and the other as corrupt as himself. Isabel always there at home keeping an eye. That Saturday lunchtime he took the coward's way out.'

'Why hasn't this Jackie said anything?' Eleanor reached past the tiny roll top desk and ran a finger lightly along the cushions on the miniature sofa at the back of the room that was Doctor Ramsay's study.

'Kath has said that if she writes anything, she will tell the police Jackie was blackmailing Doctor Ramsay. When the truth comes out, it won't benefit Jackie Masters. That's the deal. Jackie was so sure Kathleen would be pleased she had made him suffer and hounded him to death.' Chris gave a wry smile. 'Kath's not like that.'

Eleanor was a small girl again, caught up in the magic of her game. There were no dolls in the replica study. The husband doll was missing. She jogged the desk with her wrist as her hand delved deeper into the book-lined aperture. She felt along the painted panels to the right of the fireplace. Their heads touched as they both leaned closer in towards the tiny room. Eleanor pressed the little carved Tudor rose that formed part of a series ranged along the wall at picture rail height. The partition wall slid to one side.

They could only just see into the cavity they had revealed.

There was someone in there.

Eleanor squeezed her thumb and forefinger into the tiny gap and tenderly lifted out the little doll. She cradled her in her palm. Together they examined her in the lamplight. At the same moment they gave a start. Someone had knotted a strip of cotton around the doll's head. She had been gagged and blindfolded.

'He's been here,' Chris whispered.

'Yes.' Eleanor breathed deeply to stop herself vomiting. 'He must have wanted to be found out. But after that summer no one played up here again.'

Eleanor slipped the thin band of material off the doll's eyes and held her upright, gently turning her around, showing her the room.

'You know we have to tell, don't you?' Eleanor chose the words Alice would have used. Alice, who always said and did the right thing. 'We know where she is now. Kathleen is all that matters.'

'What shall we do?' Chris longed to be small again with her mother in charge.

'Let Isabel have one last party.'

Eleanor rearranged the furniture in one of the bedrooms on the right hand side of the house. This had been Gina's bedroom. Alice loved her room. She hauled the bed over to the window where the sun would shine in on Alice's pillows first thing in the morning. Then she fetched the counterpane from the master bedroom. The initials E.I.R. were embroidered on one of the small squares.

'Isabel made these bed spreads for me one afternoon when it was just us in the house. She didn't often do things with me. At the time it meant a lot.' She folded the quilt over so that it would fit the small bed in the room she had prepared. Very slowly, because no one likes to be whizzed through the air before they can get their breath, she carried the little doll over and enveloped her in the quilt. They shuffled backwards so that Chris could close the giant frontage.

Eleanor crouched close to the window of the room where

Alice was tucked up in her bed. The window was open so she could hear the soft repetitive sound of the waves on the shore as she slept. Eleanor recited from her favourite book in a lullaby voice that Chris could hardly hear:

'...Thus grew the tale of Wonderland:
Thus slowly, one by one,
Its quaint events were hammered out
And now the tale is done,
And home we steer, a merry crew,
Beneath the setting sun...'

They paused on the dark landing. Chris drew close to her Mum and, taking hold of her hand, put into it the rounded lump of glass that Kathleen had given her when she moved into Alice's bedroom.

'Here, have this. It's for luck.'

'Where did you get it?' Eleanor saw Mrs Jackson's overheated flat, Jaffa cakes heaped on a plate and she felt the warm weight of Crawford nestling on her lap.

'Kathleen gave it to me. I don't need luck. I'm going to be fine.'

'And you reckon I need every bit I can get!'

'I imagined you'd like it. It looks precious, although I don't expect it's worth anything.'

'It is worth a lot to me. Thank you,' Eleanor murmured.

Chris checked the time on her watch in the light from a shaft of moonlight slanting through the window. The fog had cleared. The century was about to end.

She knew that the Ramsays would survive. There would be more parties. She had studied them for weeks. They had given her lots of opportunities to. After all she was a Ramsay too.

The two women interlocked fingers and together they descended the stairs. The countdown for the year 2000 began:

'... ten... nine... eight... seven... six...'

Acknowledgements

A novel might start in the privacy of a 'room of one's own' but the final version involves the contribution of others.

I would like to thank the team at Myriad Editions and in particular Candida Lacey, who is a tenacious, risk-taking publisher. Corinne Pearlman's consistently positive presence, along with Candida's kindness and generosity, made the whole process of seeing a manuscript through to a book truly enjoyable. My thanks also to Colin Kennedy for his part in this process.

Lisa Holloway's unwavering belief in this novel encouraged me and her advice and feedback was always spot on.

Sarah Roberts Salon is South London's premier hairdresser; besides skilfully wielding scissors, Sarah, and her mother Ann, have been great supporters of the book.

Thanks to Katrina Heather for being the best pilates and yoga coach a girl could have.

Jeanette Winterson's comments and help have been invaluable – thank you.

Melissa Benn has long been an important friend and 'writing-companion', giving suggestions and much-appreciated support.

My thanks to Melanie Lockett for her considered perception. And for her vocal appreciation of this novel – her 'word of mouth' has given it many new readers.

None of this would have happened without the meticulous care of my agent, editor and good friend Philippa Brewster at Capel & Land. I am hugely indebted to Philippa who worked with me tirelessly with her usual skill and insight. She taught me a great deal.

Finally, starting out as a writer, and while working on this book, I would not have had the 'room' (mentally and sometimes financially) to write without the support and encouragement of my Mum, May Walker. She died shortly before publication and was not well enough to read the manuscript. However her wisdom and critical understanding, as an inspiring teacher and as a woman of the world, are with me still.

AFTERWORD:

FOR ME, writing is one element in the creation of a novel. The process is protracted and meandering and begins as a wondering: *I wonder what would happen if...* Events and scenes develop from this. *A Kind of Vanishing* began with my hearing an item on Radio 4 about how to support a child when a classmate has died. How can the children come to terms with the loss? Then there is the possibility that a boy or girl might not have liked the child. Perhaps they are secretly pleased that the child is gone. They may feel responsible for the 'vanishing'; it may be a wish come true. I populate this germ of an idea with sketchy characters.

Central to the establishment of my reality are characters and location. Since I was a child I have scribbled down my characters' 'vital statistics', continually revising their birth date, their full name and their relationship to one another as an idea takes shape. What is their role in the story? What impact do events have on them? What have they experienced? Some of this the reader will learn during the novel, other knowledge they will never know; the character's back story. My characters have lives beyond the fiction. For me, all characters do, whether David Copperfield or Lisbeth Salander. This is what makes them real. Isabel Ramsay is out there living her life. *A Kind of Vanishing*, and the novel I am now working on, dip into this life. Each time we read about Isabel we have more evidence with which to construct our own story. If I don't believe Isabel Ramsay exists, then she not is real and I cannot write about her.

To become intimate with my characters, I must know the streets through which they pass, the pavements, the paths, and the muddied grass on which they step. I must see them in their landscape. I scribble constantly in a notebook. If I don't have this with me, I ring home and leave a message, usually on the answer machine, to preserve the thought. During the writing, amongst other messages are my own: from a field, my voice lost in a gale; from a crowded bus in an urgent whisper imparting phrases baffling to anyone else: '*She does not know he has been there before*', '*The Judge likes Aeschylus*'.

I read many books and articles, adding quotes and ideas to the notebook, which grows fat with leaflets and cuttings. I mine Google. I meet people who are doing my characters' jobs. I am less interested in how they do their work than in how it feels. My characters are constant companions.

Throughout the writing, I use my camera for three reasons:

For the record: I want facts. A literal description is not integral to the veracity of the story, but a photograph will show detail that I do need to get right.

The purloined place: My photograph of a place is not of itself; it is in my novel. When I go there I am not in the present, I am in the fictional place. Be it an office lavatory, a statue or a wrought iron gate into a garden I 'take' it for fiction.

Beyond the record: The camera records what I capture through the lens. I am selective so I may miss a detail, or at the time I saw it differently. I can examine a photograph: crop it, enlarge it, perhaps heighten the contrast to see new shapes emerge.

These photographs are not illustrations of my story. Like the characters' lives beyond the text; they do not need to be included to make the story real. The text must do this.

The camera does lie. Most of these images depict scenes which happen in my story and have not happened in real life.

FOR THE RECORD :

My CAMERA captures 'reality'. This is the least important reason for taking photographs.

The Bell Steps
How many steps are there to the river?

Four up then twelve down. This odd arrangement fascinates a little boy: he has to walk up to walk down. He likes to come here.

335

I could make these steps up, but they are real. If a reader should visit the Bell Steps in Hammersmith they can follow the footsteps of my character and her child.

The Flowers

A modest bunch of flowers with no message is often propped against this headstone. Before the blooms dry and their colour fades or they become sodden from rain, they are replaced with a fresh bouquet. The headstone is only twenty-nine years old but already the epitaph is yellowed with lichen and will soon be illegible.

The Hiding Place

Is there somewhere to hide to watch for who brings these flowers? My detective finds a spot some distance from the grave. This picture confirms my recollection of the area; it is possible to crouch behind this wall and see while not being seen.

The Office Toilets

A woman runs a cleaning company; leasing cheap offices in Shepherds Bush, she has no control over the common areas. She has complained to the landlord about the unisex toilets, they give a terrible impression to clients. She should find new premises but she has become distracted by a murder case. The 'facts' are: the sanitary-ware is salmon pink and the roller mechanism is broken so that the towel spools onto the lino. These details may or may not feature in the novel. But I know they are there.

THE PURLOINED PLACE :

IN *The Poetics of Space* (1958) Gaston Bachelard describes how by polishing a table we develop a relationship with it that heightens its 'reality'. It finds a place in our world beyond its utilitarian function of 'table'. I watch a wall being built: it is comprised not only of bricks and mortar, but of the conversation I had with the young man who built it and of my thoughts as he lay each course. To me it is more than a wall.

This leads me to the second reason for taking photographs. I 'take' the real location in a photograph and make it fictional. The real place becomes the fictional location. When I visit the toilets in the last image, like Lucy in *The Lion, The Witch and the Wardrobe*, the wardrobe has no back: I have entered the cleaning company and my story is not make-believe.

I build a relationship with the location or with objects. My memories of the place are layered with the experiences of my characters. When I visit Tide Mills I 'remember' playing hide and seek there. I look for Alice and Eleanor in the undergrowth, through holes in walls, or running along the beach. When I am by the River Thames I am no longer in the present. I am no longer 'present'.

Major Incident Document

This is a photocopied page from the file of a murdered woman. Her strangled body was found at the spot marked with an 'X' in the summer of 1981. Decades later, in 2010, a woman sits in an empty house late at night. She smoothes out this crumpled sheet and by the light of an angle-poise lamp examines this image.

Wednesday
29th July 1981

The Place by the River Thames

Blinding sunshine bakes the mud to clay. Sunk into its surface are brick, twists of rope, broken bottles; flotsam and jetsam. Along the top of the wall is a trellis, a glimpse of a shrub, signifying prosaic domesticity beyond the frame of the image. Here is generic familiarity: weeds sprout from a retaining wall that is held fast with steel bolts. Some bricks are green with moss and slime, the strata pattern marking the high water levels.

I have purloined this place: in broad daylight its truth is hidden. It could be a typical riverside scene, altered little over the last 150 years. It is not. It is a shot taken by a detective and later it is given a file number. Its secret is revealed to you, the reader. If you make your way down the Bell Steps – three up, twelve down – you too might become enter the story and forge your own memories. This where a woman's life ended. This is a 'fact' that you may recall.

In 2010 my character pulls the the black and white photocopy out of her jacket pocket. She positions herself so she can see what the photographer saw.

In 2011, yet another woman is here. She snaps pictures, she makes notes in a spiral-bound book, describing the cloying odour of river mud wafting in the still air. Later she deletes 'wafting'. A person died here, she tells herself. Standing where the body was found, I believe my own story.

BEYOND THE RECORD :

THE THIRD reason I take pictures is to discover what I did not see through the lens.

In *Blow Up*, Michelangelo Antonioni's 1966 thriller, a photographer roaming a London park unwittingly witnesses a murder. He only sees this when he enlarges his picture. As he 'shoots' a couple around corners, down steps, from behind fences, the only sound is the rushing of a breeze in the trees. I had not particularly noticed this before I saw the film. Now I hear it and I am in the film.

I enlarge my images and I see what I was meant to see.

The Leaning Woman

The Leaning Woman, a sculpture by Karel Vogel, was erected beside the Great West Road in 1959. She sits on a plinth beside a churchyard, three minutes' walk from the river where the woman's body was found. As I examine the shot, I discern marks on the pockmarked concrete. I click the magnifying glass icon until the screen is a mass of grey and brown pixels.

The Jointed Carcass

Chalk lines have been scrawled over the woman's body, an attempt to erase them unsuccessful. I am told that these segments represent a butcher's jointing of a carcass. My photograph has connected two realities: the actual and the invented. My murderer has been here at night when there is no one around and drawn these lines.

OFF THE RECORD :

THESE ARE images from my characters' points of view. They are snatches of their lives. They contribute to their back story. To take these pictures I have entered my characters' lives. I sip a cup of coffee and eat pancakes with syrup in a McDonald's in Earl's Court before getting into the cab of the first District Line train of the day. As I eat I avoid the eye of other drivers – they know to leave me alone – I am my character. I know what it is like to clamber over the flint wall, trampling on nettles and rough grass before crouching down. If anyone looks over the wall they will see me. I have to assume they will not. I rest a bunch of flowers against a headstone, seeing for myself that the engraving on the stone is almost obscured by lichen. As I sit on a hillside with my notebook, I ponder the best cleaning agent for removing lily stamen stains from silk.

My characters are based on real life. I am the actor.

The Woman's View

This scrap of beach by the Thames is revealed as the tide ebbs. A woman contemplates the spans on Hammersmith Bridge, they seem to shimmer in the heat. Her husband, a civil engineer, has told her that the bridge was designed by the man who created the London sewers and opened by the Prince of Wales in 1887. Her thoughts lead her to the present Prince of Wales. Charles is getting married today.

I look at this photograph and forget that I took it. The point of view is not mine.

The Driver's View

A man with the mind of a murderer prefers darkness. He drives a London Underground train, working the Dead-Late shift on the District line. Many tunnels have not changed in over a hundred years. Always walking, always driving, he is never in one place.

He is always absent.

The Detective's View

Twenty-nine years on, a retired detective obsesses about an unsolved murder. Parked by the sea, he takes stock of what he has just learnt. He drinks coffee from his flask and, given to snacking, eats a Kit-Kat. He has a lead and imagines telling his daughter, but, grown up and grown away, she is a stranger. Absently he writes her name in steam from the cup on his windscreen. His daughter will never know her Dad did this.

As I slowly sip the scalding liquid, I am the detective.

The Boy's View

A three-year-old boy studies ants scurrying to and fro across the path and positions twigs that are tree trunks to divert them. He likes the twig's curve in relation to the square border stones. The lines in between are paths, they are short cuts, escape routes. People are not as clever as ants, he ponders. Unlike ants, their behaviour makes no sense to him. Alive with possibility this landscape is his.

The Man's View

A man comes out of the Co-op in a seaside town. It is eight-thirty-five am. He carries two soft ham rolls and a tin of coke in a plastic bag for his lunch. He has a massive heart attack. This picture is his last conscious sight.

As I gaze at this snatch of pavement I see a life passing before me.

The Beginning

These images are part of my process of writing novels. I have taken reality for use in my fiction. Using photographs such as these I believe my fiction is reality.

Then I begin to write…

MORE FROM MYRIAD EDITIONS

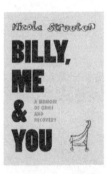

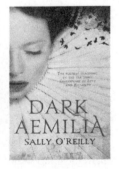

MORE FROM MYRIAD EDITIONS

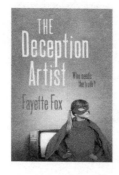

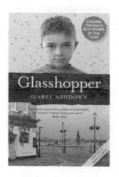

MORE FROM MYRIAD EDITIONS

MORE FROM MYRIAD EDITIONS

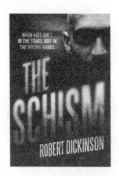

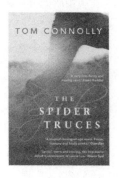